Christmas 1991

To Uncle Dan — Happy Christmas —
Seay.

REPRISAL

By the same author

The Kybe (Wolfhound Press, 1983)

Reprisal

a novel by

HUGH FITZGERALD RYAN

WOLFHOUND PRESS

Wolfhound Press receives financial assistance from
The Arts Council (An Chomhairle Ealaíon), Dublin, Ireland.

First published 1989 by
WOLFHOUND PRESS
68 Mountjoy Square, Dublin 1.

British Library Cataloguing in Publication Data
  Ryan, Hugh Fitzgerald
  Reprisal.
  I. Title
  823'.914 [F]

  ISBN 0-86327-247-9 HB
  ISBN 0-86327-248-7 PB

Cover design: Jan de Fouw
Cover photographs from The Cashman Collection, RTE.
Typesetting: Wendy A. Commins, The Curragh
Make-up: Paul Bray Studio.
Printed by TechMan Ltd., Dublin.

To Thomas, Alan, Alison, Sarah, Fergus,
Jennifer, Erika and Justin.

And also for Milo, who loved a yarn.

With the exception of the events of September 1920 in Balbriggan, all the characters and events are fictitious.

I gratefully acknowledge the help of Mr. Louis Derham of Balbriggan who made family documents available to me and was most generous with his time.

Part I

CHAPTER 1

The houses cling to The White Rock where it juts out over the strand, low, thatched cottages in most cases, with here and there a taller building whose dormer windows speak of grandeur and from which there is a spectacular view over the sea-roads and the harbour at the far end of an arc of stony beach.

The Vikings had named it as they prowled the coast many centuries before, just as they had named the village for the rocky islets off shore. The White Rock had, in its time, seen the fleets of Man and Orkney ground their keels on the stones. Wild seafaring men had come to plunder and, later, to settle on that firm shoulder of gritstone, displacing the gulls, whose habitations had prompted the name, turning to more peaceful commerce and leaving a legacy of fair-haired descendants and a sprinkling of family names from the far off Land of Lakes.

Mr Donovan was a romantic, an adventurer in his imagination, an avid reader, even in his middle years, of Henty and Ballantyne; he had soldiered with Kitchener at Kabul and at Omdurman and had set foot on desert shores with Sir Garnet. When he came to settle in the town he would live nowhere but on The White Rock, although his new wife might have preferred somewhere closer to the fine 'English' houses at the far end of the town. As he walked to and from his little pharmacy each day, a neat little man in a high, winged collar and carrying his cane with a flourish, he congratulated himself on his good fortune — a modest prosperity, an elegant and cultivated wife and three fine youngsters.

His neighbours he considered both congenial and colourful. A slouching oaf of a fisherman he might invest with the glamour of a wild sea-rover. The coalman with the sack over his head and his lumbering horse he sometimes imagined to be Odin revisiting his people in disguise, the corner of the sack concealing his conical hat. Josie Brett the stone cutter, who talked to the animals, he whom the seals reputedly came to visit, flopping out of the water at night and waddling to his door, he who carved a wooden beak for his old hen, to Mr Donovan was a man in touch with old mysteries, the deep secrets of a time long gone, when heroes walked the earth and people lived close to nature.

He cheerfully yielded the palm to old Alice Donnelly who could cure the warts by prayer, or a sty in the eye with three dalks from a thorn bush. 'They have to know,' she would say, as she ascertained exactly where the warts were located, and he wondered who 'they' might be. He had nothing of the defensive arrogance of the professional medical man, conceding that there are more things in heaven and earth than were dreamt of in his pharmacopoeia.

He listened spellbound to old Captain McNaughten who had rounded the Horn in sail and had fought polar bears with his bare hands; Captain McNaughten who could splice wire.

The White Rock was his Montmartre. Irregular matrimonial arrangements, occasional outbursts of wife-beating, or drunken shouting at night, added colour and variety to life. He saw squalor, weeds and decrepitude as 'texture', part of the infinitely varied canvas of life. And he passed to and fro each day benignly, always ready to lend an ear to a problem, or offer advice and sometimes more tangible help in the form of a few bob or a bottle for a wheezy chest.

The White Rock was his flagship, as he stood at his window, watching the rollers reaching from beyond the horizon and pounding on the beach below the house. In his mind he stood at the prow of his longship, his eyes searching for uncharted lands as he fought 'the old grey widow-maker', Kipling had said it all in that one phrase. Not that Mr Donovan was morose or without humour; there was that other deck, on which the boy had stood: 'His seward was in his hand', at least it had been in Josie Brett's version, declaimed from behind carious teeth and a glass of stout. 'He said, "I'll lave this bloody wreck and arse along the strand." ' Tellingly delivered, this line was always sure of a laugh, not least of all from Josie who grinned delightedly at the reaction.

Mrs Donovan was not too sure of the propriety of such things in a decent household, but she tolerated her husband's occasional lapse as evidence that she had in him a little gem, not exactly a rough diamond, nonetheless one with some interesting facets.

But it was not the sea that made her a widow in the end.

Striding to work one fine morning he faltered, reached for a corner-stone to steady himself and sank lifeless to the ground. Perhaps in that last instant he thought of Cuchulainn defying the men of Erin as he died by the menhir, or Byron's dying gladiator, or perhaps he wondered how his widow would survive and cope with genteel frugality and three hungry mouths to feed. It is possible that his last thoughts were guilty ones about the well that he had always intended to drill and had always postponed on the grounds that the rock was too hard and their house too high above the watertable. Whatever he thought in those last moments, he went on to his great adventure, possibly even to Valhalla, leaving work unfinished.

*   *   *

Joey looked down into the half-empty rainwater butt. His face was framed by a white disc of sky. The clouds moved in the reflection. He looked thoughtfully at the dark, almost sinister shadows on the face that looked back at him. 'We could do with some rain,' he remarked, and his voice echoed in the barrel. 'We could do with some rain,' he repeated, intrigued by the effect. 'Rain, rain,' he called again, watching minute creatures walking in little puckers on the surface.

'Hold on a minute,' said his older brother. 'I have an idea.'

Joey wasn't listening. 'Hey Kit, come and look at these spiders. They won't sink when I poke them. You'd think the water had a hard surface.'

11

'Don't be thick,' scoffed Kit. 'Here let me see.' He leaned over to see what was so interesting.

Their faces were framed together in the disc, a boy of twelve or thereabouts and an older lad looking very much more than his fifteen years in the dark shadows below.

'Hey, you'd think we were growin' beards,' laughed Joey. 'You look about twenty.'

Kit was pleased at the idea. He stood back from the barrel. 'Listen, I was sayin' that I had an idea.'

Joey turned. 'Not another one,' he groaned. Kit was always coming up with plans to make their fortune.

'No seriously, this is a good one. You've just given it to me.'

'Oh aye?'

'Well, what you said about the rain. You know the way oul' Miss Donnelly is always nabbin' us to get buckets of water from the square.'

Joey nodded. It was a sore point. 'There's no money in that.'

Indeed Miss Donnelly always promised a few coppers but never delivered. Anyway their mother would never have approved of their taking money for obliging a neighbour.

'In this dry weather everybody needs water. Now that I have the job with Mr Fedigan, we could use the bike to carry buckets in our spare time. Make a fortune.'

Joey looked thoughtful. 'What would Ma say, do you think? We don't want another row.'

Kit grimaced at the recollection. He had never seen her so upset as when he announced that he was thinking of quitting school to apprentice himself to Mr Drew. 'But Ma,' he had argued, 'this way I can be in business for myself by the time I'm twenty. I'll be my own boss.' She could not see it that way. She had hoped for better things for him: to put the Donovan name back over the pharmacy. Now he would never be anything better than a tradesman. Not that Mr Drew wasn't a gentleman after his fashion. She would not deny that, but education was the thing. 'Do you want to end up like Barney Phelan?' That was the last shot in her locker and she knew that it was futile. She lacked the resilience to continue the argument. If only the boys' father had survived. What would he have thought? Gradually she had retreated into her world of music. So she had hardly raised a protest when Kit took a summer job with Fedigans the butchers. A messenger boy. It was as if the family was irrevocably doomed. 'I don't know what your father would have thought of it all.'

Kit whistled thoughtfully through his teeth. 'Don't worry about it, Joey. She'll get used to the idea. The main thing is to make a few bob. That's capital you see. Then you can move on to something else.'

'Hmm.' Joey had gone back to watching the spiders. Sometimes they stopped as if in thought, making octagonal patterns on the dark surface, and sometimes they darted about without any apparent exertion as if propelled by hidden machinery or magnets. Joey speculatively flicked small pieces of moss into the water causing great confusion below.

'What's so interesting there?' asked Kit, stretching in the sunshine and closing his eyes.

'Nothing. I'm just giving these lads something to think about,' replied the younger boy.

'You should read the Da's nature book then, *Newton's Nature Reader*. It's very good on spiders and such like.'

'Get away.'

'No seriously.'

'I've read a good few of his books.' Joey liked to read, particularly the adventure stories. He liked to curl up in his father's old armchair, the one with the horsehair protruding in places, with the faint jangling of springs and lose himself in a world of adventure and stirring deeds.

'The ichneumon fly,' began Kit again with the air of a pompous lecturer, 'the ichneumon fly lays its eggs under the skin of the looper caterpillar, which then becomes a source of food for the growing larvae.'

'Yaah,' said Joey in disgust. He felt his flesh cringe at the thought. 'Is that true?' He left off tormenting the creatures below.

'That's a fact,' said Kit. 'It's all in the book. The poor chap has to carry them around inside him till they eat him away to nothing.'

Like Sinbad, thought Joey, except that it was not just one poor chap. Probably every looper caterpillar carried a freight of little Old Men of the Sea, wherever they went. Night and day they would feel their unwanted guests crunching away at their vitals. He shivered despite the heat. 'That's really horrible,' he murmured, more or less to himself.

'That's as may be,' said Kit dismissively. 'It's the way of the world. Everyone has to make a living.' He laughed. 'Look at us. We're going to make a few bob out of other people. It's the same thing really.'

'No it isn't,' insisted Joey.

'No, I suppose it isn't,' agreed Kit. He lay back against the wall, frowning. 'No, I suppose people are different from worms and such.'

Joey was forced to laugh at the seriousness of his expression. 'Oh, we're different all right. We've got brains, you see.' He splashed a handful of water at his brother, who scrambled to his feet to relatiate.

Joey danced back from the water barrel, keeping well out of range. Kit dashed a pail down into the depths and hurled a great plume of glittering spray at his retreating brother. Honour was satisfied.

'Right,' said Kit, putting down the pail, 'let's put our brains to work then. Let's see if we can get the bicycle for our own use too.'

'It's worth a try,' agreed Joey, pulling his braces up over his shoulders in business-like fashion. 'You can do the talking.'

The gate latch clinked behind them in the stillness of the summer afternoon. The spiders, those that had survived, resumed their clockwork evolutions on the pewter-coloured disc in the darkness of the rainwater barrel.

The bicycle was an impressive machine, heavy and black with a cage on the front fork to hold the basket and a step on the back axle for ease of mounting. A panel depending from the crossbar bore the legend *J. Fedigan, Victualler* in ornate script. The added luxury of a back carrier meant that Joey could accompany his brother on his rounds, to which Mr Fedigan had no objection, getting two messenger boys for the price of one.

They could hear the whine of steel as they approached the shop. Mr Fedigan was preparing for the afternoon's business in a blur of swordplay as he touched up his knives. He was a stocky middle-aged bachelor with a reddish face and several chins. His hair, parted in the middle, gleamed with oil.

Kit had suggested once at the table that God had granted Mr Fedigan an extra chin to compensate for the loss of his finger. Mrs Donovan thought this very disrespectful and Maureen had snorted her tea in a most unladylike manner.

No matter how he tried, Joey could not resist watching the stump as Mr Fedigan worked. It stirred and moved futilely, as if longing to be part of the activity of its fellows, and sometimes Joey felt quite sad for it. He wondered where the rest of it had gone. Had someone found an unexpected surprise in a pound of leg beef? What do you do with a severed limb? There was a story told about an old nun who had had a leg amputated. She sent it down to be buried in the family plot, even though the rest of her was to be buried with the other nuns in Glasnevin. It was no wonder that Mr Fedigan had lost it, the way he turned round from the chopping block to carry on a conversation while the cleaver continued to rise and fall.

Stubby cold looking fingers he had. Maureen said she always shivered when she looked at them.

'Ah, good lads,' he greeted them genially. 'All set for a bit of work?' He ruffled Joey's hair in avuncular fashion and Joey surreptitiously brushed it down, examining his hands for traces of meat. 'You can make a start on those orders there,' he continued, indicating the bundles on the side counter, 'and don't be too long.'

Kit tied on his striped apron and began to load the basket. Joey, as a mere camp follower, did not qualify for such grandeur but he helped anyway. It was a small price to pay for the privilege of being in on Kit's schemes. The round took them up the Dublin Road as far as the station, with sideloins for old Mr Cunningham, who had lost most of his teeth. It was a hard push up the hill but a point of pride not to dismount. The postman never managed to make it all the way. He dismounted at precisely the same spot every day and pushed the bicycle over the brow of the hill, having long ago compromised with masculine bravado. Kit would never give in to such frailty, even with his small, prehensile brother on the back.

'Ha, Donovan, ye won't make it,' jeered the familiar voice of Ned Doyle from where he lounged on the ditch with his pal Murphy.

Kit stood on the pedals, every tendon straining against the

hill. The chain groaned and clanked but did not slip. The tendons stood out on his neck as he pulled on the handlebars. 'Do you want a dig in the snot?' he snarled through clenched teeth.

Joey clung guiltily to the saddle, praying that he would not be the cause of his brother's humiliation.

The two on the ditch jeered as Kit began to zig-zag across the road.

'Ha, ye think you're great, don't ye?' roared Murphy.

With a final heave Kit took the machine over the brow of the hill and spat derisively towards the mockers. Joey exhaled in relief. It was always a relief to get safely past Ned Doyle. It was worse than passing a large dog. Doyle always had a jeer or a challenge for anyone smaller than himself, or possibly a stone idly bounced along the street to test for a reaction. There was no danger of that with Kit around, but Doyle had a way of holding a grudge.

'I hate that fella,' confided Joey as they neared the station. He did not mention the spasm of fear that always passed through his belly when he recognised Doyle's menacing figure.

Kit was still gasping for breath as they turned the corner onto Station Road. Quickly he dismounted, out of sight of the enemy. 'We couldn't give them the satisfaction, could we, pal?'

He grinned and Joey's heart warmed to him. Kit always treated him as an equal in everything they did, despite the difference in age and size.

'Some day,' confided Kit, 'some day I'm goin' to have to give Ned Doyle a hiding, just on principle like.'

'You'd be well able for him,' agreed Joey loyally, but he wondered about unpleasant repercussions on himself.

'I've a brilliant idea,' said Kit after a while, as he leaned on the handlebars. 'Why don't you let him give you a couple of belts and then I'll come along an' beat the daylights out of him?' He swung a clenched fist enthusiastically.

'I don't know. What would I get out of it, Kit?' asked the smaller boy, dubiously.

'Insurance. He'd never go near you again.'

Joey frowned. He did not like the thoughts of the initial outlay. 'Ah sure, don't worry about him. I'm not scared of •him,' he said, shelving the plan for the time being.

'It's an idea though,' persisted Kit. 'Hey, why don't we go round by Toker Hill and lob a few stones in at Barney Phelan.'

'Ah, I think we'd better go back, or Mr Fedigan will be angry. You don't want to lose your job on your first day out.'

'Aye, maybe you're right,' sighed Kit. 'Still, it would be fun, and we could get clean away on the bicycle.'

'There's stuff here for Sweeneys.' That was the decider. 'It's all right for you,' Joey pointed out, 'you're finished with school but I have to go back in September. I don't want to be scutched because you lost his meat in the ditch somewhere.'

Still, September was a long way off. The weather was fine and like the prospect of mortality, Master Sweeney was an unreal and problematic figure.

'You're right Joey, you're right,' agreed Kit. 'Anyway we can freewheel all the way down.'

There was no sign of the enemy on the way back.

'Hey Kit,' yelled Joey against the rush of air, 'are you really not going to go back to the Brothers?'

'Not a chance. I'm not goin' to spend the rest of me life travellin' in and out to Dublin every day. Two years of that was enough. Mr Drew is going to take me on and teach me the trade. I'll be able to go out on me own before I'm twenty. There'll be any amount of buildin' around here.'

Joey was filled with envy. 'It's well for you,' he shouted again. 'Do you think Ma will agree?'

'Ah she'll give out for a while and then she'll just get tired. You're the one that will have to study and be a chemist. You'll have to put the name back on the shop.'

Mr Fedigan was pleased with the speed and efficiency of his new team. As six o'clock came near he directed them to sweep up the sawdust and scraps and push up the canvas blind.

'Mr Fedigan, is it all right if we bring the bicycle home?' asked Kit as they were clearing up. 'We'd be very careful with it.'

Mr Fedigan rubbed the side of his nose as he pondered the question. 'Hmm,' he said, 'and why might ye want to do that?'

'Well it would be great to have a bicycle, like, if we had to do messages for Ma, you know,' began Kit earnestly, 'and of course it would mean we'd never be late in the morning.'

'I see, I see,' mused Mr Fedigan, untying his apron and hanging it on a nail. Joey's eyes followed the movements of

17

his truncated digit in fascination. 'Well, as long as no damage comes to it, I suppose it's all right, though mind you, ye'll have to pay for it if ye break it.'

'Oh we will Mr Fedigan and thanks very much.'

'And by the way,' added Mr Fedigan casually, 'there's a few sweetbreads for your mammy, with my compliments. A great lady, your mammy. I hope she enjoys them.'

'Thank you very much Mr Fedigan,' replied Kit politely. 'She'll be very pleased, I'm sure.'

Outside the shop he gave a little skip of triumph. 'I knew he'd lend it to us,' he beamed. 'I just knew it.'

'How did you figure that out?' enquired Joey, who had not been at all sure.

'Ha, ha, never mind. You'll understand when you're older.'

'Aw come on. You didn't know at all.'

Kit held up the brown paper parcel. 'Sweetbreads for Ma, how are ye. Oul Fedigan is daft about her. Did you know that?'

'That's stupid,' snapped Joey, repelled by the idea. He had a vision of Mr Fedigan laying his pudgy mutilated hands on his willowy graceful mother. 'You shouldn't say things like that.'

'Lookit, you don't have to be like that about it. It's just that he always gives her the choicest cuts and the odd little bit extra, that's all,' Kit back-tracked, embarrassed by his younger brother's ferocity as if he had been caught out in some shameful act. 'Anyway,' he said defensively, 'he lent us the bicycle, didn't he?'

'I suppose so, yeah,' agreed Joey, his mood improving. Sure Mr Fedigan was ancient. He must be nearly fifty. 'It's just I thought you meant he was after her, you know.'

'Don't be an eejit. Sure she wouldn't even notice him outside of his shop.' He leaned his elbows on the handlebars as he walked along. 'Still, how would you like it if they got married?' He started to guffaw at the notion.

But Joey did not join in the mirth. He felt as if a cloud had passed over the sun to think of Mr Fedigan taking the place of the shadowy dapper little figure that had been his father. 'I don't think that's very funny,' he grumbled, and contemplated throwing the sweetbreads in the gutter.

'Ah, is that youse boys?' came the familiar cracked voice from the darkness inside a cottage door.

'Yes, Miss Donnelly,' they chorused in unison. Nabbed again.

'Would yiz ever run round to the square and get me a little drop o' water?'

'Yes, Miss Donnelly, certainly.'

This was an opportunity to test out their plan even though there was no profit involved.

It was simplicity itself, and hardly a drop spilled.

'We're in the money,' exulted Kit. 'We can't miss.'

They hid the bicycle in the coalshed and went into the house. Their mother was sitting at the piano in the drawing-room overlooking the north beach. They could hear her rich contralto voice announcing her dream of dwelling in marble halls as her fingers rippled over the keys. Percy French had sat in that very room looking out at the mountains and had been moved to write his immortal song about how they swept down to the sea. Similar claims they knew had been made for practically every drawing-room as far as Dundalk, but they loyally accepted their mother's version as the genuine article and she knew about music.

She paused and smiled upon her sons. 'Ah boys, you're home. Have you had a pleasant afternoon? Now, just listen to this for a moment.' Her fingers flew over the keyboard as she resumed her interrupted melody. She gazed intently upon them, transported by the music.

Kit shuffled and wondered about tea. Joey inadvertently thought of marble slabs with round steak spread out to the view, oxtails cunningly sectioned and bound into circles, cows' tongues forever silenced by skewers, and he shivered at the thought.

* * *

Kit tugged the bell pull at the kitchen door and wished someone would answer. The corned beef was escaping through the sodden paper. 'Come on, come on,' he muttered as the brine ran over his hands and into the sleeve of his jacket. He heard footsteps on the other side of the door and hoped it might be the pretty maid again. 'Meat for Baileys,' he called urgently. His luck was in, but she was not dressed as he expected.

'Oh, hello,' she said brightly. She wore a light cotton dress with a pattern of small blue flowers, and on her head a straw hat with a ribbon around it. The ends of the ribbon trailed down over her auburn hair. 'It's the butcher's boy,' she called back over her shoulder. 'You'd better come inside,' she added, eyeing the dripping bundle.

Gratefully Kit deposited the meat on a large dish and made to wipe his hands on the seat of his trousers.

'No wait,' said the girl, and reached for a dishcloth. 'Wash your hands first. We can't have you ruining your clothes, can we?'

She was about nineteen, Kit judged, watching her with interest. English by the sound of her. A lot of English people stayed in the big houses along the terrace during the summer months, so it was logical that they would bring their servants with them. He searched for something intelligent to say to make a good impression but could think of nothing except 'Thanks' as she handed him the cloth.

'Who is it my dear?' boomed a man's voice from the corridor, followed by a clatter, like sticks falling on the tiled floor.

'What are you doing, Grandad?' called the girl, hurrying to the door.

Kit could hear scuffling and muttered imprecations and felt that he ought to offer his assistance.

'It's the butcher's boy, Grandad,' repeated the girl, and Kit realised his mistake. He could feel his face colouring and was glad the kitchen was gloomy.

'Well, have him in here at once to lend a hand,' rasped the man's voice impatiently.

Kit moved quickly to the door and saw a large bearded old gentleman struggling with what looked like a huge target, trying to extricate it from the jumble in a small storeroom.

'Good lad,' said the old man brusquely. 'Be a good fellow and carry this thing out into the garden.' His tone was that of one who was not used to having his instructions questioned.

There was no great weight in the thing, which consisted of a thick straw rope wound into a circle and faced with stiff card that had been punctured many times. With no difficulty Kit hefted the target and manoeuvred it through the kitchen and up the steps to the lawn. The girl stooped and retrieved a bundle of arrows that had spilled onto the floor.

'Over here, over here,' called the old man gesticulating to Kit. 'Keep it well out from the wall.'

He directed Kit to one end of the tennis court, where Kit extended the legs of the tripod and stepped rapidly aside.

'Thank you, my boy,' called the old man, deftly stringing a longbow, bracing it against his instep and slipping the string into a notch.

Kit came closer, watching with interest. He had never seen a real bow or arrows before.

'Well, young man,' queried the old gentleman, 'are you by any chance, a toxophilite?'

Kit knew of a great many sects and creeds among Protestants but this was a new one to him. 'Eh, no sir,' he replied diffidently, careful to avoid any inflection of criticism in his own voice. A man's religion is essentially his own business.

'Pity,' rumbled the old man. 'It's a splendid sport. Excellent for the chest and lungs you know. Give me some arrows my dear, and let me instruct our friend in this ancient art.'

The girl smiled at Kit's obvious confusion and handed a blunt brass-headed arrow to her grandfather.

'This is the cock feather,' said the old man. 'Keep it out from the bow, like so.' Quickly he notched the arrow and drew the string back almost to the tip of his nose. 'A clothier's yard,' he chuckled. 'Better not let fly, or we might damage the bathers on the beach.' He lowered the bow, releasing some of the tension and let the arrow go. The string thwacked against the sleeve of his Norfolk jacket and the arrow embedded itself in the outer rim of the target. 'Aha,' he coughed in disparagement. 'A trifle rusty. We'll soon get the hang of it again.' He thrust the bow into Kit's hand. 'Have a try yourself young man. This is the weapon that won Agincourt for us.'

The reference was lost on Kit. Gingerly he took the bow and the girl notched another arrow for him. He was conscious of her closeness and a faint perfume. Carefully he drew back the arrow, holding it between thumb and forefinger, but almost immediately it was plucked from his hand and fell ignominiously at his feet. Feeling more foolish than ever, he offered the bow to the old man, who waved it away.

The girl notched another arrow. She seemed to be laughing

21

at him. 'Now this time, hold the string,' she advised, 'with the tips of your fingers. Like this.'

Deftly she demonstrated the grip and Kit drew back the arrow once more. It swung out from the bow, through ninety degrees and escaped again from his grip. The girl laughed again.

'One more try,' she said, and picked up the arrow for him.

Right, thought Kit. I'll get it this time. Carefully he drew back the arrow again, raising his left thumb slightly to hold it in place. The bow kicked in his hand as he released and the arrow shot towards the target. It was much too low and grassed itself before it reached the mark, but it was a satisfying feeling nonetheless.

'Have another try,' offered the old man and the girl handed Kit another arrow. Carefully he notched it as he had been shown. 'Now,' advised the old man, 'look at the target. Watch where you want it to go. Pull back firmly and release smoothly.'

The bowstring sang and the arrow thudded into the target, on the outer edge of the white.

'Splendid, young man,' called the old man approvingly while the girl applauded. 'You have a natural talent.'

Kit glowed with pride. He handed the bow to the girl and shifted awkwardly from one foot to the other. 'Excuse me, but I have to go,' he said. 'I have to get back to work.'

'You must come again some time and shoot a few rounds with us,' said the old man genially. 'It could come in useful if you decide to go off to the war.'

'Oh, Grandad, don't say such a thing,' admonished the girl. 'He's only a boy.'

Kit did not know whether he was pleased or not by her defence of him and said nothing. The English spoke of little else but their war, which as far as he could gather, was not going too well. He mumbled incoherently and made his escape. Looking back he saw the girl drawing the bow and thought he had never seen anyone so graceful in all his life.

Joey was squatting beside the bicycle looking very disgruntled. 'What kept you?' he asked accusingly.

'I was engaged in conversation with a couple of tox-toxophilites,' replied Kit, pronouncing the word deliberately.

Joey's eyes became round with wonder. 'A couple of what?'

'Toxophilites,' repeated Kit archly. 'We were discussing the war.' He refused to be drawn any further and climbed onto the saddle. 'Come on,' he said, 'get aboard.'

Joey pondered on the word. It must be something like Freemasons with their peculiar oaths and ceremonies. What strange goings-on went on behind that high garden wall? He hoped that his brother would not get into any bother for consorting with them. Kit had great ideas, he had to admit, but he wasn't always the wisest man. 'Who's winnin' the war, anyway?'

'I suppose the English are. They nearly always win, don't they? But the Turks are givin' them a fierce hammerin' in the Dardanelles.'

'Where's that?'

'It's in Turkey, I think. I mean if the English are able to invade Turkey they must have the war nearly won, mustn't they?'

'I suppose so, yeah. That makes sense,' agreed Joey sagely. 'Lookit, if we get rid of all this stuff as quick as we can, we'd have time to go for a dip before we go back to the shop.'

'Now that's a good idea,' said Kit, and stood up on the pedals.

Dr Bailey was pleased with his visit to Strifeland House and his interview with old Colonel Wyndham. There was a man, he mused, who spoke the same language, a man who had seen the world and understood a thing or two. If there was anything good to be said for the war it was that people like himself could still play a useful role at an age when normally they would have been put out to pasture. And Strifeland House would be a fine Red Cross hospital for the convalescents.

He hummed as he cycled along, an imposing and dignified figure. He had extended his lease on the house in the terrace and his granddaughter had agreed to stay on into the autumn until her art college opened. This agreeable prospect went some way towards counter-balancing the dismal war news. Casualty lists grew longer day by day. It was all such an appalling waste. There was no sign now of the enthusiasm of the previous year when the first expeditionary force had set off for France 'to wrap the whole thing up by Christmas'.

But it was hard to imagine such horrors as he gently glided

down the tree-lined lane. Dr Bailey felt young again as he gained speed. He remembered such days sixty years before, when with companions long lost in the mists of time, he had gathered conkers along similar country lanes. He recalled his lost boyhood in well-worn and serviceable clichés.

At the top of the last stretch of hill he paused and, leaning on a gate, looked at the town and the sea beyond. His eye travelled over the rolling countryside and the tawny islands offshore. 'I will build a house in the high woods, within a walk of the sea,' he mused nostalgically. Not a bad idea. This could be a very agreeable place to spend the rest of his days. Below him on the road he could see two small figures engaged in some merry game, as boys will, stalking their prey from behind a wall, arming themselves with pebbles from the roadside.

Silently he glided down to observe them more closely. The brakes groaned and the bicycle juddered to a halt. He recognised the butcher's lad and another urchin and saw them launch a salvo of pebbles onto the tin roof of a cowshed below. The boys were laughing and clutching at each other and Dr Bailey peered over the wall in curiosity.

Out from the straw of the cowshed rose an apparition dressed in filthy rags, with matted hair dangling from below a battered hat, and a face covered in several days' growth of bristle. Bloodshot eyes glared up at the astonished old gentleman and the mouth opened in a snarl of hatred, revealing a couple of jagged, yellow stained teeth.

'G'out to hell owa'that, ye cur ye,' bellowed the apparition as he threshed about in the straw, struggling to his feet and reaching for something to throw.

Dr Bailey retreated in alarm as a fusilade of stones and sticks came flying over the wall, accompanied by some of the most incredible profanity it had ever been his misfortune to hear. The boys were already gone, speeding down the hill, and Dr Bailey set off after them, pedalling furiously. Over his shoulder he caught a glimpse of his pursuer brandishing a stick and starting to climb the haggard gate. There was an invitation to go back and have his block knocked off, which Dr Bailey declined. Within seconds he was safely out of sight beyond the railway arch, having suffered nothing worse than the loss of his dignity and a good tweed cap.

'Prodesant bastard,' snarled Barney returning to his lair. 'Think they own the whole bloody country, by Jaysus.' He kicked at the straw until he located his bag, shaking it vigorously to make sure nothing had been taken. 'Wouldn't put it past him,' he muttered to nobody in particular. He threshed around in the straw until he located the pile of newspapers.

He selected one at random. It was a week old and already turning yellow. The solemn faces of dead young men stared at him from the Roll of Honour. Important looking, they were, with parents who had important sounding names, but still, they had all been killed. There were lists of others too, but there were no pictures of them. It must be a fierce business all the same, not like the old days. He lay back in the straw, pondering on the matter. After a while he drew the paper over his face and soon he was snoring.

CHAPTER 2

If ever a man was suited to his job, it was Paddy Moran, who drove the traction engine that powered the threshing mill. Every autumn he appeared, from God knows where, fuming and swearing as he manoeuvred his train through narrow country roads and haggard gateways, steam engine, mill, baler and caravan almost as if the Great Northern Railway had taken to the road.

A thoughtful onlooker might have concluded that Paddy's soul was charged with the same fire that powered his mighty machine. He operated in a state of almost perpetual rage, which he vented in particular on his unfortunate assistant, Francie, and on any small boys who came within arm's length. Solicitude for their safety, perhaps, urged him to hurl coke and invective at those who seemed bent either on thwarting him in some delicate negotiation or on throwing themselves under the great cleated wheels.

Whatever their individual motives, the threshing always attracted a crowd. In vain would Master Sweeney whack the desk with the hairy end of his bamboo when the whisper went around that Paddy Moran had appeared at Shanleys' or had set up camp in the Twelve Acres. Boys fidgeted to be away, to riot in the chaff and slide on the baler chute, or just watch the grain pouring from the shuddering machine, or the 'horse's head' rising and falling, as it compressed the tumbling straw into bales. The hours of school dragged as they fretted at the thought that ricks were shrinking and that it might all be over by the time they got there. There were some who mitched on threshing days and, as is often the way of the world, the good suffered while the wicked prospered.

They calculated how quickly the mill would dispose of Moles's and of Duffs', the former a modest affair which could be sacrificed with no great loss and the latter a superior event, on the rise over the Mill Pond, where there was always plenty of barley chaff to stuff down the collars of enemies. But the essential thing was to be at the Strifeland threshing, which could stretch over two whole days. This was the time when Paddy was at his best. He had to take the mill across the tracks at the level crossing and there was always the chance that a train might happen along, not that anyone would actually want an accident to occur. The Strifeland people, anyway, had some hold over the railway company and could always arrange matters to avoid any unfortunate collision.

There was excitement enough in watching how Paddy worked the train into position, with a certain amount of diffident advice from Francie, before whisking it through the gate and across the tracks with masterly assurance. There was a certain amount of language used on these occasions, which added to the interest of the occasion and expanded the schoolboy vocabulary, as Paddy twirled the steering wheel with the heel of his hand on the little brass knob and the chains wound and unwound on the axle.

It was also an occasion when boys could legitimately walk on Strifeland soil without the old atavistic fear of man traps or salt guns, a chance to see behind the high perimeter wall and to admire the elegance of the old plantations.

The mill devoured the ricks like a shuddering monster. Pungent black smoke billowed as wheels turned and the belt hummed, going and coming, going and coming in a hypnotic figure of eight. Wheels with medusa-like spokes whirred as the men, stripped to waistcoats and shirtsleeves, forked the sheaves into the insatiable maw. Like an African kraal under the onslaught of spoilers, the conical stacks of oats lost their roofs and gradually dwindled to nothing, leaving only light circles on the ground as evidence that they had ever been. The great toothed head of the baler rose and fell, forcing the straw into the machine and the bales inched along the gleaming metal track, always with a child in front for the ride. Boys dived into the piles of chaff and stuffed handfuls down each other's shirt collars. The men moved their ladders and climbed to the ridge of a majestic rick of wheat.

Davy Bennett gazed up in admiration at his father, a sinewy, angular man outlined against the afternoon sun. His da was always the man in charge, and also the fastest man to pitch a sheaf, or bowl a ball for that matter, in the whole locality. Davy wished with all his heart to be like his da but deep down he suspected that he never would be. His da was always one for a laugh or a chat or whatever bit of sport there was about. Even a threshing became a contest so that he could show the younger lads that he was still the best man around.

Davy, by contrast, was small for his nine years. He was a quiet, observant child, used to being by himself for a great deal of the time. He knew the woods and fields of Strifeland and the creatures that lurked in the hedgerows and copses. He drew the birds and animals on the margins of his schoolbooks and jotter. He knew where hazelnuts and Spanish chestnuts grew and where the best mushrooms could be found, but he would have traded all his knowledge to be like the rowdy village boys.

Under the overhang of a rick as yet untouched, he found a fieldmouse with its young. The nest was new and the baby mice were pink and naked, for all the world like jellybabies. The mother trembled in terror, her eyes glinting and whiskers twitching. Davy drew back, sensing her fear. He looked around furtively, jealous of his secret. He had to do something before the men moved in to destroy their home. Quickly he stooped and gathered the mouse and her brood in his cupped hands. She made only a little token struggle, refusing to abandon her offspring. Davy's mind raced. There was straw in the shed at home, but the cats might get them. The Strifeland terriers would surely find them if he hid them in the barn. A weasel or a hawk would kill them if he left them in the ditch.

'What have you got there, young Bennett?' demanded a familiar voice.

Davy paled as he turned to see Ned Doyle and his pal Murphy. 'Nothin',' he mumbled backing away.

But Doyle was not convinced. 'Let's see,' he insisted, grabbing the smaller boy's wrists.

Murphy laughed. 'He's scared,' he jeered. 'He's a cry-babby. Look at him.'

Tears had come to Davy's eyes, tears of fear and frustration as he knew there was no escape.

Doyle twisted his hands open and the tiny bodies spilled onto the stubble. The parent mouse shot away into the straw.

'Jaysus,' swore the startled Doyle, and spat, to restore his reputation. 'Here, give us them.'

Davy dived to prevent him but Doyle grabbed the writhing mice and was gazing at them in wonder.

'They're alive,' he said, unnecessarily, as they squirmed and twisted on his palm.

'Give them back,' shouted Davy, 'I found them.' He held out his hands. 'Don't hurt them,' he pleaded, afraid to grab.

'Them are vermin,' said Murphy. 'Yiz should kill them.'

'That's right,' agreed Doyle, 'anyway they're no use, are they?'

'They're mine,' repeated Davy desperately. 'If you kill them I'll . . .'

'You'll what?' sneered Doyle. 'Tell your oul' fella?' He guffawed at the idea, and Murphy loyally joined in the laughter. 'I tell ye what,' said Doyle genially, 'I'll give them back after I teach them to swim.' He gestured towards the water butts lined up beside the traction engine. 'Come on Murphy,' he shouted gleefully, and broke into a run, pursued by the frantic Davy. 'Hold him there Murphy and let him see,' he ordered, and Murphy twisted Davy's arm painfully. 'One,' declaimed Doyle, and dropped the first small body into the water butt with a plop.

Davy saw it sink and rise to the surface, the limbs feebly groping for a few seconds, and then the creature slowly sank and was lost in the dark depths of the barrel.

'Two,' sang Doyle, and another mouse followed and sank. 'Three,' continued Doyle.

Davy's face burned with rage and humiliation. 'That's enough,' he said in an effort at appeasement. 'Let me keep the rest.'

'In a minute,' laughed Doyle, and tipped the remaining three into the water. 'Now,' he added with satisfaction, 'they're all yours.'

Murphy gave his prisoner's arm a final twist and pushed him to the ground. Tears streamed down Davy's face. In rage he leaped up and struck blindly at his tormentors, but Murphy pushed him casually to the ground again.

'Cry babby.'

'Come on,' muttered Doyle. 'Here's Kit Donovan and that brother of his. Let's go somewhere else.'

'What's up with you?' enquired Kit of the miserable boy on the ground. 'What are you crying for? Did they hurt you?'

Davy shook his head. 'I'm all right,' he mumbled, and wiped his nose with his sleeve, looking away in humiliation.

'What are youse doin' to that young lad?' bellowed a voice from above.

Kit looked up to see Tom Bennett on top of the rick, holding his pitchfork in the manner of the Archangel Michael. 'I never touched him,' said the aggrieved Kit, backing away as Bennett began to descend the ladder.

'Go near him again and you'll get a kick in the arse from me,' said Bennett menacingly.

'We never touched him,' insisted Kit, pushing Joey behind him and moving warily backwards.

Bennett was obviously furious. 'Yiz little gets,' he growled, 'get to hell away from here before I lay me hands on yiz.'

'Come on Joey,' said Kit angrily. 'There's no point in arguin'.'

'You're not hurt, are ye?' queried Bennett brusquely. He lifted the boy to his feet and brushed him down. 'You'll have to learn to stand up for yourself, even if they are bigger,' he added by way of concession.

'It wasn't them, Da,' sniffed Davy. 'It was two other lads. They . . .' he hesitated, unable to explain about the mice and half afraid that his father might laugh at him.

'Aye well, anyway,' said Bennett and reached for his watch-chain, 'ye still have to stand up for yourself.' He grunted and drew out an elaborately engraved pocket watch, his most treasured possession. He pressed the catch and the lid sprang open, releasing a sprinkling of silvery notes. Bennett gazed thoughtfully at the dial and then at the rick, translating its height into hours of work. 'Aye,' he muttered thoughtfully again.

Davy stared at the rainbow colours on the oily surface of the water and wondered miserably at the mindlessness of the whole episode.

'Aye,' muttered Bennett a second time and snapped the lid shut cutting off the music. 'Aye, well,' he repeated as if at a loss for something to say. He spat on his hands and hefted his pitchfork. 'Anyway,' he said again, 'ye have to stand up for yourself in this life and that's the holy all of it.' He set his foot on the ladder and grasped a rung.

The child turned away, kicking at the chaff. It's hard on them at that age, thought his father, watching him, but you can't fight their battles for them. Just as well, he reminded himself, or I would have broken that young lad's neck.

*   *   *

The warm days of autumn gave way to a grey, frosty October. It looked as if the war would see in a second Christmas. It formed a familiar backdrop to conversations, spoken of now as a regrettable necessity rather than a crusade to save civilization. There was a certain pride in the knowledge that the Irish regiments had acquitted themselves well, as was only to be expected, even if in some strident quarters it was said that this was not Ireland's fight. Recruiting drives took place with considerable success and Kitchener, stern and uncompromising, pointed an accusing finger at shirkers.

Some local men took the hint, perhaps exchanging a constant penury for some sort of security, however short-lived. There were some obvious benefits to their wives and families, who for the first time enjoyed the luxury of a regular income.

A story circulated that two of them met unexpectedly in the trenches, one leaving the line while the other was making his way up to the front. 'I wouldn't go up there, if I was you,' warned the first. 'They're fuckin' killin' each other up there.' Whereas people laughed at the retelling, it had to be admitted that this simple uneducated farm labourer, who had spent most of his life following horses, had identified the one salient feature of the war never mentioned by the General Staff. Lord Kitchener could have modified his slogan to give some idea of what your country needed you for. There was even talk of conscription.

'Would you go and fight, Kit, if conscription came in?' asked Joey, as he placed a bucket under the pump.

Kit snorted. 'Sure I'm far too young. It'll be all over long before that. They'll have to make peace fairly soon.'

'I hope so,' said his brother, 'or they'll run out of men.'

'No danger of that,' said Kit. 'There's always plenty of eejits that will join anything, just for the hell of it.'

'Not me,' grunted Joey, trying the handle, feeling for the suction. The pump made a few gargling noises and coughed explosively. He spat on his hands.

'You're right there old son. There's no money in wadin' up to your knees in muck. That's a mug's game.' Kit hunkered down on the stone kerb while Joey began to pump. Water gurgled up through the pipe and spattered sideways in a sudden gust of wind. It was startlingly cold on his face. 'I think, Joey,' he said thoughtfully, 'we might give up the water business.'

'Oh aye?' said Joey as he swung on the pump handle. 'What makes you say that?' Privately he had begun to think more or less along the same lines. It was all very well for Kit, in a way. He was kept on at Fedigans after the summer and had a few bob in his pocket, whereas Joey still had school and homework and his few hours of daylight were taken up with a most unprofitable scheme. There was frost in the afternoon air and he wished that he was at home by the fire, even with his exercise book on his knee.

'Well it's just that we seem to spend most of the time doin' favours. Every oul' one in the street has got her hooks into us. We must be owed a fortune. Oul' Donnelly must've put the word around about what nice lads we are. The ma is always tellin' me that the oul' ones stop her in the street to tell her about how obligin' we are.'

Joey stopped pumping and swung his arms vigorously, thumping himself on the back to warm his hands, the way the jarveys did it. It was nearly as cold as when they got hanks of fish and carried them home, with twine cutting into their white and frozen fingers. 'I think maybe you're right. There's no money in this game.' He thought of January and February and his spirit quailed.

'I was thinkin',' continued Kit after a pause, 'we could make a lot of money out of hens.'

'Hens!' exclaimed Joey. 'How could we keep hens? The ma would never let us keep hens.' He tried to picture his mother in a cross-over flowered apron, with a bucket of bran, standing among Leghorns and Wyandottes, but the picture did not fit.

'Not at first, I know, but she'd come around. She always comes around.' Kit spoke from experience. 'I'm startin' with Mr Drew sometime in the New Year and I'll be able to get any amount of old bent nails.'

'What for?'

'For the henhouse, you eejit. We'll have to make a henhouse.'

'We've no wood,' Joey pointed out.

'We can easily get wood.'

'What? Pay carriage on it on the train? How much would that cost? How much would the wood cost, eh?' he laughed.

'Not on the train, Joey,' explained Kit patiently. 'There's loads of timber on the island. All we have to do . . .'

'I know, I know,' sighed Joey. 'All we have to do is walk over at low tide and carry a load back.'

'On the bicycle, Joey, on the bicycle. It wouldn't be hard.'

'I bet it would,' said Joey, and laughed again.

'That's a good one,' laughed Kit generously. 'I bet it would.' He hoisted the buckets into the basket.

Joey braced the bicycle against his hip. The weight threatened to take the machine down by the head, but he managed to keep it upright. Water sloshed over his bare knees and trickled down his socks and into his boots. 'Shite!' he said with feeling. 'And shite again. You're right about this water business anyway.'

* * *

Barney Phelan had his regulars, on whom he bestowed his custom and his observations on world affairs, in exchange for a mug of soup and a few cuts of bread. Mrs Donovan had somehow acquired him as a kind of legacy from her husband, who had ministered occasionally to the old man's ailments.

'A quare dacent man, Mr Donovan,' Barney recalled between mouthfuls, 'better nor a real doctor any day.'

He took his meal outside the back door, refusing to come in, and held forth on a variety of topics as he munched, and swilled the contents of his mouth around with great swigs of tea. Maureen found it difficult to watch him but there was no escape. She made sure to stand well back nonetheless, as he rambled on about the war.

'Now I'm tellin' yiz, them Frenchies won't never hang on at Verdum. Didn't they run away the last time and leave the poor Pope on his own?'

This was still a sore point with Barney, who claimed to have defended His Holiness personally against the depredations of Garibaldi. Half a century before, he had, he claimed, seen service in the Papal Zouaves, 'the Zow-waves', and was on speaking terms with Pio Nono himself. Nobody was too sure how much of Barney's recollections were factual and how much the product of a knock on the head, sustained in some less worthy cause. It was a matter for speculation in some circles to what extent Barney's influence had transformed the radical young Pope into the infallible arch-conservative, or how much of the Phelan doctrines had penetrated into the *Syllabus of Errors*.

' "The hard man, Barney," he says to me oncet, "if it wasn't for the likes of yerself, the Church would be in a sorry state." As for the French,' Barney snorted in contempt, spraying particles of masticated bread in a semi-circle, 'ah, them'll never hould out at Verdum.'

'I'm sure you're right Mr Phelan,' agreed Maureen, anxious to terminate the interview.

Barney glared at her and the cataract swam in his left eye, like the film that slips across a hen's beady gaze. 'I know mutton from goat,' he averred. 'I know what it takes to make a soldier.' He clenched his stick and shook it towards the craven anti-Catholic French. 'Most of the curs don't even go to Mass.' He gave a last lascivious suck at the dregs of sugar in his mug and handed it to Maureen. 'I better be off about me business,' he complained. 'I'll be 'round again, Friday with a few fish.'

'Oh, I'm sure that will be all right,' replied Maureen graciously.

Barney's habit of appearing on the doorstep with a few fish for sale was something she did not encourage. The cat did very well out of it but nobody in the family would risk touching any. There was a time, before total decrepitude had set in, when Barney did a reasonable trade. 'Pinch them ma'am. Nice and firm they are,' he would invite a prospective customer, engendering interest in his wares — a rule of thumb that could be applied to many commodities. Legend had it that one housewife, having chosen a particularly firm codfish, had opened it later to find a tight wad of sacking thrust inside. On being tackled about this, Barney had sucked in his lips, looked thoughtful for a moment and pronounced in tones of wonder: 'Be jaysus, but them cod is quare ravenous craturs.'

Away he stumped, muttering to himself.

Maureen looked dubiously at the mug. It was known offici- ally as Barney's mug and the family observed the polite fiction that no one else should use it, out of consideration for a guest. Maureen rinsed it thoroughly in the rainwater barrel and replaced it in its solitary state on a scullery shelf. Then she rinsed her hands in a fresh bucket of water and sloshed it out in the yard, reflecting guiltily that she would have to overcome squeamishness if she was ever to become a proper nurse. She had no fear of blood or broken bones, and she could envisage herself soothing a fevered brow, but there were dark areas relating to hygiene and old age into which she was afraid to probe too deeply as yet. There was still plenty of time and she had no doubt that she would rise to any occasion when that time arrived. If all her patients were like the grateful young soldiers she had seen in recruiting advertisements, most of them with an arm in a sling or an interesting looking bandage set askew on a forehead, there would be no problem; but suppos- ing they were all like Barney Phelan. She wrinkled her nose, unsure of how to face such a problem. Her train of thought was interrupted by the arrival of Joey from school.

'You're home early,' he said accusingly, throwing his school- bag on the kitchen table.

'We had no school today, poor suck,' jeered Maureen. 'It's a feast day, didn't you know?'

'Oh yeah,' agreed Joey disconsolately. Girls had all the luck. He picked at the strap of his bag with little enthusiasm. For all Mr Sweeney's interest in religion, he was not very givish with days off for feast days. He could belt both large and small catechism into you, and the Mass Latin, and whole doses of litanies. He could dwell on the sufferings of Calvary when the First Friday confession was due, until your knees went weak at the thoughts of it. He interrogated closely all those who skipped the children's sodality on a Sunday afternoon — a Sunday afternoon, for God's sake — but the concept of God being love was more likely to be accompanied by a belt on the ear than a day off to worship in the cathedral of created nature with Saint Francis and Brother Sun. Joey sighed at the injustice of it all.

'Maureen,' he began hesitantly after a while, 'what do you think of Mr Fedigan?'

'I don't know. Why?' Maureen slumped forward on the table and rested her chin on her folded arms.

'Ah nothin'. It's just, well, Kit says he has his eye on Ma.'

Maureen sat bolt upright in surprise. 'That's stupid,' she exclaimed. 'He says the stupidest things at times.'

'Well I just wondered what you would say. I know he is only codding.' He had to avoid disloyalty to Kit but was relieved that Maureen dismissed the idea out of hand. Maureen would always know for sure about things in general, but then she was the eldest.

'What put that idea into his head anyway?' she asked in puzzlement.

'Ah, I don't know. It's just that he always puts in a little bit extra, "a bit of fillet for the mammy," ' he mimicked, brushing back an imaginary cow's-lick and wiping the imaginary hair-oil on his backside in Mr Fedigan's fastidious way.

Maureen laughed aloud. 'Can you just see it? All of us sitting at the table, and him with the drop on the end of his nose. "Would ye like a bit o' suet with it missus?" ' She sniffed. 'I'm always terrified of that drop.'

Joey howled at the idea. 'You watchin' his drop and me watchin' his fingers. We'd be a right family.'

A thought occurred to Maureen. 'Do you think they could play duets together and just skip one note now and again?'

Joey played a maimed arpeggio on the table and slid off his chair with the laughter. 'Now that's not nice,' he protested. 'We shouldn't talk like that.'

Again they howled at the idea, calming down, only to burst out again.

The maid could hear them laughing as she came into the yard. 'Who thrun that water in the yard?' she asked sharply.

'I did. Why?' answered Maureen.

'Well ye didn't say "by your lave" to the fairies and it's freezin'. I nearly broke me neck.'

This was the signal for renewed outbursts of mirth at the expense of the unfortunate country girl. She sniffed: 'Impident, that's what yiz are,' and clattered a few pans in a cursory inspection. She had only to leave the house for a few minutes and the whole place went to the dogs.

* * *

Tom Bennett leaned on the bill-hook with the relaxed grace of a man long used to physical work. From where he stood on the crest of the North field he could see the road from the town where it came around the cliff. It was near time for the young lad to get home from school, a brave walk for the little legs of him. He was never much of a one for the books himself, but sure who needs book-learnin' to be a labourer? A strong back and a good pair of arms is all that's wanted. A strange little fella, he thought, quiet in himself and too soft by half for his own good. Only the one, and he wasn't a bad chiseller.

He could see the fair hair shining in the bleak sunlight as the child approached with his head down against the wind. The road passed along the coast below Strifeland, running parallel to the railway, curving around the bay and on behind the trees beyond the footbridge. Bennett watched unobserved as the child plodded past below him with his satchel tucked under his arm. Suddenly the child dropped the satchel on the ground and drew a kick at it, in obvious disgust. 'The little get,' Bennett muttered. 'Hey!' He saw the face turn towards him at the shout and the child bend quickly and retrieve the satchel. Then he saw him break into a run, heading for the footbridge over the railway, and soon saw him emerge from the plantation in the dell, running as fast as he could over the rising ground towards the house. Bennett had begun again to hack back the whitethorn hedge as the child came panting towards him.

'What are ye doin', Da?' he gasped.

37

'What does it look like, son? I'm tidyin' up for the gentry that's comin' to visit us.'

'Who's that, Da?'

'Soldiers. All them that's hurt in the war. Himself has opened up the house for officers, do ye mind, to ree-cuperate. Do you know what that means?'

'No Da.'

'They have to get better so they can go back out again to get hurt.' Bennett shrugged. 'It's all daft to me I can tell ye.' He slashed at the thorns, and the raw wood flashed out from the brown bark, white, like human flesh. 'It's all daft son. How did ye do in school then?'

'I was scutched again, Da.' The child hung his head and blinked at a tear. He felt ashamed.

Bennett pretended not to notice. He paused for a moment, watching a great flight of lapwings alighting on the frost-rimed grass. Their undersides glinted white as they wheeled into the wind and buckled in a final jinking descent. They ran nervously for a few feet as they landed, then stood stock still, proud winter birds, with crests held high. 'What were you scutched for?' he asked after a while.

'Drawin' on me books,' said Davy plaintively.

'Sure what's wrong with that?' Bennett laughed. 'Don't mind that oul' master. When I was your age I was bet every day. It never done me a bit o' harm. Don't ever let them see ye cryin',' he added casually. 'They like to see people cry, them fellas.' He felt an urge to put his arm around the child and comfort him, but he thought it might embarrass him. Feck that oul' master anyway. It's a tough road the childer have to travel. 'Go on down to your mammy and tell her I'll be down in an hour or so when I get the cows in.' Already there was a bit of grass coming on and the cattle could be let out in the daytime. 'Go on home now and don't let me see ye kickin' your schoolbag around no more.'

'Yes Da.' The boy smiled shyly. 'It's just when I kick it I think it's the master. Like when you're bangin' the big drum, I always think it's someone's head that you don't like.'

'Go on outa that or I'll bang your head.' Still that's a deep class of a thought from a little fella, he thought. Begod but there's a chill in the air when ye stop workin'. What must it be like for them poor divils out in France?

A train was passing below. It gave the traditional shrill blast on the whistle, a relic of the time when the colonel's grandfather had given way-leave to the Dublin-Drogheda Railway Company with the eccentric stipulation that all trains must, in perpetuity, pay tribute of one blast in salute to Strifeland. Bennett could see the smoke plume approaching through the trees. From the sound of it, it was not going to stop at the halt and the child sprinted in order to be on the footbridge when it passed below. Bennett saw him disappear into the smoke, as the train thundered beneath him, only to emerge again laughing and waving his hands.

No doubt there would be great comin's and goin's with the house full of soldiers, and probably nurses and all, but it would be no harm at all for the colonel, the poor divil, a bit o' company for him now that he was on his own.

The child had reached the cottage on the cliff and the door closed behind him. Bennett threw the bill-hook over his shoulder with a sense of satisfaction. He liked to think of his family indoors in the evening. He liked the feel of the polished hickory handle. He always got a sense of security from the solid heft of it. A man would be all right in any bother with a bill-hook in his hand. He stamped the mud of the ditch from his Russian boots and trudged up the hill towards the byres.

*   *   *

Mr Fedigan enjoyed the feel of Saturday evening. He had his little rituals before closing. The knives had to get a careful wipe on the steel just to tone up the edges for Monday morning. Block and slabs were carefully scrubbed and wiped, evidence of his meticulous regard for cleanliness.

Kit's mother often spoke approvingly of how scrupulously clean the shop was. He had wondered about the word until he met it in the table book — Apothecaries' Measure, scruples, grains, drams, all the mysterious terminology of the alchemist. His father had been an apothecary in a sense. He wondered if there was some ominous connection there. The mincer had to be thoroughly cleaned, a job Kit preferred to the relentless

39

scrubbing. He tore up the stale bread and stuffed it down the funnel. Then he cranked the handle vigorously until the crumbs emerged through the holes, extruding the gobbets of meat that had lurked inside. After that he detached the butterfly nut on the front and removed the perforated plates and the central screw. Archimedes, Mr Fedigan had explained, had invented that screw, to push the meat along, an interesting fact indeed. Kit knew about Archimedes bathing and all that, but he never imagined that the mincer was a device of such antiquity.

His train of thought was interrupted by a familiar voice. Kit began to clatter the mincer components in an enamel basin. He coughed loudly and whistled. The caller was the old enemy, Doyle, and Kit did not want to hear.

'Ma wants to know can you give me fourpence worth of bits and the eightpence change and she'll give you the shillin' on Monday.'

Mrs Doyle was a frail, gaunt woman with a house full of kids. If Ned Doyle's father could do nothing else, he could drink and he could breed. The first Saturday night Kit had heard this request he had caught the other boy's eye and had seen in that brief glance the agony and resentment. On other Saturdays Kit made as much noise as he could and concentrated on his work to an unnatural degree.

'Would you make less noise there Kit like a good fella? You have me deafened.' Mr Fedigan wrapped a parcel with a rolling action, whipping the overlaps in neatly to form an envelope.

'Sorry Mr Fedigan. Oh! howya,' said Kit, looking up from the basin and spotting Doyle, as if for the first time.

Doyle flicked his head sideways in awkward acknowledgement and departed.

It's funny, mused Kit, how he had always intended putting Ned Doyle down, once and for all, and then, when he could have humiliated him beyond belief, merely by a grin, he could not do it. It was confusing to realise that Ned Doyle looked at the Donovans with envy, that in Ned Doyle's eyes they were the rich and pampered. He shivered at the thought of old Doyle, coming home drunk on the nights he could afford it and malevolent on the nights when he could not. What jagged kind of love, he wondered, had brought the Doyles together in the first place. Had Mrs Doyle ever been a girl, laughing at

40

the boys, swaying her hips as she swung her schoolbag?

Love, Kit knew, was a beautiful, ethereal thing, entailing suffering of an excruciating kind but joy and raptures beyond description. Not that he had experienced all that as yet, of course, but Dr Bailey's granddaughter had returned. Even if Joey had not spotted her in a pony-trap coming from the station, Kit knew that he would have sensed her near him as he went on his rounds. Kit kept his secret to himself for the time being. People would laugh if they knew of his devotion, not because she was a Protestant and a foreigner but because she was so much older, an experienced woman of the world. He could appreciate that he was at a disadvantage and, for the first time, he began to see why his mother had not enthused about his job with Mr Fedigan. That however was coming to an end. He would find ways to shine in her eyes and disparities of age, social standing and religious persuasion would disappear.

'Hurry up there Kit and stop daydreaming,' called Mr Fedigan. 'I want to get confession and get around to the band room for a game of cards.'

It was Mr Fedigan's regular Saturday routine, having cleansed his soul as scrupulously as his marble slabs, to repair to the band room for whist and an argument with Mr Drew about the affairs of the world. On matters political Mr Drew deferred to no man, not even Master Sweeney. Not everyone could just wander into such sessions, as the company was as exclusive as the group that stood on Sunday mornings at Balbriggan Street corner. You could not just expect to stroll along and occupy a place. A place at the corner was something passed down from father to son. Young lads looked up to the men, forefathers as rude as you could wish for sometimes, who knew the seed, breed and generation of everyone in the town and more besides.

'I was just thinkin', Mr Fedigan.'

'What was that, Kit?'

'Well, you know I'm startin' with Mr Drew next week and you'll be lookin' for someone to take over from me.'

'Aye.'

'What about Ned Doyle? I mean they could use a few bob.'

'Aye. I dare say. As long as his da doesn't get hold of it.'

Mr Fedigan frowned. Ned did not enjoy the best reputation

41

around the town. 'What do you think?' he asked, man to man.

In a moment of insight Kit saw the fear and desperation of the eldest Doyle, a home without warmth and a future without prospects, and understood the aggression. 'He's all right,' he said. 'I'd say he would be glad of a job.'

'Fair enough,' agreed Mr Fedigan, 'though I'll be sorry to lose yourself. I suppose Joey wouldn't be bothered?' He was reluctant to lose his immediate contact with the Donovans.

'Ah, no. Joey is goin' to be the brains of the family. He's going on to the Brothers, and who knows after that.'

'Well lock up then, Kit,' concluded Mr Fedigan. 'And by the way, there's a couple of nice gigot chops there for the mammy, with my compliments.'

Kit suppressed a smile. Deeds, not chops. That's the way to a woman's heart.

CHAPTER 3

For almost a century the trains of the Great Northern Railway
had shunted into the siding alongside the Ballast Pit to rake
out and clean their furnaces. This great amphitheatre, once a
raw gash in the landscape but now overgrown with bramble,
whitethorn and coarse grass, had furnished the gravel and
stone to build the embankment that carried the track over the
marshy ground to the south of Strifeland hill. It was a place
of adventure to the children of the town. Its bushes hid birds'
nests and colonies of rats. Its pools and reeds abounded in
newts and frogs in springtime, when the slopes were covered
with primroses and cowslips. Rabbits infested the crumbling
gravel cliffs where caves could be excavated with little effort
to shelter mitchers from school, or bands of desperadoes flee-
ing from the law, to divide the spoils of a raid on a neighbouring orchard. Many were the buckets of blackberries filled there
in the autumn, berries dark as midnight with gleaming pinpoints of light on the pips.

But the end of the Pit nearest the railway was the most
exciting place of all. Here a steep, black scarp of cinder and
half-burnt steam-coal smouldered perpetually, like a miniature
Etna. Any disturbance of the surface could cause layers under-
neath to flare into sudden life, flashing red like the entrails of
a volcano. You were well advised to wear a pair of stout shoes
if you went 'pickin' coke'. Russian boots had a way of becoming warm and sticky if you stayed too long on the slope.

Clara Bennett, like many another, came here regularly to find something to eke out her winter fuel. There was wood enough to be had from Strifeland, but for a real fire in winter-time she liked a good pile of glowing cinder. With a little help, the steam-coal could make a fair to middling fire, enough to keep out the blast of the east wind in January and counter-balance the lonely sound of the waves breaking on the Long Leg below the cottage on the cliff. Her practised eye could separate the nuggets of coal from the ash and iron-hard clinker, and her chapped hands quickly gathered the fragments into the sack that the child dragged behind her. Sometimes she started a small landslide with a stick, to uncover a hidden trove, but the railwaymen objected to this, saying that it could cause a fire under the sleepers, and then they would have to bring a wagon-load of barrels and douse the whole area. In fact the water seemed to spread the fire and make matters worse.

'Davy, lad, I think we have enough for today.'

The child twisted the neck of the sack and she tied it with a piece of baler twine. She could never manage a full sack the two miles along the track to the footbridge.

'Give us a hand up with this.' She slung the sack over her shoulder and they started up the slope, their feet sinking in the warm yielding surface.

'Come on Ma,' said the child, pulling her by her free hand.

The sack crunched on her shoulder with a sound like grind-ing teeth. It reminded her of a story. 'Do you know what a man,' she wheezed a bit, her heavy-set figure labouring under the weight, 'what a man told me once?'

'No, what?'

'If ye're ever huntin' badgers ye put cinders in your socks, 'cause the badger won't let go 'till he hears the bones breakin'. Ye fool him, do ye see?'

'Would badgers go near ye, Ma, would they?' The child had never actually seen one, but they were rumoured to be in the woods around Strifeland.

They emerged onto the side of the railway. Here on the height of the embankment the sharp, northerly wind buffeted them, penetrating their coats and stinging their knees.

'I don't know, but ye wouldn't want to go round with cinders in your socks, would ye?'

The child laughed. 'I'd much rather come here than go to school, Ma. We always have a good laugh.'

'That's true but, still an' all, we don't want the master sendin' for ye too often. Do we?'

'Da says to put no pass on him.'

'Your daddy doesn't reckon much to the books, but ye have to know a bit nowadays to get on in the world.' Still it was invigorating to be out in the air stepping along the sleepers, warmed by the work and the exercise. She always got a feeling of achievement from picking coke, and she enjoyed the child's company. She watched him stepping out, his legs too short for the gaps. He was a child of middle-aged parents, people said, a bit quiet in himself, maybe spent too much time with the mammy or on his own. It was a pity they never had another. Strange too in a way, Tom being the man he was.

'How many sleepers is there, Ma?' He was making a game of the journey, counting from one to ten, out of breath with the effort.

'I don't know, and God knows I should. I've walked them often enough.' With her head bowed under the weight she had had ample time to count them in the forty years and more that she had walked that track.

'Will the Germans come here?'

'Oh no. The only Germans I ever seen was a band like the one your daddy is in.' Admittedly, the Germans had the edge on the local brass and reed, but loyalty forced her to add, 'I didn't think much of their big drummer though.'

They had passed the bridge over the road where the track plunged into a leafless avenue through the Strifeland woods. They could glimpse the house through the bare branches. Small figures moved on the drive in front of the door.

'Did you see all the hoppy men up at the house, Ma?'

'Now, don't talk like that about the poor men.'

'Yes, but they're all over the place. They're soldiers back from the war.'

'I know and you're not to be makin' a nuisance of yourself up there. Do ye hear me? They're here for a rest.'

The child had crept close to the house after the arrival of the first batch of casualties, men discharged from hospital, but not yet fit enough to return to active service, if, indeed,

45

they ever would. His eyes had grown wide with fascination to see so many invalids in the one place. Some were missing arms, as he could see from the empty tunic sleeves pinned to their shoulders. Others, in wheelchairs, stared vacantly in front of them, or turned blind eyes towards the weak sunlight. Some struggled on one leg, with crutches, or limped heavily with the aid of walking sticks. Others lay in torpor on wheeled stretchers, which the nurses moved back indoors when the afternoon became chilly. It was more exciting even than the circus, and he could regale his envious classmates with the most vivid details, and imitate the strange accents for them, but all the time he thought that the Germans must be winning if they could do this to the most powerful army in the world.

When they reached the cottage, on the floor there was a note from the master, directing them to see to it that their son attended school regularly, at the risk of serious consequences. Clara Bennett tore it into small pieces. Better not let Tom see that, he had such a hot temper. People should be left alone to do what they have to.

* * *

There was no shortage of timber on the island, grand big baulks, too heavy to carry on a bicycle, fishboxes from as far away as Whitehaven, tattered stumps of trees, peeled white by the sea and seasoned iron hard, and now and again, a hatch cover of beautiful smooth pine, just the job for a henhouse.

'What about the roof, Kit. Can we use felt or somethin'?'

'I've just the man for that, I found them in the dump. You know those big Virol advertisements in the railway station?'

'Yeah.'

'Well I found four of them up in the Ballast Pit. They'll make a powerful roof.'

They struggled homewards over the shingle and mussel beds that lay between the island and the beach. The load grew heavier by the minute and darkness was closing in. Lights began to appear in the big houses along the terrace.

'Did you get the nails from Mr Drew?'

'Yeah.' Kit laughed at the recollection. 'I asked him had

he any oul' bent nails and he says, "No but I'll bend a few for ye." He's a funny oul' bird, but he knows his stuff.'

'Did he mind you askin'?'

'No. When I told him what we were doin' he said he always encouraged enterprise.'

'Kit.'

'What?'

'You know that word on the Virol boards, where it says that some sort of girls need it? What does that mean?'

'Oh that. That just means they're growin' up, you know. Changin' into women.' Kit gestured vaguely and the bicycle lurched under the weight of the planks.

'I see. Do you ever think about girls, Kit?'

'Women, Joey. I think about women now and again.'

'It's a funny business, isn't it?'

'If you're lucky,' grinned Kit knowledgeably.

'I bet you think about old Dr Bailey's granddaughter.'

'What makes you say that?' Kit asked, startled.

'Aha, I know from the way you talk about her, all real casual like, and ask Maureen about nursing and that.'

Kit was glad of the gathering dusk, as his face was burning, despite the frost in the air. 'I was only interested. I mean Maureen wants to be a nurse and what's-her-name is in the Red Cross. She's lookin' after fellas up in Strifeland. She gave up the art college, they say, to go nursing.' He stopped, realising that he had betrayed himself with too much knowledge.

'Aha, I have you now. You can't fool me. Did you ever talk to her?'

'Of course I talked to her.' He could have added 'once'.

The tide had begun to flow, a strong spring tide, sweeping urgently through the channel. Joey's heart quailed at the sight of the fast-moving stream. The surface was dull grey, slick and treacherous looking. There were stories of men being lost there in times gone by.

'What'll we do, Kit?' he asked apprehensively. 'I don't want to spend the night out here.' He envisaged the rats eyeing them speculatively, already thinking of supper.

'We can make it easily,' Kit reassured him, 'but it'll be a bit damp.'

'How deep would you say it is?'

47

'Well up to your waist. We'll have to take our trousers off and stuff them up our jerseys. Just keep a good hold on the bicycle.'

'I don't know about that.' Joey felt certain that already the massed ranks of voyeurs in the houses opposite were reaching for their telescopes and training them on the hapless pair.

'Come on. Don't be stupid. Nothing worse than a wet crotch. Anyway if you get your trousers wet you'll be in trouble at home.'

Quickly they removed their boots and trousers and waded into the icy water. The current tugged insistently at them but the bicycle provided a measure of support. The water rose to their waists. Their feet, numb with cold, did not feel the mussel shells cutting into the flesh, or the soft mysterious things on which they trod. Gradually the water began to grow shallow and Joey's spirits rose in inverse proportion. They were safe and triumphant with a big load of planks.

'By God, it's cold isn't it?' he remarked, the first words he had uttered since wading in.

'Sure is,' agreed Kit grimly as he trudged out onto the hard wet sand, looking and feeling slightly ridiculous, half-clothed, his backside almost luminous white in the gathering darkness.

Joey laughed and began to wipe himself down with his cap. 'Were you not afraid the one in Dr Bailey's might see your mickey?'

Kit looked down at where the member in question should have been. 'Good God!' he exclaimed, 'it's like a sultana. Sure you've none at all.'

Joey was standing on one leg trying to get into his trousers without trailing them in the wet. He looked down and began to laugh at the deficiency. Desperately he hopped about in an attempt to keep his balance, and collapsed helplessly in the shallows. He swore vehemently and began to squeeze the water from his soaking trousers. 'Dammit. Now look what you made me do.' He drew on the soaking garment and stood bow-legged as the wind whistled around his extremities. 'Come on for God's sake, or I'll get me end from the cold.'

They set off briskly again and came to the line of sand-dunes that protected the houses from the tide. Joey groaned in agony as the wet cloth clung to him and chapped his thighs.

'Joey. I've an idea,' said Kit suddenly.

'What now?'

'Well it's about that girl we were talking about.'

'Oh, aye?'

'It's just I've been tryin' to think of some way of talkin' to her and I've just figured out how you could help me.'

'Not me. I've had enough of your schemes for the moment.'

'I'll give you half a dollar.'

There was silence for a moment. Joey groaned in misery. 'I don't have to get wet again, I hope.' His teeth were chattering.

'No. Not at all.'

'Well then?'

'You know that she's up at Strifeland, looking after the soldiers.'

'So what?'

'Well, she comes down along by Toker Hill on her way home.'

'And you want me to give her a message, do you?'

'Not exactly. You see, if you put on an oul' coat and an oul' cap and pretended to be Barney Phelan I could come along and sort of chase you off.'

'Ah, don't be daft,' snorted Joey in contempt. 'Sure I'm too small for a start.'

'Lookit, I thought of that. Put somethin' under the coat to give you a humpy back. It'll be nearly dark anyway. She'll never notice. Just let a few roars out of you, that sort of thing. I'll do the rest.'

'Oh yeah. I get a hiding and you become a hero.'

'Ah, come on Joey. I'll make it three bob. It's just to give me a chance to get to know her.' He hesitated before giving way to desperation. 'Please.'

'Three and a tanner,' said Joey firmly, visions of wealth passing before his eyes. He could always jump over a ditch or up the Guttery Lane before Kit could get near him. 'Three and a tanner — in advance.'

'You drive a hard bargain, but it's a deal.'

'Are you really that gone on her, really? God, she must be something special. I mean she's ancient, isn't she?'

'Mature,' replied Kit loftily. 'She's a mature woman.'

By this time it had grown dark. The stars glittered in the clear, frosty sky. The boys' boots echoed loudly on the cobbles.

A dark shape loomed in front of them.

'Are ye the boys that were on the island?'

They recognised the soft southern accents of Sergeant Duffy.

'That's right sergeant,' replied Kit, looking up at the barely discernible figure.

'Well now that's a fierce dangerous place to be at this time o' night. Ye might have been drowned entirely.'

'Sorry, sergeant,' said Kit as spokesman. 'We went out for a bit of timber and sort of lost track of the time.'

'Hmm. Is that so? Ye've nothing there the receiver of wrecks might want to see, I'll be bound.' He chuckled.

'No sergeant, just a few planks.'

'Right so. Let ye go home now and be more careful any more.'

'Aye. We will sergeant,' said Kit politely.

Joey sneezed loudly.

'And put your feet in hot water.' The sergeant was probably an expert on the care of feet, sparing them as much hardship as possible. He faded into the darkness again, whistling tunelessly through his teeth.

By the time they reached home Joey was sneezing uncontrollably. Kit took the bicycle around to the square and surrendered it irrevocably to Ned Doyle.

*   *   *

Anna enjoyed her new vocation. She had given up the art college with scant regret. There was more important work to be done, and while she waited for a call to a teaching hospital she could do her bit as a volunteer assistant. The poor men were so grateful that at times she felt ashamed. The invalids and convalescents she dealt with were only a small sample of what was happening to millions. Those with a permanent disability were, they claimed, the lucky ones. At first she had been shocked at their cavalier attitude to the war, as if it made no difference who won as long as they were out of it. After a while she began to see beyond the laughter and the bravado. She noticed the ones that sat by themselves, reliving the horrors. She heard them shrieking in their sleep and began to understand. She accepted at face value her grandfather's view that everyone had a part to play in the 'great struggle'.

She was wary of Toker Hill and dismounted at the top. She heard sneezing somewhere behind the ditch and in a moment saw a figure clambering over the barbed wire, calling unintelligibly. It seemed to be a rickety old man with a coat many sizes too large for him and a cap pulled over his eyes. Obviously he was suffering from a bad cold. His voice was hoarse and she could not make out a word. 'I'm sorry,' she said politely, 'but I can't quite hear what you're saying.'

He gesticulated wildly, and snagged his sleeve on the fence, almost pulling the coat off himself.

'I'm dreadfully sorry, but I can't hear you.' She drew closer, and saw to her surprise that it was a young boy. 'Here, let me help you,' she called, and climbed up through the long grass to extricate him. 'You poor thing,' she said sympathetically, 'you shouldn't be out with a cold like that. You could get pneumonia.'

The boy seemed to have lost his voice completely. It was a very ragged old coat. Anna's heart filled with sympathy for the urchin. She pulled him free and helped him down onto the road. Suddenly she saw another boy, somewhat older, come running out of a laneway, stop short and then come hurrying towards them. She put her arm protectively around the young boy's shoulder and drew him close.

'Joey, are you all right?' called Kit, realising that the plan had misfired.

'I'm fine,' croaked Joey, and looked rather smug.

'No he is not fine,' said Anna sharply. 'This boy is not well. In fact,' she placed her hand on his forehead, 'I think he has a temperature. Yes. I'm sure of it.'

Joey smirked at his brother and felt the coins warm in his pocket.

'I was looking for him, everywhere,' said Kit with deep concern. 'We were all very worried.' He indicated with a circular movement of a finger at his temple that Joey was given to erratic behaviour at times.

Joey glared but could only raise a feeble squeak of protest.

'But you're a nurse,' went on Kit effusively. 'You'd know all about such things.'

'Well, up to a point,' admitted Anna modestly. 'Don't I remember you from someplace, from last summer?' Her voice had a musical lilt.

Kit's heart expanded with joy. 'In your grandfather's garden, firing arrows,' he prompted.

'Oh yes,' she laughed. 'You're the butcher's boy.'

Kit felt a pang of embarrassment. Definitely his mother had a point. 'Oh that was only for the summer, you know. I'm in building now of course.'

'Building. That must be very interesting.'

'Oh yes. I'm working with Mr Drew.'

The name did not mean anything to her. Joey coughed to draw attention to his rapidly approaching demise.

'Oh,' said Anna, 'if you come over to my grandfather's house I'll get you some linctus for that cough.'

Kit interrupted quickly. 'I think the best thing would be for Joey to go home and go straight to bed. It would be far too far for him to walk. I'll go along with you if you don't mind and collect the bottle.'

'That's a good idea,' she said approvingly. 'Now Joey, do what your big brother says.'

Joey was unable to protest. Kit shot him a warning glance. They separated at the railway bridge and Joey trudged disconsolately homewards. He could hear their voices raised in animated conversation on the still evening air and suddenly Kit seemed far away and a stranger. Joey missed him and an inexplicable sadness settled over him.

Maureen opened the door. 'You look terrible, young man,' she said. 'You'd better sit by the fire and I'll get you a cup of tea. Take off that filthy old coat.'

Joey hunched over the fire and stared at the glowing coals. He felt small and alone.

'Where's Kit?' asked Maureen. 'You went out together.'

'Ah he went off somewhere. I don't know.'

'Don't mind him. You just drink your tea and go to bed.'

Rain pattered on the roof. Joey was asleep before Kit came in. In the morning the linctus bottle was on the floor beside his bed. He was too weak for school but he did not mind.

Kit came in with a spoon and gave him some cough mixture. He was elated. 'You did a great job, Joey. I won't forget you.'

CHAPTER 4

Early every morning the train from Belfast stopped at Strife-land to unload the bread and the papers. On this particular Tuesday the orderlies stood around longer than usual and the train remained, hissing great clouds of steam into the chill morning air. Tom Bennett sensed that there was something wrong.

The guard was holding forth as he arrived. 'They've took over the Post Office and folk have been killed, murderin' bastards.'

'We know about that already, but what's happening now?' asked one of the orderlies.

'You're talkin' about the trouble in Dublin I suppose.' Bennett knew the guard well from these daily halts.

'Aye, your crowd are at it again. Bloody traitors.' The guard was in an excitable state.

'What do you mean, my crowd. I've nothin' to do with politics.' Bennett felt rattled by the assumption.

'Sinn Fein, rebels, whatever ye like. It's all the bloody same down here.'

'Don't be talkin' rubbish man. The D.M.P. will put a stop to that carry on. Why don't yiz get the bloody bread out and get on with your work?'

The guard was not to be so easily deflected. 'Because the bridge at Rogerstown is down. That's why. They're checkin' all the bridges for explosives.' His agitation, in the circumstances, was understandable. 'Youse people are all the same

53

in the end. Youse'd even side with the Germans to stab folk in the back.'

'Now listen,' Bennett could feel his temper rising. 'Leave me out o' this, ye little Belfast get.'

The guard sensed the anger in the man. 'No need for that kind of attitude. I'm not sayin' everyone down here is the same.'

'Ye were a minute ago.'

The guard ignored the technicality. 'Anyway it's a bad business altogether.'

'Aye maybe it is,' Bennett allowed, 'but if ye don't want your block knocked off, ye won't go around makin' allegations.'

The orderlies nudged one another in anticipation of another flare-up, but the episode was interrupted by the arrival of the sergeant. He came out from the woods accompanied by an old man who walked stiffly with the aid of a stick.

'All right,' called the sergeant, waving his hand, 'you can take her as far as the station anyway.'

The old man mounted the sleeper-built platform with difficulty. He glared around him impatiently. 'Well, don't stand around idle. Get the bread off and let's get a move on. Juldi, juldi.' He had obviously caught the tail-end of the argument and was in no mood for political discussions. 'Crowd of bloody lunatics, eh Tom?'

'I suppose so, Colonel. I don't go in for politics meself. I've enough to do.'

'Politics! Blasted traitors. Hang the whole blasted lot of them.'

The colonel was just the man to do it, particularly at this hour of the morning. Very wicked he was when he was annoyed. The orderlies moved smartly, heaving the trays onto the cart. The guard stepped up onto the platform, looking pleased that so important a man as Colonel Wyndham had endorsed his point of view. He looked down at Bennett with a 'there y'are now, what did I tell ye?' kind of a glance, but was wary enough not to gloat openly.

'Little Northern melt,' muttered Bennett to himself.

'You there,' snapped the colonel. 'Wave your blasted flag or whatever, and move your train out of here.'

The guard gave a quick blast on his whistle and the train

jolted forward, with a shudder running down its length as each wagon was jerked into motion. Grey smoke billowed from the funnel as it moved into the trees, with pistons whamming rhythmically, picking up speed.

'This business won't last, Colonel.' The sergeant was mounting his bicycle, with his carbine slung over his shoulder. 'Good luck to ye Tom, and keep out of trouble.'

Who the hell does he think he's talkin' to, thought Bennett. Jumped-up bog trotter. 'Aye, Sergeant. Good luck.'

Sergeant Duffy was a tall gangling man, with a reputation for directness and strength. He poled his bicycle into motion with his long right leg and rolled off down the track to the road, a sinister black figure with a touch of the circus clown in his ungainly movement.

'I'll wander up and read the papers,' said the colonel, tucking the bundle under his arm. 'Probably won't have any Dublin papers today, I gather. Walk down through the dell with me, Tom. I want to plant some trees there this year. Must look to the future you know.'

Bennett walked slowly beside his employer. The oul' arthritis was playin' hell with him, this weather. Strange, he thought, about the old man, but they never had a cross word in all the years he had worked on Strifeland. Very few could say that about the colonel, who terrified most people and antagonised the rest. Bennett felt no subservience either, even if the old man was a Protestant and one of the gentry. In fact, if he had thought about it he would probably have felt a kind of protectiveness and, very occasionally, pity. The old man had come to rely on him a great deal, now that he found it hard to get around. There was that time years ago, when he had come across him with the young one in the hay loft. 'Savoir faire, Tom. Savoir faire,' the colonel had laughed from under the pile of hay, while the young one hid her face in embarrassment. Whatever it meant, Bennett had kept the incident to himself. The Wyndhams were always a bit wild. That was a long time ago now and the colonel was not so agile. It would take him all his time to get up on the bloody ladder, Bennett thought wryly.

'No way to fight a war, Tom.'

'No, Colonel.' He was used to the old man's pronouncements,

never questioning him on anything outside his own experience.

'The only decent kind of a war is the cavalry. You should have seen us in the Sudan.' He chuckled at the recollection of happier times. 'What they have to do here,' here being France, 'is punch through with their artillery and let the cavalry loose in the rear. That should shake things up a bit, eh?'

'Could be just the job, Colonel.' Everybody was an expert on strategy nowadays, even the poor bastards in the wheelchairs above in the house.

'What did Duffy mean by those remarks, by the way?'

'I don't know. He doesn't like some of the lads I have a jar with.'

'Watch it all the same, until this trouble blows over. Duffy's a hard man.'

Bennett laughed. 'Don't I know it.' He did not expand on the remark.

They discussed the planting of trees for a while, agreeing on the need for shelter where the east wind whipped up from the bay in winter, slanting the ancient elms and sycamores away from its fury. The sound of hammering from the direction of the haggard interrupted them. There was a lorry at the level-crossing and a man in uniform was coming towards them. He was not one of the inmates of the house.

'Colonel Wyndham, sir,' he addressed the old man, saluting respectfully.

'Yes. What is it young man?'

The officer produced an envelope. 'I have orders, sir, to requisition your barn. The situation may become grave. You will find a receipt in here and a guarantee that all damage will be made good.'

'What the devil do you want my new barn for?'

'As you can see sir, the barn commands a view of the coast road, the railway and the railway bridge. My men are at this moment cutting rifle slots.'

'But Colonel,' interrupted Bennett, 'the barn will rust away in no time.'

The officer ignored him, addressing his answer to the colonel. 'This chit guarantees that your property will be replaced when the present emergency has passed.'

'Frankly, I think you're wasting your time,' said the colonel,

56

thrusting the envelope into his pocket, 'but do whatever you have to, young man.'

The hammering was joined by the strident sound of hack-saws as the officer returned to his men. Daylight appeared through rectangles high in the walls of the barn and here and there a rifle was waggled through to try out the arc of fire.

'They're makin' an awful balls of your shed, Colonel,' muttered Bennett in disgust.

'Don't worry Tom,' said the old man with surprising cheerfulness. 'We haven't sold the pass yet to Home Rulers and Sinn Feiners.'

'Whatever about that, Colonel,' replied Bennett, 'it's near time for me breakfast so I'll leave ye for the moment.'

'Right you are, Tom.' The old man turned towards the house, whistling tunelessly through his teeth and swinging at the occasional weed with his stick.

Begod, thought Tom, but he'd enjoy a row even at his age.

* * *

Everyone was talking about the rebellion: the Volunteers had taken the centre of the city and had struck at targets all over the country; Dublin was said to be in flames; hundreds had been killed. One story was better than the next: the wireless huts in the mill field had been, or were about to be burned to the ground.

A crowd had gathered on the windmill hill by the time Joey arrived. People were pointing excitedly, explaining to each other where the attack was likely to come from. Joey spotted his brother in his new overalls and ran to join him.

'What's happening?' he gasped.

'Nothing yet,' said Kit, 'but they say the Volunteers are going to burn the wireless huts.'

'Why would they tell everyone?' asked Joey, puzzled.

Kit shrugged. 'I suppose you have to do the decent thing and give the men time to get out an' that.'

'I suppose so,' agreed Joey, relieved at the thought that no real harm would be done.

There was an air of excited anticipation, like the half hour or so before the start of a football match. 'Where are they?' somebody asked impatiently. A ripple passed through the crowd and people pointed. Children were lifted up to get a better view. There was some movement away to the right towards the railway line. And far to the left they could see a line of soldiers advancing on the double from behind the old church. The sun glinted on bayonets and equipment. 'This is it,' said one of the watchers and his voice was hushed. 'No it isn't,' said another, disappointed. 'They're soldiers over there too. There won't be any battle here today.'

The boys watched in fascination as the troops deployed around the perimeter of the field and in the bakery buildings. As if on a parade-ground drill, they filed into the millrace and took up position, the line opening out like a string of beads. The sluice gate had been closed and the water in the mill-race began to drop, although the soldiers seemed indifferent to it anyway. In minutes the field was ringed by armed men.

A team rattled a machine-gun into position near the sluice gate and the muzzle traversed in a wide arc that included the people on the hill. A sullen silence descended on both the watchers and the soldiers. It was obvious that any attempt to attack the wireless huts would be suicidal. Anyway there was no sign of an attacking force.

'Let ye all move along now. Ye've no business here.' It was Sergeant Duffy moving through the crowd, almost diffident, and the people backed away from him half-reluctantly, but in a way glad that someone had decided to put an end to what had been a pointless and potentially dangerous situation.

'South Staffordshires,' said a voice. 'Wouldn't you think they'd have something better to do?'

'Aye,' agreed those nearby. 'Where do they think they are?'

The crowd began to break up and drift away conversing in little groups.

'What did you think of all that?' asked Joey.

'Well nobody's going to tackle them head on, that's for sure,' said Kit. 'I'd say they know their business.' He shoved his hands into his overall pockets and kicked at a stone. 'There's no answer to that argument, is there?'

'Still an' all, it's not fair. I mean, I never saw so many guns in one place.'

'Who ever said things had to be fair? It all seems to come down to the big guns, in the end.'

'I dare say that's the end of it then. The Volunteers have had it, would you say?' Joey looked at his older brother.

'Sounds like it,' he shrugged. 'Whatever about the soldiers, I sure don't fancy a boot in the arse from the sergeant.'

That was something they could both understand. They looked back at the sergeant. The people had moved away, leaving him, a tall, isolated figure on the brow of the hill.

* * *

Maureen scratched away diligently at her homework. She liked a Waverly nib. It gave a bit of style, a bit of a flourish to her handwriting. The nuns cautioned her on her flamboyant capitals but still she persisted. She dipped her pen in the ink-bottle and shook an excess blob from the tip. Looking up thoughtfully for a moment, she noticed her younger brother's expression of misery. He had finished his homework and was disconsolately running the tip of his pencil up and down the grooves in the soft grain of the white deal table. Tiring of that activity, he occasionally drew the pencil across the grain, making a small washboard staccato.

'Don't do that please, Joey,' said Maureen. 'I'm trying to think.'

Joey sighed and went back to the lateral movement. He sighed again, a little louder.

'What's up, Joey?' asked Maureen, responding to the obvious gambit. 'You look very fed up.'

'Ah,' grumbled Joey, 'there's nothin' to do.'

'Oh,' nodded Maureen, 'I see.' She lowered her gaze to the page again, waiting for Joey to expand on his complaint.

'I mean, all I do is go to school and come home and do lessons. It's boring.'

'You have your hens to look after.'

'Ah it's not the same, you know.'

'I know. Not since Kit started his new job.'

Joey was silent for a moment. He ran the pencil up and down a few times. 'It's not just that. I mean I wouldn't mind the job but I never see him at all now.' He lapsed into a glum silence.

Maureen knew what was troubling him. All her classmates knew too, how Kit was mad about the English one and how he hung around the terrace hoping to meet her on her way home in the evening. They all agreed, particularly those who had sought her friendship in order to scrape acquaintance with Kit, that he was making a right eejit of himself. It did not worry Maureen as much as it worried her schoolmates. She adopted a lofty and tolerant attitude to her brother's infatuation, but she felt sorry for Joey. He was a bit like a lost soul moping around the house, particularly at week-ends, complaining of having nothing to do. He could not adapt to the idea that Kit saw himself now as a working man with a man's interests and little enough time for boyish escapades. And he was inclined to talk a little too expansively at times about his plans for the future. Under the tutelage of Mr Drew he had even begun to pronounce on political matters. The metamorphosis was too much for Joey.

'All I get to do is feed the hens and muck out the henhouse,' he groaned again. 'And go up to the mill for bran. He never wants me around anymore.' He was close to tears and blinked furiously. 'He even gave his job to Ned Doyle.' He shook his head in puzzlement.

'Never mind, Joey,' said Maureen sympathetically. 'He's just going through a childish phase. He thinks he's in love, you see. You're still his best pal. Just you wait and see.'

Responding to her sympathetic attitude, Joey searched for further evidence of guilt on his brother's part. 'You know that henhouse we made?'

'How could I miss it? It's not the most elegant structure, is it? I mean, Virol signs on the roof. Kit will have to brush up on his building techniques. The poor hens must be deafened in there when it rains.'

Joey laughed for the first time. 'I never thought of that. I'll tell him that too.'

'Whenever we see him,' added Maureen drily. 'What about the henhouse anyway?'

'I wondered about that word. You know the one about these girls need it, the Virol?' He trailed off self-consciously.

'Oh, anaemic? That's 'em, if you haven't enough iron in your blood.'

'Iron? In your blood?'

'Yes. The iron makes your blood red. If you haven't enough iron you get weak.'

'Go 'way. Is that a fact?' Joey thought hard for a moment. 'The dirty liar. He didn't even know.'

'Who? What didn't he even know.'

'Kit,' said Joey accusingly, 'he said it was somethin' about girls turnin' into women.' He blushed and his eyes involuntarily strayed to where Maureen's breasts strained against the constrictions of her bodice and gym slip. His face burned with embarrassment.

Maureen broke into a peal of laughter. 'So he's an expert on that too is he. Never you mind him.'

They heard the back gate banging shut and had barely time to compose themselves before Kit burst in the door. He was dressed in dungarees and was liberally dusted with hardwall plaster. In the long pocket on his thigh he carried a folding rule, the badge of his trade, as a medical student brandishes his new stethoscope. Maureen kept her head down and Joey concentrated on the table top. Kit looked at them suspiciously and Maureen snorted in an attempt to stifle a laugh.

'What are you two laughing at then?' demanded Kit, looking from one to the other truculently.

'Oh nothing,' said Maureen airily. 'We were just talking about Ned Doyle.'

'Oh him. What's so funny about Ned Doyle?'

'It's the way he tries to copy Mr Fedigan all the time, rubbing his hands, all businesslike. Anyone would think he owned the place.'

'I'll tell you a good one,' said Kit relaxing. 'Ma went in there the other day. You know the way she can be very grand and that?'

The other two nodded as Kit imitated their mother's stately walk.

'"Young man," she says to Ned, "I need a capon for the weekend."'

'What did he say to that?'

'He just looked at her for a minute, like a sheep lookin' at a turnip, and says he, "Yes madam. I'd say it's goin' to be a bit chilly." '

They laughed helplessly and Kit gave them his version of their mother's frosty stare. 'Mr Fedigan gave him a clip in the ear and said, "I shall look after Mrs Donovan's requirements in person." Poor oul' Ned couldn't make out what he'd done wrong.' Kit drew a chair in to the table. 'Hey, what do you think?' he went on rapidly. 'How would you fancy him for a stepfather?'

'Don't be daft,' said Joey dismissively.

'What would it matter to you anyway?' challenged Maureen. 'You'll probably be married yourself by then, to the English one.'

'I might an' I mightn't,' replied Kit airily. 'If it suits me. There's other things to be done first though.'

'Such as?'

'Well, for a start, there's Ireland's freedom to be won.'

'Oh no,' groaned Joey. 'Not you? We get nothin' else all day from Master Sweeney.' He leaned his head on his hand.

'I'm serious,' continued Kit, ignoring the interruption. 'Mr Drew says the Volunteers will try again and this time they'll succeed.'

Joey snorted.

But Maureen turned pale. 'You're not involved in that, are you?' she asked apprehensively.

'Not at the moment,' conceded Kit, 'but more blood will be spilt if they execute the leaders.'

'Ah they're always goin' on about blood,' snorted Joey, standing up impatiently. 'Is it red or white blood?' he asked pointedly, with a conspiratorial wink at his sister. 'I'm goin' to feed the hens. Our hens, I might remind you. It's about time you did a bit of lookin' after them.' He slammed the door after him and in a minute they heard the frantic cackling as the hens converged on him for their evening meal.

'What's up with him?' asked Kit in puzzlement. 'What did I say wrong?'

'He's only a little lad,' said Maureen seriously. 'He just wants a bit of your attention now and again.'

'Oh,' said Kit and looked rather guilty. 'I see.'

'You're not in the Volunteers, are you?' asked Maureen, going back to what was worrying her. 'I mean, that's all finished and done with, isn't it?'

'Maybe it looks that way now Maureen, but the day will come when we will have to rise up against England again.'

'And what will your fine English woman think of you then?'

Kit scratched his head in some confusion. 'I don't know. That's different, sort of. I mean.' He was not sure what he meant. 'Anyway it would only be against the government, not ordinary people.'

'Ordinary people got killed at Easter though, didn't they?'

Kit drummed his fingers on the table. Mr Drew would have the answer to that one.

* * *

People paid the milkman on the doorstep. None of your dockets and receipts. When you heard the rattle of the cans at the door you got down the milk money and your jug, and there was always a tilly for the cat. Tom Bennett enjoyed delivering on Saturdays and Sundays when the regular man was off. He took a childish pleasure in driving the cart with its big wheels and the floor slippery with the drips from the churn. It was like one of those chariots they used to have in the old days. He enjoyed the chat and the gossip as people came from their breakfast for the latest news or his weather predictions. What he picked up at one house as rumour he could report at another as gospel truth.

Mr Drew was always good for a bit of news or an argument. In his capacity as general handyman, undertaker, and politician he knew about most things that went on in the world. He always wore a dark suit and a high collar. With his straggling grey moustache and round glasses he was an impressive figure. No one would lightly call him by his christian name.

On this particular Saturday morning Mr Drew was glazing a window in Dublin Street. 'Well Tom,' he began directly, 'what do you make of all this business?'

Bennett was directing a stream of milk into a jug for the woman of the house. 'The way it is, Mr Drew, they had no chance at all from the start. They was mad if you want my opinion. And a tilly, mam,' he finished, giving an extra dart into the jug.

'Well now, I don't know about that.' Mr Drew stood back

63

and admired the new window frame. 'Look at that. You'd think it grew there.' He took up a piece of glass. 'Eight be six, eight be six,' he muttered, and flicked his rule around with practised ease. There were eight small panes to be replaced. 'Now I've been in politics all me life Tom, and a lot of good it's done me. . . .'

Bennett waited respectfully. Mr Drew had stood on the same platform as Redmond.

'But the executions last month made me think long an' hard about it all. Cut that for me, Tom, while I have a cigarette.' Mr Drew never descended to slang. Where others had a drag or a fag, he would take a cigarette, with the permission of the ladies, if any were present. He handed Bennett the glass-cutter. 'Just straight across from them two nicks.'

'All right, but I'm not much good at this.' Bennett put the glass on the stool and, using a lath as a guide, began to saw backwards and forwards. The glass crunched under the point.

'Now just snip it off.'

Bennett grasped the edge uneasily, imagining razor-sharp splinters slicing through the ball of his thumb. He bore down and the glass broke, for two thirds of the way, clean along the line, but inevitably a jagged piece snapped off at the end, ruining the whole pane.

'Tasty bit o' work Tom, tasty bit o' work.' He was inclined to speak in duplicate, as a man used to measuring. 'Measure twice, cut once' was his motto.

'I told ye I was no good at this,' said Bennett defensively.

'Never mind, never mind. I have the eight of them cut already in the hand-cart.'

'Well what the blazes did ye ask me to do that for? I could of lost a finger.'

'Look at that, Tom. That's a diamond, the hardest thing on God's earth.' He drew the cutter firmly across the glass and snapped the jagged piece clean off. 'That's the way it's done Tom. Cut firm and make a clean break. No chewin' away at the edges — like politicians.' He handed the piece to Bennett for his approval.

'Oh begod, I see what you're getting at now. But you've the queerest way of makin' a point.'

'I think it will come to that yet. Maybe I've been barkin'

64

up the wrong tree all me life. We'll just have to see what transpires for a while.'

There was a scraping of hobnails beside them. The sergeant was trailing one long leg on the limestone kerb, by way of brakes. He had arrived unnoticed, pedalling slowly and silently as usual, taking in everything he saw. Now the freewheel clicked rhythmically to announce that no deliberate surveillance was intended. 'There ye are men, and isn't that a grand morning?' He remained on the saddle, not presuming to dismount, looking like someone bound for somewhere else.

'I was just sayin' as much to Tom here,' replied Mr Drew, 'how the weather is changeable like. You never know what to expect.'

'True enough Mr Drew,' agreed Bennett, enjoying the notion of conspiracy. 'Ye wouldn't know what coat to wear this weather, would ye, Sergeant?' Maybe he was too subtle for Duffy, as there was no reaction.

'Aye well, God bless the work, and see you don't cut yourself there Tom.'

Bennett looked down in surprise. He still had the jagged piece of glass in his hand. He dropped it into the hand-cart, where it shattered into splinters. Was the sergeant smarter than he looked, he wondered. Were they all starting to talk in riddles?

'Dangerous oul' stuff that Tom,' said Duffy, already in motion. 'Good luck to ye Mr Drew.'

They watched him turning into Barter Row, heading for the barracks.

'I'd be wary of that fella', Mr Drew. I wouldn't cross him in a hurry.'

'Give it time. Give it time. Things is changin' around here.' Mr Drew returned to his work, enspatulate fingers kneading the putty in the palm of one hand, drawing it into a rope which he rapidly worked into the frame with thumb and knife. 'I'll talk to you again, Tom.'

Bennett felt dismissed but flattered in a way, as if he had been drawn into serious councils, where his opinion was held in esteem. He stepped into his chariot and slapped the reins on the pony's back.

* * *

65

Things began to look up with the coming of summer. Normality of a sort had returned although the centre of Dublin was said, by those who had been there, to be in ruins. Politics and executions meant very little to Davy Bennett but he was sorry that the soldiers had left the barn. They were a cheerful bunch who had spent of a lot of their time playing ball against the corrugated walls. The echoing thump of a bald tennis ball had drawn him to investigate and gradually they had let him become part of the game. They played three-and-in. Davy enjoyed their good-natured horseplay, even though he knew that his mother was not happy about his hanging around the soldiers.

Now the barn was empty except for bales and the sunlight struck long diagonal shafts through the high rifle slots. Davy went back to his solitary amusements.

He crouched over the copybook, drawing carefully with a hard HB pencil, scratching rapidly at the paper, trying to impart to it what he saw before him. The image was sadly grey and faint on the lined paper but he worked intently, his tongue moving in unison with the pencil. He was unaware of the figure coming up behind him until a shadow fell across the page. He looked up in alarm to see one of the nurses from the house, in a long navy cloak and a hat with a red cross on it. Hastily he shut the copybook and tried to hide it.

'May I see?' she asked gently.

'It's no good,' he muttered in an agony of embarrassment.

'Oh, I don't agree,' she replied. 'From what I could see it was very good indeed. Let me just have a little peep.'

She smiled at him winningly and he offered her the book, awkwardly, but feeling an unusual urge to have somebody see what he had done. Anna turned the pages slowly, studying the drawings, while Davy looked around feigning unconcern. He felt a strange apprehension that she might laugh or make some disparaging remarks that would stop him drawing forever. She might well say that it was ridiculous for a boy to waste his time drawing animals, birds, plants or vistas of woods and farmland when there were more useful things to do.

Strangely, she said, after a careful study: 'You really look at things, don't you?'

'I just like drawing,' he mumbled in some confusion.

'I mean the clouds. You really look at them.'

Davy wondered at first if she was laughing at him. His schoolmates would have found it hilarious. Master Sweeney would have found in it more evidence of intolerable laziness in a boy who daydreamed and looked out at the clouds. 'They're just there,' he said inadequately. 'I just try to draw them.'

'Why don't you try watercolours? I imagine they would suit you?'

Davy's mind raced. Watercolours, what were they? He had little or no experience of colours, a bit of distemper on a wall, red lead on a cart, but painted pictures were unknown to him. There was a coloured print of the Sacred Heart at home with a little red lamp in front of it, but that had always been there. It obviously came readymade. On inspection he had found that the colours were made up of millions of tiny dots, but for the life of him he could not imagine how it was done. He shook his head, ashamed of his ignorance. 'I never seen watercolours.'

Anna looked at the child with pity. As a student she had realised that she would never be more than highly competent, but even so, painting was a physical pleasure. She could not imagine living without access to colour, particularly in a place as beautiful as Strifeland. 'You really should try watercolours.' She added: 'Your drawing is very good.'

She looked down at the scene below them, the path stretching down from the old gate lodge, the cornfield bounded by the ancient plantations of elm, beech, and oak and the rambling old house nestling among dark rows of yew. Beyond the house lay more woods and the bay glistening in the sunshine. Long, lazy waves curved in towards the beach. The horizon was rimmed by the rugged grey line of the Mournes. The brown soil of the cornfield was dusted by a fine mist of green where the seed had just shot, thin on the ground before them but foreshortened into vivid greensward in the middle distance. 'I would like to paint this scene,' she said. 'I haven't got the time. Perhaps you might do it for me sometime.'

Davy shifted uncomfortably and rose to his feet. 'I wouldn't be able to,' he mumbled, wishing she would go. He wanted to finish his drawing and regretted having shown her his copybook. People always seemed to want an explanation of a picture, as if it could not speak for itself.

'Well anyway,' she said, 'I must get back to my charges.' She handed him his copybook and started down the slope to where two men were hobbling along the rutted pathway.

One walked with the aid of crutches, poling himself along slowly while the other inched along beside him, gingerly, like a very old person. Davy wondered why she called them charges as they could barely make headway. He noticed how they straightened up as she approached them and he could hear their cheerful greetings. He sketched the trio rapidly into the scene with a few quick strokes. The lead of the pencil snapped and a small tear appeared where he had been drawing. In a spasm of frustration he ripped out the page and tore it into little pieces. The shreds of paper scattered in the breeze as he threw them, swirling like the snowflakes in the little glass globes with the minute Swiss cottages that he had seen in a carnival stall.

CHAPTER 5

A sluggish nondescript river winding through gently rolling countryside became synonymous, that fine July, with carnage of an unprecedented nature. The Somme. The very name sounded like a bell, the death knell of a generation. It reverberated through every conversation. It dwarfed the battles that had gone before. It brought new strategies, new weapons and new armies, driven like brutes to the slaughter. The insane arithmetic of warfare transmuted the horrendous casualty lists into steps towards the final victory. A gain of a hundred yards of shell-pocked enemy territory, a shattered farmhouse or devastated hamlet, was hailed as a major victory in the papers and headlines heralded an imminent breakthrough. But neither steel hats nor steel tanks made any difference in the long run and the armies settled once more into an equilibrium.

'Do you think they'll try and bring in conscription over here Mr Drew?' asked Kit.

'Hand me the hawk, Kit,' replied Mr Drew, looking judiciously at his handiwork, as they perched in the valley of Dr Bailey's high roof. 'Blue Bangors, Kit, Blue Bangors,' he repeated, tapping the slates with a trowel. 'Always use the best and,' he paused, 'leave a bit of your heart.' There was a poetic streak in Mr Drew. He dabbed mortar around a loose hip-tile with a quick slicing movement. 'That should hold her,' he grunted with satisfaction. 'No,' he continued, adverting to Kit's question, 'that wouldn't do at all. Haven't they had enough of our young men for their cursed war? People would never stand for conscription.' He stood up slowly and stiffly, holding onto his hat in the brisk sea breeze.

Kit looked down on the garden from his vantage point. The archery target stood there. The tennis net drooped slightly in the centre of the well-trimmed lawn. He knew about leaving a piece of his heart when he worked on a house. He knew better than Mr Drew, who had a lifetime of such work behind him. 'But what if it's necessary? I mean, if England loses the war where would that leave us?' He sensed imperfectly the dilemma of the nationalist position. 'How would we manage under the Germans?'

'Nonsense boy,' snorted the older man. 'The Germans are not interested in us. If we make trouble for England that suits them fine.'

'But do you want the Germans to win? I mean, after all they did in Belgium an' that?'

Mr Drew looked at Kit sharply. 'Gather up them tools there and let's move along.' He glanced around with some satisfaction. 'There's another hundred years in her now,' he pronounced. 'There's ship's timbers in that roof boy, solid oak purlins. The divil himself wouldn't shift it. Aye, that's a fact.'

The sun's heat reflected off the slates and Mr Drew felt an inclination to linger. Kit collected the tools and stowed them in the sack.

'Fine houses,' mused Mr Drew, 'but built from the tears and sweat of the poor.'

'How's that Mr Drew?' Kit respected his employer's position as unofficial chronicler of the town's past.

'Oh, now. Wasn't it always the way? Any little bit of good we had wasn't it took away by the ascendancy.'

'How do you mean?'

'When I was a chiseller all this place was cottages, grand little cottages, with the beach behind them and the fields in front. A grand place entirely.'

'And what happened to them?'

'Didn't the landlord move them all out, down to Barter Street, a dark gloomy hole of a place, where the ice lies on the ground all day in winter. Look at the way the moss an' damp climbs up through the walls. His voice trembled with indignation. 'He took the best place for the grand houses an' thrun the poor people out.'

'I never knew that,' said Kit, looking around with new interest. 'Why did they agree?'

'Didn't have any choice, did they?'

'Like conscription, I suppose.'

'Aye, like conscription.'

They heard suddenly the sound of hooves below and a pony and trap appeared from the direction of the town. Kit recognised immediately the figure of Anna in her uniform. The driver he did not recognise, possibly someone from Strifeland. Kit stood up and called out as Anna passed. She smiled up at him and waved. The ground below rotated and he stumbled in the roof valley. Mr Drew's strong hand seized him by the slack of his overalls.

'Sit down for God's sake. D'ye want to break your neck?'

Kit grinned sheepishly. 'It must be the heat,' he muttered.

'Heat, me arse. You wouldn't be the first young fella to break his neck over a pretty young woman.'

'I wasn't,' protested Kit, but could think of nothing else to say.

'Heh, heh,' chuckled the old man. 'Time was I might of showin' off a bit meself. Heh, heh.' He smiled, remembering youthful gallivanting. 'Time was. Ye'd have had your work cut out for ye then, me bucko.'

'I don't know what you're talking about. The heat got to me, that's all.'

'I knew a steeplejack once that couldn't go aloft without a couple of balls o' malt under his belt for the vertigo. You have to be careful or you'll come a terrible cropper.'

Kit pondered his words wondering if there was some hidden meaning. 'I'll get used to it soon enough.'

'I don't doubt it. You've a good head on them shoulders. Ye won't go far wrong.' He rose and stretched himself. 'I think we can pack up here,' he said, gathering his tools into a leather hold-all. 'You go ahead of me and just look straight in front of ye. Don't look down.'

'I'm grand, I'm grand,' said Kit, feeling the tall ladder spring under his weight. 'I'm grand,' he repeated, grinning to reassure himself and to impress anyone who might look up from below.

* * *

71

Perhaps it was the posture, thought Clara, but thinning turnips seemed to bring the gospel to mind. It was still as clear as when she had learned about it during her year with the nuns. 'Many are called but few are chosen'. She shuffled forward on her knees, glad of the sacks to protect her from the stones. It would have been handier to tie them on like the men did, and one or two of the women, who wore dungarees, but it didn't seem quite proper. Not that she was vain about her appearance, but it was more dignified in a way, to make a kind of a prayer mat and move it along with you, a hassock, like the Protestants were reputed to have for kneeling on in their church.

She singled the seedlings expertly, flicking away the weakest and leaving the strongest standing in full possession of ten inches of furrow. 'To him that hath shall be given'. Wasn't it always the way? She remembered the nun explaining the puzzle of 'him that hath not, even that which he seemeth to have will be taken away and he will be cast out into exterior darkness'; and there they lay where the hoe had passed along, blocking the seedlings into clumps, shrivelled and wasted, the rejects of the crop. 'Blessed are the strong for they shall possess the land' and have all the competition removed and have air and water let in at their roots. She wondered if it was blasphemous to think like that, perverting St Luke, but it was the way things seemed to go.

She levered herself along, not straightening her back. It wasn't worth the pain to straighten up and then have to bend again to the earth. Better to stay down till the end of the row. She looked back at how far she had come. Always look at what you have done already. Don't look forward at the row stretching interminably ahead. Still she liked to test her resilience now and again and look the task square in the face. From so close to the ground, the horizon was a slight rise in the field not twenty yards ahead, hiding the miles and miles of seedlings that lay before her. It was cheating, in a way, to pretend that the work ended there, at the bottom of the sky as Davy would say, but it was a help to imagine yourself coming to a halt on top of a mountain, gazing down on a magical landscape of meadows and woods with the sun glinting on the sea beyond.

The roots gave way with a slight tearing sound. Her hands stung from the young nettles. No more than two leaves and a

72

purple flower on them as yet, but they hurt as much as the big ones. Still, swedes weren't as bad as the white turnips. They stung nearly as much as the nettles. 'Sufficient unto the day is the evil thereof.' They had a funny way of putting things but it was true for them. Nettles and backache were enough to be going on with. She wondered what the other women thought about as they inched along. Probably the few shillin' that made the work worthwhile. There was more money to be made in the hosiery factories in Balbriggan but you couldn't manage a full-time job, even if you could get one, and look after a man and children too. The bit of farm work was useful even if it paid only the same as the schoolboys got. Agricultural day-rate (women) was fixed by some immutable law. 'Did I not contract with you for a penny, so what are you complaining about?' They have you every way. What would you be doing in a vineyard anyway? Jumpin' up and down on the grapes? She laughed softly to herself. There was a vine on the west wing of the house. She looked involuntarily over to where the sun glowed yellow on the stone. For a moment she sat back on her heels, her eyes clouding with the memory.

Their footsteps rang in the tunnel as they ran. The sound rebounded from the cobbles and the massive stones of the archway. 'Wait for me. Wait for me, Watty,' she gasped, laughing and short of breath. Her heart pounded with excitement. They were under the drawing-room, where the great important people were probably sitting just then, the colonel and his lady and the colonel's father, the wicked old man in the wheelchair. He had always been in a wheelchair it seemed, with a plaid rug over his knees and a stout cane with a silver knob on it for pounding on the floor or on the furniture, whenever he wanted something. What would they do if they could see their darling Walter, looking again like any scruffy urchin, chasing around with the labourers' children and leading them on one foray after another, raiding the grapes or the orchard or throwing stones at the hens or sharing a tobacco pipe in the barn. Watty was always the leader, naturally, as everything belonged to him in a way, but it cost him many a hiding from his father and a scolding from his mother, who felt that besides every other consideration, it was his duty to give good example to the other children, rather than lead them astray.

The grapes were the best. In theory they would sneak through the stable yard and into the tunnel, where the only light came from small thick panes of glass set into the lawn, make a quick dash under the house and emerge beside the west wall with time to snatch a bunch of grapes before the gardener lit on them. In practice they became a horde of screaming dervishes whose chances of success were severely minimised by the noise they made. She knew about dervishes because Watty's father had fought them in Egypt, not very successfully, it seemed, and still spoke of having another crack at them someday.

'Yiz little gets. Gowa that, yiz little hooligans.' The gardener swung at them with both hands, flailing in all directions, putting her in mind, even as she ran, of the windmill beyond in Skerries. She snatched at a bunch of ripe, black, dusty-looking grapes. There was always a fine powder on them. Danger heightened her perception. She saw the gardener's hand connecting with Watty's ear. She heard the sharp stinging slap and his cry of pain as he fell. He was up again, dodging the heavy boot, and in a moment they had reached the safety of the shrubbery. The others scattered in various directions into the woods to share their loot. You could sit into a clump of canes, like in an armchair with a high back on it. They lay back gasping and laughing with excitement, but there were tears of pain in Watty's eyes, which he blinked furiously away.

'Damn flies,' he said, rubbing with the heel of his hand. 'Did you get any?'

'I did,' she replied. 'You can have half, if you like.' This, besides consoling him for his failure, had the advantage of lessening the guilt of the sin of theft and, presumably, the punishment, in the afterlife.

'Let's have them then.'

They lounged back on the canes, eating with almost lascivious pleasure, peeling the grapes with their teeth, examining the translucent green with the shadow of pips at the centre and bursting them against the palate to let the juice flow.

He turned sideways and laughed. 'This is the way the Mohammedans live,' he said, 'lying around on couches with women and eating grapes.'

She felt sort of embarrassed and yet pleased and excited at the idea. For the first time ever with him she felt self-conscious and awkward.

'Of course they marry them all first. That makes it sort of all right.'

'Would you like to be a Mohammedan with all them wives?' She put her head back and watched the moving lacey pattern of the branches against the sky, feigning indifference to his answer. She felt the urge to reach out to him, to hold his hand, even touch his cheek. The feeling confused her. Perhaps he felt the same and could not speak.

'No,' he drawled. 'I don't think so. Women are so stupid. You'd have no fun at all. Of course I'll probably have one wife anyway, when I own Strifeland.' He took a penknife from his breeches pocket. 'Sharp as a razor. German steel. Father killed a dervish with this. Cut his throat. Aaagh!' He made horrible gurgling sounds and rolled around, in a manner appropriate to dervishes with severed jugulars, until the canes gave way and spilled him onto the ground. He rolled onto all fours, peering through the shrubbery, on the look-out for the Mahdi's fanatical followers. 'Aha! got one.' He threw the knife with a rapid flick of the wrist and, by great good fortune, the blade stuck into the bole of a tree and remained there. 'Skill,' he said nonchalantly, plucking it out and beginning to carve his initials in the smooth grey bark — W.W. 1889, with the nine backwards, making it eighteen eighty-p.

'Put mine there too, will you?' Perhaps in some magic way, this would make them inseparable. The bark would curl in around the edges of the wound, sealing the contract as long as the tree should live.

'Right,' he said, proud of his skill, and began to carve C.R. with elaborate care. Typical of women to have curves in their initials, where a chap has good straight lines.

She leaned her head against the tree and ran her finger over the fresh, damp lettering. In years to come, as lady of the house she would stroll here on a summer's day with her parasol and remember this time, or perhaps at night she might steal from the house by moonlight and cross the lawn, barefoot on the dewy grass, ghostlike in flowing chiffon, to relive this moment.

'I was thinking', he said, snapping the blade shut again, 'of a better plan.'

'Hmm.' She wasn't really listening.

'If we try from this side the next time, we could have the grapes and be away before he knew we were coming.'

But she was no longer interested in grapes.

Clara rubbed the backs of her hands where the nettles had stung. It was strange the way things had gone after all. As a girl she had heard her father tell how Strifeland had once belonged to their family, long, long before the Wyndhams had come with their penny whistles, in the rear of Cromwell's army. 'All this land', he used to say with a sweep of his arm, 'was Regan land, in oul' God's time!' He said it with pride, as if former greatness compensated for a life of unremitting labour and subservience. And yet he had always been fiercely loyal and grateful to the Wyndhams for his job and a roof over his head. She wished she knew the whole story, half-believing what he had said, half-embarrassed to think that she had ever hoped to be a lady.

Davy came clambering over the gate with a bag in his hand. 'Da sent me over to lend a hand,' he said. 'I brought something to eat.'

She stood slowly, pain shooting through her spine, and stretched with a sigh of relief. 'Well then, we can have a little picnic.' She smiled. Perhaps her father had been right. There was a touch of the gentleman in Davy, a certain refinement in his manner, that in all honesty he never got from his father. It was strange all right. Here she was with her child, closer to the land of Strifeland than poor Watty in his lonely grave on some South African hillside. In the Protestant church there was a memorial to his gallantry, but she had never seen it. 'Don't you be goin' off for a soldier,' she said suddenly.

Davy looked at her curiously. 'No fear,' he retorted quickly. 'And I don't want to be a patriot either.'

And what's a patriot, when he's at home?' she quizzed lightly.

'Master Sweeney says that patriots are men who love their country and die for it.'

'Only men?' she raised her eyebrows.

'Well that's what he said anyway,' replied the boy.

'I'm sure Master Sweeney knows what he's talkin' about, but if we were all patriots who would be left to thin mangold?'

She rubbed the dried clay from her hands. She didn't love the clay very much, she thought. Maybe she loved the place and a few people around her, but she did not feel the master's enthusiasm for dying. 'He's looking healthy enough on his patriotism,' she sniffed. 'Anyway we have work to do.'

Davy wiped the crumbs from his mouth with the back of his hand. 'Right then,' he said, tucking in his shirt-tails, 'let's see if we can reach the top of the hill.'

CHAPTER 6

In the warm clammy days at the end of August the mushroom spawn began to run. Barney Phelan was the first to know, possibly hearing it in the small hours, where he lay in the straw, close to the earth. It pushed upwards inexorably and the damp white buttons appeared in the meadows, probing urgently through the roots of grass for a few brief hours of life. By mid-morning the weevils had invaded the stalks and by early afternoon the pink, frilled cups had turned to withered, wrinkled plates with ragged undersides the colour of a witch's cloak.

Joey sat among the yellow buachallauns and contemplated his harvest. Carefully he punctured each cup with the end of a plantain stalk and added it to the hank, concentrating on his work. His mother would be glad of the mushrooms, not just for the taste but as a memory of her husband. He got itchy feet, she said, at the mention of wild mushrooms and would always take a ramble through the fields when Barney brought the news.

There were very few days of summer left and Joey was not sorry. Soon he would begin a new chapter in his life, travelling on the train to Dublin to the Brothers, as Kit had done before him. He was looking forward to it. There was not much else to do anyway. Kit was either at work or out somewhere. He was no fun any more. Joey paused in his task.

There was a time when they used to collect whole baskets

of mushrooms and take them down to Kerrigan's shop and sell them. Kerrigan bought just about anything. There always seemed to be a tub outside, filled with blackberries with spiders lolloping around on top of them. For all his business acumen, Mr Kerrigan never caught on to the fact that while one Donovan boy was haggling over his pail of berries inside the shop, the other was filling a can from the tub outside.

Sacks of winkles leaned against the wall awaiting collection and trickling a white, salty stain across the pavement. Winkles, as Kit had discovered, were good value. You could have a feed of them and then mix the empties in with a bucket of full ones and still make money. He never gave a thought to the hundreds of disappointed Cockneys with pins poised in readiness, only to find that the door was gone and the shell tenantless.

In the fetid darkness of Kerrigan's, with the smell of old organic matter, cats and innumerable scruffy children, there was money to be made, by a little chicanery and sleight of hand, but Kit was no longer interested. For most of the time he just moped about. If that was what love was like, thought Joey, you could keep it. Anyway, it was obvious that she looked upon Kit as no more than a schoolboy. Kit was the only one who could not see it. From where he sat among the yellow weeds, Joey looked down on Barney Phelan's lodging. He wondered what drove a man to opt out of normal life. There was something attractive about the idea on a warm August day. Barney was no lily of the field but someone provided for him nonetheless.

* * *

Cricket had settled in Fingal and flowered, like an unlikely seed blown to some chimney top or lodged in a high crevice on a cliff. Like a fly in amber, the mystery was how the devil it got there. But it had. And the Fingal league excited passions as fierce as any football match or boat race. Strifeland and its environs fielded an indifferent team, but they had the advantage that their opponents, the Black Hills, came to them, so that any interpretation of the rules should naturally lean in the direction of those who owned the field. Stumps were driven in on the meadow before the house and batsmen strode to their creases.

The crowd, at this end-of-season match, was augmented by the convalescents from the house, young men who had grown up with the game on English village greens and public-school playing fields. They added their enthusiasm and appreciation to the general hubbub, with occasionally a touch of condescension or laughter.

Strifeland, all out for a reasonable one hundred and twenty, began their assault on the stubborn Black Hills' defence. Two stalwarts at the wickets began to lay about them to the delight of the visitors, hitting almost every ball to the boundary. Strifeland's pride was in jeopardy. Colonel Wyndham rose stiffly from his deckchair and paced the sideline, twitching a cane and fuming with impatience to have at the enemy.

A voice from the crowd asked the question that had begun to form in the minds of the knowledgeable. 'Why don't yiz let Tom Bennett bowl?' The voice quavered with the puzzlement of long-suffering wisdom. 'Isn't he the only man yiz have that knows how to bowl a ball?'

There was a murmur of agreement and the captain, whose appointment had been a sore puzzle to many, quickly remedied his oversight.

Bennett snapped his braces over his shoulders and pushed up his sleeves, grinning to acknowledge the cries of encouragement.

'Me sweet man Tom.'

'Me life upon ye.'

The colonel nodded in approval.

Bennett paced out his run, pensively polishing the ball on his shirt. He turned and fixed his victim with an intimidating stare. He gave his characteristic little shuffle and began to run. The batsman braced himself for the onslaught. Bennett's right arm swung through a great arc and the ball hurtled from his hand. There was a shout as the bails were scattered and the batsman's head dropped in anguish.

It was as if defeat was a communicable disease. The Black Hills men felt their resolve crumbling. Uncertainty invaded their ranks and men doubted themselves. In the same over another man fell to the mighty Bennett and the tide turned for Strifeland.

Clara Bennett beamed at her son. 'It takes your da, Davy, to show them how,' she said with justifiable pride.

By mid-afternoon the result was a foregone conclusion and spectators began to drift homewards, leaving only the *cognoscenti*, those who appreciate the loneliness of the man at the crease.

The excitement of the game and the badinage of the spectators had put Kit in better form. There was some of the old gleam in his eye. 'Joey,' he said suddenly, 'do you want to go home with Maureen and her friends?'

Joey looked disparagingly at the group of giggling schoolgirls. 'Not me,' he snorted. 'Why do you ask?'

'I just thought we might wander up through the woods. Nobody'll notice with the match on. There's pheasants in a wire cage up there.'

'Hey, that would be great. Maybe we could get a few bamboos in the cane wood.' It was too good a chance to miss, to explore the normally forbidden territory of Strifeland's woods without fear of being caught. Joey felt a weight lifting from his mind. It was just like old times again, the old partnership, the unbeatable Donovan team. 'Why do you want to see the pheasants, Kit?'

'It's called reconnoitering, Joey,' said his leader loftily. 'Information like that could come in handy.' He winked conspiratorially.

Joey could see the fowl already in the pantry, their brilliant feathers giving a touch of oriental splendour to the chilly little room.

Dead twigs crackled under their feet as they made their way along, crouching under low hanging branches and peering around at the unfamiliar surroundings. It was not only the clandestine nature of their expedition, but also the atmosphere of the woods that gave them a thrill of excitement.

The landlords, when they planted their boundary groves, did so with what seemed extravagance to later generations, to the townsman with his few square feet, or the smallholder eking a living from a few poor acres. Thousands of acres are given over to woodland, groves of beech, oak, sycamore, or elm, interspersed with holly and laurel and a rich undergrowth of fern and bramble, with apparently wasteful prodigality, but these woods give a charm to the landscape and harbour a profusion of wildlife as well as providing timber. The foresight of those early planters determined the appearance of the Irish landscape for centuries.

The two boys moved almost reverently, as if in some great natural cathedral. They tended to converse in whispers, not only from considerations of prudence, starting at the sound of a woodquest whirring from the branches overhead, or sudden rustling in the undergrowth.

'Stop a minute, Joey,' whispered Kit urgently.

If it was a gamekeeper they were in serious trouble. He would probably shoot them on sight.

Kit grasped his brother's arm and drew him back behind a clump of laurel. 'Shh . . .' he whispered, 'not a sound.'

Joey peered through the shiny leaves at the woodland track and soon he could see two figures approaching, a woman whom he recognised as Anna, and a young man carrying a cane, which he used to hold back the brambles that tugged at her cape. They were laughing and talking together softly but the boys could not hear what was being said. Presently they paused in a small clearing beside the laurels and the young man took the girl in his arms and looked down at her. The sunlight slanted through the branches onto the upturned face. Gently the man unclipped her turban-like headdress and her auburn hair fell free and shining over her shoulders.

'God, you are beautiful,' he exclaimed as if discovering some wonder.

She leaned her head against his shoulder and he stroked her hair gently. She moved in closer and he held her to him. For a few moments they stood quietly with their arms around each other. Joey's face burned with shame. He felt that he was engaged in some furtive and sordid act. He glanced at his brother and saw the expression of pain in Kit's downcast eyes. The older boy's freckles showed startlingly clear in his pallid face. He was trembling.

'Oh Frank,' the girl was saying, 'must you really go back?'

'Not for a long time, my love,' he replied in a melodious West-Country accent, 'not if I can help it.'

'But what can you do? I mean, won't they just send you?'

He gave a low, ironic laugh. 'Play their own game. I've

applied for transfer to the Machinegun Corps. That will take a while. Maybe the whole damn thing will be over by then.'

She did not seem convinced. 'Machineguns,' she said anxiously. 'Wasn't that what wounded you in the first place?'

'If you can't beat them, and all that.' He smiled. 'Look, this is how I see it.' He sketched three semi-circles in the leaf mould with swings of his stick. 'Each machinegun has a fan-shaped field of fire, interlocking with the gun on either side. That gives us a wall of bullets from Switzerland to the sea. I just intend to be on the right side of it this time.' He laughed drily. 'They can come to me this time.'

She shook her head as if not really convinced. Joey leaned forward, intrigued by the diagram on the ground. Kit grasped his arm again and Joey almost cried out with pain.

'Sometimes I hope that you never get well,' she said gently. 'I know it's selfish, but I would like us to stay here together forever and forget all about the war.'

'My very sentiments,' he murmured, 'but I wouldn't have any choice now anyway, with conscription. We simply must make the most of the time we have left, before I have to go off again. You wouldn't want a conscientious objector for a husband, now would you?' He took her face in both his hands and looked at her earnestly.

Anna slipped her arms around his neck and pulled his face down to hers. Joey heard her give a low moan and suddenly Kit had turned and was threshing his way through the laurel grove, thrusting the branches aside and letting them swing back at Joey, who followed in hot pursuit. The man started after them with a shout but soon abandoned the chase.

'Schoolboys,' he reported, grinning. 'I'm afraid we probably disappointed them.'

Anna readjusted her headdress, tucking her hair out of sight with the side of her hand. 'It's lucky we weren't doing anything,' she remarked.

'Hmm. Your reputation is still safe — worse luck,' he grunted.

She gave him a quick glance.

'If I had two good legs under me I would have caught them, little blighters. Give them a clout in the ear.'

'Oh don't be silly. They were probably looking for chestnuts or something like that.'

'I suppose you're right.'

'You were a boy yourself, at one time I imagine,' she teased. 'Don't be a grumpy old man.'

He relented, and tucked her arm through his. 'Perhaps we might hobble down and see how the match is progressing.'

'If you don't hurry you'll be late for tea and all the evening papers will be gone. Then you'll be even grumpier.'

'Like the old man, you mean? He's a funny old bird.'

'I quite like him. He says what he means.'

'I'd better not leave you near him then when I'm away. Who knows what might happen? May and November and all that.'

'Well don't be too complacent. I'm not going to wait around forever, you know.'

In the distance they could see the figures on the cricket pitch, like white clothespegs on green baize, and hear the click of leather on wood. As they approached there was a ripple of applause and the umpire stepped in and withdrew the stumps. The players strolled towards the house, arguing volubly and the last few spectators drifted away, already talking about next year.

That night Kit made no mention of the events of the afternoon and Joey was just as glad. He had enough to think about with a new school year starting next morning. He was apprehensive about finding the place and about the Brothers' reputation for hard work and hard discipline. Carefully he checked his satchel, for about the tenth time. Everything was still in order.

'Don't worry about it Joey,' said Kit. 'I'll go in with you on the train and show you how to get there. You'll have to run from Amiens Street to be in time.'

'Hey, thanks. That'll be great. I don't want to be late the first day.' He laughed nervously. 'But what about Mr Drew? Don't you have to work tomorrow?'

'Ah, he won't mind. He can spare me for a while. Probably better off without me.' He slouched in the chair and stared into the fire. 'I won't be missed.'

Joey frowned at his brother's bleak tone. He wanted to offer encouragement. 'Doyle's dog got one of the hens today but Maureen bandaged it up again,' he said, hoping that this might constitute good news. 'She says it will be all right if the other hens don't pick the bandage off.'

'Aye,' sighed Kit. 'That's good.'

'Maureen's great at things like that, isn't she? She fixed a boil for me with a hot bottle.' Joey rolled up his sleeve dramatically to show the spot.

But Kit remained staring into the labyrinth of the fire. Blue jets of gas shot out from the coals and ignited, making miniature dragons' breaths. Tar sizzled and crawled, dripping into the white hot passageways, causing momentary black spots, only to disappear in spurts of flames. Abruptly Kit took the poker and began to demolish the fire, bashing the coals down and raking them out onto the hearth where they hissed and crackled in protest. Ruminatively he prodded each jet of flame, extinguishing it with the steel and separating the rapidly cooling coals, until there was nothing but a scatter of smouldering cinder.

'The da always did that, didn't he?' remarked Joey. 'Always raked out the fire at night.'

'Cracked all the tiles too,' muttered Kit. 'Ah well.' He prodded again at the cinders, pushing them back to let the chimney draw the last wisps of smoke. 'It's time for bed,' he said, rising suddenly. 'That's the end of that.'

Joey heard his footsteps on the stairs and the creaking of floorboards above. He was conscious of the faint hum of the oil lamp and was glad of its warmth. Suddenly the world outside the circle of light seemed dark and foreboding. For a long time he sat alone with his thoughts. When he went upstairs Kit was already asleep.

*   *   *

The evenings drew in and people said how they wouldn't feel it now till Christmas. September gales blew and thatch was mended against the winter. It was difficult to imagine that there had been a summer, that cricket and sandcastles and bathing had ever been possible. October brought early frost, crunching ice on the puddles and iron-hard ridges of dung on the street, that could turn an ankle, or trip an old person, tottering to first Mass in the dark. A man needed the warmth of the pub, a bottle and a bit of quiet conversation to keep a bit of life in the old bones.

'Tom,' said Mr Drew, frowning, 'isn't it the comical oul' world.'

'That it is,' agreed Bennett. 'That it is.' He waited for the other man to expand on his generalisation.

Mr Drew rooted with absorption in his jacket pocket and eventually produced a cigarette, one that had seen better days, a definite knee-bend halfway down and shreds of tobacco dangling from one end, like a jackdaw's nest in an old chimney 'These things will be the death of me.' He lit a match and cupped the flame in his hands in the manner of a man used to working out of doors. Gratefully he drew in the smoke, savouring the tang of sulphur and coughed, a long rending cough, that reached far down into the lungs, rummaging the interstices, pillaging every corner. Mr Drew spat discreetly onto the sawdust floor. 'Ah, that's better,' he gasped, and took another lungful. 'But it is though, isn't it?' he continued adverting to his introductory remark.

'Aye, that it is,' agreed Bennett again, and took a careful pull from his glass.

'Things'll be worse, mark my words, before they get better.' Mr Drew emphasised his point with his index finger. 'There's lads we know locked up in Wales. There'll never be peace till they're let home.'

Bennett grunted. He had heard all that before. 'What about the conscription?' he asked mischievously. 'Would you go to war if you was called up?'

Mr Drew glared at him. 'Now Tom, that's all me arse and parsley. I'm too ould for that, as well you know. But more's to the point, would you go?'

'Ah,' said Bennett, stuck for an answer. 'I never gave it much thought. Not that I wouldn't be up to it, by Jaysus,' he added truculently. 'They've took older men nor me.'

'And God's curse on them,' retorted Mr Drew, 'they've took a quare few young lads too.' He went silent, looking into his porter.

'Aye,' agreed Bennett. 'No, that wouldn't be my line o'

business. I'd stand up to any man face to face but I'd never want to kill anyone. I mean . . .' he trailed off. The whole business was beyond him.

'There was a grand young lad, young Donovan that worked for me, just went off and joined up. Never said a word.'

'Aye. I heard about that. Wasn't he too young though?'

'A big lad. Probably gave a false name an' that. Broke his poor mother's heart.'

'I dare say.'

'Aye. He just went into Dublin with the little brother and never came back. Fair dues to Duffy though. He tried to track him down.'

'No luck, I suppose?'

'No. He was probably sent off to England right away. They won't keep any Irish regiments in Ireland no more.'

'Not since the rebellion, I suppose.'

'Not rebellion, Tom, the rising. There's a difference. A rebellion is against a lawful gover'ment. A risin' is a down-trodden people standin' up for their rights.'

'I see,' said Bennett unimpressed by verbal nicety. 'Amounts to more or less the same thing for the poor huers in the front-line.'

'It's a question of justification,' insisted Mr Drew. 'Master Sweeney is very good on the subject, at the meetin's. You should come along sometime.'

'I'm sure he's a great man with the words all right,' admitted Bennett grudgingly. He changed the subject. 'How did that young lad's mother take it?'

'The whole family is very upset. I mean, a widow-woman and now the eldest lad gone off.'

They sat in sympathetic silence.

'Duffy tried to find him, you say?'

'Aye. Pursued enquiries, as he'd say himself, but I suppose they wouldn't be all that fussed if a young lad gave the wrong age.'

'The way it is,' agreed Bennett, shaking his head sadly, 'the boots last longer than the poor lads wearin' them.'

Again they lapsed into silence. The curate appeared and wiped the wet rings from the counter, lifting their glasses diffidently. Seeing the two sombre faces, he refrained from his usual inanities.

'A peculiar genius, Duffy. I never know what to make of him.' Mr Drew frowned at the ambiguities of the sergeant's situation.

Bennett smiled as if at some private joke. 'I'll tell you somethin' that happened a good few years ago,' he began. He fingered his jaw, instinctively probing a gap where a tooth should have been. 'It's a while ago now. I was goin' along by the bridge there at Strifeland when I met Duffy on the way back from Balbriggan. Anyway we got to chattin' like, ye know. "Tom," says he, "I've often wondered about somethin'." "What's that?" says I, like an eejit. "Well," says he, "I often wondered which of us is the better man." ' Bennett took another pull from his drink and wiped the froth from his lips with the back of his calloused hand.

'What happened?' Mr Drew was intrigued.

'Well sure, nothin' would satisfy him but to have the coats off in the woods there an' then.' Bennett chuckled at the memory and fingered his jaw again.

'Well come on. Who won?'

'By Christ, I can tell you, that was quite a fight. He's a hardy man, the sergeant.'

'Yes but come on. Out with it now.'

'Well now,' Bennett grinned, 'that'd be tellin' ye wouldn't it? We had a gentleman's agreement ye see. It's a matter for meself and the sergeant.'

Mr Drew snorted. 'Well you're the quare bucko all right. I'll have to form me own opinions.'

'A gentleman all the same. "I'm obliged to ye Tom," says he, when we were finished our manoeuvres, as if I was after lendin' him a pound.'

'Civil enough, I'll grant. He did his best for the widow Donovan. You know she stopped playin' the piano the day the young lad went off. Never touched it since.' He stubbed his cigarette butt out on the wet counter and slipped from the stool. He hitched his trousers up and drained his glass. 'Friend Fedigan wouldn't be too pleased if he thought the sergeant was sniffin' around the widow-woman though.' The observation was accompanied by a salacious chuckle.

'It's comical all right, as you say.'

* * *

Davy opened the box again and gazed in wonder.

Windsor and Newton: Watercolours. Japanned Tin, he read on the little brass plate. Two dozen tubes reposed in grooves inside. Wonder of wonders, the lid itself opened out to form a kind of tray with compartments in it and a hole to put your thumb through.

His mother said a lady had called to the door and left a parcel for him. Experimentally he unscrewed the caps. In the lamplight it was difficult to make out the actual colours. The names meant nothing to him and most of them he could not pronounce. Gamboge, vermillion, alizarin, a kind of red, though the name made him think of green or brown like a lizard. Lamp black. Now that made sense. Ultramarine. Marines were something like sailors. He had seen them coming off a gunboat in the harbour one time, at least the fishermen said they were marines. That was obviously like navy blue. At least it looked like that in the tube. He wiped a smear of paint on his copybook and, even in the yellow lamplight, the blue vibrated on the paper. He felt a thrill of excitement. He licked his finger and rubbed the stain. It spread and thinned out. The white showed through from below giving a lighter skiey shade. He tried a yellow in the same way. It overlapped the blue and to his amazement, a deep green emerged, in places like new leaves of early summer and in other places dark like the moss that hung from the dreeping clay cliffs below the cottage, a kind of midway vegetation, permanently wet but not quite seaweed.

He tried some more, smudging one colour into another with his fingers, afraid as yet to use the brushes. Violets and browns emerged unexpectedly. Orange flared between red and yellow and the realisation began to dawn on him that she had given him a priceless gift, the ability not just to use the colours in the tubes, but to liberate a myriad of colours that lurked invisible at first, like clients dependent on their more powerful neighbours for the right to exist.

He longed for daylight to see them as they really were. With a start he realised that he had covered a whole page with streaks and scrawls of paint. Guiltily he tore it out and turned to its fellow at the other end of the copybook, removing that too, lest jagged ends might give the game away and call down the wrath of the master for further evidence of slovenliness.

The door opened and his father came in, blowing a little after his long walk and shaking the rain from his coat.

'Gettin' a bit of a nip in the air,' he remarked by way of greeting to his wife and son.

Quickly Davy slipped the paper and paints out of sight. He was not prepared to explain just then what to anyone else would surely appear as a mess.

Part II

CHAPTER 7

The chaplain hesitated. He had no easy words for the task before him. He saw no end to the conflict that had already entered its third bitter winter. He leaned forward, gripping the edge of the pulpit. His face was lined and tired. He was close to despair. Overhead the evening clouds fled across the sky, showing vivid orange through the shattered rafters. The men shuffled restlessly, easing their kit on their shoulders. It was cold in the ruined church. The smell of stew wafted to them from the field kitchens, distracting many from the solemnity of the occasion. There were those who resented the delay and muttered with self-conscious bravado.

The purple stole fluttered in the sharp November breeze. 'I won't detain you long, men.' His voice carried, harsh and rasping, to every corner of the church. 'It is my job to offer comfort and encouragement to you as you go into battle, and to implore God's blessing on the work you have to do. Let me remind you that there are chaplains on the other side,' he pointed vaguely in the direction of the line, 'doing exactly the same.' Is this the dark night of the soul? He wondered about the God he served. We are made in God's image. What must He be like? An act of God? It made a certain sense. 'You are crowded in here now, but it won't take a very big chapel to hold what will be left of you in a few days' time.'

His words struck them like a blow in the unearthly silence.

'I will give general absolution to those who are truly sorry.'

He made the sign of the cross abruptly, 'Ego vos absolvo in nomine. . . .'

His words were drowned in the deafening thunder of the guns. The name of God was lost as the preliminary barrage erupted. The evening sky was torn apart by flame from the hidden batteries and the deafening roar of projectiles overhead. A lethal rain of high explosive began to fall on the enemy positions, levelling all obstacles, annihilating the already demoralised opposition.

Nothing could survive such an onslaught.

'Well lads,' said the corporal, 'youse all must be cheered up by them few words.'

The boys grinned self-consciously. It was all right for an old regular to speak disrespectfully of a priest but they were still too close to their origins to take such liberties. They were the men of the New Armies, not yet battle-weary veterans who had earned the right to swear and criticise. Their battles had been theoretical matters, played out on the stubble fields of England, where horsemen represented the creeping barrage and a few token strands, well marked with tape, indicated wire.

'Get some of that stew into yiz lads,' continued the corporal in avuncular fashion. 'It might be a while before yiz get another hot meal.'

They sat around on boxes or squatted on their heels, examining the contents of their mess tins. There was some muted laughter at the quality of the victuals. The corporal was warmed by their innocence and bravado and inwardly cursed the priest for coming so close to the truth. Kit looked at the older man, who caught his eye and winked.

'Here son,' he said, 'try a drop o' this.' He held out a half-finished naggin. 'De Kuypers,' he explained. 'A couple o' darts o' that and we'll go through them like shit through a goose.'

Kit grinned in reply. The liquid burned a fiery track down his gullet. He gasped and passed the bottle back.

But the corporal declined it. 'Buy me one in Bapaume tomorrow,' he said offhandedly. 'Keep a nip for the morning. It'll keep the chill out o' the bones.'

Kit's thanks were drowned by an intensification of the barrage. The ground reverberated around them and the corporal stood up, slinging his rifle over his shoulder. Drinks all round in Bapaume; he was not so sure.

They trudged forward through the dark approach trenches, following their guides, their boots squelching in the mud, except where duck-boards made the going a bit easier. Men stumbled, cursing under their heavy packs, and hurried to regain contact with those ahead. There was a tendency to crouch, although the trench sides formed a black horizon above their heads.

The ground shook under the impact of thousands of shells and the air vibrated until sound became a continuous roar, like a never-ending express train hurtling past. The stench of cordite and overflowing latrine sumps assailed their nostrils. As they neared the forward positions a light rain began to fall. The men being relieved began to file past in the opposite direction. In the intermittent flashes of light their faces showed gaunt and white. Their eyes were dull and rimmed with weariness. They made a few attempts at jocularity but got little response. The relieving troops had adapted already to their dark, sub-terranean existence, inching forward like a long blindworm, oblivious to everything around them.

Joey woke with a start. He was sweating. He listened for the sound of the piano but the house was silent. He heard the soughing of the wind and the steady patter of the rain on the window. It must have been a dream. He lay still for a long time but there was no sound of anyone moving downstairs. For a time he stared at the pale, grey squares of the window. Sometimes they seemed to recede until they were miles away and then they gradually grew bigger again. He wondered if he had woken at all. If he moved, he thought, he would know for certain, but the old childhood fear returned. The creatures that hid under the bed would know that you were there. You were all right as long as you lay still. When he was small he used to sit on the stairs in the dark, with his eyes shut and his fingers in his ears, until it was time for Kit to go to bed. He forced himself to sit up and look around at the empty bed. It was just a blur in the darkness but there was no rustling or sound of breathing. He knew then that he was awake and the loneliness engulfed him. The sleep was gone astray on him.

Hours later he saw the first pale glimmer of dawn lighting the bedroom wall.

Whistles shrilled all along the line and suddenly they were going over. The dreadful momentum of battle had taken hold. Grey-green smoke drifted ahead of them down the slight declivity as the deafening barrage leaped further on, like a moving wall of flame, pounding the approach trenches and pulverising what remained of the village of Beaumont-Hamel.

Apparently the guides and wire parties had done their job, as gaps were visible and men began to work their way through, stepping high, like marionettes, over the broken coils. There was no question of running, weighted down as they were by half a hundredweight of equipment, although the desire to get it over with was strong. Visibility was further reduced by the drizzle and figures loomed grotesque and hunch-backed, out of the overcast — Dublin's clerks, students, slum-dwellers, become hunters, stalking their victims through the primordial mist.

With shocking suddenness the barrage ceased and the air began to clear. The steely grey light of dawn revealed a lunar landscape of shell-holes and craters strewn with impenetrable thickets of wire, broken wheels from some previous advance and the skeletal trunks of what was once a forest. The feeling of being exposed was accentuated by the eerie silence, as if a reassuring voice had been stilled.

Unbelievably, machineguns opened up from the enemy trenches, sweeping the advancing figures with a deadly scything fire as the men in grey swarmed up from below the ground.

Kit felt his stomach lurch in dread. It was not fair. They never said anything about this. A cold, grim fatalism gripped him: going back was impossible; he would get into trouble; it was out of his hands; in a moment he might be dead, cancelled, irrelevant, but yet he could not do anything about it. He clenched his rifle like a talisman. That was his only protection.

Men stumbled and fell, some suddenly as if poleaxed, others slowly, apologetically, cringing or shuddering as if swallowing some foul-tasting medicine. Shouts and cries filled the air amid the chatter of small arms. Kit saw a man suspended from the wire, and his mouth opened in horror as he watched blood

96

flowing from the man's groin. Another sat with his legs stretched straight in front of him, the way a child sits, staring glumly at his boots.

The corporal writhed on the ground, searing the air with curses. 'Go on, go on, for fuck's sake. Don't stop here.'

The depleted line inched forward over no-man's-land. Kit saw the machingun emplacements, grey-green, like a ragged hedge of sea buckthorn and just as impassable. Yellow needles of flame spurted out. He felt a blow on the hip, spokes of pain shooting out from his lower back. He fell slowly forward, crumpling under the weight of his pack, taking in the scene in vivid detail as he drifted downwards.

Brown geysers of earth erupted from their own line as German 5.9 Howitzers, from somewhere far away, began a counter-barrage. White smoke rose in pillars, revolving in the light wind, turning to gauze as it drifted away. There was a gash of blue above Kit and, as if in a dream, he watched a scout-plane droning across, the sun shining upwards on its struts and wires, until it became an iridescent dragonfly. The sky revolved as he looked upwards and he pressed himself closer to the ground, feeling the security of even the smallest hummock. The battle, for what it was worth, went on around him. He was conscious of men walking and crawling past. He heard their shouts from a long way off and the relentless hammering of the machineguns.

Sometimes at early Mass in the little chapel on Toker Hill he used to feel his head swimming after the climb up the hill. It was the fasting of course. Waves of blackness would flicker across his vision and the droning of the priest would become a buzz. Once he had lost consciousness and woke to find himself sitting on the step in the porch with someone pushing his head down between his knees. There had been cowdung on the man's Sunday boots. 'You're game-ball now son. You won't miss the Consecration.' There was a smell of hair oil overlying the smell of dung. Racing down the hill after Mass. Sliding on the ice in wintertime, on dark November mornings. Breakfast frying. His father used to make breakfast on Sundays, whistling through his teeth as he worked. If people get up for early Mass they're entitled to have breakfast ready when they come home. 'We could break off long elder branches and knock the icicles off the railway bridge.' 'No use, Joey. Elders are too soft. They're only big weeds.' A grey curtain fluttered across Kit's mind. 'Did you see that aeroplane, Joey?' He felt that he had spoken aloud. The enemy might have heard. An egg should not be turned over when frying. His father was a perfectionist. It should be lightly basted to give a white film over the yolk. 'Get that into you now!' There was always a speck of shaving soap that his father had missed. He used to walk around the house as he shaved, calling people, getting things on the move, admonishing the cat. The sharp smell of shaving soap brought tears to the eyes. They always sat in the crook of their father's arm, turning the pages while he read to them. 'It's not fair on the poor caterpillar. Is it, Daddy?' His father pensively brushed the nap of the fabric on the arm-rest. Small haloes flickered under his fingers. 'Life isn't always fair, Kit,' he said gently. 'It's not fair, though. Is it, Joey? But Joey was already asleep. Kit felt the tears run over the bridge of his nose and trickle down the side of his face. Slowly he drifted into unconsciousness.

A light drizzle began to fall.

The advance had been halted and the survivors withdrew slowly to their own line, crawling and slithering gratefully into the safety of the trench. They were pathetically few, as became clear when platoons and sections tried to reform. Walking-wounded and stretcher cases were moving to the rear. Those not so badly mutilated were in high spirits, detached from the battle and rejoicing in having copped a 'blighty one'. Medical orderlies laboured incessantly as dressing stations overflowed and supplies began to run out. There was extraordinary gentleness between those who could fend for themselves and those who could not. Men lit cigarettes for others, remarking, 'You'll be home for Christmas, oul' son,' or 'You'll be as right as rain in no time,' particularly to those who knew that it was not so. Sometimes though, it was impossible to look on the contents of a stretcher and do more than mumble a few incoherent sounds of sympathy and encouragement. The best you could do was pull the groundsheet up over the lad, against the wet, and hope that someone further down could do something for him.

There was water in the bottom of the shell hole but it was a small price to pay for the security. By bracing his good leg against a tangle of wire and wood Kit could keep himself on the upper slope. It had been worth the agonising struggle to get there.

Another man lay with his back to Kit and one foot in the water. He might even be dead. The battle appeared to be tapering off. Occasional bursts of machinegun fire whistled overhead. A gigantic railway howitzer punctuated the artillery duel. Thump. Kit counted. Thump, again. Two rounds per minute. He had seen it in action on the way up; Canadians, one of them in carpet slippers. 'We've got the goods for them today boys,' he had said, rubbing his hands. Kit figured that it must be mid-afternoon. The sun was only a blur of white behind the overcast. He thought of the naggin of gin. That would warm him. His teeth chattered. His head was clear again. Someone would find them when it got dark and soon they would be going home.

The other man stirred and appeared to be trying to speak. His shoulders twitched.

Kit took a mouthful of the gin and felt it burn its way down, dulling for an instant the pain inside him. The grateful warmth branched out and he imagined it creeping out to his extremities. Things could have been much worse. 'Would you try a drop of gin?' he whispered, wondering how close they were to the enemy lines. 'Do you good.'

There was no reply.

'I'll throw it across.' There was a definite stirring. He gathered a handful of wet clay and flipped it sideways. Movement brought fresh pain, and fear that he might slip down into the water, where the blood would be drawn from him, leaking uncontrollably into the mud.

The man shuddered.

'Here goes.' Kit lobbed the bottle above the man's helmeted head so that it would slide down in front of his face.

It thudded into the slope and the wet earth began to slip. The man rolled on his back. The skull under the mud-caked helmet lolled hideously, devoid of flesh. The black eye socks regarded Kit with cynical amusement. He felt a scream rising inside him. The tunic burst open and a fat, grey rat emerged, disturbed from its work in the chest cavity. Its nose twitched as it sniffed the air. There were pinpoints of light in the inquisitive eyes.

Kit screamed, a long ululating vowel of pure terror. He was so utterly alone. His legs would not move. His hands clawed at the clay as he thrust backwards.

The cry carried to the men on either side, in the dusk of the winter afternoon, sending a chill through those who heard it. Somewhere out there was a man confronted by some unspeakable horror. It could have been themselves. It might be next time.

Another and another rat emerged, with obscene scuttling sounds. They lumbered around the corpse, jostling each other, climbing back and forth. Filled with loathing and revulsion for both man and rodents, Kit hurled handfuls of clay at them. If only he had his rifle he would be safe. The rats retreated, hopping over the rim of the hole, eyeing him malevolently. They would be back. Time was on their side. He had stopped screaming but he was gasping for breath. His throat contracted in a dry painful retch but nothing would come. He was conscious of warm wet blood on his thigh and a roaring sound in his ears and the darkness came again.

'Mach schnell,' said an urgent voice and Kit felt himself being jolted around. He could see a figure in grey in front of him and realised that he was on a stretcher. His heart sank at the realisation that he was in the hands of the enemy. 'Mach schnell,' said the voice again, and he caught a glimpse of a man, obviously an officer, gesticulating at the bearers. 'Pompous sod,' said another voice in the darkness. ''Ere China, 'ave one o' these.' He felt the cigarette being placed between his lips and a match flared for one instant. Gratefully he drew the smoke into his lungs. There was no taste like it in the world. 'You'd think the bastard was in charge, wouldn't you,' the English voice remarked. 'Mach schnell, my arse. Move these blokes along or so help me. . . .' Words failed him for a moment. 'Where the hell am I?' asked Kit. 'Don't worry Paddy. You're on your way 'ome.'

The nurse looked down at him. 'We can only patch you up

for the moment. There's some lead in there that will have to come out.' There were dark circles under her eyes, accentuated by the lantern that hung from the tent pole. She was almost staggering with exhaustion, but her fingers moved efficiently. Finally she stood to call for the bearers, and as if as an afterthought she turned again to Kit. 'And tell me my man, did you take Bapaume?' Her manner was haughty and intimidating.

'I wouldn't know,' he replied apologetically. 'I've been out of action all day.'

'Hmm, Irish aren't you,' she sniffed. 'Well anyway, you're going back to base hospital. You'll be out of action for quite some considerable time.'

From somewhere there was the smell of rashers frying and he realised that he was hungry. 'Thank you very much ma'am,' he said.

The grey-clad prisoners took up the stretcher. They were glad to be out of it too.

CHAPTER 8

There was a cold wind coming off the sea as Bennett left the pub. He was angry and confused. He felt diminished by something he could not understand. In a stand-up fight with anyone, by God, he could hold his own, even Duffy, but there was another world where he would never win, a world of clean collars, a world of smooth words and people looking down on you. What was it the little get had said? 'You must appreciate Mr Bennett that the boy's education is being put in jeopardy by this scavenging.' That was the one that had hurt. He had been ready to take the little bastard by the neck and throttle him. Nobody minded a few scutches now and then when a child deserved them, but it wasn't right to scutch Davy for helping his mother. Tears came to his eyes — God, but it was cold.

'Clara,' he had said, when the child came home from school, once again still crying with the pain, 'it's time I had a word with the master.' She had tried to stop him, saying there would be trouble and that Sweeney would only take it out on Davy, but he had been adamant. They hadn't even asked him into the hallway, left him standing at the door like a tinker. Polished furniture and ornaments in the hall. An umbrella stand, and Mr Sweeney coming out from the parlour with his: 'Ah Mr Bennett. You've taken your time about answering my letters,' as if he had been sent for.

Bennett clenched his fists. I should of grabbed him straight off, he fumed, but the initiative had been lost. Scavenging. It was like a slap in the face. Didn't everyone do it when times were hard? The way he said *Mister* Bennett, a kind of a jeer. What kind of a man sent his wife out scavenging? He was ashamed in spite of himself. He stopped for a while, looking out at the grey, white-capped sea and the distant line of the Mournes. The wind whistled through the dry twigs and the salty yellow grass along the shore. He could have done with his coat. It came to him all of a sudden. They were poor. People looked down on them. They probably laughed at the child going to school in cut-down clothes. They had no hallway with polished furniture. He couldn't even find them a decent place to live. People laughed behind his back. 'There's the great Tom Bennett, workin' his arse off for the gentry and his wife scavengin' through the fields.' It was true too. Anger welled inside him. He could imagine the laughter in the pub after he left. He'd tell them, if only he had the words. By God, but he'd make a few changes from now on. The whiskey warmed him.

Clara heard him closing the wicket gate. At least he wasn't in jail, thank God. She pushed the pot onto the stove. He'd be glad of a drop of soup. She saw from his expression that he was not in the best of tempers as the door slammed behind him. Best not to say anything for a while.

'It's smoky in here,' he growled.

'I'll open the window.'

'No leave it. It's bloody freezin' outside.'

So that was how it was. 'Will you have a drop of soup?'

'What?'

'I said, "will you have a drop of soup?" '

'I know what you bloody said. I'm not deaf. Is there nothin' decent to eat in this bloody house?'

She was hurt by that. She had gone to a lot of trouble over the dinner, walked all the way into Fedigans. Mr Fedigan always threw in a few bones and a bit of suet for nothing. 'I've potato cakes with a bit of ox liver.' That should sweeten him a bit.

His face was grim in the flickering firelight. It was still too early to light the lamp. 'That little bastard Sweeney.'

So things hadn't gone well at all.

He reached for a chair and stumbled over the half-sack of

coke. 'Jesus Christ. This place is a bloody pigsty. Get this dirt out of here.' He kicked viciously at the sack, scattering the contents over the floor. His voice trembled with rage.

She drew back in fear.

'And you can keep this bloody swill too.' He seized the pot and hurled it at the wall.

Brown trickles of soup ran vertically from the stain. Clara stared at it, imprinting it on her mind. It was like a painting of a forest, glistening in the firelight, a great cluster of branches and the tall, thin trunks of strange and stately trees.

'And keep your brat out of me sight or I'll take me belt to him.'

Suddenly he was gone, slamming the door again. The cottage quivered in the unearthly silence. She knelt amid the wreckage, too shocked to move. She was conscious of the child staring at her with large, frightened eyes. She could not understand what she had done. The sea groaned on the beach below the cliff and a curlew piped sadly in the evening sky.

Bennett swore as he left the pub for the second time that night. 'Goin' round in bloody circles,' he muttered, rubbing his hands vigorously.

It was bad enough to have missed the band practice, but to have endured the sly grins and looks of complicity, when the barman suggested that maybe he had enough, was more than Bennett could take. He lurched into the street, bemused and resentful of the world. He had gone far beyond self-justification, and would have welcomed a row with anyone. Time was when not a man in this goddamned town would have crossed him, but there was no adversary in sight now, only the barest glint of moonlight and the sharp sea wind with a touch of frost in it. She'd better have the place tidied and a bit of grub or she'd hear all about it. He shivered and turned his jacket collar up.

It was a long trudge home, for the second time that day.

The door was bolted and locked. She wouldn't answer, no matter how hard he kicked it with his hobnailers. He had fixed the bolts himself and they were good.

'Open this bloody door, woman, or I'll break it down.' His tongue slurred on the words.

There was no answer. The cottage was in darkness.

'So help me Bob, if you don't open it. . . .' He lurched against it with his shoulder. 'Davy,' he heard the pathos in his appeal. 'Open the door.' Give them time.

Still there was no sound. He felt his way around the corner of the wall and opened the shed. At least there was some shelter there. There were a few logs on the floor. He sat down with his elbows on his knees, and his head in his hands. He felt miserable and sick. The shed seemed to sway and he toppled sideways onto a pile of sacks. He got the sickly smell of jute and gagged violently. It was too difficult to move and sleep overtook him.

It was almost light when Tom awoke. His mouth was dry and furry and his head seemed about to split when he moved. He subsided again onto the sacks. He was shivering but not so violently. His overcoat lay across him and the child was sitting a few feet away, watching silently. When he stirred again the child moved back, as if ready for flight.

'Don't be afraid Davy.' Only yesterday he had prepared to strangle the master for frightening the child, and now, he realised, his son was afraid of him. It added another dimension to the surge of remorse. He had never offered violence to Clara or the boy before. If only the roof would fall in and bury him.

'Ma says you're to come in when you're ready.' The boy was watching him warily. His father was grey with cold, unshaven and old looking. He looked shrunken and weak. 'Are you all right Da?'

'Aye, I'm fine.' His joints groaned with stiffness from the hard earth floor. He got slowly to his feet, huddling the coat around him. 'The coat,' he mumbled. 'Thanks for the oul' coat.'

The stove door was open and the fire made a cheerful blaze. The wall was wiped down but the stain was still visible. Clara was lifting the kettle from the hob. She paused for a second, uncertain of what to say. Bennett looked glumly at the floor.

'You don't look too good.' She broke the awkward silence. 'Go in and lie down and I'll bring you a cup of tea in a minute.'

'Aye, that would be nice,' he mumbled. 'I don't feel so great.'

'Give your daddy a hand with his boots Davy.'

Bennett sank onto the bed and the child tugged at the laces and began to pick the loops out carefully, loosening the thongs. The long brown tongues lolled out like cows' tongues in the butcher's window. The child silently recalled Master Sweeney's perennial riddle: 'What has a tongue but can't talk, unlike the boys in this class?' The boots thumped on the bare floorboards and Bennett rolled gratefully onto the bed, pulling the covers around him. The bed had not been slept in. They must have been up all night, afraid he would attack again.

'There. Drink that, before you shiver the place down.' There was almost a hint of humour in her voice, now that her fear had subsided.

He drank gratefully, avoiding her eyes. The warmth began to return to his body.

She sat on the end of the bed. 'It didn't go too well then, with the master?'

He could not bring himself to bluff. 'He made me feel like a pauper.'

She saw the pain in his eyes. The ground had shifted under his feet. Th rules had been changed. She said nothing for a while, understanding.

'The little huer.'

She looked directly at him, willing him to meet her eyes. 'He knows all the words, Tom, but he never sung the tune.'

He was startled by the uncharacteristic flight of fancy and looked up. He saw pride in her worn features and a kind of radiance around her, offering strength.

'You lie there for a while till it's time for the milkin'.'

'Aye,' he said, lying back, 'I might do that.'

'Do you think maybe it's time we put a lick of distemper on the kitchen? I'd sort of fancy a nice green for a change.'

'Aye, green would be nice,' or tartan with yellow spots or whatever. It was a small price to pay. 'Would you ask the lad to bring us another cup o' tea? Maybe you'd explain to him about the education while you're at it. It's supposed to be good for people, whether they like it or not.' He settled back in the bed. It would be nice to be able to lie there all day but that wasn't for the likes of the Bennetts. Nobody could ever call him a slacker, he thought, feeling a small vestige of pride. The cheek of the little melt. By God she kept them warm and fed when others couldn't. He won't get away with a remark like that again, by Christ.

* * *

Winter took its toll of the old and feeble, while those who survived, retrenched, husbanding their strength and resources. Old women like Alice Donnelly took to their beds to avoid the snows of January and the harsh east winds of February, and like the old women who went before them, they looked for the first weak sunshine of springtime and a bit of a stretch in the day. Faces grew gaunt and pale and gentian violet covered chilblains and unrelenting cold sores.

Rain slanted down on the deserted streets of the town. A smudge of smoke from the school chimney marked where the master, reigning supreme in the atmosphere of farts, powdered ink and the musty smell of damp clothing, had strategically placed his table directly in front of a reluctant fire, and the children shifted their feet and snuffled as they looked out at the bleared image of the black and naked trees.

The year took its toll on the colonel's barn too, assailing it with rain and damp and salt sea-air. A braid of rust formed round every rifle slot and long streels of red ran down the corrugations.

'You see, the way it is Colonel,' said Mr Drew, 'rust isn't a class of a disease, the way some people think. It's an explosion.' He expanded his hands expressively to simulate the process.

'A what?' asked the colonel. 'An explosion?'

'Yes,' repeated Mr Drew, warming to his subject. 'All your little grains of metal start expandin' with energy. Molecules they call them nowadays, molecules.' He savoured the word. Education is a great man. 'They all burst out and change the iron into rust. A remarkable business.' He tapped a patch of rust that extended from one of the rifle slots in the side of the barn. 'You can see how the rust is bigger than the surroundin' metal.'

The colonel leaned over, stroking his moustache thoughtfully. 'I see what you mean. Yes. Is there anything you can do about it? We can't have the damn thing rotting into the ground.'

'Think no more about it. A stitch in time and all that. What I'll do is clean off all the rust and slap on a bit of red lead. That'll keep out the wet. Then I'll put a bit of corruget on every hole and bolt it through onto a brace. She'll be nearly as good as new again.'

'Well get on with it then, man. We've wasted enough time already.' He had reason to be impatient. Months of correspondence had given him no satisfaction. It had become obvious that no one was going to supply him with a new barn. The O.C. Gormanston, whose predecessor had signed the original chit, passed his letter on to the Quartermaster General, with a note about some farmer looking for a free barn. From there the matter had been successfully passed on to the new Ministry of Reconstruction, which seemed an appropriate place to lose such a query. The final result was a letter expressing His Majesty's Government's regrets that due to the exigencies of the war and the overriding priority of the munitions industry it was not deemed possible at that time to honour the commitment in full. At such time as the present hostilities should cease it might become possible to review the situation in the light of the circumstances then obtaining etc. etc. A draft for ten guineas was enclosed to effect essential repairs. Mr Drew's 'bits of corruget' would in the opinion of His Majesty's Minister for Reconstruction, Mr Addison, have been better employed against Ludendorff on the Western Front.

'What do you think, Colonel?' It was Tom Bennett's voice at his shoulder, arousing him from his thoughts. Tom had been observing the job in silence.

'Well it's the best we can do at the moment I suppose. There is a war on.'

'Aye,' agreed Bennett, looking up at Mr Drew, who was reaming out the rust with a rough file.

Mr Drew thrust the file into his coat pocket and blew away the dust. 'Do you know a bastard when you see one, Tom?' he called down with a twinkle in his eye.

'I know a goddamned Skerryman when I see one,' replied Tom in puzzlement.

'No, no,' said Mr Drew innocently. 'I mean a bastard file. There's one there in the box. Just pass it up to me.'

What next, wondered Tom, rooting in the toolbox. Bastard

files! As if there wasn't enough bastards in the world.

'What do you think Tom? Will it do?' asked the colonel.

'Do you really want my opinion?'

'Why not? You've never been slow to give it before.'

'Well, Colonel, it's the English way of doin' things. They tear your barn apart to protect your interests, you bein' a unionist and all that, and then they give you pot-menders to put it back together again. Bloody pot-menders.'

'You know,' chimned in Mr Drew from aloft, 'he's got a point there. That's what they'll do with the whole country in the long run. Tear it to bits and then tell us to get on with it.'

'Nonsense man,' expostulated the colonel. 'This is the greatest empire that ever existed. It's not going to fall apart because of a few demagogues and fanatics.'

'The empire the sun never sets on,' declaimed Mr Drew. 'Do you know why that is, Colonel?'

'I imagine you're going to enlighten me,' said the colonel tolerantly.

Tom listened with interest. It wasn't often the colonel was put on the defensive.

'Because God couldn't trust the huers in the dark.' Mr Drew chuckled and drew the file across the metal with a screeching sound.

The colonel was obliged to laugh, a dry rattling cackle. 'You're a cynical man, Drew.'

'Cynical enough about some things, but I'll tell you something. It's the unionists I feel sorry for. They'll be dumped in the ditch by their friends. At least we won't expect any better.' He clambered down to the ground and picked up a tin of lead. 'We won't be able to paint over the cracks when that day comes.'

The colonel was irritated by the direction of the discussion. It made him uneasy. 'Well I've no time to stand around engaging in airy persifflage. You'd better get on with your work.' He rapped the side of the handcart with his cane and turned away, muttering to himself.

Begod, thought Tom, but isn't it great to hear two educated men discussin' things. Molecules. Airy Percy Fladge. Maybe I should of stayin' on at school a bit longer.

CHAPTER 9

The Saturday half-day always had something of an air of holiday about it but on the last day of term it was a blessed day indeed. The weather was in keeping with Joey's spirits as he contemplated almost three months of freedom. The whistle screamed in the station, echoing under the vaulted iron roof and a great gust of smoke whirled back from the engine, carrying smuts through the open windows. Joey grabbed the strap and hauled up the window. A face appeared, framed in the doorway and he felt his knees go weak with the shock. He stared speechless and Kit looked up at him in astonishment, from under a cap that was still a shade too large for him. He was in uniform and carried a knapsack over his shoulder; his face seemed leaner and older than might have been expected, but gradually a grin of delight betrayed something of the old Kit. The train gave a lurch as the guard's whistle shrilled again and, turning the handle quickly, Kit opened the door and threw his gear onto the carriage floor. Awkwardly he clambered aboard as the train began to move.

'It is you, isn't it?' Kit said, grabbing his brother by the shoulder. 'This is just great.'

Joey blinked, recovering from the shock. 'I don't believe it,' he stammered. 'I just don't believe it.'

Kit shook him violently. 'My God, Joey but you've grown like a dirty great weed.' He signified his joy by pounding his brother on the back.

110

'Dirty great?' repeated Joey in puzzlement and tentatively pounded in reply.

'Just an expression,' laughed Kit, and stood back. 'By God,' he said, 'I would hardly have known you.'

'Nor you either,' replied Joey, and he smiled broadly. 'Christ,' he continued, emphasising his new maturity, 'but it's great to see you.'

They sat down on opposite seats and stared at each other, lost for something to say and occasionally laughing aloud. The train trundled over the viaduct, past the mean, rundown streets, and gradually gained speed as it reached open country. The Saturday lunchtime express got people home in thirty minutes, as hot and weary office workers and day-trippers to the sea-side fled from the broiling city heat.

'We got your letter,' Joey began after a pause. He tried to inject reproach into his tone, but he was too filled with happiness to succeed. 'The ma nearly died with relief.'

'I wonder what she'll say,' said Kit and a spasm of apprehension passed over his countenance. For a moment he was a small boy. 'I suppose she was a bit upset, you know, about eh, everything.'

'A bit upset? That's putting it lightly. I suppose I'd better tell you that she nearly went mad with the worry. Hardly said a word for months.'

Kit lowered his eyes. 'I know. I was sorry about all that,' he mumbled.

'Still,' went on Joey gently, anxious not to cause offence or appear ungrateful, for fear that his brother might vanish, 'everything will be fine, now that you're back.' It was like catching a butterfly. You had to go slowly and carefully. If you snatched at it suddenly it would either flutter through your fingers or be crushed beyond redemption. There was a question that he dreaded to ask. On one level it would seem unmannerly to say: 'How long have you got?' and on a deeper level perhaps, if he did not ask, Kit might stay for good. It was like putting your fingers in your ears and closing your eyes. If you refused to acknowledge the presence of the monster it could do you no harm.

'I got some leave after I left hospital,' Kit volunteered as if reading his brother's mind.

111

'Are you all right now?' asked Joey, wondering how he had not thought to enquire before.

'Oh yes, just a bit stiff here and there.' Kit waved his hand dismissively. He lounged back and stretched his legs out on the seat.

They had the compartment to themselves and Joey followed suit.

'How did it happen? How long were you in hospital? What was it like out there?' The questions tumbled out of him all in a rush. 'I mean, is it like it says in the papers? Who would you say is winning?'

Kit avoided his eager gaze. 'I'll tell you about it sometime, maybe. It's not very interesting really. I never really knew what was going on. We didn't get to see very much.' He paused as if thinking hard and his eyes glazed over, remembering. 'Anyway,' he resumed after a while, 'I was in hospital for about five months on an' off. Not really a hospital, most of that time. A kind of a rest home.' He grinned wryly. 'Like an oul' fella, on a pair o' sticks.' He sat up straight and watched the familiar landscape between the clouds of smoke. 'It's a beautiful day,' he said at length, 'really hot, isn't it?' He unbuttoned his tunic and threw it beside the cap on the seat. 'Won't be wanting that for a while.'

Joey felt a guilty surge of relief. Already Kit, with his sleeves rolled up, looked less obviously a soldier. It was not the most universally admired profession at that moment.

'You know,' said Kit as if again reading his mind, 'I don't think the uniform is such a good idea around these parts, somehow. I've had a few dirty looks since I came in at Kingstown.'

'Ah, don't mind that. Sure everyone knows you're all right.'

'I suppose I should be encouraged by that remark,' grunted Kit, and stood up.

The train had changed its note as it began to throttle down for the station. Suddenly they were over the railway bridge and the town lay before them with the sea beyond. Joey watched his brother intently as Kit's eyes devoured the scene, steadying himself with a hand on the luggage rack as the train lost its momentum.

'Look, Joey, look,' he cried excitedly. 'There's Barney Phelan, with a leg at each corner.'

112

This odd description shot out as he watched the old man stumping up the road and the appropriateness struck Joey. Indeed he had never noticed before how the arthritis had splayed Barney so that he walked with legs wide apart, as if they were hinged separately to the body without meeting at any point. Even from that distance they could see how Barney stopped every now and again to give his characteristic little shrug, adjusting his layers of clothing and the sack that went everywhere with him, clutched over his left shoulder.

'Barney and his Indian bag. Now I know I'm home.' Kit swung his knapsack over his shoulder and shrugged in like manner.

The regatta provided a welcome excuse to escape from the house after dinner.

Their mother had taken the surprise quite well, considering. At first she had been speechless when Joey went in ahead to break the news, and then tearful when she saw her eldest son darkening the kitchen doorway. She noted how he dragged his right leg somewhat and put her hands to her face in alarm. 'Oh no,' was all she could say at first. 'It can't be.' She sat down abruptly, scraping the bentwood chair on the tiles and stared in disbelief.

Kit dropped his gear on the floor and bent down to kiss her awkwardly on the forehead. Extravagant displays of affection had never been commonplace in their house. 'I'm sorry, Ma,' Kit said, and took her hand in his, noticing how cold it was. 'I should have let you know.' She did not appear at first to take in what he was saying and merely nodded in agreement.

Gradually she had regained some of her usual composure and remarked that it was as well that he had come in time for dinner. She uttered no word of reproach. 'One of your brother's famous hens,' she added with the ghost of a smile.

Joey spread his arms in a rueful gesture and said, 'If they won't lay they have to be good for something — can't eat the bread of idleness. Not quite the fatted calf though —' but then checked himself, thinking that he was talking too much.

The tension had noticeably eased and they drew in to the table. Mrs Donovan was unable to concentrate on her food

113

and, directing them to finish everything, she excused herself to go and telegraph Maureen.

The brothers were free then to stroll among the crowds at the harbour and enjoy the excitement of the races.

The band marched past with a spirited rendering of 'St Patrick's Day', inappropriate to the time of the year, but by far their best piece. Tom Bennett, leaning back to take the weight of the big drum, swaggered in the rear and twirled his drumsticks stylishly. He stared grimly ahead, ignoring the small boys who trotted beside him, proud of the effect he created.

'Well, by Jaysus,' said a familiar voice, and the brothers turned to see Mr Drew bearing down on them, hand outstretched. 'The only goddamned redcoat I'd want to shake the hand of.' He wheezed benignly and pumped Kit by the hand vigorously. 'Be the Lord Harry.' He paused and repeated the oath, gazing at the younger man.

'How are things, Mr Drew?' enquired Kit cordially, man to man.

'Ah not so bad, not so bad,' said the older man. Diffidently he lowered his voice: 'You got a bit of a tip, then, I see.'

'Aye. I was lucky enough, I suppose. Could've been worse.'

'Aye. Aye. Well the mammy must be very glad anyway, to have ye home in one piece.' There was the unspoken question in his remark.

Joey, with nothing to contribute to the exchange, had been watching the preparations for the races. The lifeboat was being launched from a trailer with great duodecagonal wheels, clumping ponderously down the slipway as the line was paid out. The crew, magnificently burly in cork lifejackets, held their oars upright with nonchalant assurance. The craggy figure of Sergeant Duffy sat behind the stroke. Although he dreaded the water with the instinctive fear of the countryman, it was known that he had a medal for bravery in a rescue at sea. The bow went down into the water and rose again as the craft floated free from the trailer. At a word from the cox the oars found their rowlocks and the lifeboat moved to its station on the circuit.

The call went up for the first race and all eyes were turned towards the starter.

'We'll talk again Kit,' said Mr Drew and moved away into the crowd.

The crews rested on their oars as they waited for the starter to finish his preliminary harangue. He stood in a small dinghy and repeated the instructions that were so hallowed by time that all the spectators could recite them by heart, but there would be no point in having a megaphone if you didn't give instructions.

The Balbriggan men, greatly outnumbered, sat dourly, with brows knitted in concentration, and endured such jocularities as 'half shirts', alluding, no doubt, to their major industry and their sartorial elegance, and worse insults suggesting that their ancestors, if such could be traced, had been less than merciful in their treatment of shipwrecked mariners. All this served only to release great surges of adrenalin into their outraged blood, as they gripped their oars and swore to teach the hereditary enemy a lesson he would never forget.

'They're off,' was the shout as half a dozen assorted craft leaped forwards with the initial heave. Rowlocks groaned audibly and timbers creaked as the contestants shot towards the first mark, spurred on by the excited shouts of the crowd. Around the first flag they veered with much jostling, and abuse, some nice points of seamanship being debated, but fortunately the language could not be heard by the watchers on the shore. Away they streaked towards the north shore and the second mark, the field stretching out now as stamina and pride began to tell.

Around the second flag came the two leading craft and began the long haul back to the pier. On this leg they were within yards of the crowd that lined the road. Neck and neck they surged along, Balbriggan men and Skerrymen in a life and death struggle. The Balbriggan men, the huers, were definitely the pick of the bunch in this heat. Gradually they drew ahead as the din became almost unbearable and deftly, with insulting ease, they crossed the line and backed water, to enjoy the expressions of their dejected rivals, who collapsed over their oars in shame and frustration.

It was an afternoon of sun, bunting, excitement and laughter. The Donovan boys wandered through the crowds, watching by turns the swimming and boating races, or extracting more than their money's worth of amusement in the arcade at the tower. For a penny the laughing sailor dispelled the world's troubles, good value at ten times the price. The posters heralded the imminent arrival of George Formby and a season of diverting entertainments — *High Jinks* and *Ye Gods*, titles needing little explanation, and *Daddy Longlegs*, a sad and humorous tale of a little orphan, with ample amounts of pathos and some very pleasant songs. The season catered for all tastes.

The late afternoon sun had begun to cast long shadows as they ambled along the shingle towards The White Rock. Reflections of whitewashed walls shimmered in the water. The trees of Strifeland hill stood out in pale silhouette through the haze. Imperceptibly everything began to take on the bronze and gold tinges of evening.

Idly Kit skimmed a slate along the surface, watching the circles spread as it leaped and zig-zagged. A seabird languidly detached itself from its reflection and laboured into the air with a single shrill cry.

'I used to think about days like this when I was out there. I didn't ever think I'd get back here.'

Joey did not reply. He looked up at the house on The White Rock. The window facing onto the strand was open and clearly he could hear the sound of his mother's piano. He stood still, listening intently. It was almost as if he could see the notes drifting through the casement and settling on the flood tide.

'Listen,' whispered Kit. 'You've no idea how often I imagined I could hear her playing, just like that.'

There was a terrible poignancy in the music.

Joey could not tell him of the silence that had reigned in the house for so long. 'I think', he said slowly, 'she has the idea that you're home for good.'

As if in answer to his words, a light wind ruffled the surface into cats' paws and the shadows seemed to lengthen visibly, bringing a chill to the corner of the strand under the dark shoulder of rock.

A match flared in the dark rectangle of Josie Brett's cottage door and his old dog barked lazily. The glow of the lamp showed the gaunt figure foostering around inside and the two brothers, from old habit, veered to give him a wide berth.

'Don't want to be put in a sack,' muttered Kit wryly, recal-

116

ling their mother's oft-repeated warning.

By virtue of his interest in children and despite his uncanny rapport with God's dumb creatures, which fascinated those very children, parents admonished their offspring of both sexes never to accept anything from him and to run if ever he went near them. In a world where spontaneous generosity is rare enough, it was a puzzle to young minds why Josie Brett's offerings of sugar barley were so strictly out of bounds. As they grew old enough to understand a little better they exorcised their old fears by laughter and innuendo.

'Better not to say anything for a while yet,' said Kit quietly. 'There's just the chance that I mightn't be passed fit.'

'And if you are?'

'I've no choice.' He paused, and with an effort at casualness added, 'unless of course it's all over by then.' He clambered up the rough grassy slope from the beach, making heavy going of it with his bad leg.

Joey found himself hoping that the leg would not get better and paradoxically that his brother was not faking in order to gain a discharge. He pushed the thought aside as unworthy. Why should his brother, or indeed any Irishman, abide by their absurd code of honour in order to fight England's war. Better to lie and cheat and get safely out of it. 'What did Mr Drew say, by the way?' he added suddenly.

'Oh the usual. If the lads like me put our weight behind the cause we could throw the English out.'

'And what do you think?'

'He's talkin' through his arse. It's the usual thing, the oul' fellas doin' all the talkin' and the young lads gettin' killed.' His mouth set in a hard line and he said no more until they reached the gate. 'That was a tough oul' hen Joey,' he remarked, relenting. 'Did they ever do any good?'

'Not much really. I just kept them, you know, for old time's sake, somethin' to do. I like the sound of them, especially in the morning. You needn't think', he added laughing, 'that I owe you anything for your share. Anything I ever got for eggs was spent on feed. Now that I think of it, you probably owe me a few quid.'

'Ah me oul' China,' said Kit, slipping an arm around his shoulder, 'I'll make a businessman of you yet.'

* * *

117

Clara Bennett watched her child as he worked by lamplight, painting, with silent absorption, what he had seen that afternoon. In the daytime Davy painted in colour but at night he confined himself almost to monochrome, dark brown shading to black or conversely giving way to a glowing burnt sienna. The wet paper allowed the paint to crawl, spreading tendrils of pigment from the central mass, growing organically as he controlled it with quick brush strokes until, from the apparent chaos, there emerged a pattern, a shimmer of light on water, a tumble of cloud over the Mournes or a shine on the quarters of a ploughhorse. Even to her uninformed eye it was obvious that here was a rare gift, an untutored natural feeling for light and colour and a capacity to render what he saw in such a way that the observer felt the rightness of it and wondered how it had not been noticed before.

Casually she rose and leaned over, as if to adjust the lamp. She studied what he had painted. Instantly she recognised her husband standing at ease beside his drum. A deep shadow from the cap covered much of his face but it was unmistakably Tom's angular frame, awkward but arrogant. Yet there was something vulnerable about the stance of him. What was it, she wondered. She noted the light falling on his shoulder and the fold at his knee as he stood with one leg slightly bent. Living with him all these years, she had always thought of him as the same jaunty Tom who had strolled into her life, but now she saw, for the first time that he was, in fact, getting on a bit. It was as if the drum had got too heavy for him. The child had enabled her to see it, this strange gift of a child who had come late to them. He seemed all in all to be made of a finer material than his parents, almost like a changeling, she thought, quite unlike herself, or her husband with his rough ways and calloused hands. 'It's very good,' she said as he looked up at her. He never asked for approval or criticism, pursuing his own way at all times. Neither did he try to explain, and she was wise enough not to ask. 'I think it's time you went to bed now,' she added, turning down the lamp. 'I'll wait up for your da.' She heard the brush chime on the rim of the jamjar as he rinsed.

'I'll give you this one,' he said unexpectedly. 'I think I'm beginning to get the hang of it at last.'

118

'I'll keep it,' she said gently, 'until you're a famous artist, and then I'll sell it for a thousand pounds.'

'No,' he said seriously. 'You keep that one. I'll give you lots of others to sell if you like.'

'I will. I was only joking. I wouldn't sell this for all the world.'

The child smiled shyly. 'That way you can keep this day forever. That's what I would always like to do when I am happy.' He shook the brush dry and carefully smoothed the fine sable hairs. 'I really think that I would like to spend my life doing this kind of thing.'

'When you're big and finished with school you can do anything you like,' she replied, and felt a fierce determination forming suddenly inside her.

* * *

Dr Bailey swam seawards with a deliberate and determined trudgeon, breasting the grey incoming rollers with snorts of enjoyment and shaking the water from his beard like a grampus. September seawater, brown and murky though it might be, contains invaluable iodine; as a medical man he appreciated its benefits.

As he reached his limit and turned to drift in with the waves, the houses of the terrace seemed a long way off from his new perspective. The vantage point determines our perception of things, he thought to himself. From a safe distance the war seemed a straightforward struggle between the forces of good and evil. Prussianism was a malignant force which all civilised countries had united to destroy.

A correspondent of *The Times* had calculated that it would take forty million shells to destroy the four lines of fire trenches and communications on the thirty-mile front at Ypres. During the last two weeks of July the artillery had tried to comply, pounding away night and day, serving notice of one of the bloodiest and most irrelevant onslaughts of the war. What the strategists could not see from their maps was how the bombardment had pitted and scarred the soft clay of Passchendaele, destroying the drainage and trapping the early rains in a moonscape of craters.

The tank corps on the Menin road had a closer perspective as the land turned to ooze and their vehicles, one after another, bogged down and degenerated into useless piles of metal. Infantrymen knew at a glance that the situation was hopeless but those who had a more lofty view decreed that the advance should proceed. Victory, as always, was just out of sight beyond the next rise.

Dr Bailey pondered on the futility of it all as he rose and fell on the waves. A test to destruction they were calling it now, a war no longer of armies but of nations. He had discussed it at length with Anna's young man, whose views on the matter, if they could not be called cynical, were certainly bleak and foreboding.

Frank, temporarily seconded to the Grenade School in Dublin, repeatedly turned the discussion to the morality of the war. He maintained that there were many among the serving officers who shared the view that the whole effort had long since become pointless; that it was maintained by men who were not so much evil as insane. Ludendorff, according to Frank, was openly known to be mad and had a psychiatrist permanently in residence at his headquarters; yet there was a logic to that general's theories of total war. He had for instance given his submarines a free hand against merchant shipping, to destroy Britain's capacity to supply an army in the field.

At the thought of submarines Dr Bailey looked around at the horizon, wondering what sinister dangers might lurk beneath the heaving surface. He felt stray strands of weeds brushing his legs and flinched. Once the imagination began to work . . . .

Following Ludenorff's logic, every man, woman and child was a belligerent; every building and ear of corn was a legitimate target; aerial bombardment need not discriminate; the conventions on the treatment of prisoners and non-combatants became pointless claptrap. But this, as Frank insisted, was the logical conclusion of mechanised industrial warfare; machines of greater destruction could be looked upon, in a sense, as beneficial in that they hastened the inevitable end.

Inevitable, that was Frank's word. Sometimes Dr Bailey was profoundly disturbed by the young man's views. He feared Frank was developing a morbid obsessiveness.

The young fellow had adopted an unfashionable and permissive attitude also to the conscientious objectors, refusing to deride them in the vitriolic language of the popular press. He had admitted in an unguarded moment that he sometimes envied their moral courage, deflecting the surprise of his hearers by adding that he was put off the idea of pacifism by their paltry allowance of eightpence a day and their prison diet. The old man believed there was a dark and brooding corner in the boy's mind and that Anna should have put off all thoughts of marriage until the shadow of war had lifted. Now his granddaughter had begun to form disturbing, radical views on the whole 'Irish question', as the situation was invariably called. Imperceptibly she had moved from uninformed dismissiveness to a conviction that a great wrong had been done. How this had come about the old man could not say, surrounded as she was by her own kind. She maintained with some vehemence that the execution of the rebels in the previous year had been a grave mistake and that the military authorities had done a bad day's work for the continuance of the empire. At times he was inclined almost to agree. The sight of the devastation in Dublin had shocked and disturbed him but, nevertheless, he reasoned, the rebels had been in league with Great Britain's enemy. It was a puzzle that these mercurial people who had sent a quarter of a million men to the standards when the call went out, were now hailing as martyrs those men who had stabbed their country in the back. And here Anna differed with him in heated terms, maintaining that Ireland should be regarded as a separate entity. All very confusing.

His feet touched sand and he stood upright, bracing himself against the waves. Symbolic, he mused. It is difficult for a man to find a secure footing in these changing times. He waded carefully ashore to where his bathrobe lay folded beneath a stone.

'Doctor Bailey, sir.'

The old man left off carefully drying between his toes. A young chap stood between him and the sun, with his cap respectfully in one hand.

'Yes? And what can I do for you, young fellow?' Obviously a local lad.

'I don't know if you remember me. I've been out in France for a while. I just wondered if . . .' It was not quite clear what he wondered.

The doctor peered more closely. 'Good heavens,' he exclaimed, 'the butcher's boy, isn't it? What's this I heard about you?' He reached for Kit's hand and pumped his arm vigorously. 'That's right, yes. Doing your bit, eh? Proud to shake your hand young man.' Indeed he was a young man too. How long ago had that been? Seemed only yesterday.

Kit grinned somewhat awkwardly. 'Still doing the archery sir?'

'By Jove, yes, archery.' Now he remembered clearly. 'Weren't you very young to join up? You were wounded, I understand.' Something of a professional frown came across his features.

'I'm afraid I told a few lies, sir, in the beginning. I don't think I'm the only one.' Kit flexed his leg instinctively. 'I'm grand again. I've been passed fit,' he added.

'Ah,' replied the doctor, pensively towelling his beard. 'I see.'

'So I'm going back, and I just wondered how you were, and Miss Bailey, because I have to leave this evening and I just wanted to say goodbye.' The prepared speech came out in a gabble and Kit stopped suddenly.

'How very kind of you,' replied the doctor. 'I see.' He slipped his feet into a pair of rather monastic looking sandals. 'A bit of a via dolorosa, this.' He indicated the stony section of the beach. 'You must come inside. My granddaughter would be exceedingly annoyed if I neglected to bring you in.' He ushered Kit towards the wicket gate in the garden wall. 'She doesn't get about very much at the moment.'

Kit frowned in puzzlement. He began to wish that he had not come. This part of town was still alien territory. He regretted the impulse that had brought him here. He stuffed his cap into his jacket pocket. His old jacket was much too tight for him. He felt awkward and gawky.

Anna was on her knees in the garden, rummaging with a trowel. She looked round at the sound of the hinges screeching in protest and gave a gasp of surprise. 'Kit! So you've come to see us at last.' Slowly she rose to her feet. She wore a long flowing smock that did nothing to disguise the evidence of her pregnancy. 'Well, this is a surprise,' she added, coming forward and taking both Kit's hands in hers.

'Hello,' he managed to exclaim, detaching his tongue from the dry roof of his mouth. His eyes met hers but seemed to

122

be inescapably dragged downwards. She looked lovelier than ever. He swore inwardly at the gormless impression he was making.

'Is that all you have to say, after all this time?' She took his astonished face in her hands and kissed him gently on the forehead. Standing back she surveyed him, suddenly serious. 'You have changed, though, haven't you?'

'Our young friend has been convalescent,' interposed the old man, surveying the weeding. 'I hope you haven't been overdoing things, my dear.'

'Oh no. Anyway, hard work, you always say, is the best thing for someone in my, ahem, delicate condition.'

The old man grunted.

Anna caught Kit looking at her. To her he seemed very grey in the face, tired looking. 'That's how he always refers to my bump,' she added, patting her belly.

'I didn't know you were . . .' Kit trailed off with an ineffectual gesture. It was not something to be talked about just like that. Why had someone not warned him? It would have been better to have stayed away.

The doctor ambled away, saying something about being peckish.

'Oh yes. You mean married, of course.' She laughed lightly. 'Not long after you ran away, actually. I'm Mrs Surtees now.'

Kit struggled with the ashes in his mouth. All that time that he had been faithful! He knew that was stupid. Even when he was lying in the mud, she had been. . . . He forced himself to be calm. 'And how is, how is your husband?' He had said the word. The unfairness of it all hit him again.

'He's fine,' she said quickly, 'but what about you? You don't look very well. Hadn't you better sit down?'

'I'm grand, grand.' He gave a grimace of a smile. 'In fact I've been passed fit again.'

She laid her hand on his arm. 'I heard that you had been hurt.'

'Well that's all fixed up again. In fact I'm going back again tonight. That's why I came here. I wanted to see you before I left.' His tongue was running away again, but it was all pointless now.

'Oh Kit, I'm so sorry.'

123

What did that mean? Was it that she realised now how he had felt; that she was the reason he had almost been killed; that he very well might be? He felt anger rising in him but she was so beautiful and so vulnerable. It was hopeless, he knew, and even sinful to think about her now. 'I have to go,' he mumbled, stepping back a pace. 'Maybe I could write to you sometime.' He gave a sort of awkward wave, a kind of half-salute.

She lifted her hand in reply. 'Yes do please,' she said, gazing after him with her hand still raised. Still only a boy, she thought. It wasn't right to send him out there at his age.

The gate screeched again and Kit stepped out onto the foreshore. The sea looked grey and bleak. The waves rolled the pebbles with a hollow rumbling sound, like distant gunfire.

I hope he gets killed. The thought rose involuntarily within him. I hope he is blown to bits.

Bile rose in his throat and he leaned his back against the wall, wiping a cold sweat from his forehead with the back of his hand. Oh, God no. I don't mean that. I don't mean it like that. If he gets killed I will look after her. She would need me then, he rationalised.

I could shoot him. Somehow, somewhere, I could shoot him. No one would ever notice. In the uproar of battle somewhere, a bullet in the back of his skull. One more wouldn't make any difference.

Oh, Jesus! How could I think like that? A mortal sin. He felt the void opening beneath his feet, dark, yawning to swallow him. He could never look her in the eye again. He would have to go to confession, do penance. The thought did not belong to him. 'A firm purpose of amendment'. He pulled his cap from his pocket and jammed it on his head. I need a drink, he thought.

Anna turned the trowel thoughtfully in her hand, wiping the clay from the blade. The metal shone under the cloth. Now she understood. There must have been something more she could have said. She could still see the pain in his eyes. She hurried to the gate and dragged it open again, but he was gone. The hinges keened softly as the gate stirred in the wind.

CHAPTER 10

With the satchel over his shoulder and a full bucket of water in one hand Joey felt at a decided disadvantage. Strangely though, having the responsibility of Miss Donnelly's water supplies was a kind of reassurance, something that could not be shirked or abandoned even in the face of The Skinner Doyle. Ned, by virtue of his profession had acquired a nickname and wore it with a certain panache. Despite the twinge of an ancient fear, Joey continued along the pavement. Splashes of water stained the kerbstones.

'Still here then, are ye?' The Skinner's grin had an ugly twist to it.

'How d'you mean?'

'Haven't taken the shillin' yet, like the brother?'

'Mind your own business,' retorted Joey, with a spurt of anger.

'I seen him goin' off the other day.'

'Oh aye.' Joey cursed the hygiene mania of Miss Donnelly that forced him to go so slowly.

The Skinner walked slowly backwards, not quite blocking the way, but making the point that he could if he wanted to. 'He wasn't too happy about goin' if you ask me.'

'Well I didn't ask you, did I?'

'He looked a bit jarred to me.'

'Why don't you mind your own business.' It would have been nice to knock the smirk off that fat ugly face.

'Yeah. I'd say he was well jarred.'

'No he wasn't,' snapped Joey. His arm was tired and he longed to put the bucket down for a minute but would not give the older lad the satisfaction. 'Anyway Kit can do what he likes. He's a soldier, not a bloody messenger boy.'

It was a telling point but Doyle merely laughed. 'He's on'y a bollix,' said The Skinner. 'He took the shillin'.'

'Watch your mouth Doyle,' said Joey furiously. His arm muscles ached with tiredness and with a gasp, he lowered the bucket. Water splashed over The Skinner's boots.

'You shouldn't of done that,' he said menacingly.

Joey lowered his gaze. 'It was an accident,' he mumbled.

'Oh yeah? Well so is this.' Doyle pushed the rim of the bucket and it clattered onto its side in the gutter.

The water swilled away, picking up a scum of dust and straw as it spread over the cobbles. Joey's heart thumped with hatred and frustration but most of all with the humiliation of knowing that there was nothing much that he could do about it. For a time during the summer, it seemed as if Kit and Ned Doyle were actually friends. They had drunk porter together and had even gone to a concert in the tower.

'So now,' said his tormentor, 'you'll have to go back to the square and get some more water for poor oul' Donnelly. Won't ye?'

'That was a lousy trick,' grunted Joey retrieving the bucket. He resented almost as much the time wasted, what with thirty lines of Virgil to prepare for the morning and God only knows how much Algebra.

'That's how we treat traitors around here,' declaimed The Skinner, 'and traitors' brothers.'

'What do you mean "traitor"?'

'It's simple, me son.' Doyle leaned down and thrust his face at Joey. 'Any Irishman in the King's uniform is a traitor and we know how to deal with the like o' them.'

As if detached from it all, Joey felt his fist clench and smash with all his strength into the leering face. Suddenly he was being lifted and was hurtling against the wall. He felt a stinging blow on the side of his head and he sagged to the ground.

'And let that be a lesson to ye,' concluded Doyle, turning on his heel. He had gone further than he had intended, but luckily there was no one else around. It would not be too good if word of this got back to Mr Fedigan. 'And you can tell your big brother he'll get the same,' he added in bravado.

Joey sat by the wall trying to collect his wits. The Skinner made no sense at all. He put his fingers to his forehead and felt the warm stickiness of blood where the bricks had grazed him. Like Algebra, it made no sense. There was no concrete information to go on, just an evil miasma of abstractions in which x offered the illusion of an answer. How could a fellow like Kit be a traitor in anyone's eyes, even those of an eejit like Doyle? A traitor to what? He rubbed his head in both puzzlement and pain.

The truth of the matter was that Kit had been a bit drunk the evening he went away. It had been a very painful evening all around and his mother was still pale and silent from the shock. She spent a lot of time at the window overlooking the sea, with a rosary twisted in her fingers, not so much praying as pining. It was a quiet house. The music had faded again. There was nothing for it but to keep going. Wearily he retrieved the bucket. Was it only two years ago since they had set out to make their fortunes out of water carrying? It seemed like a lifetime. Joey hated the thought of another winter, the darkness and the cold. It seemed worse with the change in the time. The evenings were drawing in earlier and earlier.

Still there were some good sides to it all, the bit of a laugh on the train in the morning with the lads. There was the mad neighbour who stayed in bed until he saw the smoke of the train at Gormanston and then sprinted for the station with breakfast, collar and tie in his suit coat-pocket. It was always a laugh to peep into the compartment and watch him peeling his hard-boiled egg and blowing the shreds of tobacco off his toast. He worked in the brush factory in Talbot Street. Was that where the saying 'daft as a brush' came from?

I must be going a bit daft too, thought Joey, quickening his step. He fingered the bump on his temple. The blood was drying. He tried to think of a plausible explanation for the injury. A good three hours' work to do, at the very least. He did not relish the prospect. It was stupid to pay any attention to The Skinner Doyle. When Kit came back he could sort it all out. Involuntarily he shivered. Kit would come back. There

127

was no alternative. He would never be asked to go into action again. It would not be fair. They would probably give him some safe job in England. It was somebody else's turn now. That was the way it worked. He trudged wearily back to the pump. Why could there not be a well or a pump on The White Rock? Now there was an idea. Let x equal the number of buckets of water. . . . Definitely, he thought, that bang on the head did me no good.

*   *   *

Frank stood at the rail straining his eyes towards the dark rim of land astern. His eyes caught a faint flicker of white to the north. Abel Rock, he concluded. From the bedroom on the terrace he had watched that light, shining red on the landward side, reaching a long finger of reflection towards them on calm summer nights. Perhaps at that moment she was standing at the window, watching that same light. He counted. Five. She would see it now. Ten. It flashed again. He counted again, a tenuous link. The white water churned below the stern. Smoke eddied around him from the funnel. Phosphorescence glistened and vanished in the wake and gradually the light sank out of sight and the horizon was dark.

The rail was cold and wet with dew. He stepped back, wiping his fingers fastidiously and began to pace the deck, thinking of Anna and the child as yet unborn, whom he might never see. A great sadness filled him at the idiocy of the whole business, the lunatic irrelevance of everything he did: how much ghee a camel driver should get each day; the finger method of target location; aiming off for a man walking, doubling, running. With all the knowledge gained it should be a simple matter to reduce human relationships to location of target, recognition and marksmanship. The world had settled into a permanent state of war, an industry in its own right. Schoolboys completed their studies and marched off to the front. It saved a lot of uncertainty, the anxiety of finding their own way in the world, success or failure. The religious chaps had it all figured out, souls gathered to God's banquet. No wonder they preached so mightily in support of the whole affair. 'Our prayers go with you'. He gave a short chuckle, surprised at his

128

own turn of mind. *Army Book 4039* had a space for prospective employment after the present war in which he had inscribed 'professional fatalist'. It seemed as good an idea as any other.

In the well-deck men, huddled in great-coats, were singing softly and passing a bottle around. The song lilted with the long axial roll of the ship, 'All round me hat', a song of Ireland's freedom. They looked up as he passed, young lads from Dublin.

One held up the bottle. 'Will ye have a dart, sir?' His teeth grinned white in the half-light.

Frank raised his hand. 'No thank you lads. You'll need it to keep warm out here.' He smiled upon them as they sat on the boxes. 'Just go ahead with the song.'

He wandered on as they called 'goodnight sir', and soon the singing started again, gentle, plaintive, another of their old ballads, 'We may have brave men but we'll never have better, Glory o, glory o to the . . . .' A gust of wind swept the last words away.

* * *

Tom Bennett scratched his head and looked at the pictures. 'Begobs Davy but you're a remarkable genius alright.' He grinned in astonished recognition at one of himself by the drum, all angular strength in the threadbare uniform. 'Begobs, but ye have me there, right enough.' He was not so sure that he was flattered. He looked kind of puzzled, maybe a bit of a gawm, gazing around like that. 'Remarkable. I don't know where you get it from.'

'It's just a knack,' said the boy. 'It doesn't have to come from anyone.' It was almost abrupt, as if he had been correcting a child.

'Aye, aye, remarkable, all the same,' replied his father carefully. There was one of Clara sitting by the fire. Just right. There was a faraway look in her eye that he had never noticed before, as if she could see something in the glow. The shadow and the soft yellow light changed her to a pensive stranger, yet still undeniably Clara. He looked at her where she sat darning by the fire, with a cowrie shell from the South Seas peeping through the heel of a sock, and she caught his eye. 'This fella', he remarked, looking for reassurance, 'this young fella-me-lad has us dead to rights Clara.'

Clara beamed with pride. 'I knew you'd be pleased. That young Englishwoman says he's very good.'

'Is that a fact?' Tom was impressed. She'd know about such matters. He looked at his portrait again. It was a pity in a way he didn't do it when the band was on the march. Might have looked more dignified. Still, he wondered about the man in the picture. 'We should put these on the wall, ye know. What do you say, Davy?'

The boy was pleased. 'You'd have to get frames for them Da. Frames cost money.' It would be exciting, though, to see a picture of his own in a real frame. 'I suppose you'd have to go to Dublin for that.'

'I could always ask Mr Drew, I suppose. He'd have a rabbitin' plane.' He dropped the word casually to show that he knew a thing or two also. He looked again at the two pictures. People might laugh at the idea of homemade pictures on the wall, but by God, they were good. They deserved a frame. It would be nice for the Christmas. 'I'll have a word with Mr Drew on the matter.'

'You mean a pint with Mr Drew on the matter,' said Clara without malice.

'I might have the one,' he conceded. 'Always an interestin' man to talk to on any subject.'

*   *   *

A great deal is asked of the committed Christian, at times far too much. It is easy to respond to the Christmas story in the comfort of our own firesides. Of course the candle in the window assures the Christchild and His weary parents of a resting place, but out of a perverse desire to try us He comes in the guise of the poor, the down-at-heel and, perhaps worst of all, the malodorous.

'And may I wish you an' all belongin' to you the blessin's of Jaysus for the Christmas.'

Barney's sentiments and sense of timing were impeccable. King Wenceslaus and his ilk would have skull-hauled him indoors and plied him with food and drink for the twelve days

130

of the festive season. The legend says nothing about what happened to the poor man for the rest of the winter. Barney, perhaps, preferred a modest but regular largesse the whole year round, rather than sporadic outbursts of princely generosity interspersed with long spells of starvation. Nevertheless, Mrs Donovan always iced a cake for him at Christmas.

As always the cake disappeared swiftly into the dark recesses of his sack.

'Aw, the blessin's o' God on ye ma'am,' he said, hefting the sack, enjoying the weight. 'No better man to keep body and soul together.'

'Well I hope you enjoy it Mr Phelan,' replied Mrs Donovan. 'But seriously, would you never consider going into the Union, even if only for the winter?'

'Aw Jaysus, missus, I couldn't abide that. Sure the doctor has me persecuted to go into the hospital for me chest.' He coughed by way of illustration, one of his long, grinding hawks. Undoubtedly there was cause for concern. 'But,' he gasped for breath, like steam whistling through a valve, 'but I was never much given to that class o' thing.' He made it sound like some secret vice. He leaned closer, flicking his eyes sideways to see if he was being overheard. He lowered his voice. 'They take people away in them places. God's truth, in the middle o' the night, they wheel them away — never seen again.' His eyes rolled at the horror of it all. The cataract flickered. 'As long as God gives me the health, I'll stick where I am.'

Mrs Donovan gave a slight gesture of resignation, an expressive turn of the hand on her delicate wrist. 'I just thought —' she trailed off.

'Don't worry about me missus,' Barney reassured her. 'I'm as comfortable as bedamned, not a bother on me. There's others worse off than meself.'

'I'm sure you may be right,' she agreed, hugging her elbows. There was frost in the afternoon air.

'I was just thinkin' of your own young lad that went for a soldier. It must be cold enough for the likes of him.'

Mrs Donovan looked away. The same thought was rarely absent from her mind. 'It must be cold indeed,' she whispered as if to herself. She shivered again.

'I do say a prayer for him now and again.' Barney spoke

out of concern, as one who understood the power of prayer and had stood close to the fountainhead. There was none of the wheedling, cringing piety of the professional pauper.

'I appreciate that Mr Phelan.' Mrs Donovan was genuinely moved by his concern.

Barney scratched luxuriously with his free hand, raking his armpit, taking maximum pleasure from the itch, as if in a pre-amble to some other topic. Eventually he desisted from the investigation. 'There's yourself too if you don't mind me sayin'' so. I mean a poor widda woman with no man in the house.'

Mrs Donovan hardly heard him. Her mind was elsewhere.

'Isn't it time you thought of another man, not to say but what Mr Donovan wasn't a quare dacent man, God be good to him.' The circumlocution implied that the late Mr Donovan had in fact been a decent man indeed.

'Oh yes, of course, of course.' Mrs Donovan had barely caught the gist of his last few words. 'He was a very good man, God rest his soul.' She was at a loss as to the direction the conversation had taken.

'I mean, there's Mr Fedigan, there, the butcher, with a good business behind him,' continued Barney in his other alias as Cupid.

'Yes, indeed, he is a very hard-working man,' agreed Mrs Donovan, mystified.

'Well there yiz are then,' Barney concluded with an air of satisfaction.

He shifted the sack to a more comfortable position. The weight of the cake pressed against his back and his mouth watered in anticipation. He imagined the crunch of the icing between his few remaining teeth and the hard snap of a cachou encountered by surprise. The sweet fleshy pulp of raisins beckoned him onward. He knew that he would stop at the stile beside the school, where he frequently halted to rest, and there he would surreptitiously break off a few lumps, rummaging in the sack, not officially producing the whole cake until he arrived home. From somewhere in the dim recesses of his child-hood he still recalled the strictures against eating in the street, 'tenement fashion', but the raisins and sultanas lured him on.

Mrs Donovan closed the door quietly. The old fear gnawed at her, the fear that woke her in the silence of the night and walked beside her through every waking hour. Still there was something else nagging at the back of her mind, something Barney had said. She stood by the window watching the darkness move in over the sea. The room grew dim but she did not light the lamp. Gradually it dawned on her. Mr Fedigan had designs on her. She smiled. What a simple poor man! She began to laugh, silent quivers of laughter that shook her frame. Tears came to her eyes and flowed down her cheeks. It was too ridiculous for words. The laughter seized her in great spasms as her tears flowed freely. She felt the loneliness close in around her and she longed for her husband with his consideration and optimism. She thought of his elder son, so like him in many ways and wondered where he might be at that season of goodwill and she longed for someone to talk to.

When Joey arrived home he found her still sitting in the dark. The fire had gone down and the room was chilly.

'You shouldn't be sitting here in the dark, Ma,' he said anxiously. He took a spill and lit the lamp, turning it up to fill the room with its comforting glow.

She looked at him gratefully. 'I was just thinking of something rather funny,' she said.

He saw the tears and was puzzled. 'I'll see if Nan has done anything about the tea,' he offered.

'She's not here this afternoon. We can poke up this fire and make toast if you like.'

'I'll do it,' he volunteered, surprised. She was actively asking for his company for the first time in a long while. Oddly enough she looked better than of late and seemed more animated, or perhaps it was only a trick of the lamplight. He hurried into the kitchen to get the bread and long-handled fork.

'And light a candle in the front room,' she called after him. 'Maybe somebody will . . . .' She left the thought unfinished.

* * *

'Christmas or no Christmas,' the captain said, a peppery little man with mud-spattered uniform, 'we maintain an aggressive posture towards the enemy.' He practised what he preached, unlike the splendid creatures from base who occasionally honoured them with a visit. Night and day he prowled his sector like a terrier straining to be let go. 'Counter-attack is the soul of defence,' was his maxim. 'It is necessary to close with the enemy to achieve results.' He spoke like a textbook, whether under fire or in times of relative quiet.

The men shuffled their feet and blew on their hands. It was bitterly cold, with only the faintest glimmer of moonlight.

'Individual fire, gentlemen. Use your initiative. Pass the word along quietly.' Like a terrier, the captain had a nose for the enemy. He knew that there would be a raid that night and no one doubted his word.

Kit peered into the blackness of no-man's-land, letting his gaze travel slowly and deliberately from side to side, trying to isolate recogniseable shapes. From somewhere to the left a flare soared into the air and burst, illuminating the tangles of wire and the rims of dark shell-craters. A machinegun chattered speculatively, but nothing moved. The flare dimmed and began to descend. Fear gripped Kit as darkness reclaimed the ground in front of him. Something moved, a shapeless grey object, almost indistinguishable from the earth. Kit fired instinctively, his shot merging with others of his section. The figure reared like a beached seal, turned a pale blur of face toward their position, then flopped forward without a sound.

'Got him!' whooped a jubilant voice. 'Got the bastard.'

'Be quiet, that man,' snapped the captain.

Another flare burst overhead. The machinegun chattered again, then all was silence. The flare dimmed and fell.

'A star in the East,' muttered the man beside Kit, and gave a dry laugh. 'Merry Christmas, oul' son.'

CHAPTER 11

The last springtime of the war brought no welcome greenery to the shattered landscape, no hint of new life, of regeneration. Abbey Wood stood like a palisade against the sky.

Under appalling fire, Ludendorff's March offensive had taken the ground, placing the railway junction at Amiens in peril. During the night the counter-attack by the Australians had hit the exhausted German defenders without the customary warning of an artillery barrage. A giant pincer had begun to close on the Germans as the Thirteenth Australians groped and clawed their way towards their compatriots in the Fifteenth Brigade. Artillery had pounded the railway cutting, sealing off the German escape route to the rear. Allied reinforcements had arrived at daylight.

Machineguns worked steadily forward and, like the skilled fingers of a surgeon excising a cyst, the bulge of the German advance was gathered in at the base and cut cleanly away. Now grinning French Moroccans were shepherding bedraggled prisoners.

General Debeney and his resplendent staff arrived to offer their *felicitations*, careful to keep to the hastily laid duckboards. There were a few derisive cheers from a group of diggers who had captured some *schnapps*, legitimate spoils. 'Good on yiz mates,' came a voice in the strident accent of the Antipodes, 'up here when it's all over.' The implication seemed to be lost on the visiting dignitaries.

Captain Frank Surtees sat on an ammunition box. He was bone-weary. The cold mist of morning penetrated to the core. He shivered with fatigue and anti-climax. It was time to go home. He drew his cigarette case from his pocket and pensively tapped the end of the cigarette on the lid. He stared at it absently for a moment and then struck a match, inhaling the smoke in a great gasp. He stared, unseeing, at the activity around him. His feet were cold and wet and his eyes were filled with grit.

'Excuse me sir.'

Someone had spoken to him, several times it seemed, before he understood.

'Beg your pardon sir.'

A young chap stood in front of him, diffidently, finger to his cap. Frank noted the elephant badge of the Dublins and the old man's eyes in the boyish face. 'Yes?' There was something vaguely familiar about the lad.

'Captain Surtees sir, isn't it? Donovan is my name, from Skerries. I don't suppose that would mean anything to you sir.'

'Donovan. Donovan. Of course. My wife mentioned you several times. Yes of course.' Frank peered at the young man's exhausted face. 'Well I'm damned.'

Kit grinned awkwardly pleased, despite himself. 'If you don't mind me asking sir, seeing as how I just met you like this, would you have any news from home?'

Frank moved aside, making room on the box. 'Sit down Donovan. We needn't stand on ceremony this morning.' He offered a cigarette and Kit gratefully accepted. 'I don't know much about local affairs, I'm afraid. Not very familiar with the political scene in your part of the world.' He was surprised at how glad he was to see even this vaguely familiar face.

'Yes sir,' mumbled Kit awkwardly. It was a bit like when Mr Sweeney would stop him in the street, consciously dropping his schoolmaster guise to engage in avuncular chat.

'There is one thing,' exclaimed Frank, brightening with a flash of enthusiasm. 'Proud father and all that, must excuse me.' He took out his pay-book and flipped the stud open with his thumbnail. 'My daughter,' he declared expansively, producing a photograph, already creased at the corner from much handling.

Kit felt something lurch inside him. Anna was standing in the garden on the terrace, flanked by winter-shorn shrubs and holding a bundle of shawls, from which peered two dark inquisitive eyes. Kit stared, devouring the image greedily.

'Inordinately good looking, I'm told,' continued Frank. 'Still I mustn't bore you.' He closed the book and snapped the stud shut again.

Kit felt an urge to snatch the photograph and run.

'And what word of your own people then?' went on Frank, although he had no idea who they might be.

'Oh, they're fine, thank you sir.'

Frank drew pensively on his cigarette and let his eye wander around the confusion of wreckage and exhausted men. 'You know,' he confided, 'I don't think this whole business was such a good idea. It's not really getting us anywhere.'

'You mean the last couple of days sir?' Had they not scored a major success?

'No, no,' Frank smiled wearily, 'the whole shooting-match, the war itself. We'll bang away for a while more, and then we'll talk. Inevitably someone will have to talk to someone on the other side. Look at them for heaven's sake.' He nodded towards a file of bedraggled prisoners. 'Did you ever see such a miserable bunch? What's the point of scoring a victory as you call it, over poor devils like those?'

'They were nasty enough yesterday.'

'Only because we were there. If we all went home there would be no problem, would there?'

Kit looked at him strangely. 'That's dangerous talk, sir. You could get into trouble for that.' He tried to say it lightly. People were shot for — what was it? — alarm and despondency, despair and presumption, to encourage the others.

Frank laughed, a dry hacking laugh and coughed on the smoke. 'No, you're right. We wouldn't want to get into any trouble, would we? He looked at the boy quizzically. 'Anything for the quiet life, eh?'

Kit grinned at the irony. 'I see what you mean.' I could have had him there, if I wanted to. The dark thought lurched upwards from the deeper recesses of his mind, but it made no sense. In a way the officer was right. If they all decided to bugger off home the generals could sort it out among themselves.

They sat for a moment or two, until each became conscious of the incongruity.

Kit rose suddenly. 'I must get back to my unit, sir. Thank you for talking to me.'

'Very glad to have met you Donovan,' said Frank. 'Take care of yourself now.' The inadequacy of the words struck him as he said them. Might as well tell him not to go near any gunfire. Look out for shells, that sort of thing. He watched the young fellow picking his way over the debris and the rutted ground. Better really to send him home out of all this.

Kit trudged back to his unit. A field kitchen had been set up and his mates were swilling mugs of hot sweet tea. Involuntarily he felt sorry for Anna's husband. He looked sort of lost and bewildered. The image of Anna was still before his eyes, the grain of the paper softening her features almost to a blur. In his mind he could see her moving about her garden. Absently he accepted a mug of tea and sat down on his pack. He was with her in their private garden. The child was his. He could feel the sun on his back as he bent protectively over them.

'Get fell in there lads,' came the corporal's voice, breaking into the reverie. 'We can't stand around here natterin' like a seragly of oul' ones.'

Muttering curses, the men hoisted their packs and shuffled into line. When Kit looked around the captain was still sitting on the ammunition case, with a cigarette smouldering between his fingers. It occurred to Kit that that might be dangerous and yet precautions seemed so pointless. I hope someone looks after him though, he thought. He looks as if he has reached the end of his tether.

*   *   *

A man alighted from a car at the corner of Balbriggan Street. The car pulled away and the man straightened his Norfolk jacket carefully, plucking at the hem with finger and thumb, repeating the movement at the back with a twist of the hands. He wore riding breeches and gaiters and carried a cane.

'There's somethin' about your man.' Mr Drew spoke confidentially. He leaned his elbow on the chopping block, picking up some small particles of suet on his sleeve, as he observed the stranger through the open door.

'Oh aye?' Mr Fedigan was not particularly interested. He drove a skewer in with the heel of his hand. 'One and fourpence a pound. I don't know how people can afford to eat at all at all,' he remarked mainly to himself.

'Aye, he's a quare bird. He's no summer visitor and that's for sure. I've seen him around before.' Mr Drew's eyes were still on the stranger.

'Right enough,' agreed the butcher, 'now that you mention it, I have seen him around. I suppose he's somethin' to do with the English people up the way.'

'Aye maybe, but he spends his time askin' directions and just strollin' around.'

The man was talking to a woman outside the shop. She was pointing. He smiled and raised his hat, nodding affably.

'Time was,' muttered Drew, 'anyone comin' into town from that direction had to report to me.' He flexed his shoulders, aggrieved at the drop in standards. Young lads nowadays. No pride in their own place. 'Anyway, what was I goin' on about? The meetin', aye. You'll be there of course?'

'Oh aye,' the butcher nodded.

Chop, chop. The cleaver rose and fell, crunching through bone. The sound rang like a bell in the empty shop.

'The master wants a full account of our local organisation to pass on to the brigade.' Organisation. He liked the sound of the word. It signified that they were in business and serious about what they said. 'And a couple o' sweetbreads,' he added, 'if ye have them.'

'I'm afraid the sweetbreads are all gone. I'll keep you some on Monday.' This was not entirely true, but the sweetbreads were spoken for, nonetheless.

Mr Drew scuffed the sawdust pensively with his boot. His eyes were still on the diminishing figure of the stranger. A thin veil of rain drifted across Church Street, dimming the outline of the belfry. 'He's not here for the good of his health,' he mused. 'Not on a day like this.'

A dog scuttled across the street, pausing to look speculatively towards the shop, thought better of it and went on.

'This weather won't bring the visitors,' agreed the butcher.

'Begod!' exclaimed Mr Drew, 'but I know what it is.' He

punched a fist into the palm of his hand. 'Begod but I knew it all along. That fella is a spy if ever I saw one.'

'A spy!' The butcher paused in astonishment. 'A spy, do you say? But sure,' he scratched his head, 'spies don't look like that.'

'I'm tellin' ye he's a spy. It all fits into place. Didn't the young one in the hotel tell me he sat down to dinner with his hard hat on. That means he's some class of a policeman. I keep me ear to the ground too, ye know.'

'But I mean to say,' replied the butcher, 'what in the name o' God would he have to spy on around here?'

The dog made another foray past the door and lifted his leg derisively against the doorpost.

'G'out to hell owa' that,' roared the butcher, advancing from behind the counter in a flurry of apron, as the animal fled to avoid the retributary boot.

'I'll tell ye what,' continued Mr Drew, unperturbed by the interruption. 'There's you and me and any o' the lads that might be involved with the Movement. The Castle keeps tabs on everyone.'

Mr Fedigan frowned. He had never considered that aspect of it. The Castle was a much more sinister proposition than Sergeant Duffy. Duffy was human, a man you could talk to, even in some circumstances regard as a friend. There was that time of course when he had worried about Duffy and the widow Donovan, but there had been nothing in the sly remarks let slip in the Band Room over a game of cards. The Castle now, that was a horse of a different colour. He felt a little spasm of fear and looked covertly at the other man: Mr Drew seemed quite elated with his deduction.

'Begod,' said the builder, 'he's goin' into The Central. He won't find out much in there.'

The Central Bar was a by-word for discretion. Best drinks certainly. There was no water in the malt there. Pints were not topped up from the slop tray. Civility at all times, except when a customer became obstreperous, but most of all discretion. A man might drink himself under the table, leave his wife and children hungry, insult the Church or the government or talk inanities from one end of the day to the other, but no word of it would be heard outside the confessional privacy of The Central.

140

'He won't find out much in there,' chuckled Mr Drew, 'the dirty spyin' cur.'

The stranger had been tried and judged without a hearing.

'Still an' all, he doesn't look like a spy does he?' The butcher returned to his original objection. 'I mean spies kind of merge with the background, don't they?' He put the point tentatively.

'Merge how are ye,' expostulated the builder, 'and where would you leave Mata Hari then?' It was a telling point. 'No, spies adopt diversionary tactics. You always take them for something else, but I know a spy when I see one.' He was not to be shaken.

The butcher abandoned the argument. 'Still an' all it was a terrible thing to do to that poor woman, I mean even if she was a . . . .' He searched for a suitable phrase.

'A spy, do ye mean?'

'No, a woman, ye know like . . . .'

'Of dubious morals, sort of. I know what you mean. A nod is as good as a wink.' Mr Drew grinned lasciviously in spite of himself. 'Ah no, she wouldn't deserve the death sentence for that, God knows, or there'd be a quare few put up again' a wall.'

They chuckled at the unintended *double entendre*, men of the world together.

'But a spy's a spy and in time of war the sentence is well known.' Mr Drew paused.

Both men looked involuntarily in the direction of the pub.

'Arrah' not at all,' snorted the butcher self-consciously after a long silence. 'He's just a day-tripper, probably on a skyte.' The idea was reassuring. A skyte made sense, a decent normal thing for a man to do. He began to chop again, methodically, left hand flipping the meat into position, right hand rising and falling with machine-like precision.

'Maybe you're right,' conceded Mr Drew, 'but we'll put the word around to have an eye kept on him. You can't be too careful these days.' He hefted his parcel of meat and twirled it pensively by the loop of string. 'Indeed you can't be too careful.' He pulled his hat brim down and stepped out into the drizzle.

* * *

It was some perverse compulsion that drove Frank to see Bapaume. It had so long been a strategic objective, so many had died trying to secure it, that now that it was in their hands he wanted to see if it had been worth the effort.

The horse reared in alarm and Frank gathered the reins to keep it under control as the gun-carrier lurched past on the rutted dusty road. The cheerful gunners perched precariously on the vehicle. One sat astride the six-inch barrel of the Howitzer like some priapic God of war. Things were really moving now as the armies drove relentlessly onto the Siegfried line. All through August success had followed upon success as the German morale began to break. Ludendorff's black eighth of August had stretched into a black week and then a black month as the fabric of his armies began to crumble. They could see the writing on the wall as the word surrender became commonplace.

The traffic was incessant. Motor lorries streamed towards the front while columns of disconsolate prisoners trudged in the opposite direction, their illusions as shattered as the landscape through which they walked. The industrial reality of the twentieth century had destroyed their dream of invincibility. Poor, bare, forked creatures, thought Frank. How Lear would have felt at home here. There was nothing terrifying about these Prussians. Dirty and shabby, their faces gaunt with weariness, they plodded listlessly by.

He pulled the horse aside and headed across country, towards the grey pile that had once been Albert. The famous leaning Virgin was missing from the ruined church. The war must be going to end at last. A sign from Heaven, or maybe a celestial joke. He negotiated the tangle of metal which marked where the railway junction had been.

A troop of cavalry, their horses laden with equipment, put him in mind of a band of tinkers carrying their wares to some village fair. The scurrying wind picked up the dust and flung it in their faces. The horses snorted and tossed their heads. Above the roar of the lorries there came to them the distant pounding of the artillery. Their round, wide-brimmed helmets made him think of Agincourt, and Harfleur, history and fashion repeating themselves. 'And gentlemen in England now abed will hold their manhood cheap'. Shakespeare knew it all. 'What did you do in the war, Daddy?'

The Romanesque ruins stood out from a great scarp of debris, bricks and tiles that still trickled downwards in minor landslides.

From Albert to Bapaume his route lay across recently captured countryside, pitted with shell holes and the hastily dug trenches of the August fighting. In places he noted fields where crops long-neglected had re-seeded themselves and had grown rank and choked with weeds. The ground was strewn with abandoned wagons and the corpses of horses and mules. Occasionally he caught a glimpse of human remains, a leg protruding from the earth where hasty burial had been undone by shellfire, or a head, turning grey, with the lips drawing back from the yellowing teeth.

Strangely, he felt unmoved by it all. It was as if he passed through a dream world. He noted what he saw, the untidiness of it all. Someone should try to clear it up, but he felt unequal to the challenge. There was no starting point. The chaos went on to infinity on all sides. Rust and decay, he mused, would gradually absorb everything back into the earth. In time there would be nothing but mounds overgrown with green, nourished by the flesh that lay beneath and by the minerals released by the decomposing metals. The thought comforted him. It was all part of an inexorable process of growth and reclamation. It mattered not at all how any creature should live or die. The contribution lay in being and then decaying, as part of a great cycle of existence. It was as if a light of understanding had gone on in his mind. At last he felt detached from the events around him, almost like a mystic, experiencing some strange religious ecstasy.

By now he had completely lost sight of the road. He navigated as if by instinct along narrow country lanes, through the skeletons of trees and the litter of the German withdrawal. Occasionally he came upon areas that had been relatively untouched by the fighting, places where trees had kept their leaves, which were beginning to turn gold in the autumn sunshine. He dawdled along at such times, imagining himself on a leisurely country ride.

The horse shied suddenly, almost throwing him from the saddle. An emaciated figure in mudstained grey was blocking the pathway. He was holding both hands high above his head in obvious surrender. Startled out of his reverie, Frank fumbled for his Smith and Wesson. Before he could produce the weapon, the expression on the man's face registered with him. The huge eyes staring from the gaunt and exhausted face, entreated him silently. Frank levelled the revolver at the man.

'What are you doing here?' It seemed such an inane question but he could not believe that an enemy could remain undetected in territory captured over a month before and over which three army corps had gone like gleaners over a field.

'Freund,' said the man urgently, gesticulating, and pointing into the trees.

It was not clear to Frank whether he was claiming friendship or indicating the presence of a companion hidden in the undergrowth.

'Freund,' he insisted again.

Frank dismounted warily, keeping the gun pointed at the man and interposing the bulk of the horse between himself and the copse. His heart was thumping at the shock of being taken unawares.

'Nein, nein,' said the man again, obviously trying to communicate as much reassurance as possible by his tone. 'Ein mann geschossen.' He spoke clearly, obviously devising an acceptable pidgin.

Something about him made Frank relax. It was unthinkable that he should attempt an ambush almost fifteen miles behind the lines. For this German the war was over. Quickly he conducted Frank through the bushes until they came to a rough shelter, made from pieces of abandoned ammunition cases and a couple of oilskin capes. Crouching down, Frank saw another man lying on the ground, staring at him with expressionless eyes. Immediately he got the nauseating smell of putrefaction, the unmistakable reek of gangrene. The man's trouser leg was torn apart and a filthy rag formed a crude dressing on his thigh. The flesh visible on either side of the dressing was swollen and discoloured, black and yellow. Gas gangerene. Frank knew enough of hospitals to recognise the symptoms. Wet gangrene, not surprisingly, had been invaded by bacteria which were living off the body's fluids and the natural sugars of the tissues, in a nightmare process of fermentation.

An odd domestic detail struck him: a coalscuttle helmet,

half filled with berries and mushrooms lay beside the man. It appeared that they had been living off the land for weeks, probably in the hope of a counter-attack and eventual rescue. There were two rifles also, to which the first soldier pointed and shook his head vigorously. Damn, thought Frank. What am I to do with these two? It struck him that the injured one would probably die, but he still had to deal with the other. He could hardly leave him to wander around behind the lines, and yet if he took him prisoner he would have to return to Albert. It was all so inconvenient. He was tempted for a moment to remove their weapons and ride away, leaving them to their own devices.

'Nicht gut,' said the first man anxiously, appealing for help.

'Not good,' agreed Frank, pondering what he should do. 'Not good at all. We'll have to try to get him to a doctor. Doctor,' he repeated loudly. 'Medico,' he added, cursing his lack of linguistic accomplishment.

'Ja, ja, Doktor,' agreed the other, nodding vigorously. He was obviously prepared to fall in with whatever Frank might suggest.

As gently as possible they lifted the injured man, who moaned feebly in protest. Frank took him by the shoulders while the other man lifted the legs as carefully as he could manage. Frank was relieved to be at the other end when he saw the full horror of the leg with the boot removed. The man had soiled himself repeatedly, no doubt as a result of his diet. He thought for a moment of the saint who dismounted from his horse to kiss the leper. Ruefully he admitted that he was no candidate for canonisation. He had thought kissing lepers an unhygienic practice when the master in school had told them the story with such enthusiasm, and had wondered if the teacher had done a bit of it himself. He recalled vividly the smell of the old man's breath, like turnips, when he would lean over a pupil to offer advice on a knotty problem in Euclid. Incongruously, he began to chuckle and the soldier smiled at him, anxious to please.

With difficulty they lifted the man into the saddle. He seemed to have become unconscious, for he emitted not even a groan. They leaned him forward onto the horse's neck and turned back towards the distant silhouette of Albert, holding the injured man in position on either side. It was a mercy that he was unconscious as the horse lurched over obstacles and negotiated the ridges and hollows of the terrain. Frank was perspiring with the strain of anticipating these jolts. From his own experience he could imagine the pain. He squinted anxiously into the sun.

At length they came to a road where a large group of Canadians were lying with their feet up on their packs, waiting to move up to the front. They crowded around in curiosity when they saw the strangely assorted trio approaching. Some swore in astonishment when they saw the suppurating wound. It was as if they had become inured to casualties by the thousand but that one individual enemy, so far gone, made an extraordinary impact on them.

Some muttered sympathetically, while others reached up gently to lift him down. Orderlies appeared as from nowhere, with a stretcher and clean dressings, and a doctor came bustling over to take control. Very soon a passing lorry was waved down and Frank saw his two captives loaded on board. As the lorry pulled away the first soldier stood up and saluted him. He called something but Frank did not understand. The picture of the German saluting him remained with him for a long time. He couldn't have been more than forty-five, he thought, but he looked seventy.

He retrieved his horse and gingerly wiped the saddle and flanks with his handkerchief. With a feeling of disgust he mounted again and kicked the horse into a trot. Bapaume remained a mystery.

CHAPTER 12

Irritability, the doctor said, was an inevitable concomitant of the condition. Colonel Wyndham had suffered a massive heart attack and his face had been disfigured on the right side when he fell into the hearth. Now the eye stared from its socket with an expression of preternatural rage. To add irritability to any Wyndham was bringing coals to Newcastle and he was living in a constant state of almost unbearable frustration. A fastidious man at all times, the indignity of the bedpan was almost insupportable. A succession of nurses, fools and cretins by his sayso, came to Strifeland and left again, having borne for as long as they could the brunt of his invective.

The highlight of his day was the outing in his wheelchair, as far along the lanes as the nurse could manage to push him, so that he could see how the work of the farm was progressing. This would entail long conversations with Tom Bennett, who would lean on a spade, while the nurse would stand impatiently by, clucking her tongue or foostering with the rugs around his legs.

'Jesus Christ woman, I'm not a child. What was that again Tom?' The injured eye flashed with anger as he turned his basilisk stare on the interfering female.

'I just was thinkin' Colonel, that maybe you might be wantin' someone to lend a hand with the business end of things,' Bennett suggested the idea diffidently, not wishing to offend or underscore the old man's helplessness. 'I'm not much good at

147

that class o' thing meself, like. The money end and that.'

The old man glared for a moment and then frowned. He snatched the rug from the nurse's hand as she tried to get in a furtive tuck around the knees. 'Leave it, leave it, for God's sake. Don't fuss woman.'

She retreated in dudgeon, doubtless plotting some Macchiavellian revenge, some vile medicine or, worse still, some indignity relating to hygiene, to which he would have no choice but to submit. Perhaps even a week's notice to quit.

'Hmm,' he mused. 'A manager, secretary. That sort of thing.' There was some merit in the suggestion. Some intelligent company with a bit of luck. Someone who could read the paper without eviscerating it or making vapid comments, like these women, sent to pester him. Yes indeed, Bennett was a sound fellow. 'Good idea Tom, I'll see to it at once. If we go down, we go down with flags flying, hey?' He turned his eye on the nurse. 'Don't stand there idle all day, woman. Get a move on.' Bloody hell. Why did he have these incompetents visited on him in his old age?

Bejasus, thought Bennett watching the progress of the pair along the rutted lane, but he's not gettin' any sweeter. Puts me in mind of his father. He recalled an earlier patient, incredibly old, grinding his teeth in fury, his fiery and domineering spirit reduced to the confines of a bathchair. It would be better he mused, to go quickly, not straggling on for years, a burden to everyone, especially one's self.

Clara wouldn't go near the old man. She always said he was too hard on his son. That was probably because she was born on Strifeland and was a little bit afraid of the lord and master. Bennett recalled the son, a nice enough young chap, a bit standoffish, but that was only to be expected. The father had sent him into the army 'to straighten him out'. It was a pity the way he had been shot. Now the family was dying out with no one to carry on the name. They said that the old man was clutching the son's photograph when they found him after the heart attack, so he must have been fond of him all the same.

*   *   *

The path from the footbridge led down to the edge of the cliff and soon Anna found herself near the cottage on the point. Her eye took in the scene: a woman struggling with a clothes-line as the washing filled with wind and cavorted around her; old stone walls blotched with green and saffron lichen, a loose slate here and there; tall devil's pokers making a splash of colour where a rivulet trickled through ferns to fall over the cliff.

'Can I help you, Mrs Bennett?'

The woman turned with a start at the voice. 'Oh, it's your-self miss, missus. I didn't hear you coming.' She let go of the prop in surprise.

Anna ducked her head and laughed as the pole swung wildly backwards and forwards. She snatched at it with both hands.

'Oh I'm so sorry, miss,' exclaimed Clara apologetically, as much embarrassed to see a young lady engulfed in the Bennett washing as she was alarmed at the possibility of knocking her on the head. Blushing, she unstepped the pole and the line became a thing inert under its weight. The sleeves of Tom's grey flannel shirt trailed on the grass. She was conscious of the darned heels of socks and the worn state of some of the items on view. 'Won't you come inside and have a cup of tea? You've walked a long way.' For a moment she thought that Anna might refuse, possibly to remind her of her place, but she accepted gratefully.

The cottage was dark after the bright sunshine. It was sparsely furnished. A plain deal table was covered with oilcloth, the pattern of which had all but vanished due to constant washing and wiping, and the dowelled chairs had small cushions tied to the seats. There were two armchairs that sagged in the middle, from which the stuffing peered in small grey tufts. There was a fire in the stove under a blackened kettle.

'It won't be a minute,' said Clara, poking at the coals. 'Won't you sit down.'

She gestured towards one of the armchairs and Anna sank into its depths. Springs groaned beneath her. The room was warm and, in a way, homely, but she was disconcerted by the smell. It was the smell of age, of old timbers and old furniture; the smell of people living close together with few of the modern conveniences. She wondered uncharitably about eat-ing in the house, but it was evident that the place was kept

149

scrupulously clean. No speck of ash lay on the hearthstone. The linoleum shone with a metallic gleam. Her eye was drawn to a pattern on the wall where attempts had been made to cover a stain but it seemed to have reasserted itself at each painting, lifting the distemper off in flakes of salt. It was probably a damp patch from outside. She imagined that it looked like a flock of ostriches standing close together, ruffling their plumes and flexing their spindly legs. She noted the two watercolours in the heavy dark lacquered frames.

'Davy's work,' said Clara catching her eye. 'My husband put the frames on them,' she added proudly.

Anna got to her feet to look more closely. The frames were wrong for the pictures, draining the colour from them and drawing the eye to the sombre black border. 'He really is very good,' she remarked, leaning closer to the pictures, 'which in a way is what I wanted to talk to you about.' She accepted a cup of tea. 'I was hoping you would let me take him into Dublin, to the art gallery to look at the paintings. I'm sure he would find it very interesting.'

'Oh!' replied Clara with a start. 'I'm sure he would love to go.' For a moment she was tempted to refuse, almost as if Davy were being taken from her into another world of different interests, different people. 'But wouldn't it be an awful lot of trouble?'

'Oh no, not at all. I often go myself.'

Clara felt at a disadvantage. This young woman took for granted something that she herself had never thought of doing. She could have given her child this experience but it had never occurred to her. She wondered what Tom might have said if she had gone off to Dublin to look at pictures. He would probably have laughed. Anyway, she had no idea where the gallery was. She would have to see to it that he was clean and tidy. That at least she could give him.

'Shall we say Thursday then?' queried Anna, unaware of the older woman's misgivings. 'Thursday is excursion day of course.'

'That would be lovely.'

It was agreed.

They sat again and drank their tea. Inevitably they talked about the war and how it must be drawing to a close. And afterwards? At least the government could give its attention to Ireland. It would be good when people could get back to living normal decent lives again.

This naturally led to Colonel Wyndham and his problems. He would be very lonely when the convalescents went home, as they surely would at some stage.

'He is an interesting man though, isn't he? He holds very strong opinions on everything,' said Anna.

It was as if a cloud passed over the sun for a second.

'Aye that he does,' agreed the older woman. 'He can be a hard man when he wants to be.'

Anna sensed some resentment.

They talked of Anna's own child, already learning to stand and displaying several fine teeth, and Anna warmed to the subject of how it would be when they were all together again when Frank came home. Her vision of family life was like water carried in cupped hands, in constant danger of being spilt, yet she refused to believe that it could be otherwise. She had never talked so openly to anyone about such matters. It was a relief to find someone who could listen and understand. She had hardly, until then, realised how much she loved her quiet, diffident soldier and how much she had built her life on the certainty that he would always be around.

They were interrupted by the arrival of Davy with his schoolbag under his arm. He had begun to grow. His knees and elbows protruded awkwardly. He was puzzled at first and then pleased at the invitation to Dublin, although he wondered what he would say to her for a whole day.

'Your mother tells me you are getting to be a great scholar.'

'Mr Sweeney doesn't think so,' he replied, unbuckling the straps, 'but I'll show him.' He pulled out his books and dumped them on the table. 'I'll get a scholarship, just for spite.' He laughed at the idea but there was an edge to the laugh.

'I can see you both have a lot to do,' said Anna and took her leave.

Clara went back to her washing, thinking of a young man who had gone off to war a long time ago.

* * *

151

Dr Bailey made his rounds as usual. November and the thought of winter filled him with a certain foreboding but still it was good to feel useful, not on the scrapheap yet. A young volunteer was shaving one of the convalescents, if an amputee, blinded by mustard gas, could ever be described as convalescent. The blade scraped a smooth track along his cheek. One of those safety razors — throw away the blade after a couple of days and insert another. Not something he would ever feel the need of, the doctor thought, fingering his rather luxuriant whiskers. There was something repugnant about using things and then throwing them away. Profligacy was the word for it, a fitting symbol for these times of disposable and replaceable people. How many million was it? Twenty million wounded, possibly five million dead or missing, and the Central Powers had lost almost as many.

How could such things happen between the greatest empires in the civilised world? Civilised? But it was a fact. The resplendent dynasties of the ancient continent had clawed themselves down into the slime like the most primitive African savages. The glory of civilised warfare was gone forever. He looked at the boy's sightless eyes and shook his head.

What time-serving shirker would step into this young fellow's rightful place in the land fit for heroes? The claptrap of the orators had a hollow ring. The nurse chattered brightly to her charge, towelling him gently under the chin. Would any young woman, her hair falling around her shoulders, submit to his embraces? 'Hands lopped off on the grunsel edge'. That was Milton, the sacrifice of the first-born to Moloch. Or was it Belial? There was nothing new under the sun.

The sound of cheering in the outer hall interrupted his morbid train of thought. The nurse went to investigate and returned with eyes shining.

'It's an armistice,' she cried to all the room. 'The war ended this morning.' And she burst into tears.

The news had just come with the afternoon train. Men leaped or clambered from their beds and converged on the door. Some seized the hands of those nearest and shook them vigorously. There was uproar throughout the house. Wheelchairs were waltzed around by those who had legs under them.

The colonel emerged from his private apartments, propelling

himself in a fury. 'What the devil is all this Mafeking about in my house?' he bellowed, but his voice was lost in the cheers.

Three times three they roared their delight and congratulated each other again and again. Some were too overcome to say anything. Some threw their arms around the nurses and swung them wildly in a swirl of skirts and aprons. Others went to ring the estate bell or simply to be outside on that glorious day. There were a few who were unable to move or to add their voices to the general hilarity.

The colonel plundered the remains of his cellar and insisted that everyone drink to victory.

'The old fox Ludendorff has gone to earth,' he confided to the doctor, 'But, by gad, they'd dig him out and make him pay dearly. Make the whole damned lot of them pay. Crush the Hun so that he will never lift his head again. Germans, Dutch, Boers, all the blasted same. Only thing they understand is a good hiding.'

Dr Bailey mumbled something non-committal and raised his glass to the ceasefire. He had no desire to be the skull at the feast. 'Fourteen points, eh,' he suggested. 'A settlement along those lines should be the answer. Should have been done years ago.'

'Fourteen points, be blowed,' snorted the colonel, glaring up from his chair. 'Damned Americans coming in at the eleventh hour, thinking they can set the world to rights. Like as not every tinpot demagogue in Europe will want to set himself up as a king, not to mention the crowd we have here, clodhoppers, schoolmasters. Now's the time, I tell you, to root them all out, Bolsheviks, agitators, the whole damned lot, and let things get back to normal.'

Dr Bailey gave silent thanks that his granddaughter was not around. Even his milder version of normality was denounced by her, as reactionary, setting the clock back. What would she make of the old man's feudal triumphalism? Indeed the colonel was only a few years older than himself. He was glad that his was not that fiery spirit trapped in a brokendown body in this crumbling old house. Everything had changed during those short few years. What had happened to the regal plumes he had seen bobbing through the streets at the late king's funeral? Sceptre and crown. He excused himself and stepped outside, away from the hubbub of voices.

Frost lay in the shadow of the house. He stood with hands clasped behind his back and stared unseeing at the winter sea. The simple faith that had maintained him through all his professional life, belief that he should at all times sustain life, came like a thin and futile voice. The gnarled branches stirred and whispered over his head.

'So it's all over then, Doctor.'

The voice broke into his reverie, of Bennett, the foreman, plodding up the path from the byre.

'Yes indeed, thank God.' It was not an expression that he used frequently, but he felt it would be an appropriate sentiment to Irish ears.

'Aye, thank God.' Bennett raised his hat and scratched his poll.

A renewed burst of cheering came from the house. Horseplay had broken out again.

'And them's the winners, God help us.' Bennett shook his head. 'The poor huers. May the Lord look down on the losers!'

A Christian thought, mused the doctor. Were there any winners at all? 'Yes indeed,' he murmured in agreement.

'What was the point of it all, Doctor? I'm fucked if I know. I mean, you're an educated man. There must be a reason for things like that.'

I'm fucked if I know either, thought the doctor, savouring the turn of phrase. 'Well at least it's hardly likely to happen again.' It was the standard answer, the war to end war. 'The world has learned a lesson it will never forget.' The words sounded hollow and unconvincing to his ears.

'Maybe you're right, Doctor, but I'm not so sure.'

'You don't mind if I walk along with you for a while. My patients have no need of me. One way or another they've had a dose of a tonic today.' His gloomy mood abated. He began to question Bennett about his life and listened with interest to his description of the cycle of birth, ripeness and decay repeated year in year out. 'You're a fortunate man Bennett. It must inculcate a great respect for life. I can sense it in the way you speak.'

'That's as may be, though I never gave it much thought.'

'It's just a theory of mine, people who make things grow,

154

more than likely, are more humanitarian.'

Bennett scratched his chin and chuckled. 'I don't know so much about that. Did ye ever hear about the Rushman on the jury?' He snapped a switch from a hazel as if from force of habit and swung it at the rough yellow scutch.

'I can't say that I have. Is he an apocryphal Rushman by any chance?'

'I couldn't answer to that,' said Bennett, frowning, and he pressed on with his story. 'Rushmen can make things grow, as ye probably know, where nothin' on God's earth was meant to grow. There's men that know about growin' things.' He paused in momentary awe at their undoubted skill. Sanddunes blossom in Rush. Scallions grow in little fields hardly the size of a handkerchief.

'Our friend was on a jury, you say.' The doctor brought him back to the main thrust of the story.

'Aye. On a jury, he was. Some famous murder trial, if I remember rightly.'

'And?'

'Howan'ever, the jury was locked. Couldn't reach a verdict, right or wrong. Three days they was in there arguin' the toss.'

'And our friend resolved the issue, I take it.'

'In a way, I suppose. Up he stands at the end of the third day, and says he straight out, savin' your presence, "Hang the fucker. I've carrots to weed." '

The doctor laughed in spite of himself. 'Aha! I take your point.'

'Comical times, Doctor. It's comical times we live in.'

Comical times indeed. 'And wretches hang that jurymen may dine.'

A stroke of a pen, one hour either way probably cost lives that very day. As if there had not been enough to put up with, there was influenza to cap it all. He had read the latest papers on viruses and the intelligence dismayed him: in simple cultures the viruses roamed at large, invading, infecting and reproducing a hundred fold in the time it takes to smoke a cigarette. No wonder the old continent was on its knees. The life of any one of us, he mused, is nothing more than an accident, a random quirk in some great cosmic process that could just as easily be terminated by a wandering virus as by a bullet or a hard-pressed market gardener. There was nothing for it but to soldier on. He turned up his collar and shoved his hands into his pockets. 'Dereliction of duty,' he murmured ruefully. 'I must get back to my work.' He looked up the hill towards the house. Lamps were being lit in the windows, casting a cheerful glow.

'Well sure,' Bennett touched his forehead with his forefinger, 'I dare say things will get better from now on. I'll say good day to ye, Doctor.'

'And to you Bennett. I sincerely hope you're right.' He felt tired. It would be enough to look in on the influenza cases and then go home and turn in early.

The bleak afterglow anatomised the trees around the house in dark silhouette. Rooks rose in unnecessary alarm at the distant whistle of the Belfast express. All over, bar the shouting, he thought, aware of the sounds of singing and a piano being subjected to a merciless pounding, as young voices rejoiced in being alive. With a rustling of wings the lapwings drifted in with the dusk, piping plaintively on the newly turned soil, harbingers of winter.

CHAPTER 13

So this is it, thought Kit. This is what it was all about. He stood back under the eaves of the cottage, behind a curtain of drips, and let his eye wander along Church Street. The rain pelted down, like glass rods shattering on a gun-metal roadway. The small houses hunched under the steady downpour. Drain-pipes gurgled and splashed small torrents into the cobbled gutters. Piles of horse-dung melted and ran yellow in the gullies. A high-wheeled car was stopped outside The Central. The pony drooped its head disconsolately; the water streamed from the bit of tarpaulin on its back. Miss Gearey would be having her port wine in the snug, as she did every Wednesday after-noon, after delivering her butter to Kerrigan's, beautiful salty country butter that always ended up with a few red hairs from oul' Kerrigan's streel of a wife, or finger marks from some of her snotty kids. How in the name of God had he ever eaten anything from Kerrigans?

Jesus, she's a plain woman, Kerrigan's wife. No eyelashes, or at least hardly any you'd notice. It was a wonder how she had six children. Love is blind they say. Maybe oul' Kerrigan steeled himself to the deed in the dark of the night. Maybe he stoked himself up in The Central and then ran across the road before the effects wore off. Six times he had faced the pros-pect. There should be medals for that kind of courage. There was no doubt but the children favoured their mother. There must be more to life than huckstering in a dark little shop with the rain teeming down into your soul.

Kit wiped a drop from his nose with the back of his sleeve. A small figure cut across the intersection at Barter Street, leaning forward into a sturdy car umbrella. Sweeney! Look at him, the little sleeveen. The man of words, always secure and snug, laying down the law to all and sundry. There was a time when Kit had promised himself that he would get his own back, give him a taste of what he had dished out, but now he couldn't be bothered. It wasn't so much that Sweeney hammered his pupils, which he did now and again, it was his way with words. He could always make a lad feel small, and the parents too. They never went near the school, always greeting him politely and smiling because they knew he had them beaten.

The older generation spoke with reverence and affection of Mr Mac, the previous master. They learned a lot from him. They recalled the times when he would go on a bit of a tear and the school would be shut for a couple of days, but that was in the old days. There was none of that about Sweeney. Like a spider he scuttled out in the morning and scuttled home in the afternoon, and those whose lives he touched flinched from him. But they obeyed, thought Kit. Everyone feared Sweeney because he used his bit of knowledge like a weapon, a stick to keep people in their place — people like Mr Drew, a skilled tradesman with his own business. Mr Drew was a decent enough sort with his opinions on the divil and all, but what did he really know about anything?

What did any of them know?

He had been part of something so big that no one could assess its importance. He had made a commitment and had seen it through, he thought, rather self-importantly, but it would be nice to know where it had all led to. He had no wish to settle back into this one-horse town, to be the lad again, to listen to village loudmouths and tedious old bores going on, over their porter, about what it was like in their day, and the fight for freedom and The Movement. They didn't know their arse from a hole in the ground when it came to a real war. He could tell them a thing or two — if he was bothered.

Skinner Doyle came to the door of the butcher's and lobbed a handful of scraps to the disconsolate looking mongrel that sat outside. It looked as if Skinner deliberately aimed the scraps for the deepest puddle. The dog shuffled to its feet, shook itself in a futile effort at drying its coat and splashed after the meat. Doyle caught Kit's eye and gave him a nod. Time was, he'd have been glad of those scraps himself. There was a kind of a self-satisfied smirk about his fat face. Incongruously, Kit noted that he still seemed to have all his fingers intact. In fact he had even grown an extra chin.

The dog retreated under the shelter of the eaves and began to worry a large bone. Its jaws were flecked with sawdust and saliva.

'And you wouldn't call the Pope your uncle,' muttered Kit, pushing the bone away from him with his boot. It's a sad state of affairs when a fellow ends up talking to dogs.

He fingered the few coins in his pocket, exploring for milled edges. There was just enough for a few jars and after that he would have to think seriously about what he was going to do. There was always Mr Drew of course, but the prospect of shovelling cement and carrying blocks for the rest of his life did not appeal to him.

Of course he could drive the horse and cart with the planks and the poles and the gravel. Who ever said it was a one-horse-town? Judging by the streets, there was a fair few horses. They used to collect the dung, himself and Joey, for the vegetables, another of their schemes. He smiled, remembering the time Skinner had challenged them on their tub full of manure. 'Are yiz goin' to eat that for your dinner, eh?' And the reply that had come by inspiration: 'If your oul' one thought you could eat it she'd be round to borrow some.' Skinner had crumpled in a very satisfactory way and Kit wondered why he had regretted the remark. Even Joey, though he had laughed, had said it was a bit rough. Joey could be self-righteous too at times.

To hell with it! He still had a few bob to postpone the evil day. The bar smelled of damp coats and stale porter. There was a stranger there, an agreeable sort of a chap, with a military cut about him, who insisted on buying him a drink. Sure what harm? He seemed to know a bit about the world outside, a bit more than fishing and spuds and village gossip and he listened with intelligent interest to a fellow's opinions.

*   *   *

159

'Mr Drew,' said the sergeant, 'there was another matter I've been meaning to broach with you.' The rain spilled from his cap brim and ran in rivulets down his cape.

'Another matter? You mean the crack in the gable isn't all that's wrong. You know, sergeant,' he emitted a dry cackle, 'I sometimes think any class of a dunt would bring the whole thing down around your ears.'

'You'll be referring to the barrack, I take it.' The sergeant looked at him quizzically.

'Aye, that too,' replied Mr Drew, giving him a queer look. 'And what was the other matter you had in mind?'

'Well, there's that young lad Donovan, just out of the army?'

'Oh aye?'

'I'd as lieve you kept an eye on him yourself, as see him in bad company elsewhere.'

'I take your drift, Sergeant. There's work in plenty for him as far as I'm concerned, whenever he has a mind for it.'

'If he has to get into bad company — though mind, I wouldn't want him to — it would be as well for him to be with his own kind.'

'Well, I'm sure it's a compliment, in a back-handed class of a way.'

The sergeant dislodged a puddle from the folds of his cape. He hiked the left pedal around to the ten-o-clock position, preparatory to moving. 'Right so. I dare say you'll have a word with him in due course. It's odious weather, isn't it?' With that innocuous remark he was gone, on whispering wheels, down the rain-sodden street.

A remarkable man, mused Mr Drew, watching the receding figure, a remarkable man altogether. He scratched his straggling moustache, trying to clarify his thoughts. He could never be sure of his attitude to Duffy. Policemen had been shot in Tipperary and the Volunteers made no secret of the fact that they intended to shoot many more. The days of rhetoric were over. Those who were friendly to the Movement were known, and who were not were marked men. Where did Duffy stand, inflexible in his respect for duty, yet concerned for the welfare of one confused young lad?

Step in close, the experts said, and make no mistakes; through the temple at close range. Mr Drew grimaced. He subscribed to the ideal of a republic, hated oppression, as any Irishman would, but he could not see himself putting a revolver to Duffy's head and bringing him down in a tangle of spokes. He envisaged the scene as it might be but could feel no enthusiasm, no passionate sense of justice. Maybe I'm just too old, he thought, too old to be certain any more.

*   *   *

The locals used to call it the Mill Field but gradually, because of the three black huts and the tall masts, its name was changing.

Frank closed his eyes and lifted his face to the sun. Insects hummed all around. He could not remember when last he had been so at peace, as he lay with his little daughter in the lush greenness of the Wireless Field.

The stream proper and the mill-race divided the lower field into segments, joined by small bridges made from railway sleepers. The stream teemed with pinkeens, the prey of children with jamjars and nets made from old lisle stockings with the holes carefully repaired. The mill-race, more sluggish and sedate, where it emerged from its tunnel below the mill, abounded in frogspawn and tadpoles, under its green carpet of cress. Buttercups and their royal cousins, the kingcups, among clumps of rushes, gave evidence of the marshy nature of much of the field. Forests of umbrella-like plantain covered the sloping banks of the stream.

He lay back in the long grass and the little girl climbed over him and sat astride his chest. Miranda. To be wondered at and admired, her name meant. Her fingers were yellow with pollen from her posy of daisies and buttercups. Her hair was fair like his own. He opened his eyes and looked at her in wonder. This was how life should be spent, in a meadow in springtime, with one's own child. He lifted her up and she waved her arms and legs.

'Wimpf, wimpf. G'andaddy wimpf,' she shrieked in delight.

Grandaddy, or strictly, great-grandaddy, had already begun his determined swimming, to the child's enormous admiration.

'Big waves,' agreed Frank, rocking her from side to side, so that she laughed and dribbled down at him. 'Hey,' he gasped, and put her down. 'I don't want to be drowned, you know.'

161

They became absorbed in watching a green insect crawling up a blade of grass which gradually bowed under the weight, so that the creature, having achieved its objective, was deposited back on the ground. It immediately began to climb another blade.

'A kind of entomological perpetual motion,' said Frank gravely.

Miranda spluttered and lost interest. She was watching the great mill-wheel turning in its slow, deliberate way under a white veil of water.

A mill worker was grinding tools on a grindstone that turned on a shaft protruding from the wall. At first the blades protested with rending screeches which gradually turned to a long singing note as they took an edge. That was the secret of life, thought Frank, things working in harmony. Water, the life-giver, imparted the power and went on its way unchanged. Human intervention borrowed that power and made it work, transmitting it by fly-wheel and belt throughout the building, to grind grain or metal, and all aspects of the work sang in harmony. He felt strangely humbled at the thought. What wonders could be accomplished by people working in harmony.

He raised himself on his elbow to make sure that Miranda did not wander too far. The sun gleamed on the fresh tar on the little huts. The wire struts of the masts hummed in the gentle breeze. There it was again, the harmony, the human mind borrowing the great forces of nature, the invisible waves that encircle the earth at the speed of light itself. Shakespeare knew it so well in his time, 'a thousand twangling instruments', the music of the spheres. The child came toddling back to him again. There was no Caliban there to frighten her.

It was almost like a religious experience, a blessing to feel so much at peace with the world. Ugliness, pain, horror and degradation were behind him for ever. The world was purged of its filth. He smiled at his daughter and at himself. Mustn't get carried away, like some of those mystics the Catholics went in for. He rose and stretched, taking his daughter by the hand.

There was a man in shirtsleeves sitting on the doorstep of the nearest hut, a civilian by the look of him. He raised a hand in greeting and they passed the usual civilities about the weather.

'Interesting business you have here,' remarked Frank. 'I saw a bit of it in France.'

162

'Aye surely,' agreed the man, with a Northern twang to his accent. 'As a matter of fact I rigged most of it myself. Thon fellas in th'army don't understand the workin's of wireless telegraphy.' There was a cocky assurance about his professionalism, 'I know what I'm talkin' about.'

A key tapped in the darkness of the hut.

'Come on in then,' he invited, 'till I show you.'

There was a young fellow in a coastguard uniform, listening intently to the transmission and scribbling on a pad.

'What exactly is the purpose of it all?' asked Frank, looking around as the man, who introduced himself as Rushe, spoke of oscillations, electro-magnetic waves and the thermionic valve. He indicated each component with the assurance of long familiarity.

'Oh, communications generally. I just put it together and keep it goin', like. These omadhauns in the army and the coastguards break it all up again.'

The young fellow grinned. 'We keep track of shipping and that,' he volunteered. 'It's standard practice nowadays.'

'I see,' said Frank, impressed. 'There must be a lot of shipping to occupy three huts.'

'Oh thon's the army,' said Rushe dismissively. 'They spend all their time talkin' to theirselves. The other wee hut's the generator like y'know.'

The two of them laughed at the absurdities of the military mind and Frank indulged their good humour. Indeed what he had seen of military communications had left a lot to be desired. Talking to the ships though, there was a wonderful innovation.

'Wonderful, marvellous,' said a voice, echoing his thoughts as he blinked again in the sunlight. A bedgraggled old character with a sack over his shoulder was looking up at the swaying mast. 'Sendin' messages through the air, bejaysus. Penetratin' solid stone walls. Wonderful, marvellous!' He shook his head in astonishment and lurched away, hefting his burden.

'I was just about to brew up,' remarked Rushe. 'Maybe you'ld care for a cup. Would her ladyship be able for a sugar barley?' He extracted the stump of a bar from his pocket.

Miranda grasped it eagerly.

The strong sweet tea, boiled up in the kettle, brought Frank's thoughts back to those times in the war when he had been grateful for life's small pleasures, when a basin of warm water in which to wash and shave had been a luxury almost unimaginable, when a few hours of quiet to sit and read had made him want so much to stay alive, to come back to his wife and family and to show them how much they were loved.

Now his contentment extended to all.

Miranda had been amusing herself by poking the bubbles in the tar of the hut. Now her hands were covered in the stuff and there were black streaks on her petticoats.

Rushe went into the hut and emerged with a rag soaked in spirit. 'This'll do the trick,' he volunteered. 'Many a time and oft I've had to clean it off my own wains.' Deftly he removed the stains adding, 'You never know what clabber they'll be in.' Obviously he was an experienced hand with children.

'I fear I have a lot to learn,' admitted Frank. 'Her mother would have my life.'

'Wains, is it? You'll still be learnin' when they're carryin' you out in the box.'

He poured another mug of tea and they sat back again enjoying a smoke. The warm day beamed around them. The key tapped in the darkness of the hut. The metal of the mug rim had a sharp taste to it where the enamel was chipped.

'So you're home for good then,' said the technician, inquisitively. 'Not tempted to put in for a regular commission?'

'Not a chance,' retorted Frank emphatically. 'No more soldiering for me.' He put his arm around Miranda and drew her close. ' "My zenith doth depend upon a most auspicious star".'

Rushe blinked in puzzlement. 'Aye, I dare say. You have the cut of a soldier about you though.'

'Won't be long getting rid of that,' scoffed Frank, rising to his feet and brushing down his jacket. 'Come along, young lady.'

Miranda stretched up to him and he hoisted her onto his shoulders.

Part III

CHAPTER 14

In the dead of the night the lorries came rumbling over The White Rock hill, soldiers from Gormanston camp as it transpired. The small houses reverberated to the convoy passing through to the square. In the stillness people strained to follow their progress and wondered who the quarry might be. It was the first time that they had felt the threat in their own homes. Children woke to the noise of boots pounding through the streets and the shouts of alien voices. Doors banged and footsteps receded. Engines coughed and thundered into life again. Headlights cut the darkness, tilting their beams towards the clouds as the convoy raced back over the hill, speed and noise creating the maximum shock, but they had not found the men they wanted. On a lugger at anchor the hunted men heard the distant motors and knew that they were safe for another night.

This kind of operation had become commonplace in many parts of the country within months of the Armistice and the much talked about return of normality.

Joey turned from the window, letting the curtain fall back into place. 'Now do you believe it?' he demanded, his voice trembling.

Kit's face showed like a white blur in the gloom. He searched for the matches and lit the candle, at a loss for words.

'I'm tellin' you,' Joey insisted, 'they're playin' for keeps now. Christ don't you understand?' He could not recall a time when he had talked down to his brother like that.

'All right, all right,' snapped Kit. 'I believe you.'

'This is all your man's work, you know.' He almost added that he hoped Kit had no hand or part in it.

Kit's mouth was dry. 'Jesus,' he whispered, swallowing hard. He could feel the sweat on his upper lip. 'Do you think they got anyone?'

'How would I know? You don't understand the way things are, do you?'

'I think I'm getting an idea of it now,' said Kit slowly. 'Is your man really a spy, the way Mr Drew says?'

'You can bet your life on it. They say wherever Jack Straw appears there's always a raid. You were a very foolish man to talk to him.'

Kit exploded. 'How the bloody hell was I to know anything? I was only home a couple of days. He racked his brain, trying to recall if he had said anything at all to the stranger in the bar. 'Anyway I don't know a damn thing about the situation here, so don't be looking at me like that.'

The candlelight flickered on his face and Joey could see that he was angry. He relented. 'I wasn't suggesting anything,' he muttered. 'It's just that you can't be too careful.'

'So I see. You're too young to be mixed up in this sort of thing, Joey. It's all getting out of hand.'

Joey sat on the edge of the bed and his shoulders dropped. 'I'm not really involved, not yet anyway, but I don't see much choice. It's not the same as before you went away. Some of the lads say we should all join in together and get it over with.'

Kit lay back, propping himself on his elbow. 'You don't know what you're talking about.' His voice was bleak. He saw a grey shape rising from the ground and heard the rattle of rifle fire. The figure flopped forward, as it had done many times in his dreams, but the eyes remained open, gazing at him. 'That's the greatest army in the world out there, and you, Joey Donovan, are going to take them on. Lookit,' his voice rose, 'they could wipe this town off the map in twenty minutes. You have no idea.'

Joey was silent for a few moments. 'Mr Sweeney says that blood must be shed —'

'Don't give me that,' interrupted Kit. 'It won't be his blood, you can bet. It will be poor eejits like you and the likes of you. Do you seriously want to fight anyone, Joey? You're the most peaceable bloke I know.'

'Nobody wants to fight, but supposing those lorries stopped outside our house. Do you think they'd listen to reason? It's out of our hands Kit. It'll be worse before it's better.'

The door creaked open and their mother looked in. Her candle cast a soft halo round her face. 'What are you arguing about at this hour?' she whispered.

The brothers looked at each other.

'Nothing much,' said Kit. 'It was just the motors outside that woke us.'

'Go back to sleep then,' she whispered, withdrawing.

They listened to her footsteps on the landing and the click of her door. They lay in silence for a long time. Eventually Joey spoke.

'You never did say anything to your man, did you?' He felt like a traitor for asking, but there was always the danger after a few drinks.

'There's no need to ask me that, Joey.' His voice was cold again. 'Do you think Mr Drew would have given me the job otherwise?'

'Sorry,' muttered Joey. 'I shouldn't have asked.'

'No you shouldn't,' growled his brother.

There was silence, and gradually Joey drifted into sleep. The candle guttered and went out. Kit lay awake, his mind confused by images of amorphous things creeping towards him out of the darkness. He had come to dread the dark, noises in the night, sudden awakenings. He longed for morning to lighten the window panes. He reached for his cigarettes and struck a match.

* * *

A crowd had gathered in Talbot Street where the soldiers were searching the rooms over a shop and Anna had to pause in her hurry to the station. Over the heads of the children she could see the steel helmets, the dull glint of fixed bayonets and the legend in raised white lettering on the window panes, *Kennedys' Bread*. Incongruously, Davy's derogatory rhyme came to mind with the warning:

169

'Don't eat Kennedy's bread
It'll stick in your belly like lead.'

The children, ragged and barefoot for the most part, were jeering the soldiers, some of whom looked decidedly sheepish. The adults muttered more ominously and scowled. In reply the soldiers held their rifles square, forming a fence and pushing the crowd back. A boy yelped when a heavy hobnailed boot descended on his toes. Anna felt a fierce resentment rising inside her.

'Be careful of the children,' she called angrily.

People turned to stare, making way for this imperious young woman, an English woman by the sound of her.

'You deliberately trod on that child's foot,' she snapped, glaring into the soldier's impassive face.

'No missus, I did not,' he retorted stolidly. 'Just stand back please.'

The crowd grinned in anticipation of a scene.

'Is this how His Majesty's forces behave towards civilians?' she went on, knowing that her anger was making her over-state her case.

'Just stand back, missus, please,' repeated the soldier, tensing his grip on the rifle. 'Keep back now.' He reiterated the formula like an incantation.

An officer emerged from the shop, thrusting his pistol into the holster. He had drawn another blank. The bird had flown — if it had ever been there. He noted the elegant young woman in an altercation with one of his men.

'That's right, missus,' called an encouraging voice.

'What's the problem?' he asked. She was a lady of some quality, deuced good looking too.

'Your men, sir,' she retorted, 'are behaving like Prussians. Do you make war on children?'

He was stung by the comparison. Was she siding with street-Arabs against her own kind? Angrily he ordered his men back to the lorry. They clambered into the wire cage, the latest protection against missiles.

'Nuts for the monkeys,' sang a derisive voice in a descant, the note falling on the last word. 'Take them back to the ezoo.'

The crowd laughed and Anna recovered her composure.

'That's the style, missus,' volunteered a ragged old shawlie. 'Prussians is too good for them. Bowsies is what they are.'

She had no desire to linger in conversation. The crowd began to scatter, the entertainment over. She hurried towards the station, anxiously watching the minute-hand on the big clock. A train passed on the metal bridge overhead. 'It'll rumble like thunder an' your mother will wonder, so don't eat Kennedy's bread.' The ridiculous rhyme stayed with her as she hurried up the steps, fumbling in her purse for the ticket. She kept thinking of the bayonets and the excited faces of the children.

The rhythm of the train syncopated the rhyme, 'It'll stick in your belly like lead,' the engine accelerating with explosive gasps of steam. Irish history, according to some of the polemicists, was a long series of children bayoneted, infants impaled on pikes, roofs pulled down over the heads of the starving, but that was all long ago, in barbarous times, not in the twentieth century. In a moment of clarity she saw that the soldiers could not win, simply because they had the weapons. It was so obvious that she wondered why nobody had pointed it out to them.

She would put the point to Frank, if he had time to listen, given his new-found enthusiasm for the job of estate manager with the wild old man at Strifeland. His conversation tended to drift towards Peruvian guano and the new Whiting Bull tractor, tested by officials from the Ministry of Agriculture itself. It was good to see him so occupied and so cheerful, even if the job was doomed to be short-lived. The Land Commission would take the estate. Too many hungry men looked longingly at the fertile fields. The twentieth century could not tolerate the old ways. The twentieth century, the age of science and progress when hunger and disease would be banished and the great powers would set the world on a firm path to peace and prosperity.

Mankind had turned a corner, he maintained. Anything could be achieved by men of goodwill — and women over thirty, he always added, in deference to the new suffrage laws. The Atlantic had been conquered by airmen and messages could be transmitted through the aether by means of electricity, drawing the whole world closer together.

* * *

171

There she goes again, said Skinner Doyle to himself, like a fuckin' cuckoo clock. Every time Kit Donovan goes up the street she's out the door; worse than oul' Donnelly with the water buckets. Library books, how are ye! Lending Daddy a hand by cleaning the windows. Inwardly he mimicked Dolores Kerrigan's careful accent. Oh, Dolores is moving in very nice circles since she's been away to boarding school.

People in nice circles didn't stravage the streets flaunting themselves at ex-soldiers. He savoured the term. An ex-soldier, a common labourer, too fond of the bottle by far. One of the Donovans from The White Rock. Who the hell do they think they are? All the same, there was something about her . . . the way her skirts swirled around her slim figure when she turned to call across the street . . . the way she clutched her library books in front of her chest. He watched her, time and again, during the ladies' bathing time around near the tower, her long costume clinging to her as she climbed up the ladder, her fair hair peeping from under her cap. He had even shouted remarks from his vantage point on the rocks outside, with some of the other lads. In desperation he had thrown winkles at her as she trod water, but she was immune to such blandishments. Donovan wouldn't have to resort to such tactics to gain her attention. God! the way she wiggled her arse as she polished the glass. She'll wear a hole in the fuckin' window. Donovan didn't take much notice. She was watching him in the reflection.

Skinner knew the pain of loss, the torment of the damned, Satan's exclusion from the very nice circle of the elect. 'Ouch,' he yelped. He had nicked his finger. 'Blast it,' he muttered and went in search of a plaster.

*   *   *

'He may be a judge accordin' to the Sinn Fein gover'ment,' said Bennett, 'but he doesn't have the power o' life and death over people.' He tapped Mr Drew on the arm to emphasise the point. 'An' I don't care who hears me sayin' it.'

'Ah, now Tom,' replied the older man. 'That's why they made him a judge. He's not goin' to lose the run of himself all of a sudden.' He put his hand on the side of the cart because the pony was restless and the cart swayed back and forth with the motion of a boat on the moorings. 'We have to rely on the likes of Sweeney to set up the machinery of government.'

'I don't know about that. He's the class of fella that gets carried away with his own importance. In no time he'll be orderin' people around and handin' down the law for further orders.'

'Now Tom,' Mr Drew assumed a more cautionary tone, 'Sweeney could turn out a very important man in these parts. You don't want to antagonise him.'

'Judge or no judge, Mr Drew, I'm not afraid of Sweeney or his law.' He paused again as an idea occurred to him. 'If any harm comes to the oul' fella out there, I'll hold youse responsible. He's always been fair to me and I won't stand by and see him harmed. It's one thing to blow up railways but . . . .'

'Ah now, Tom, there you go again. Who said anything about harmin' the oul' colonel?'

'Nobody yet, but I'm just thinkin' ahead. And you can pass the message on to Sweeney. He won't catch me on the hop the next time.'

Mr Drew detected some old antagonism, some specific affront into which he was not prepared to probe. 'I respect your opinions, Tom, and your loyalty. No. The colonel will go in the natural way, like I said. His class is a dyin' breed. I'm more concerned for yourself.'

'What do ye mean? Why should you be concerned for me?'

'Well it's like this. You've always been in the middle, like, even between Balbriggan and Skerries. You played football with one and beat the drum for the other. You've a split personality. Do you know what that is?'

Bennett chuckled, prepared for a scientific explosion.

'I mean you have to support one side or another. That's the way things are now. It's a simple choice, change or stay as we are, and I'm not talkin' football now. Which is it to be?'

Bennett rubbed his chin. 'I wish I could see it as simple as all that. Are you sayin' we'll all be better off in a republic? Will all the murders be all right then?'

'Not murders, Tom, acts of war. In wartime that's the way it is. We have a real army now and we have the beatin' of England in this kind of a war.'

'I don't know Mr Drew. You used to be a man for political solutions. Supposin' yiz bomb their cities, like in the war, would that be all right too? Isn't that the way wars is won nowadays?'

Mr Drew hesitated. 'That's not the way it'll be. There's no question of that. I don't suppose you ever saw a bullfight.'

'I can't say that I have. They don't go in much for it around these parts.'

'Well it's not that I have myself, but I've read about it.'

'What's that got to do with anything?'

'It's the way they do it. Just jab away at the one spot, tire him out, bring the head down.' He indicated the spot and twisted his neck expressively. 'Finish him off with a little bit of a sword the size of a knittin' needle.' He gave a little flourish.

'Just like that? And yiz have enough men?' He was not convinced.

'This is man to man, level peggin'. They won't be prepared to lose men over whether we have home rule or a republic.' He mused for a moment, assessing the odds. 'And who the divil did they ever beat anyway, but a few poor niggers with bows and arrows?' The odds were obviously satisfactory.

Bennett laughed. 'So we have them on the run then, have we? I hope you're right. Just remember what I said though, about himself. Any harm comes to him, I'll deal with Sweeney meself.'

Mr Drew felt strangely confused. He could not decide whether Bennett was an obsequious lackey of the ascendancy, as the official line might suggest, or an independent-minded individual, who prized loyalty above his own reputation. The man, he suspected for the first time, might have hidden depths. Maybe he had a split personality. Schizophrenics or something, they called them. He resolved to delve further into the tortuous world of psychology. A remarkable business entirely. He regretted the lack of time available to him for reading. It was as if all pleasures had to be postponed until more pressing matters had been disposed of.

Bennett was preparing to go. He gathered the reins from the peg.

'I'll be in touch Tom, and remember what I said about Sweeney. Don't cross him. He's an influential man right now.'

174

'Indeed, I'm not lookin' for a row with anyone. Good luck now.'

The iron rims crunched on the cobblestones and with a clanking of churns he was gone.

Mr Drew scratched his head. Bennett's words disturbed him. He recalled his reaction to the death of the first policemen. They were guarding a cargo of dynamite. That was another thing. He rubbed his chin. He imagined the men buckling and falling into the ditch as the bullets hit them. He always pictured policemen on bicycles. It must be right if the top men said so, a necessary evil, as the master said, to make it clear that an Irishman must choose for once and for all.

He had never actually fired a gun himself, except for an old shotgun years ago. It was probably better that these things should happen down the country, where passions ran stronger, where the issues were somehow clearer, where people were maybe that little bit more obviously Irish. He could not pin down the rationalisation. People were different down there all the same, different accents, a different way of looking at things.

There was something about the colonel though. Where was the point of going through a revolution only to end up tipping your cap to the gentry? Mr De Valera said that he was no revolutionary, meaning that things would be the same generally after the republic was gained. What use would that be to the hungry men that looked over the ditches at the fine fields of the gentry? Connolly had the rights of it even if he was led astray by a crowd of poets and mystics. A child should have shoes on his feet. People should have a roof over their heads and food in their bellies.

Colonel Wyndham, he reflected, was no obstacle, but his class was still around, still talking down to the peasantry, still raising sons for the imperial army and looking to the East for a sign. Not that it had done them a lot of good. The colonel had lost his only son in South Africa. Tom Bennett said he was holding the boy's photograph when he had his attack and fell into the hearth. Maybe he kept it on the mantelpiece like other people kept a holy picture. Anyway he was clutching on to it when they found him, half burned to death. Momentarily he saw a picture of St Joan, clutching a crucifix amid

175

the flames. 'Her last word was Jesus!' the caption read. Not surprising, he thought irreverently. It was hard on the poor old fellow, but as a class they deserved little sympathy. They had seen the good days in their grand houses. They would all have to go, like they were going in Russia, though please God it would not have to be so violent. A little bit of physical force — a better word that — would be enough to scare them off. There were enough decent people at the top on both sides to see that it was kept within reason. The thought comforted him.

In the meantime there were matters of business to attend to. Great affairs went on one way or another, but a man has to make a few bob.

CHAPTER 15

' "Donovan and Drew", now that's got a nice ring to it.'

'Are you sure you don't mean "Drew and Donovan"?'

Mr Drew scratched at his moustache. ' "Drew and Donovan", aye. Not that I'm sayin' yes, now, young fella.'

'I tell you what,' said Kit, pressing his advantage now that the older man was interested, 'we could just say "D and D Coal Merchants". Has a good ring to it.'

'Aye I dare say, but what put this into your head?'

'Well I've been thinking. I've been arsing around for the last year, not doing very much really, except for the job with you, of course,' added Kit hurriedly, 'but I'm not going anywhere. I'm too old for a proper apprenticeship. All I do is hang around the pubs.'

The older man nodded. 'I know what you mean. You want to make something of your life. That's a very good thing, but why coal?'

'Well, I'll tell you, I've always wanted my own business. I want to buy and sell. Everybody needs coal and nobody around here does it on a big enough scale. You have that bit of a yard over near the harbour, that you don't use much. All we'd need is a few horses and drays.'

'A few horses? Where would we get the money?'

'Well, one more horse, to start. My mother would go security for a few bob.'

'Would she now? What does she think of the idea?'

177

'I think she'd be glad to see me busy. She's nearly given up hope of me amounting to anything.'

Mr Drew stood up, absentmindedly opening and closing his rule. He scuffed his boot in a pile of gravel, removed his hat and replaced it several times.

'You'd do the navvyin'?' he queried dubiously.

'I would. We could take on a young lad to help. Just think of it, "D and D Coal Merchants" in red and black with a touch of yellow. You know that kind of writing that sort of stands out.'

'Three-dimensional, they call that.' Mr Drew nodded again. He took a few paces then spat on his hands. 'D and D it is. Put it there, young man. By God we'll show them yet.'

If I have to work every hour God sends, thought Kit, I'll show them yet. Occasionally he saw Anna and her husband and child. It looked as if they might settle in the town for good. He still thought about her all the time but deep down, he knew that she would never be his. Yet she was a spur to his ambition. Someday she might look at him and realise what she had missed, with her grand airs and her husband with his head in the clouds. For a brief, malicious moment he thought of how people said that Frank was not the full shilling. All in good time, he thought, he would show them.

* * *

Doctor Bailey buffetted the newspaper into some semblance of its original shape. He had never known a woman who could read a newspaper without dismembering it.

'A curious thing this,' he remarked to Anna, who sat at the other side of the fireplace.

She looked up from her book.

'This League of Nations business. All very fine sentiments of course, but these Japanese are carrying it all a bit too far.'

'How do you mean?'

'Well they're suggesting a formal declaration by all intending members, forbidding any form of discrimination on the grounds of race or nationality. Needless to say, our people are resisting it forcefully.'

178

'Would that not be a good idea?' She put her finger on the page and closed the book over.

'Not in practice. I mean, the empire would fall apart. There are adequate guarantees for the rights of colonies and accountability by the colonial powers.'

'That of course has no bearing on Ireland, has it?' she replied tartly.

'A different case, my dear. Ireland is not a colony. It enjoys all the benefits as part of the United Kingdom.'

'Supposing they don't want that?'

'I don't know,' he sighed, 'you take a very simplistic view. Who would want to leave such a great family of nations to go it alone? Tariffs would bring them to their knees in six months. They will come to realise that, when the present trouble blows over.'

'I don't think it will be as simple as all that,' said Anna dubiously. The wind gusted in the chimney and she picked up the tongs.

'There's a perfect example,' said the doctor, 'your English, or more correctly, Welsh coal. Independence would make Swansea a foreign seaport. Trade would be crippled.'

Anna silently pondered the point. 'Well we'd better make the most of it while we can then,' she smiled, placing a large piece of coal into a cavity where the fire had subsided.

The doctor went back to his paper, muttering something about the Japanese.

The clock chimed in the hallway. It was nearly time for Frank to come home, probably bone weary and even wet to the skin as he so often was. 'Learning the job from the ground upwards', as he always said with enthusiasm, bringing a lot of it home with him too, stamping his boots, leaving great trails of mud on the scullery floor. It was a small price to pay to see him so well and so optimistic about their future. He even spoke about acquiring some land himself, getting someone like 'that splendid chap Bennett' to work for him, making 'a go of things'. She had never thought of Tom Bennett as splendid before, but there you are. She would have to speak to him about the long hours however, or his health would suffer. And it would be wiser too to keep off the roads after dark.

* * *

Comparisons were made with India, where demagogues were influencing the people -- an illiterate rabble by all accounts — to stir up trouble against the imperial government. A stern line had to be taken to prevent the dissolution of the empire. Similarly in Ireland, as isolated incidents of terrorism became more common, the authorities spoke of a campaign of murder against servants of the Crown, with a concomitant heightening of tension and outbreaks of civil strife. A new Government of Ireland Act saw the best solution in splitting the country in two. In the language of the press, the situation was explosive.

'Step into the hall a minute Tom, till I get your money,' called Mr Drew.

Bennett placed the large enamel jug on the floor and took out a pencil. 'Right you are Mr Drew,' he replied. 'Two and two as usual.'

The sizzle of frying eggs came through the open door. Mr Drew emerged from the kitchen with the money and a bundle tightly wrapped in oilcloth. He dropped the bundle quickly into the half-filled jug.

'Two and tuppence Tom,' he said loudly, and added under his breath, 'hold onto that for us Tom. We'll pick it up again.' He offered no explanation and none was needed.

Whether he liked it or not, Tom was an accessory to whatever 'the boys' had in mind. He felt his heart pounding and imagined that every window in the street harboured a spy. This was what Mr Drew had been leading up to for so long. He was caught. He could drive the cart round to the barrack and hand the parcel over to Duffy, but he had no doubt as to what would happen to him if he did. He could hardly pretend that he had lost it. Whatever it contained, and he had a shrewd idea, there was no choice.

Glancing furtively around, he refilled the jug from the churn and stood it on the ledge of the cart. He slapped the reins on the pony's rump and moved on. His perceptions seemed heightened by a feeling of guilt. He could scarcely take his eyes from the jug. Microscopic black midges swam on the surface of the milk, the same lads that get into old musheroons and riddle them with holes. Clara always rejected any that had weevils in them, although Bennett always maintained they'd be well dead when they were cooked. It was always a cause of argument between them that she always seemed to throw away the biggest ones.

He caught a glimpse of black out of the corner of his eye. Duffy as usual. The man seemed to be everywhere. Bennett nodded noncommittally, not anxious to stop for conversation. He fancied that Duffy gave him an odd look and when he stopped at his next customer he glanced back. The sergeant was still there, leaning on his bicycle and apparently observing the trickle of people heading up the street to early Mass. It was a relief to Bennett to turn the corner and escape from that all-seeing eye. Christ, he thought, I'm too old for this game. He could feel the perspiration on his forehead and was glad of the cool breeze when the horse broke into a trot. The milk slopped from the jug and trickled over the floor of the cart. He could see the edge of the bundle and felt himself consumed with a desire to know what was in it. The best place for that would be the shed, in a hole in the wall, where Clara wouldn't find it. There'd be hell to pay if she thought he was mixed up with that class of thing.

His confidence began to return as he left the houses behind him. Women never understand these matters but there comes a time when men must make a stand. He wasn't sure where he had heard that, or what precisely it meant, but it sounded appropriate to the occasion. He began to smile with satisfaction, fabricating a little legend: 'Right under the sergeant's nose, not a bother on him.' He imagined men slapping him on the back and laughing: 'We knew we could count on you Tom.'

He hid the bundle behind some boxes, where bricks had fallen out of the wall. Two sticks of dynamite. He could hardly believe his eyes. That would cause a bit of a stir alright. Best to wrap it up the way it was and say nothing. He stacked the boxes again and made a bit of noise.

'I'll tidy that shed one of the days,' he said to Clara when he went inside, making an elaborate show of dusting himself down. 'I nearly broke me neck in there just now.'

'Oh yes,' she replied off-hand, busy with her own thoughts, 'and put a bit of wire on the window to keep the hens out of it then.'

'Aye. I'll do that. And what's on the menu for today?' The morning air and the excitement had given him an appetite and the Sunday stretched before him like a holiday. He was in rare form. He rubbed his hand vigorously and looked out the window, crouching slightly to see under the lintel. 'There's your man out there again,' he said, 'lookin' at the hay. He's always on the go.'

Clara was pleased to see him so animated. 'You'll be startin' the hay soon I suppose.'

'Aye if this good weather holds.' He laughed. 'Unless your man gets it all done this afternoon, before we get a chance.' He gave her a playful slap on the rump. 'What about somethin' for a hungry man. There's a bit o' kickin' this afternoon. I thought I'd take the lad in to see it.' He sat down at the table. 'Bejasus I'd nearly have a go meself, I feel that good.'

'Will you go 'way out o' that, an old man like you.' She put a plate of stew in front of him. 'Youse men never grow up.'

'That's what keeps me young, girl,' he replied through a mouthful of food. 'You have to have things to do. Remember the way I used to tackle. I'd still be able for it too.'

He chuckled, as if at some private joke and for an instant she caught his eye. There was something there that she had never seen before, something secretive, almost sly, that caused her a vague unease.

*　*　*

'What these fellows have achieved with their de facto government, young lady, is the effective fragmentation of this island.' Colonel Wyndham rustled the newspaper on his knee to emphasise the point.

'You mean partition. Do you really think that would last?'

Anna had come to enjoy their morning walk and the arguments that ensued about the day's news. She was sitting on a bench in front of the house enjoying the heat of the sun.

The old man in the wheelchair was squinting against the light. 'Do you see that line of mountains out there?'

She followed his gaze to the misty blue ridge of the Mournes, almost lost in the haze. 'Yes, I do.' She waited.

'I've been looking at them for most of my life, I suppose. I've seen them so near that you could see the fields on their slopes. I've seen snow on them when there was none any-where else, a beautiful sight. Sometimes, like now, those huge

182

clouds sit on them for weeks on end and we have this hot weather. Anti-cyclonic weather.'

He watched her to make sure that she was following what he said, and she wondered if the bad eye that glared at her so threateningly was by any chance his weather eye. She felt a smile beginning to tug at the corners of her mouth.

'They say around here that the more you see of the Mournes, the worse it's going to be.'

'Are you by any chance speaking metaphorically?' She sometimes adopted his own idioms, playfully letting him know that she would not be done down by rhetoric.

'If you wish, young lady, but there's a breed of people behind those mountains that will prove a thorn in the side to your republicans and my imperial government.'

She waited for him to develop his theme.

'When they make their demands, and believe me, they'll back them up, then we'll have a recipe for civil war on this island. Two conflicting mythologies, two versions of christianity, each conferring the absolute right to kill in the interests of the greater good.'

'Don't tell me you're putting yourself forward as an advocate of gentle Jesus.'

'Don't mock, young woman.' There was an edge to his voice that had not been there before. 'I believe Christianity is an excellent idea, but it takes little account of human nature. Nevertheless it should be given a try sometime.' He gave a dry, grunting laugh at his own cynicism.

'But surely,' she persisted, 'the northerners will have to fall in with whatever your imperial parliament decides. And if they decide on home rule, then that will be the end of it.'

'Ah, but you see, your republicans . . . .'

'I wish you wouldn't say "my republicans".'

'Very well then, the republicans, have driven the other crowd into a corner. They'll defend their heritage of outside privies and triumphant bigotry against Rome, English rulers and Irish scholars, and parish priests with blackthorn sticks, violently, if need be.' He had managed to use phraseology calculated to inflame both sides even further. 'Even a rat will fight when it's cornered.'

The picture he painted was bleak and ominous. If it proved

true there was little hope. She could not let him dismiss every-thing so caustically. 'And where do you fit in? Which side will you support?'

He sat for a while, deep in thought. His eyes wandered over the fields and the woods and the sea beyond. 'Ah, there you have me, I'm afraid. I am a dinosaur, a southern unionist. My kind will be the jetsam of whatever settlement comes about. There aren't enough of us to pose a dilemma. We must face the reckoning of a three-hundred-year-old vendetta.' He looked directly at her. 'I was brought up as a British citizen, an officer and, dare I say it, a gentleman, but my country will dispose of me when the time comes, in the interests of expediency. I can hide behind those mountains or I can wait here till my neighbours burn the roof over my head.'

'Oh for heaven's sake, this isn't the seventeenth century.'

'I know which century it is. They have the machinery now to do what they tried to do in other centuries. Minorities should present no great problems.'

A silence descended between them. Anna closed her eyes and lifted her face to the sun.

'You're sulking now, I suppose.' His voice broke in on her thoughts with almost an anxious tinge.

There was something she ought to say. 'Since you mention outside privies . . . ' She hesitated. Dare she go on?

He looked at her, frowning in puzzlement. 'Yes. Go on.'

'The Bennetts . . . one of your cottages. . . . None of my business really, but it's a bit primitive.' It had to come out.

He was drumming the fingers of his left hand on the arm of the wheelchair. 'Indeed,' was all he said. People treated the old like simpletons, told them how to conduct their affairs. The woman had been born in that cottage and had brought her husband into it without complaining. Everyone knew what was best for everyone else nowadays. He was thinking of a long time ago, of a boy on a pony and a young girl look-ing up at him. He remembered talking about duty and obliga-tions, saying nothing directly. He had sent him away for his own good and had made a fine man of him in the long run. It was all clouded now, as if in a mist, and he could barely recall the pride at seeing him commissioned, or the reason why his bones had been left on some far off hillside. The girl had got a decent man and had thickened into middle age. She was the fortunate one. He had nothing with which to reproach himself. It was so long ago as to be of no importance any more. 'Hmm,' he murmured absently. 'I dare say.' His bladder was troubling him, bringing him back to the more urgent present. 'I'd be obliged,' he began, tugging at the wheels, 'be obliged if you'd assist me indoors.' A bit primitive, she said. Never complained about it before. Let the Land Commission sort it out in their own sweet time.

CHAPTER 16

Kit reined in the horse on the lane above the Wireless Field.
He felt entitled to a smoke. A thrush fluted somewhere in a
whitethorn. The sound always recalled the tangle of bushes
below the railway where they used to go bird nesting. He
recalled the musty smell of the soggy ground where the mill
stream widened just before it entered the culvert under the
railway bridge. That was a long time ago. Thrushes always built
in the thorn there. Their song was like a summons, almost a
challenge, to go clambering in the branches to catch a glimpse
of sky blue eggs held in a little bowl of moss and down.

He exhaled the smoke slowly, thinking about Joey. He was
no longer the little brother. He had filled out into a powerfully
built young man, now in his final year in school, with ideas of
his own. He had the brains. He was destined for university at
least. That would be no problem from the money point of
view. Business was going well, but there was the other matter,
his growing involvement with the Movement. Kit had argued
about it but his brother was adamant. He went his own way
now, no longer tagging along as a disciple. Kit had come to
accept the hopelessness of the argument when he had finally
taxed Joey about getting involved in violence. 'And where the
fuck were you two years ago?' Joey had replied, taking him
by the lapel. 'Don't talk to me about violence.'

It was impossible to explain. For an instant Kit had seen
the dark shape rearing up in the mud and the white blur of a

186

face turned towards him. 'It's not as simple as all that,' was all he could say in reply. With luck, things would not get any worse.

He took the duplicate book out of his pocket and riffled the pages. It was nice to see how it was filling up. The bakery was a good contract to get, a regular customer, summer and winter. Already they had a second dray on the road and were thinking about a motor lorry. With that they could haul road metal for the council and gravel for the building. His partner often laughed at his plans. 'Hould your horses there a minute, Kit. Let's pick one bush clean before we move on. Pick the bush clean.' Even so, Mr Drew was just as excited at the way business was expanding. There was a spring in his step and a bit of divilment, as he would say, in his eye.

Kit watched the blue cigarette smoke dispersing in the still air. There was a soldier lounging beside one of the huts in the field below. They were all over the place nowadays. It was strange to see the familiar khaki and to feel no affinity towards it. It would be better all round if they went back where they came from.

Two men emerged from the other hut, one in waistcoat and shirtsleeves and the other he recognised as Captain Surtees. He had dropped the military title but even in tweed jacket, breeches and gaiters, he had the unmistakable bearing of a soldier. Kit could never think of him as anything but Captain Surtees. He watched quietly, drawing on his fag. Their voices carried to him but not clear enough to make out what they were saying. The smaller man pointed to the aerial, gesticulating as he spoke. Frank was nodding. The soldier had straightened up.

It was ironic thought Kit that he still thought about Anna. He had no doubt that someday he would achieve the eminence he had always wanted in order to approach her and lay his heart at her feet, but he had come to terms with all that. In her eyes no doubt he had gone from butcher's boy to coalman. It was doubtful if she ever gave him a thought. He laughed wryly at the memory of how he had lain in hospital hoping that somehow she might find out and come to his side to nurse him back to health. He remembered how, even lying wounded in the shell-hole, he had thought about her and about how he would go back a hero and she would be there with all his family and friends, even The Skinner Doyle, holding out their arms to greet him. How he had hated that man down there for taking her away. It was embarrassing to think of it now. He knew that Maureen's friends used to laugh at him about it, especially that Kerrigan one, Dolores. She wasn't bad looking either, considering where she came from.

The cigarette burned his fingers. He flicked it away. He wouldn't mind laying his hands on Dolores Kerrigan, even if they were black and shiny with coal dust. Black handprints on her white skin and freshly ironed clothes. That would ruffle her up a bit all right. He wondered why he dwelt on the idea.

'Mup there,' he remarked to the horse, slapping the reins on its rump. The animal reluctantly tore itself away from cropping the weeds of the verge and the wheels crunched on the loose stones.

Captain Surtees was walking around by the old church, obviously on his way home. There was a motorcar parked in the shadows under the dark old trees of the churchyard. Two men approached the captain and spoke to him. Even at a distance Kit could see that there was some sort of argument going on. Eventually however, the captain was persuaded to get into the motorcar. Strange, thought Kit. Motorcars were rare enough. That was not the old motor from Strifeland. He would know that anywhere. He heard the engine starting and the car drove off in the opposite direction from the terrace.

Some other figures approached around the corner at the church. 'Blast it.' It was Maureen and her friends, including no doubt that Kerrigan one. They were bound to meet him at the ford when he let the horse stop for a drink. Maureen always called him Jack Johnson. She thought the coal business was a great joke. She would be laughing on the other side of her face someday.

* * *

'The problem', said Mr Drew, 'is how we interpret the orders.' He spoke with a ponderousness in keeping with the importance of the occasion. 'Am I right Tom?'

Bennett shrugged, saying nothing.

The two men in the cloth caps looked curiously at Bennett. They were young lads from the Fingal Brigade of the Volunteers, or, as they were now styled, the Irish Republican Army. If Drew said he was all right then it must be so, and the wife too. She was sitting by the fire, looking more puzzled than alarmed by the late-night intruders.

Bennett watched the two lads. They seemed very young to be sent on any class of a dangerous job.

'What is there to interpret?' said one of the boys. 'It's all perfectly clear to me. We blow the bridge. That's all there is to it.'

'Now wait a minute, me son,' interpolated Mr Drew. 'I won't be comin' with you, for obvious reasons.' He was not in truth fit for active service, where speed and agility might be required. 'So I want you to be clear on what to do. The correct term is *blow up* the bridge.'

Railway bridges had become a standard target. The Great Northern Railway served the camp at Gormanston but the metal bridge over the Delvin was too heavily guarded, so the smaller bridges had begun to attract the saboteurs. Strifeland bridge was to be the next.

Mr Drew continued. 'A bridge is held up be its own weight fallin' on the keystone.' He dipped his finger in his cup of tea and sketched a diagram on the oilcloth.

Bennett leaned forward, intent on the problem. He could see it now. You blow up the keystone and all the other blocks fall inwards and collapse. The practical mind again. Mr Drew indicated the effect graphically with splayed fingers. Blobs of tea radiated from the arch as the bridge disintegrated.

'I don't know about that,' said one of the boys, shaking his head. He spoke with a confidence beyond his years, as one who had seen danger and had downfaced it. He was not over-awed by Mr Drew's grasp of technicalities. 'If we want to knock a bridge down we put the dynamite on top.'

His companion nodded agreement.

'The question is then,' Mr Drew conceded reasonably, 'does dynamite blow up or blow down?' He frowned, admitting the problem.

Clara watched them covertly. Was this, she wondered, what they meant when they talked about the war. There was an air of unreality about it all, an old man and her good-natured husband and two boys arguing about how to use explosives.

189

Whatever about the two boys, the older men knew precious little about the matter. More disturbingly, she was now party to a secret she never wanted to know, a secret that could prove a threat to her family. On another level, it irked her that Tom had so little to offer in the discussion.

As if he had read her thoughts he piped up: 'Why don't yiz have a look at the dynamite and see if there's any instructions on it. I mean, surely they'd put instructions on it.'

That seemed like a practical suggestion to Clara, with the added advantage that it would remove the discussion to wherever the dynamite was being kept.

'Why not?' agreed Mr Drew. 'Have you got it handy Tom?'

As if in a dream she heard him reply.

'Aye. It's in the shed.'

She felt her pulse pounding with the fright. He pushed the chair back and went outside. They could hear the shed door opening and the sound of boxes being moved against the wall. The scuffling continued for a few minutes and then they heard him returning. He was laughing softly and carrying a package in one hand.

'You won't believe this,' he began, 'but the oul' broody hen was sittin' on the bundle. I had the divil's own job to get her off. She tried to pick the hand off me.'

Mr Drew took the package and unwrapped it. It was warm. They were laughing, the four of them, as Tom exhibited his wounds.

'Don't ever say I didn't fight for Ireland.'

There were no instructions on the greyish yellow sticks so the argument was at a stalemate.

'I still say it blows up,' averred Mr Drew.

'I'll tell you one thing,' volunteered one of the boys, 'it's as well we're goin' to do this job right away. Them sticks are sweatin'. That's very dangerous you know.' He claimed to have dealt with dynamite before, which was probably true as he had been entrusted with the lengths of fuse.

Even Mr Drew was impressed by his superior knowledge.

'Them little drops are nitroglycerin. Very dangerous stuff.'

They peered closely again at the sticks.

'I think,' whispered Mr Drew, 'I think, maybe we ought to remove this stuff outside and hide it in the ditch. I have to

190

get back before anything is done, or I'll be missed.'

They agreed in whispers, afraid to alarm the sticks by any sudden noise. Mr Drew wrapped the dynamite again in the cloth, very gingerly, his teeth tightly clenched.

'Good night Mrs Bennett,' he whispered.

Clara did not reply. Her eyes were rivetted to the bundle, which he held in both hands, almost like an offering.

Tom opened the door and the three men stole outside.

He could not meet his wife's accusing eyes. 'I didn't have a choice,' he muttered lamely. He could not explain what he really meant. What else could any Irishman do when the sides are picked?

'That thing,' she said, and her voice trembled as if with shock, 'has been on the other side of that wall for God knows how long.' She could see the house disintegrating in her mind's eye, bricks and beams expanding outwards amid a cloud of thatch, like Mr Drew's diagram. Her home was being thrown to the wind. The thatch was caught in a gust and was whirling skywards. 'How long was it there?'

He cleared his throat. 'Only since that Sunday we were talkin' about the hay. The day I took Davy to the match,' he added, anxious to please her by his accuracy.

She was aghast. 'You mean there's been a bomb in there the whole summer?' She went to the door and opened it. The night was clear and starry. She stood for a long time, looking at the sky. Her mind was racing. She thought of Davy, dismembered and bleeding and she was overcome by a feeling of helplessness. What could be more important than protecting your own family? What cause was worth the mutilated body of a child? Strangely she felt no alarm on her own behalf. 'What if someone gets killed? Have you thought about that?'

He coughed again and began awkwardly: 'Sure that won't happen. It's only to destroy the bridge. Nobody will get hurt.'

'Supposing the train crashes. People could get killed.'

He was not prepared to accept the possibility. 'Not at all. Sure half the county will hear it and the trains will all be stopped.'

'Maybe you're right. I hope so. How will Mr Drew get home? He'll be in trouble if he's seen on the road.'

'Aw, he'll cut across the fields. Nobody'll see him, don't worry.'

'I'm not worried about him. I just don't want Sergeant Duffy comin' lookin' for you.'

Tom did not reply. He came and stood beside her. They were both wondering about the two young men out there in the darkness. They could see the lights of the big house shining through the trees.

'What's next on your list?' asked Clara, with a hard edge to her voice. 'After you get rid of the soldiers won't you have to start on the gentry? Isn't that what this is all about?'

Tom resented that. He was being accused of attitudes that were foreign to his way of thinking. 'We're not a crowd of bloody Russians,' he replied. Subconsciously he was already identifying himself with the others, the lads, your men. 'There's none of that class of thing.' He felt that he had failed to reassure her, and put his hand on her shoulder.

'Leave me alone,' she said, turning away. 'I'm going to bed.'

She lay awake for hours looking at the dim squares of the window. Sometimes the image receded to a pinpoint of light and sometimes it loomed over her. Gradually she drifted into sleep.

The distant sound of an explosion jolted her into wakefulness. The window rattled in its frame and the house shuddered. Tom had not come to bed. She rose and put her coat around her. It was still dark. She found him sitting in his chair by the ashes of the fire. The room was cold. She knelt beside him and took his hand in hers.

'I don't want you involved in this business,' she said, 'but if you are, I won't let you down.'

'It's not like that,' he replied slowly. 'I don't understand how it started or an'thin', but I've been thinkin' about it. I'm not cut out for a soldier, but if they need help I can't turn away. I wish to God I was a readin' man like Sweeney or in the politics like Mr Drew.' He felt like a man groping in the darkness, looking for the right path, which he knew had to be there somewhere.

'Maybe it'll all blow over fairly soon,' she said, sensing his distress. 'Or blow up or down.' She tried to say it lightly.

'I wouldn't want to hurt a body really. You know that. I

feel sick, I don't mind tellin' you, about the dynamite. I never knew that could happen.'

'I think,' she said, 'you should get some rest. You don't want people to see you all bleary eyed in the morning, as if you'd been up all night.' It was strange, she thought, how quickly the guilty mind adapts to lying and deceit. She was already anticipating the inevitable questions that would be put to them. She could imagine Duffy's slow and deliberate speech, the formal phraseology and the thumb hooking the notebook from the breast pocket.

'Aye,' said her husband. 'You're probably right. I could do with a nap.' He shuffled into the bedroom like an exhausted man and kicked off his boots. He lay down on the bed but sleep eluded him.

Clara climbed the ladder to the attic.

Davy was awake in the low-ceilinged room. He was sitting up peering through the little window. 'Did you hear a noise?' he whispered.

'Yes,' she said. 'It was only thunder. Go back to sleep.'

He yawned and lay down again. 'It gave me a bit of a fright. I hate thunder.'

'Don't worry son. It's a long way off.' She patted his head.

Davy hunched the blankets round himself. 'You'll get cold Ma. You should go back to bed.'

'Aye, I'll do that.' She went down and slipped into the bed beside Tom.

Within minutes she was asleep but the man beside her lay staring at the ceiling until the grey light of dawn showed him every line and mark on the ancient plaster. Quietly he rose and pulled on his boots. War or no war the cows would still have to be milked.

CHAPTER 17

The explosion rattled the windows on The White Rock and the sound echoed around the bay.

Kit sat up suddenly in the darkness. He felt sweat on his forehead. Artillery? The familiar surroundings reassured him. 'What was that?' he said to the dim figure in the other bed.

'Probably one of the railway bridges,' yawned Joey, 'or maybe someone had a go at the barracks.'

'Good God! What do you want to bring trouble on our heads for? The place will be swarming with the military.'

They lay silently, listening to the sounds of the old house.

'Where would you say it was?' asked Joey after a long pause.

'I don't know but at a guess I'd say Strifeland bridge or that direction.'

'Might have been an ambush?' suggested Joey.

'Why ask me,' retorted Kit. 'I thought you were in on all this business. It's a wonder you're not out at night yourself, blowin' up half the country.'

'I just might one of these days,' snapped Joey, offended. 'If I'm ordered to.'

'Oh, that would be great,' Kit said, his voice rising with anger. 'When you've finished drilling with your broomstick. Don't be a bloody fool.'

'Mr Drew says —'

'Mr Drew says. . . . That's all he ever does. You shouldn't put any pass on that old fart.'

'Don't you underestimate Mr Drew. You may not know this, but he is one of the head men around here.' Joey paused for effect. 'Anyway I shouldn't even tell you that much, seeing as how you're not with us.' It was his most telling shot and he intended it to hurt.

'All right, all right,' said Kit after a moment, 'don't start all that again. I just don't want you to get into trouble.'

Again there was a long silence as each lay still, busy with his thoughts.

'Anyway,' said Joey, 'I know you're all right.'

'Thanks a lot,' snorted Kit. 'That's nice to know.'

'Ah, I don't do anything really,' admitted Joey, in a conciliatory tone. 'Maybe pass on the odd message for Mr Drew.'

Kit grunted.

'Like about your man, Jack Straw,' continued Joey, eager now to impress.

'Oh yes. You mean the spy?' Kit laughed in the darkness. This was one of Mr Drew's favourite theories.

'You can laugh all you like, but the lads know all about him. They had him picked up last night.'

'How do you mean?'

'Mr Drew ordered me to deliver his description to an address in Dublin. A squad picked him up last night. We've been watching out for him and a quick telephone call was all that was needed.'

'You mean he's going to be shot?' Kit felt the fear crawling inside him. 'That's murder, Joey, and you'll be involved.' His tongue stuck to the roof of his mouth.

'He'll be court-martialled first,' said Joey airily, but there was a tremble in his voice. 'Anyway, spies know the risk they're taking.'

It was like a nightmare. His brother's voice was unreal. They could not be talking about a man's life. 'Don't you realise what's going on? Where will they hide him? There's nowhere around here. Jesus you'll all be found out.'

Again there was a long silence.

'We haven't got him.' Joey spoke deliberately, trying to steady his voice. The Movement was no place for men who cracked under pressure. 'A Dublin squad is holding him until they decide what to do with him.'

'So it's all right then, so long as somebody else shoots him. Is that it? You're all gone mad.'

There was no answer.

'Were you anywhere around when they picked him up? Is there any way that you can be connected with it?'

'No, not at all,' drawled Joey, sounding less concerned than he felt. 'They just stuffed him into a motorcar and took him off to Dublin.

'Last night?'

'Sometime yesterday evening. He was in town all day, snooping around.'

A chill realisation dawned on Kit. They had the wrong man. It was Captain Frank Surtees who was probably lying bound and gagged in some tenement room or perhaps already face down in a ditch with the back of his head blown away. Kit sat up and swung his feet to the floor. He put his head in his hands. 'Jesus Christ,' he whispered, envisaging the scene. A fierce surge of elation overcame him. It was not his responsibility. Someone else would do what he had wanted to do himself. Now she would need him at last. She would be helpless and alone. It would make up for all the hurt and the loneliness. She would learn to love him as he always had loved her.

No, she would not. She would return to her own kind and he would never see her again. She would hate everything connected with this country and the people who handed her inoffensive husband over to be murdered. The crime would be justified, excused or perhaps dismissed as a tragic mistake. Say nothing, a voice whispered in his brain. He hesitated, remembering the pain. It was like touching an old scar, or fingering a bruise.

Old soldiers, he thought, comrades in arms. He remembered that misty morning in March. When was it? A lifetime ago, when they sat together on the ammunition cases. There was a photograph, a blurred sepia image. The photographer's hand had trembled. He could imagine the old doctor cupping his hand around the viewfinder of his box camera. Everybody did it, part of the mystique of photography.

He could see the photograph clearly in his mind's eye, even clearer, he realised, than he could see Anna herself, whom he saw frequently around the town. It was as if he himself had

196

carried her image with him for years, not noticing that it had become dog-eared and creased, still seeing it as it had first appeared to him. With a shock he realised that he did not love the wife of Captain Surtees at all. He loved a young girl who no longer existed, an image to which he had been faithful for years, a picture that has sustained him when everything else had seemed bleak and hopeless. It was not the fear of mortal sin and imminent death that had kept him from the whores of Warminster, when the new recruits were let loose for the evening. It was a pure, burning devotion to this girl who barely knew that he existed. Now she would never know how much she had meant to him.

'Maybe it is too late,' the voice whispered again. 'You have a second chance. Take your time.' He had accepted a cigarette, that morning on the outskirts of Abbey Wood. They had shared in the exhaustion and anti-climax of a victory. They had seen the tide turn together and the beginnings of disintegration in the enemy. What was it the corporal had shouted? 'Get a move on. Yiz are like a seragly of oul' ones.' He rubbed a hand over his face wearily and reached for his breeches.

'Come on Joey,' he said, 'you have the wrong man. We'd better go and see what can be done about it.'

Joey was aghast.

'He does fit the description though,' he said lamely after his brother had explained.

'Get your boots on quick. We'll have to find Mr Drew. I hope to God we're not too late.'

A ragged line of cloud scudded along the eastern horizon where the dawn was just beginning to show. The streets were deserted. Josie Brett's old dog barked at the sound of their footsteps.

An upstairs window opened as they pounded on the doorknocker.

'Name o' Jaysus, don't wake up the whole barony,' whispered Mr Drew, looking furtively up and down the street.

They heard his boots clattering on the stairs and he was still hooking his braces over his shoulders as he opened the door just enough to let them slip inside.

* * *

197

The constable rubbed a hand across his face, conscious of the stubble. He never felt right until he had a shave in the morning. 'Let you not distress yourself, young lady,' he said. 'I dare say Sergeant Duffy will have some word for you when he returns. There's been some disturbance out that direction during the night.' He did not wish to elaborate. The young woman was agitated enough as it was.

Anna looked around the bare day-room. She twisted a handkerchief in her fingers. Her eyes were red with lack of sleep. She knew that something terrible had happened. She had heard the distant explosion as she sat waiting in the darkness. With a terrible certainty she felt that it was connected to Frank's absence. She had dressed immediately and made her way to the barracks, relieved to see that there was a lamp already lighting in the room downstairs.

'Perhaps you'd be partial to a cup of tea, ma'am,' suggested the constable gently. He would have welcomed the activity.

'Oh, no thank you. I wouldn't want to put you to any trouble.'

'Sure, it's no trouble. Wasn't I thinking of having one myself?'

He disappeared into a room at the back and she could hear him poking the range. Anna paced to the window. The sky was lightening. The glow from the oil lamp looked weak and yellow but it kept the chill from the air. A map of the district showed the townlands in different colours, where someone had improved on the Ordnance Survey, for convenience sake. Her eyes wandered over the strange-sounding names, The Salmon, with not even a stream, Strifeland, Ballaghstown, where no town ever was. Her attention was drawn to the sound of the sergeant's bicycle rattling against the wall outside. The room darkened as he stepped inside, stooping slightly in the doorway.

'Oh good morning ma'am,' he said in some surprise as he removed his cap. 'And what can I do for you?'

Suddenly Anna felt foolish. There was nothing in the sergeant's manner to suggest that he had any bad news about Frank. 'It's just that my husband,' she began awkwardly stumbling over the words. 'It's just that there was some trouble and my husband didn't come home last night.'

198

'Ah,' said the sergeant slowly, 'I see.' He drummed his fingers on the desk. 'Well, as to the disturbance, you may set your mind at rest. There was precious little harm done. Nobody hurt at all, thanks be to God.'

The constable appeared with the tea. 'You'll be having a drop then, Sergeant?' He disappeared again.

'Your husband was nowhere in the vicinity, I'm pretty sure. The house is empty of course, now that the old man has gone into that home in Dublin.'

Anna put the tea untouched on the table. 'Well, where is he then?' she said miserably.

'There now,' said the sergeant gently, 'there did many a man take a vagary now and again. He wouldn't be given to the occasional drink, I suppose?' It was the most common explanation in such cases.

'Indeed not,' she replied shortly, offended by the implication.

'Good, good,' he said gently, thinking that the English could never do anything normal. It would be so much easier if he could enquire around the pubs and track the man to wherever he had taken refuge, after a bit of a bender, postponing the evil hour when he would have to face the consequences. He was an odd young man though, a bit airy, people said. Maybe it was shell-shock or something like that. 'I will make enquiries and let you know what transpires. In the meantime you should go on home. It may well be that he'll be there before you.'

'Thank you, Sergeant Duffy,' she said not really convinced. 'I should be most obliged if you would let me know.'

He watched her closing the garden gate behind her and felt a depression coming over him. It was part of the job to reassure people even when he was not so certain. There were strange goings-on on the roads, especially at night. It ill-behoved a man to be stravaging in these troubled times. He cupped his hands around the untouched mug of tea. It was still hot.

The constable reappeared, buttoning his high collar. There was a small patch of newspaper covering a nick on his cheek, evidence of a hasty shave. 'What way did you find things beyond, Sergeant?' he asked without preamble.

'Somebody had a go at the railway bridge at Strifeland.

Not a very professional job in my opinion. They managed to dislodge a rail and a couple of sleepers.' He reached for a pen and rubbed the back of the nib on the blotter. 'I'd better enter it in the book straightaway.' He dipped the pen and wrote carefully. 'Nothing happening here, I suppose while I was away?'

'Just the young lady, of course, and one or two people moving about, old Drew and the young Donovan lads. He's a terror to work, that young chap. He'll own half the town some day.'

'Hmm,' said Duffy thoughtfully, chewing the handle of the pen, which showed evidence of similar attacks before. 'Hmm,' he mused again, and resumed writing.

'I'll take a turn around,' volunteered the constable. 'It might be that I could get word of that young gentleman.'

'Aye, do that,' said Duffy, half listening. Something was not quite right about Drew and the two lads abroad at such an early hour. It would be no harm, he resolved, to have a word in that quarter before very long. There was no great harm done and, if they were involved in any way, a bit of a fright might keep them out of trouble. Carefully he blotted the entry in the book and replaced the pen. No rest for the wicked, he thought ruefully, and stretched luxuriously. The tea had gone cold, with an oily brown scum on top. He shoved it aside with distaste.

* * *

'Footing turf,' said the man to himself, 'the worst job God made.' He cursed aloud as he straightened his back.

He was a small dark-skinned man with a drooping black moustache. Working alone on the mountain often made a man talk to himself. Sometimes it was the only intelligent conversation a man got. He groaned and looked about him. The low evening sun picked out the white bog-cotton and the deep purple heather flowers. Millions of long spider webs covered the bog, gleaming like silver threads in the light. He gazed at the beauty of the scene, woolgathering, enjoying the rest. Shadows of cloud flitted, dark green on light, over the slope of Glenasmole. There was not another sinner to be seen on the whole mountain.

Reluctantly he crouched again to the task. The turf was still wet where it lay, but he had to get it up off the bog or his labour would be lost. It would bend under its own weight but with luck it would dry before the autumn rains could wash it back into the ground. Patiently he built and roofed the pyramids. The breeze was cold but it would suffice.

A movement flickered in the corner of his eye. He squinted into the sun. There was a motor coming along one of the rutted bog tracks, an unusual sight. With a sense of premonition he stooped lower. It was stopping at the junction with the paved road. Two men alighted, one with his hands raised. Even at the distance of a hundred yards or so, the watcher heard the click of the hammer over the idling engine. The man with his hands raised stepped three paces forward. The turfcutter clenched his teeth, waiting for the report. Oh God, he thought, if they see me I'm done for. Surely they could not avoid seeing him, probably silhouetted against the horizon. It was too late to run.

The second man stepped smartly backwards to the car, holding what was obviously a gun in one hand. He said something to the other man then opened the door with his free hand. The engine roared as the door slammed. The car threw up a cloud of dust as it raced away in the direction of the city. The man stood where he was for at least a minute then he appeared to be removing a blindfold. He looked about him, rubbing at his wrists and flexing his knees.

The turfcutter took up his slean and held it across his chest, just on the offchance. He felt his bowels churning with the fright. The man had spotted him and was approaching. He gripped the handle tightly and waited.

'Hello there,' called the man. He was blinking as if he had been kept in darkness for a long time.

The turfcutter watched him as he clambered over a cutting, sheer and smooth, seven-spit deep, with a trickle of black water at the bottom.

'Hello,' called the man again, 'can you give me some idea as to where I am?'

'By Jesus,' said the turfcutter, 'I thought you was a goner that time.' Reluctantly he bent and gave the man a hand up onto the bank, still keeping the blade well in view.

'So did I,' replied the newcomer, 'though for the life of me I don't know what it was all about. What did you see anyway?'

'Nothin', nothin'.' The man shook his head vigorously. 'It was too far away. I'm getting very lampy.' He blinked furiously by way of explanation.

'Our friends said something about new orders coming down from brigade. Brigands more likely. Still I can't complain.' He smiled wearily. 'I'm rather anxious to get home though, if you would be good enough to point me in the right direction.'

'Aye, me ould son.' A common danger had created a kind of affinity. 'In fact I'll go one better. I'll lend you me oul' bicycle. I dare say there's them as would want to hear from you.' He was not anxious to know too much and was prepared to risk the bicycle and even more, to sacrifice the pleasure of the long downhill trip home with the mountains spinning around him. He hauled the machine out from behind the bank. 'It's a bit of a push to the top of the hill but you can free-wheel the five miles into Rathfarnham, no bother. Leave the oul' bike with the peelers and tell them I gave you a lend of it.'

Frank shook hands with him and lugged the bicycle over to the road. He swung his leg over the saddle and was on his way. The man watched him dwindle into the distance.

'Frightened the shite out of me,' he said aloud, as if rehearsing his account. Suddenly he felt an urgent need to relieve himself. He clambered down into a cutting and dropped his braces.

* * *

Clara looked out the window in puzzlement. There was a lorry lurching across the field, coming towards the cottage. She could make out the familiar figure of Mr Drew behind the wheel. He was grinning like a boy with a new toy. There was another man with him and the back of the lorry was piled high with piping and tools.

'There y'are Mrs Bennett,' he greeted her. 'What do you think of her, eh?' He slapped the lorry with a proprietorial air. 'It's a far cry from the oul' handcart.' He was in jovial mood.

'Is it your own Mr Drew?' Clara was impressed.

'She is an'all. And won't I be needin' it with the magnitude of the contracts I'm handlin' nowadays.'

'Do you tell me so?' He was obviously keen to give her the details so she obliged by affording him an opening.

'Aye. And the first one is for the colonel himself regardin' this very premises.'

She felt a twinge of fear at the words. They seemed to augur some abrupt change.

'There's nothin' to worry about Mrs Bennett,' said Mr Drew, noticing her surprise. 'It's just a matter of a bit o' plumbin' himself directed me to look after.'

'I don't know what you mean.' She sensed an intrusion.

'The way it is, I have orders to sink a well here and install a septic tank over beyond.' He indicated the extent of the job with a sweep of his hand. 'Then he tells me to install a sink and basin and ah, other accoutrements,' he phrased it discreetly, 'on these premises, if you have no objection.'

She began to understand. The estate was going to be taken over by the government. Everybody said so, and a house with modern conveniences would command a better price on the market. All her ancient bitterness towards the old man came back. He always did things his own way. She began to wonder where they would go when Tom's job was gone and their home was sold over their heads. 'I don't suppose I have any choice, have I?'

'I suppose not. Him that pays the piper and all that.'

The other man had begun to unload the lorry, swinging the lengths of piping down and stacking them in pyramids. Mr Drew joined him and they discussed the details as they worked. They agreed that it would take a fair amount of pumping to raise the water from the well to a storage tank but the tank could be augmented by rainwater, cunningly directed by chutes. They argued at length about the head. Mr Drew inevitably had answers to all objections and solutions for all difficulties. He expatiated on microbes, which could be eliminated by boiling the water, and aquifers from whence a never ending supply could be drawn, provided the well was competently sunk.

'You'll be the envy of half the barony, Mrs Bennett,' he assured her, 'what with runnin' water and indoor plumbin'.'

He tapped the piece of plumbing in question and raised and lowered the seat by way of demonstrating its versatility not only as a convenience but also as a fine piece of furniture in its own right.

'And how is the colonel?' Clara felt obliged to ask out of decency. 'We haven't heard anything since he went away.'

''Deed an' he's not a well man at all, at all,' said Mr Drew with a suitable sympathetic tone. 'But sure, he's well looked after up there in Dublin. Another winter up yonder would have finished him off altogether.' How Mr Drew deduced all this from the brief note from the colonel's solicitors must remain a mystery. 'Anyway he's better off out of harm's way.'

He had a point, with the country in a state of confusion and parts of it too dangerous for the government agencies to show their faces. Even with the reinforcements, which had already acquired a reputation for ferocity, the rebel army, as it was now openly recognised, held large areas of the south, where the king's writ no longer ran.

'What about Captain Surtees, the manager like? What does he say about all this?' She indicated the piping.

'Ah he just says to me to go ahead. "It appears that you are the man to fix things around here," he says to me.' Mr Drew gave a sly chuckle. ' "I'll leave things in your capable hands," he says. True for him, too.' His eyes twinkled at some private joke.

Davy came trudging towards them across the field. There was obviously something bothering him although he looked with interest at the lorry.

'What's up, son?' asked Mr Drew. 'You look as if you found a penny and lost tuppence.'

'Ah nothin',' replied the boy, hanging his head.

'What is it, child?' said his mother gently. 'You weren't in trouble in school again I hope. It would be a bad way to start the new year.'

'No, no,' mumbled the boy. 'It's just that one of the soldiers gave me a belt in the ear.'

'Who did?' asked his mother in alarm.

'One of the soldiers over at the barn. He told me to get to hell out of it. They've knocked some of the patches off it. Wait till da hears about it.'

'What class of soldiers are they son?' asked Mr Drew quietly. 'Was there anything strange about them?'

Davy frowned. 'They were dressed sort of different, a bit like policemen.'

Mr Drew sucked a breath in through his teeth. 'Be the hokies,' he muttered, 'I don't like the sound of them. Them's the Black and Tans by the sound of it.' He took the boy by the shoulders. 'Steer well clear of them lads, Davy me son. They're a bad lot.'

'Are they as bad as people say, Mr Drew?' asked Clara.

'Well,' said the builder thoughtfully, 'takin' the long view, you might say we've already won if they have to resort to this kind of carry on. Counter-terrorism they call it, but it's a poor day when a government has to employ murderers to enforce the law. By the way,' he paused and looked at the boy, 'did you have a look at me new lurry? Climb aboard there and see what you think of her.'

Davy grinned, his injury temporarily forgotten, and hopped up into the cab. The other man moved aside to let him try the steering wheel.

'It's about Tom,' said Mr Drew quietly. 'Now there's no need to be alarmed. We need a few men of his standing to give weight to the new institutions, like the courts and that.' He waved a hand to indicate the scope of the new institutions.

'But Tom doesn't know anything about the law,' said Clara.

'Ah, that's not the problem now. We need men who are respected, not the young hotheads. Men who can serve a summons and have people take it seriously! Kind of special constables if you like. Otherwise the Sinn Fein courts won't work. You can't have flyin' squads enforcin' the civil law now can you?'

'I suppose not,' she admitted, not too sure at all about the distinction. 'I just don't want him to get himself into any trouble.'

'Now don't worry on that score. It's not like active service. Tom has a good head on his shoulders. Everyone has a job to do at a time like this.' He tugged at his moustache. 'All the same,' he went on, 'don't say anything to him about Davy gettin' a belt in the ear. There's others will take care of the Tans, in due course.' He tapped a length of piping with his toe. 'Aye, all in due course.'

'I'm afraid at times that things are going to get much worse

205

before they get any better.' Clara wondered if she would even be there to see the improvement. If the farm went and the house with it they would have to go somewhere else, even to England. It was as if a cloud had darkened the sun. She shivered. There was a definite touch of autumn in the air. 'I'd better let you get on with your work,' she said and left him to his unloading.

There was a box of coal in the corner beside the fire, real coal from D and D. Tom would not allow her to pick coke any more. There was a lot to be said for modern conveniences, she admitted as she added some lumps to the fire. Maybe as you get older you will pay to have things the easy way. What used to be a point of pride became merely an irksome task to be avoided if possible. She poked the fire and pulled the kettle across.

CHAPTER 18

Sergeant Duffy was in a benign mood. Considering the amount of trouble in other parts of the country and the proximity of Gormanston camp with its army of Auxiliaries and Tans, it was surprising that his area was so free of trouble. He was even inclined to be indulgent towards Tom Bennett, although the man persistently trailed his coat, trying to get himself into trouble.

'You know what you need, Tom?' he began, hiding a sly smile.

Bennett turned suddenly, looking alarmed. He had been peering in through the window of the bar, trying to see over the ornate Jameson mirror that hid the occupants from the curious gaze of passers by.

A pub is a place where a man is entitled to some privacy to commune with his fellows or enjoy a contemplative jar. There was little fear of discovery through the grimy window of that particular premises. The fitful oil lamp illumined the faces of the patrons, in colours worthy of Rembrandt, as they gazed into their porter. There was a desultory argument in progress with one voice predominating.

'What was that, Sergeant? I didn't catch that remark.' Bennett was polite but wary.

'I was just thinkin' Tom, that you should get yourself a good bicycle. Now, I'd recommend a Rudge. That's a powerful machine.'

'Well now, that's not a bad idea. But why, particularly, do you think I need a bicycle? I'm well used to shanks' mare.'

'Now Tom,' Duffy continued in his deliberate way, 'you can't be a policeman without you have a means of conveyance.' He chuckled to himself.

'I don't know what you're talkin' about.' Bennett was glad of the darkness that concealed his expression of surprise.

'Tom, Tom, I'm not a fool.' Few would have disagreed with him. 'I know what you're up to, you and Master Sweeney and old Drew. I don't mind if you call yourselves the alternative police. I don't mind even if the master calls himself a judge, if it keeps a few hotheads out of harm's way. It might even make my job easier,' he conceded generously, 'but if you're to be a constable, even a Sinn Fein constable, the least you could do is get yourself a decent bicycle.' He laughed throatily at his own wit.

Bennett saw that the game was up. 'I'm lendin' a hand. That's all. It's no business of yours.' Somewhere within him he felt a surge of indignation that surprised him. He saw himself with sudden clarity as an arm of the legitimate power. Not for the first time he cursed his inarticulateness. 'Things is changin' Sergeant,' was the best that he could manage.

'That's as may be, but the law is still the law and if I ever find you or any of your lads with firearms, I'll have to proceed according to the law. Take that as a piece of friendly advice.' He turned as if to go, then hesitated. 'I don't make the laws Tom, as I've said before, and it's not for me to comment on them that do, but until they come up with a better one I have my job to do.'

'Aye. That's how it is, but we all have to do what we think is right, eh, Sergeant? We mightn't always like what we have to do.'

'That's true enough, Tom, but without the law it's a jungle. Listen,' he added after a moment's thought, 'there's an old bike out the back of the barracks. You're welcome to it. It's a bit of a high-nelly, and it needs new tyres, but it will get you around.'

Bennett laughed. 'I might be interested, at that, though I don't know what me superiors might think.' It struck him that he would have liked to ask Duffy's advice on a few points, but it would have been incongruous.

He wondered if Duffy was laughing at him, but there was a vein of stubbornness that prevented him from explaining himself. After all, Duffy was supposed to be the enemy, an agent of the Crown. It was all a bit confusing. Duffy sorted badly with his picture of the terror squads and arsonists in the Crossley tenders, the sweepings of England's jails, as the people called them.

There was a case of cattle maiming at Killalane to be investigated. They had opted for the Sinn Fein court and the acerbic justice of Master Sweeney. He would have to go out there to serve summonses. It was a long trek. 'I'll take you up on that offer, Sergeant,' he said suddenly. They were, in a way, comrades in arms. I must be mad, he thought, lettin' meself in for all this bother. Was Clara right when she said that he hadn't the courage to refuse? He shrugged at the thought. You couldn't always leave things to other people.

'Right so, I'll root it out for ye.' It would be no harm, Duffy reflected, to keep in touch with Tom. He'd be a safer man to deal with than the wilder young fellows or the implacable and relentless old men, the men of theories and of visions. His benign mood had passed. He felt uncertain and worried at the thought of wild men. 'We have to spare the old feet in this game. And by the way, I can give ye a pointer or two on that hamstring business, if ye have to look into it.' He made the offer diffidently.

Bennett laughed. 'By God, Sergeant, but we'd make a brave team, yourself and meself.'

Duffy clicked on his bicycle lamp. 'We'll see Tom, we'll see,' he remarked.

The Skinner tilted the stool backwards and regarded his pint. The dowels creaked under his weight. He had a good few in him and his mood fluctuated between joviality and truculence, as was his nature. Kit wished he would just shut up or go away. The Skinner had an opinion on everything.

'Hunger-strike! I'm tellin' yiz. The hunger-strike will be the beatin' of them. If your man dies . . .' He took a long swig from the pint and his jowls trembled. 'If your man dies . . . .'

'You'd know a fair bit about hunger-strikes,' said Kit, but

the irony was lost.

'Lookit. What I'm tryin' to tell yiz,' he glared around at the lamplit faces, looking for support.

'What you're sayin' Ned, is if McSwiney dies it'll stir things up so bad the British will have to give in because of world opinion. The Yanks won't wear it. Right?' Kit thought he could bring the discussion to a speedy conclusion.

'That's right.' The Skinner nodded.

'So you want the poor bollix to die. Right? So you can settle back in comfort.'

'That's not what I said,' snarled Skinner. 'You can always twist things around. Always the clever man to twist things around your way.'

Kit made no reply. The drink was not agreeing with him. Neither was the company. The other patrons were content to let the two of them argue it out.

Skinner lapsed into morose silence. Presently his mood brightened. 'How's business this weather, anyway?'

'All right.'

'Often thought about the coal business myself. Good money in it.'

'That a fact?'

Skinner looked at him suspiciously. Donovan never gave much away even when he had drink taken. He could prod away with questions, manoeuvring an opponent but he never let himself go. 'I'll probably stick with the butchering though. Set up on me own one of these days.' There was another way to get at Donovan.

'What would Mr Fedigan think of that?'

Skinner looked slyly at the other men at the bar. 'Ah sure, he has his mind on other matters. Gettin' to be a great dandy nowadays, a real Mickey Dazzler.' The men grinned in anticipation. Something in Kit's expression warned Skinner that he had taken the wrong tack. 'I'm thinkin' about it though,' he repeated, and let the subject drop.

'You do that, Ned,' said Kit unsmiling.

Silence descended again. The curate worked his way along, lifting glasses and wiping the rings of porter off the stained mahogany.

Skinner laughed. 'That was a good one about your man.'

'Your man?'

'Yeh. The English fella. I'd say it frightened the shite out of him.'

'What was that?' asked a prompter from further down the bar.

'Did ye not hear about it?' Skinner guffawed and the questioner shrank in shame. 'He was kidnapped for an informer, it seems, but they let him go. Had him up again' the wall when orders came through to let him go. They got the wrong man, it seems.' He drank again and wiped his mouth. 'Seems like a lot of bother about a fuckin' Englishman. Could have shot the huer for all the differ it would make.'

'Aw Jays, no. He's a harmless poor divil,' protested the other speaker.

'All the fuckin' same. Isn't that right. Once a redcoat, always a redcoat eh Kit?' Kit made no reply. Through a haze of alcohol Skinner saw the logic of it. Donovan was an ex-soldier too. Took the shillin', a shillin', 'Fourpence-worth of scraps and she'll send you the shillin' on Monday'. He caught Kit's eye and in a flash of inspiration knew he had him at last. 'Of course it might've suited yourself if he was done in, mightn't it? You could be sniffin' around a fine young widda-woman.'

He reached for his glass in triumph but his hand never reached it. Porter splashed in his face and the glass shattered against the wall. The stool splintered as he was borne backwards under the onslaught and Kit was upon him, pummelling furiously. Skinner caught a glimpse of his attacker's face contorted with rage and he began to fight back desperately. Tables overturned as they rolled together on the tiled floor and men swore as glasses and bottles smashed to the ground. Skinner rolled over and struggled to his feet, swung a wild roundhouse at Kit and his fist hit bone. A searing pain shot through Kit's nose, he tasted blood and staggered back, his nose spread to one side and rapidly swelling. Spittle sprayed from Kit's lips as he gathered himself for another attack. Skinner looked around for a weapon.

There was a roar as the door burst open and Kit was lifted bodily against the wall. Tom Bennett had him by the lapels and was threatening to bang his head against the plasterwork if he tried to resist. The warning was unnecessary. The sudden surge of adrenalin had passed and Kit sagged, exhausted and panting. Blood streamed from his nose. Duffy had Skinner by the arm and was squeezing and twisting until the bottle fell from his grasp. As quickly as it had started it was over.

'That's enough of that,' Duffy said grimly. 'Let ye both come along with me now.'

Outside on the pavement again, he looked at Kit, who was gingerly feeling his nose and wiping the blood from his face. Skinner looked similarly crestfallen. 'Young buckoes that can't hold their drink. Maybe we should bang their heads together, Tom, and send them home.'

'Aye,' growled Bennett, 'bloody disgraceful.' He shook Kit again by the lapel, but not too roughly. 'You'd better get that nose seen to.'

'That was a mighty blow,' said the sergeant, examining Kit's injury. He turned to Doyle. 'You have no need to be using weapons if you can strike a blow like that.'

Skinner hung his head, ashamed, but pleased by the compliment. He was still panting for breath and his heart pounded.

'Let ye shake hands now and that'll be an end of it. I dare say there was a measure of right on both sides.'

Kit hesitated and extended his hand.

Skinner hung his head and mumbled, 'Maybe me mouth ran away with me.' He winced as they shook hands.

The curate emerged with his dishcloth, the symbol of his office. 'Yiz'll have to pay for the damage,' he shrilled.

'That's fair enough,' nodded Bennett. 'Will there be any charges, Sergeant?'

'I don't think so,' said Duffy. 'It would be more of a disagreement between two gentlemen.'

'And yiz are both barred,' added the curate, flapping his cloth dismissively, reasserting his authority.

Skinner felt the porter rising in his gullet. Hastily he took himself round the corner into Barter Street, from whence came the sounds of repentance as he gawked elaborately into the gutter.

'A sadder and a wiser man in the morning, Tom,' said Duffy. 'And you get yourself off home, young man, and keep out of trouble, or you'll be hearing from me.'

Kit grunted. His face throbbed with pain, but worse than

that was the knowledge that Skinner had touched a nerve, a hidden vein of guilt that he had not wanted to admit, even to himself. He turned away and started up Church Street, holding a blood-stained handkerchief to his face. He got the taste of porter mingling with the blood and sat down on a low window-sill to recover. He felt alone and sorry for himself. Maybe Skinner was right. He was a low conniving creature, whose sole thought in life was huckstering, making a few bob. He tilted his head back to stop the blood that still trickled from his nose. Jack Johnson would have taken it in his stride. The stars glinted down at him in the immense silence.

Dolores Kerrigan heard voices in the hallway and the sound of the front door opening. That would be Captain McNaughten on his way home. When he was ashore he always came around in the evening for a read of the paper and a chat. It was something that was accepted as natural, an old man, of indeterminate relationship with the Kerrigan family, who occupied an armchair on one side of the fireplace at regular intervals throughout the year. He had been there as long as she could remember, probably with the same jokes and the same remarks on how big they were all getting and how they resembled various uncles and aunts, as if nobody existed in their own right but merely as a sprig on some vast and rambling family tree. 'Good girsha,' he always remarked when she brought him his tea. 'Your granny will never be dead while you're alive.'

And presumably, as well as home-cooked meals, he was the main beneficiary of the Rosary trimmings when they prayed for all those at sea.

Captain McNaughten was timeless. He had always been the same age, with tendons standing out in his neck and a maze of little purple veins in his nose. When she was young she had imagined that there were spiders living in his nose. The black hairs that protruded were their legs, as they tried to brace themselves like old-time chimney sweeps so as not to fall out. She used to imagine him sneezing, perhaps in a storm, and all the little spiders flying with the wind.

Sometimes, on very special occasions they used the good tea service that he had brought back from Japan when he was

213

on the big clipper ships. Each time it appeared the story was told again of how the potter had packed each delicate piece in straw and paper and then thrown the lot down the stairs to prove that they would not be broken on a sea voyage. Then he unpacked the lot and, would you believe it, not a thing was broken. The tea service had an enhanced value because of its precarious origins.

Captain McNaughten had fought polar bears in the Arctic when he went to the Klondike. In fact he had run out of musket balls. The little Kerrigans had sat spellbound to see if he had escaped alive. Nobody could escape from polar bears if the gun was empty. 'Didn't I think of me old mother, that I'd never see again, and all me old friends,' which seemed a reasonable reaction in the circumstances. He would look around at the rapt and expectant faces. 'And didn't I start to cry out loud.' His voice would rise as the climax approached. 'And the tears rolled down me face and fell on the snow and froze. And what did I do then?' The older ones smiled, knowing the secret, until one of the younger listeners took the prompt. 'That's right. I put them into me old musket and shot all the polar bears. And that's how I'm here today to tell yiz all about it.' The denouement was greeted with varying degrees of laughter and incredulity, depending on the ages of the listeners.

But Dolores was too old for such stories any more. She wanted her own excitement. In the Dublin office the other women, girls they called themselves, were far advanced in years; and the men, most of them in their late forties, were too old to interest her, so she rejected contemptuously their cumbersome and frowzy compliments. The girls on the shop floor seemed to have more fun in life, even if they were regarded as quite common. Sometimes she envied them as she looked down from the office and toyed with the idea of striking up an acquaintance by means of messages sent pneumatically in the little brass money cylinders. She could have been a sales assistant if her parents had let her, but she was a cashier, living high above the others in her little glass office, sending money and receipts whizzing through the pipes to all parts of the shop. It was not fair, she complained, to no one in particular, especially as she spent a fair amount of her spare time behind the counter in their own shop, or weighing out goods in the storeroom at the back.

She liked the storeroom, of course, and its rich variety of smells. It was part of her earliest memories, the smell of tea and meal and the sweet taste of sultanas or demerera sugar. The brown sugar crawled and subsided in the bags as she filled them with the little scoop. She could never resist licking her finger and dipping it in the sugar.

Captain McNaughten had been, he claimed, in Demerera. He had a bone-handled knife which he swore, had been used in an attempt on his life. 'There's a long story attached to that knife,' he would say as he cut his tobacco. 'I got that in Demerara.' She asked him once: 'What's the long story?' He had looked puzzled for a moment. 'Well a fella tried to kill me with it. That's the long story.' There was a faraway look in his eyes. 'Oh,' she said, disappointed. 'Is that all?' He continued cutting the plug. 'He won't be needin' it any more. That's where the sugar comes from.'

She dipped her finger again and licked the sugar slowly, feeling guilty like a small child.

The front door closed.

'Are you nearly finished in there, Dolores?' her father called from the hallway.

'In a minute,' she replied, and began to fold the bags closed, her long fingers working automatically, gathering the edges in and making a neat triangle in the middle. She sighed at the routine.

'Bolt up before you go to bed.' She heard his step on the stairs.

'Yes, Daddy,' she answered.

Labels, gold with black lettering, gleamed on the mahogany drawers along one wall, relics of former times, strange alchemical terms — bismuth, aloes, manna. That was a disappointment. When she first heard of the Israelites in the desert she was prompted to look in that drawer, to see the glistening food that fell from heaven. There was nothing in it but balls of string. Life, it seemed, was rather like that. She had expected a job in Dublin to lead to independence and adventure. The most exciting thing so far was watching the chief cashier taking snuff, spilling half of it down his waistcoat and sneezing mightily into a none-too-clean handkerchief.

She put down the scoop and went through the hall to the

front door. She heard her father's boots hitting the floor and the creak of the bed-springs. She opened the door and stood for a moment, enjoying the fresh night breeze. The street was in darkness, except for a gleam of light from the doorway of the pub, where some people were engaged in conversation.

She leaned back against the door-jam and looked upwards. She could see the Pleiades. The old sea-captain had told her about them, the Seven Sisters, and the Plough, the most important of all because if you could see the Plough you always knew where you were. It seemed far-fetched, to say the least, that a light millions of miles away could . . . She started suddenly. A figure moved in the darkness almost beside her. She put a hand to her mouth, stifling a cry.

'Ssh,' said a voice. 'Don't be afraid. It's only me.'

It was Kit Donovan. He sounded as if he had a bad cold. 'Were you sitting there, watching me?' she challenged in a whisper. She could feel herself blushing, although she had done nothing wrong.

'I can hardly see you in this light,' he sniffed.

She was disappointed. She had imagined that she was looking pale and interesting in the starlight. She peered at him closely. 'What happened to your face?' she asked in alarm. 'You're in a dreadful mess.'

'Ah, nothing.' He tried to grin. 'A bit of a barney you might say.'

'I'd say it was more than that,' she whispered.

He felt her fingers gently exploring his battered nose and despite the pain, he was glad.

'I'd better have a look at you,' she whispered more urgently. The blood was sticky on her fingertips. 'Come inside, but don't make a sound.'

Suddenly they were conspirators together. She made much of slamming and bolting the door. The family could sleep soundly in their beds. They tiptoed into the storeroom and closed the door quietly. Dolores fetched a bowl of water and a cloth and turned up the lamp.

'Jesus, Mary and Joseph! she exclaimed when she saw the state of Kit's face. 'What in the name of God happened?' For a well-bred young lady her language was a bit extreme.

Kit put a finger to his lips. 'Easy now,' he whispered. 'What will your oul' fella say if he hears you and comes down?'

She looked towards the door in fright. 'There'd be hell to pay,' she admitted, 'but he won't budge again tonight.' She giggled. 'He keeps a po under the bed.' It was not very loyal but reassuring nonetheless.

Kit felt the laughter bubbling up inside him. He snorted and winced with pain.

'Here, let me look at you.' She pushed him backwards onto a teachest and began to dab at congealed blood.

The water was cool and refreshing and her fingers were gentle. He put his head back and closed his eyes. There was a sensual pleasure in being attended to like that, being treated almost like a baby.

'I don't think it's broken,' she said after a careful inspection. 'The little wobbly bit in front is bent all right, but I wouldn't say the bone is broken.'

Kit hoped she did not mean that she was finished, but he need not have worried. Dolores carefully wiped his forehead and dabbed at his hair. He could feel the warmth of her knee against his thigh. He wondered if she had noticed. He was aroused and trying desperately to conceal the fact.

'There now,' she said slowly. 'I think you'll survive.'

She made no attempt to stand back and Kit waited a long moment swallowing hard. He would have to say or do something. There was a strange taste in his mouth, salty but not blood. A pulse throbbed in his battered face. He realised that his arm was about her waist and that he was drawing her sideways onto his knee. She made no attempt to resist and turned towards him. He kissed her violently and inexpertly, ignoring the stabs of pain.

'What took you so long?' she laughed quietly, drawing back.

He felt foolish and juvenile. 'I'm sorry,' he mumbled, wishing that he had more experience. She stirred on his knee and he could feel her warmth anew. She was laughing at him but he was not offended. He realised that she was always laughing at him and he smiled at her, shifting discreetly to relieve the agony in his groin. She was a fair old weight all the same, being practical about it, and teachests were not designed for such manoeuvres.

'Here's something for the poor little boy.' She spoke in baby talk.

217

She put her finger between his lips and he tasted the toffee taste of sugar. Slowly she withdrew her finger, all the while looking at him directly, even challengingly, in the eye. She dipped it again in the sugar and this time lasciviously put it into her own mouth. Momentarily he remembered his old fear of Kerrigan germs but this was another matter entirely. The pain was unbearable. He struggled to get up. She still regarded him quizzically, with her finger in her mouth.

'Don't do that,' he said.

'Do what?' she queried, pushing in close.

He put his arms around her again. 'Supposin' somebody hears us.'

'Don't worry.'

He looked at the pile of sacks and she caught his eye. They listened again. She was fingering the top button of her blouse.

There was a rumbling sound and suddenly the house shook to the thunder of lorries. There were three of them at least, tearing along the street and screeching to a halt in the square. Voices shouted outside.

'Put out that light.'

Dolores heard her father's voice upstairs, urgent with fear, and suddenly she was pushing Kit into the darkened shop. 'Lie down behind the counter. I'll let you out when things quieten down.

Old Kerrigan was in the storeroom in a long nightshirt, scratching himself. 'The light,' he hissed. I told you to put out the light.'

Dolores did as she was bid with alacrity.

'Get up to bed,' said her father again, angry with her for no good reason but his own fear.

Running feet passed and repassed the windows, but nobody tried to force an entry.

Kit crouched behind the counter, listening to the uproar outside. Blast them, he thought. Everything was going wrong. Not quite everything, he corrected himself. In fact taken all in all, it was not such a bad night at all. He smiled broadly in the darkness feeling an uncomplicated happiness flooding through him, for the first time in a very long time. Dolores Kerrigan! He must have been blind.

*　*　*

Mrs Donovan heard the door click shut and called softly from the kitchen: 'Who's there?' Her voice quavered with alarm.

'It's me,' said Kit, groaning inwardly. Awkward explanations and a little judicious embroidery of the truth would be called for.

She came shuffling out to the hallway in dressing-gown and slippers. Her eyes were haunted in the candlelight. 'Oh Kit,' she said, near to tears, 'they came looking for Joey. The Auxiliaries or whatever they are.'

A cold fear gripped him. 'Oh Christ,' he said. 'What happened?'

'They were all over the house.' She felt soiled and violated. 'I couldn't stop them.'

'Joey. What about Joey?' He gripped her arm. He felt that he should have been there to do something about it all. 'Did they take him?'

'He got out the back window when he heard the lorries. I heard him on the roof of the shed. He just said "I'm off now", and was gone. Oh, Kit, what are we going to do?' She gave way to the tears that she had been holding back.

'Did you hear anything outside?'

'I don't know. There was so much noise in the house.' She dabbed at her eyes. 'He's only a little boy. What could they want with Joey?'

'Don't worry,' he said, awkwardly patting her arm. 'They won't catch Joey.' He would have gone over the shed, rattling the Virol boards, and alarming the last few hens, and then across the rocks and away into the fields. 'Nobody could find him,' he said reassuringly. 'I'll go and look for him.'

For the first time she looked at him properly. 'What in God's name happened to you? And where were you?'

'Ah, I had a bit of a fall,' he said shamefaced. 'It was very dark.'

'And what have you been doing till this hour?'

'Well, I heard the lorries and kept out of the way for a while.' It was difficult to say if she believed his lame story, but Joey was her primary concern.

'Drinking again,' she sniffed, with some of her customary disapproval.

'Look, I'll go out and see if I can find him. I have a rough idea where he might go.'

She sat down at the table again, twisting her handkerchief between her fingers and gazing at the candle flame. A pool of grease spilled over the crater and ran down the side of the candle. She watched it gathering into a knob and congealing, becoming hard and opaque again. 'They wanted to know where you were,' she said quietly.

There was a long silence.

'Why me?' He sat down heavily. 'Why the blazes would they want me?' He shook his head, trying to clear his thoughts.

'The fact that you weren't at home at that hour, that's what one of them said.'

He looked at her suspiciously but there was no query in the remark. She was not trying to trap him, he realised guiltily. But he could not explain without another lie. 'There's no curfew here,' he said defensively. Rain pattered on the window. He looked at the kitchen clock. It was only four in the morning. Rain before seven, fine before eleven.

'He didn't even have a coat with him,' she said and again burst into tears.

'Don't worry Ma, I'll go and find him.'

'Oh Kit,' she whispered, 'mind yourself. I don't know what we're going to do. I just don't understand what's going on.'

Joey crossed the railway at the cinder heaps, keeping low, although it was almost pitch dark. He could see a light in the signal-box and gave the station a wide berth. His heart was pounding and he gasped for breath. There must have been a whole regiment of them, he thought wildly. He kept moving, his mind in a whirl, heading toward the dark outline of Hatton's Wood.

He heard cattle coughing in the darkness and his heart leapt with fright. A light rain began to fall. There was a fingernail of moon, surrounded by a halo, in the west and the trees stood out like black filigree against the dim light. His teeth chattered with the cold and the rain was getting worse. They never said anything about this in the drill sessions. He realised that he was hungry.

The dark outline of a chestnut tree loomed in front of him and he stood in gratefully under its shelter. He knew the tree of old. There were probably conkers galore over his head, not yet ripe enough to fall. The thought distracted him. There was a time when those conkers would have been important to him. It was important to get the best ones. Many a time he had climbed that tree to shake the branches. He could see them in his mind's eye, shining and wet in their white shells. He tried to bring his mind back to the immediate problem. Where would he go? Where would he sleep from now on? What about university? He could hardly walk the streets with the Tans looking everywhere for him. Panic gripped him. He would have to go on the run. The realisation left him feeling lost and alone and close to tears.

If only Kit was there it would be alright. It was all very well for him, he could stay in his warm bed and go to work every day. Resentment rose in him. Kit was too cute to put himself out. Rain dripped through the leaves and he huddled back against the bole of the tree.

Far away across the field he heard the whistle, two notes, almost like a cuckoo's call, the old secret signal from years back. Everything was going to be alright. He answered with the same two notes. The signal came again, closer this time. He answered again, relief flooding through him. He heard Kit's voice and he stepped out into the rain.

'Over here,' he shouted. 'Over by the tree,' and soon he could see his brother, his collar turned up and rain dripping from the peak of his cap. He ran towards him and shook him by the hand. 'I knew you'd come,' he said, almost choked with emotion.

'I brought your coat,' said Kit gruffly. 'I gather you left in a bit of a hurry.'

Barney Phelan stirred under the straw. He pulled his coat around him. Rain drummed on the roof of the shed. He heard a movement nearby.

'Who's that?' he snarled, reaching for his stick.

'It's only us Mr Phelan, the Donovans. We had to come in out of the rain.'

'Donovans. And what might youse be doin' out at this hour? Why aren't yiz at home?'

'It's the Tans, Mr Phelan. We can't go home for a while.'

The words hung in the silence.

Some battered memory of hospitality and manners tugged at Barney. He cleared his throat. 'All right then,' he grunted, 'but don't make any noise.' He burrowed again into the straw, grunting and grumbling, keeping a wary hand on his sack.

The brothers nudged each other and settled down warily. Cattle stamped and squelched in the adjoining shed. The smell of dung was almost overpowering. The brothers lay quietly, trying to hug themselves warm. The straw stirred again as Barney sat up.

'Are yiz only goin' to sleep now?' he enquired.

'That's right Mr Phelan. We've been out all night.' It sounded suitably plaintive.

'Well, get up yiz little cunts and say your prayers.'

He threshed about until he was in a kneeling position and began an incomprehensible gabble, which they deduced to be the rosary. Sheepishly the brothers followed suit, trying to stifle the hysterical laughter that rose inside them. Gradually the rosary petered out.

'Keep us all safe till morning. Amen,' added Barney.

'Amen,' they answered together.

There was a long silence and they settled down again.

Not just till the morning, thought Kit. It was almost morning already. He fingered his bruised nose. He had almost forgotten about it. The rain hissed down outside. The cattle stirred and snorted. Barney snored under the straw and Kit smiled, thinking of sugar and Dolores Kerrigan.

CHAPTER 19

'Young lady,' said the colonel, 'I'm very glad to see you. This place is full of old people.' He glared around the garden. 'They can be very tiresome, you know.'

Anna laughed. 'The kettle and the pot situation,' she said. 'I'm sure that you make everybody hop to it yourself.'

'They've no conversation,' he complained. 'I can never even have a good argument.'

Anna fidgeted with her gloves. 'I heard what you did about the cottage. It was very kind.'

He gestured dismissively. 'A small matter. Been with us a long time. We'll see the jackdaws moving in on Strifeland soon.'

'I'm so sorry,' said Anna, 'you love the place so very much.'

He put his head back and stared at the drifting clouds. 'Strifeland,' he said. 'We made it. Planted all those trees. I was still planting five years ago. The continuity, you see.'

She said nothing.

'My son, you know, had this notion that we should give the land away, give it back to the descendants of the original owners. A lot of cant, really.' He laced his bony fingers together, talon-like hands with the tendons standing out like strings. 'Very fine young fellow, but not a bit practical.' He grunted a little laugh. 'I would like to see it again though, before I go.'

Anna looked away.

'No need for any of that now,' he reprimanded. 'The old order changeth, hey? You've had your own troubles I understand.'

223

'Oh yes,' she said. 'I was very frightened. Frank, of course, doesn't hold any grudge, which is typical of him. Nothing ever seems to upset him, but I don't feel easy here any more. People seem to think that all English are the same. You can sense it in the way they look at you.'

'The mistake,' he said vehemently, 'was to make concessions in the first place.' He was off again on a familiar tack. 'I can see that you're smiling,' he said after a while.

'Was I?' said Anna innocently.

'Oh, yes. You're thinking that I'm only an imitation Englishman, fulminating about the empire, while your friends the republicans, don't regard me as Irish. Neither fish nor flesh, as they say.'

She shrugged, at a loss for words. She thought of him suddenly as a fish stranded in some dwindling tidal pool, cut off from the great ocean surge. It was an odd thought and she looked at him again. He had not long to live. He opened and closed his mouth, saying nothing. Stranded, marooned.

'The whole damn place is going to fall down about our ears one of these days,' he said after a while. 'You'd do well to take yourselves out of it.' He gasped for air, tired from the exertion of talking.

'Perhaps I should take you indoors,' suggested Anna.

'Perhaps, perhaps. This damp air does not agree with me.' He pulled the rug around him, plucking impatiently at the folds in the fabric. 'We must arrange that expedition before it's too late.'

'I'll see to it very soon,' said Anna, standing up and taking hold of the back of the wheelchair. It struck her that he was as light as a feather, as if he might blow away in a gust of wind.

* * *

It was odd, thought Joey, that the actual reason why he was lying behind a ditch on a country road should be a chance remark in a pub, but then again, where else would matters of great weight be discussed?

A certain landlord had complained to one of 'the boys' that business was in a perilous state since the Tans had come to Gormanston. The Auxiliaries were fair men to put away their

224

drink but they were not always meticulous about keeping tally, and since they moved around the country at short notice there was little hope of collecting anything on the slate. They could be noisy enough too when they had a drop taken, but worst of all they scared off the regulars, on whom the landlord depended for his basic income in both good times and bad.

And this landlord's *bona fide* trade too was ruined. This institution, devised by wise and far-seeing rulers in days gone by and hallowed by ancient tradition, provided that a weary traveller could obtain refreshment at any hour of the day or night, to sustain him in his peregrinations. Lest such a venerable custom should lapse through disuse, *bona fide* travellers felt obliged to rouse themselves from their comfortable firesides, without thought for their own convenience, and trek the minimum three miles to avail themselves of such refreshments. These nocturnal perambulations had dropped off of late, as people were afraid to go out at night even for essential purposes, and hostelries in country areas were feeling the pinch.

A pattern had emerged. Patrols of Auxiliaries and RIC had taken to stopping at this particular pub in the late afternoon on their return from the north suburbs. Such regularity was not in character, but as they were near their home base they could afford to relax. These quiet back roads saw little activity of any importance.

Under some overhanging chestnut trees, whose broad leaves, tinged with the first russet of autumn, cast a deep shade over the narrow twisting road, a cartload of bales straddled the bend. A motorist would not see it before his eyes adjusted to the sudden twilight. It was a perfect trap.

The five men, dressed like any of the local labouring men, lay behind the stone walls and ditches on either side of the road. Joey, as the inexperienced one, was in the group of three. He stroked the stock of his rifle. The time had come at last. He could not have said whether his mouth was dry with anticipation or fear, but he wished that they would come.

The slight breeze rustled the leaves overhead. The voice of the country carried on the afternoon air, the sound of hens, a distant train, an ass braying somewhere towards Knockbrack. That's how they measure distance out here, he thought, with the townsman's condescension. 'Tis two asses' roars from here sir.' The Tans were not even half an ass's roar away, right at that moment, knocking back beautiful black pints, pints like a line of parish priests, black suits and white collars. The sound of the train was surprisingly clear, given the distance to the railway, about one ass's roar perhaps?

The section leader motioned to him. The look-out had signalled that something was happening. They must be on the move. Joey gripped the rifle more tightly. He could feel the sweat on his forehead. There was no danger, he assured himself. Sitting ducks, they all said. A nagging voice told him that that was not his fear. He wondered if he would be afraid to pull the trigger — no, squeeze the trigger. They always said, 'Take your time and finish the job.' The blood roared in his ears and he bit his lip, to help himself concentrate.

They weren't men anyway. They were monsters, invaders, violators of his native land. The noise of the steam engine seemed alarmingly close. He could hear the hiss of steam and the rumble of wheels. Incongruously there came a long warning blast on the whistle.

The men looked at each other in alarm. They could not understand. As one they raised their heads above the walls. There was a deafening screech of iron-shod brakes and a cacophony of rattling, clanging metal. Steam was released in a hissing white cloud and straw and splintered planks flew in all directions.

A great black traction engine, coming from the other direction, had smashed into the impromptu barricade and was even then trundling the shattered remnants before it as it gradually slowed down. The assemblage of machines which followed had jack-knifed one into the other and was careering from side to side, in imminent danger of overturning into the ditch. Only the skill of the driver, a diminutive and grizzled character in a shining black coat, a patina acquired from his trade, prevented total disaster. Gradually the brake-shoes took hold and the procession came shuddering to a halt.

The men watched in fascination. It did not occur to them that they might have been crushed to death where they lay.

Along the line of vehicles came a man on a bicycle, who obviously bore the same relationship to the driver as the acolyte does to the prelate. This cyclist had had a narrow escape and was even then trying to bring his machine under control.

The driver had by then dismounted and was in the act of treading his headgear into the hard road metal. 'Jaysus Francie,' he began without preamble, 'what class of a fuckin' eejit are ye?'

Only the calibre of eejit was in doubt. Francie, whose fault it obviously was, had still not regained his composure and made no reply.

'A short cut, how are ye! A glass o'stout at "The Man o' War". Are ye tryin' to fuckin' murder me?' He kicked at what had been his cheese-cutter cap and lofted it over the ditch.

Francie looked shamefaced, as well he might.

The section leader was the only one who seemed to have remembered the purpose of their mission. The others were grinning broadly at the scene, awaiting developments with detached amusement. The officer stepped forward.

'Get that contraption out of the way at once,' he said with all the authority he could muster.

The driver turned on him a baleful eye. So close was the officer that he could see the driver's veins criss-crossing the white of the eye like red cracks in the glaze of old china.

'And who the fuck might you be?'

A reasonable enough question in a way, but the driver's reaction was one of satisfaction that he had been presented with a more worthy target than the unfortunate Francie. With luck this young countryman might even be the owner of the vehicle that had caused all the trouble. It might be a question of damages even, or summonses.

'Never mind that,' said the officer. 'Just get this machine moving and be quick about it. This road must be cleared.' He reflected that there was a paradox there somewhere.

'Indeed!' remarked the little man tolerantly. 'Do you tell me so?'

'That's right,' said the officer, glad to see that reason had prevailed. 'Get a move on there.'

The little chap clambered back onto the footplate, as if to comply with the order, but in a flash he was down again with a short, square fire-shovel, a navvy, as it is commonly called, clenched in his fist. 'Now maybe we can start again,' he began with menacing politeness.

'I said . . .' The officer had no chance to finish. A horn blared behind him and he leapt aside as an open touring car shot past, dodging swiftly around the obstructions.

There were four uniformed men in it. Their laughter drifted back to the group on the roadside and one of them called out mockingly: 'Nice work Paddy. Keep it up.' It was no grief to them if a few bogtrotters brained each other with spades; made life easier for everyone. In an instant they were gone in a cloud of dust and straw.

The little man paused in astonishment. He stared in the direction the car had taken. 'Tans,' he spat. 'How dare they adopt that familiar tone with me?' He was offended not by the generic insult, but by the assumption of first name terms by people to whom he had not even been introduced. 'No fuckin' breedin',' he muttered to himself. 'A good kick in th'arse is what they need.'

The officer spoke fiercely, furious with himself. 'If you hadn't ballsed everything up we'd have given them more than a kick in the arse.'

Realisation dawned in the little man's bloodshot eyes. 'Ah ha,' he croaked, 'be Jaysus, but I get it now.' He looked at the others who had emerged, with their weapons carried casually. 'Why the fuck didn't yiz say that in the first place and we could of blockin' the road good an' proper.' He hurled the shovel onto the ground in chagrin. It rang on the stones like a bell. 'Youse young lads,' he said in disgust, 'yiz have no notion o' stragety.'

The men grinned sheepishly, looking at each other. Joey tried to look disappointed, but he could not deny the sense of relief that filled him.

The officer was getting them on the move again. They had a long way to travel, mostly on foot. The engine had got up a head of steam. No great damage had been done, except to the cart, a small price for any farmer to pay for the achievement of an historic aspiration. The ever-faithful and long-suffering Francie had retrieved his employer's shovel and battered cap and the traction engine moved off again with a great clanking and rumbling. Francie fell in behind, drawn along like a speck of dust, subsumed into the tail of a great comet as it drifted across the sky.

'Right lads,' said the officer, 'we'll split up for the moment.

We'll have another go, but not here. Don't worry,' he added to Joey. 'You'll get a bit of action soon enough.'

* * *

Clara Bennett looked at the letter in disbelief and shook her head, unable to take it all in. The shock left her almost unable to think. 'I can hardly credit it,' she said again.

Anna was puzzled and alarmed by her confusion. 'I don't want to pry, Mrs Bennett but I hope it isn't bad news.' She was anxious lest, as the bearer of the letter, she might come in for a share of the blame.

'No, no,' said the older woman slowly. 'It isn't bad news at all. I misjudged him, that's all.'

Anna was relieved that she had not been the instrument of some malicious or heartless action by the old man. She waited for further explanation.

Clara crumpled the letter and her eyes misted over. 'He's signed over the cottage to us, and the field, so the Land Commission won't turn us out. And he's put aside money for Davy, for his education, he says.' She put her hands to her face, quite overcome. 'I misjudged him,' she said again. ' "My good friend Tom Bennett" he says.' She said it with awe and was at a loss.

'Oh! Mrs Bennett,' said Anna, 'I am very happy for you. I really am.' She took the other woman's hand and squeezed it. 'This is wonderful news and wonderful for Davy. He is such a bright boy. You'll be very proud of him, I've no doubt.'

They sat for a while in silence. The sun streamed through the cottage window.

'And what about yourselves, Mrs Surtees?' asked Clara after a while.

Anna gave a kind of half-shrug. 'Well grandfather is leaving soon anyway. He felt he was useful here during the war but now. . . . Anyway, he's very old. Slowed down a lot. As for us . . .' She paused, 'I just don't know. It's difficult to say. We'll probably stay on until everything is settled about the land.' She spread her hands. 'After that I just don't know. Probably go home I suppose.' It struck her as strange that she should say 'home', meaning England. This in reality, had

229

become her home. This was where her child had been born and where she had known happiness, more than anywhere else. Frank had made no plans. He spoke vaguely of getting a piece of land, but would never define exactly what he wanted, beyond the immediate task in hand, which absorbed him utterly.

'We'd be that sorry to see you go,' said Clara. 'You've been very good to us, you and your husband.' But her regret was drowned in the realisation of their own good fortune. What would Tom say? In a way she felt that she had got back the land her father had spoken of, or at least part of it. A sizeable part too, she thought, glancing out the window. The field was in stubble, glistening after the rain, and it was all theirs.

'If I see your husband I'll tell him to come home,' Anna was speaking from the doorway. She was pulling on her gloves. 'Mind you, I'll say nothing about the letter.' She smiled again and was gone.

Clara stood watching her. She heard the intestinal gurgling of the plumbing system. Somewhere, Mr Drew had said, there was a bit of an airlock. He had pursued it, banging on the pipes with his hammer, but its ghost returned occasionally, like a playful poltergeist, to emerge in great gasps from the tap or, conversely, hold the water back for half a minute until the patience gave way. Strange how impatient people became with modern conveniences when they never complained about lugging buckets from pump or well every day of their lives.

When her husband came home Clara silently handed him the letter to read.

Tom gazed into the fire. He could not identify the feelings that rose inside him. He could not grasp the idea that he was a man of property. People were always interfering in his life, telling him what he should do and what he should think. Mr Drew had even hinted that he might be in line for a slice of the estate, through the Land Commission, that Master Sweeney would put in a word in the right quarters. He began to grin at the thought. He was one jump ahead of them all this time. They would get the quare gunk when he told them not to bother. His mind was racing ahead, making plans, as every proprietor must. He thought maybe he might do like the Rush-men, and go in for vegetables, maybe even throw up a bit of glass. No more bother to him. It would be good to have the last word with Master Sweeney after all these years. Stand a few bullocks in a bit of the field. A couple of cows maybe. He hooked his thumbs into his waistcoat pockets and leaned back importantly. 'What with the prices cattle are fetchin' nowadays, Master Sweeney,' he would say. 'Yes, the lad is doin' very well above in the university. A credit to yourself, Master, if I may say so.' He could be magnanimous in victory.

An occasional jag of doubt flitted across his mind. Something worried him, a vague feeling that it had not been his own doing. It was an indefinable feeling of failure. He had never amounted to much in his own right, despite his efforts and his hard work. Even the plumbing was put in without his sayso.

'You didn't read all the letter, did you?' Clara broke into his thoughts.

'No. I'm not much good at the letters.'

'He thinks very highly of you. He mentions your scupulous honesty and diligence. He says it has been a privilege to work with you all these years.'

Tom felt a painful constriction in his throat. He had never realised what the old man had thought. 'Scrupulous honesty and diligence', they were good words to have said about you. 'Work with him' not 'work for him'. That was an important distinction. He shook his head, whistling softly through his teeth. 'Davy will do well,' he predicted, changing the subject. 'He won't be an ignorant clodhopper like his oul' lad.'

'If he's half as good a man,' replied his wife, 'I'll be well satisfied.'

He grinned broadly. 'I'll tell you one thing an' not another.'

She waited expectantly.

'I don't give a damn what goes on either in Balbriggan or the Skerry tonight. Someone else can look after it. I'm goin' to sit here be me own fireside with me wife an' family, an' to hell with the lot o'them.' He stretched his stockinged feet towards the fire and wiggled his toes. He pulled out a packet of Waverlies and lit one with an expansive gesture. 'Run that young lad up to bed,' he ordered imperiously, 'and you and me can have a confabulation.'

* * *

'The way it is, Mr Drew,' said Kit, 'I don't have much choice. You might as well count me in.'

'Aha,' said the older man, 'I always knew you'd come round.' He spat on his hands. 'Me life upon ye.' He beamed, shaking Kit's hand vigorously. 'We can use men with your experience.'

'Well that's just it,' replied Kit. 'I want to keep an eye on the brother, really. He shouldn't be let out by himself. As for putting a gun in his hands.' He shrugged expressively.

'That's it, that's it,' said Mr Drew. 'Lads like yourself will make all the differ.'

'The way it is,' went on Kit, anxious to clear up any mis-understanding, 'I can't just stand still. Even the sergeant has warned me about the Tans. He was askin' me about that dynamite business. Sure I didn't know the first thing about it.'

'Oh, that,' said Mr Drew, archly. 'No you wouldn't know anything, at all, at all.' He looked around innocently, inspecting the horizon. 'No sign of Captain McNaughten,' he mentioned, as if embarking on some other train of thought.

Kit gazed around the horizon. Only a sail or two could be seen beyond the lighthouse. 'My father used to get on great with old McNaughten,' he said. 'He had any amount of yarns. Did you ever see that bone-handled knife? My father said he took it off a Chinaman that tried to kill him in Shanghai.'

'That's a fact all right,' agreed Mr Drew. 'He told me about it himself. A Lascar it was, jumped on him in an alley.' He paused. 'Your daddy would be proud of you this day. The business and all.'

'It's not what he had in mind for me though, as far as I can gather.' He pinched at the leaves of a small succulent plant that lodged in a crevice of the harbour wall. Idly he watched the tissue suffuse with juice and burst between his finger and thumb. 'Well anyway, if the Tans are lookin' for me I can't stay at home and, with Joey more or less on the run, I'd like to be able to keep an eye on him.'

'Ah sure, I know what you mean. Everybody has their reasons. Still, you could be a useful man. What was that you said about Duffy?'

'Just that he came around to the house the day after the raid. Said he had been meaning to talk to us. That's what he told the Ma. He said the Tans have their own sources of information. I wondered, to tell you the truth, if I ever said anything to your man, you know.'

'Oh yes. Jack Straw.'

'It's a long time ago. I honestly don't think I ever said anything. I was only just home at the time.' It was not the first time that he had racked his brain trying to remember. He had drunk a good bit in those days.

They stood in silence, leaning on the wall.

'They got him, you know,' said Mr Drew, after a long time, without turning his head.

'Are you serious?'

'Aye, above in the County Meath. Found on the side of the road.' He kept his gaze averted, not meeting Kit's eye. It was something that happened a long way off. It had nothing to do with them.

A jovial, convivial man, not slow to buy a pint or crack a joke. Kit could see him with his elbow on the bar, with froth droplets on his trim moustache. 'County Meath, you say?'

'Aye. He got around. Somebody got to him in the end.' Mr Drew rubbed his hands, where flakes of whitewash had clung to them. He brushed at his sleeve. 'He got around alright.'

'Aye.' So that was Jack Straw. Was it King and Country or just the usual thirty pieces of silver? Or maybe it was just for the hell of it, a game to see who could outwit the other, the ultimate gamble. Did he look at his executioners at the last moment? Maybe he reared up like a beached seal in his final agony, turning a white face towards the one who had shot him. Kit shivered. 'Anyway, you can count me in, but not for that kind of thing.'

'Good God, no. Nothin' like that at all, at all. Joey'll be all right by the way. You can carry on here during the day but just be a bit careful at night. Move around a bit.' He underplayed the possible danger, anxious not to let Kit have second thoughts.

'Easier said than done.'

'You'll have the Movement behind you. The business will run itself.' That at least was reassuring. 'If all comes to all, Joey can ship out on the coal boat. He could be very useful to us, goin' over an' back all the time.'

'There she is.' Kit pointed towards a grey smudge of smoke

beyond the lighthouse. The collier was still hull down. He felt a thrill of excitement. Here was a ship coming at their behest, with their coal. It would cause a stir in the harbour, towering over the fishing smacks. Black-faced men in heavy boots would stamp on the iron deckplates in an arrogant and lordly manner, the envy of the small boys who scrambled for the fallen lumps of coal at low tide. Great buckets would swing across, overflowing with coal. Horses would strain in the shafts. He could already hear their hooves as they scrabbled for a grip on the road metal. Old fishermen would suck their pipes and point knowledgeably at the rust-caked superstructure. And all this was at the beck and call of Donovan and Drew or Drew and Donovan. It was no matter. He grinned broadly, imagining the scene.

Mr Drew caught his mood and smiled. The young lad's heart was all right. He need never have worried. He hawked mightily and spat over the harbour wall. 'And we'll haul that down too,' he said, pointing his thumb towards the coast-guard station.

Kit looked up to where the Union Jack cracked in the stiff breeze, at the end of the yardarm. It was suddenly unfamiliar and offensive, a gaudy piece of bunting afflicting the eye. 'You know I never even noticed it before.' He thought of stockades all over the world where the flag flew in defiance of Zulus, Pathans, and assorted foreigners. The image came from his father's old books, tales of adventure, where white men, empire builders, planted their standards in other people's soil and defied anyone to pull them down. He could see them in their Norfolk jackets and pith helmets, laying down the law, always pointing with canes, while the natives cringed. In the old etchings it seemed the natural order of things. 'Yes, by God, we will,' he said suddenly and clenched his fist. The sound of the collier's siren carried to them over the water and his attention returned to the business in hand.

CHAPTER 20

The man stood in the alleyway safe from the light. He fingered the pistol in his pocket, feeling the ridges on the butt with his nails, deriving comfort from the weight of the weapon. The noise from the public house was increasing as the men inside became more and more drunk. There was the occasional smashing of glass. He wondered what was keeping his partner. He didn't fancy the idea of tackling that lot by himself. The phone call from Dublin had warned them to be on the lookout for the local sergeant and his brother, promoted that day to District Inspector, and a half-dozen Black and Tans who had latched onto the celebration. They had apparently made a regal progress through Santry, stopping at every pub along the way and becoming more arrogant and offensive as they went. By the time they reached Mrs Smith's in Balbriggan there was no holding them. She had already sent for the police to try to get them off the premises and protect what was left of her stock.

A party of RIC came up from the barracks and stopped outside. The watcher in the shadows heard their hasty consultation. They had not expected to find their own sergeant and a DI involved in such behaviour and were reluctant to interfere. Even less did they want to get involved with the Tans. Their reputation for ferocity impressed friend and foe alike.

Go on, urged the man silently. Do something. The whole thing was getting out of hand. The policemen looked at each other and shrugged. The light from the window showed their expressions of embarrassment and helplessness. One of them muttered something to his companions. One by one they began to drift away, shamefacedly. The man watched them with contempt. The blood pounded in his temples.

Suddenly the street door opened and a group of men stumbled out singing and laughing. A few of them clutched bottles that they had apparently removed from the shelves. They began to clamber into a car that was parked by the kerb.

Thank God for that, thought the man with relief. He felt a nudge beside him.

His partner had arrived, stealthily. 'Do we take them?' he whispered.

Suddenly the door into the alley was flung open and they could see the two brothers within, arguing with the landlady and one of her daughters. The women were obviously terrified. The younger one held the door.

'We'll take their guns,' said the first man, moving forward quickly.

In a flash they took in the scene of destruction. Chairs had been thrown everywhere and tables knocked over. Broken glass littered the floor. The room was empty except for the two men, far gone in drink, and the frightened women.

'Let's have those guns,' said the first man, pointing his pistol.

The brothers looked at him, not understanding at first what was happening. A look of complicity passed between them and they realised their danger. No words were necessary. As boys and as men, they had never needed to explain things to each other. Together they had tackled the world and beaten the toughest. They sprang apart and grabbed at their holsters, but it was too late.

There were several sharp reports and tongues of flame stabbed towards them. A bullet entered the inspector's left side and he fell instantly. His brother staggered into the street, severely wounded and shouting for help. Blood was pumping from his thigh. There was a high-pitched note of panic in his voice. He could not believe it. Less than a minute had elapsed since their companions had left the bar.

Suddenly the place was again filled with the pounding of boots but the mysterious gunmen had vanished. A red pool was spreading from the body on the floor, oozing across the stained

236

linoleum, seeping into patches where the hessian backing had been laid bare by the tread of hobnails. There was nothing to be done but remove the injured sergeant and the body of his brother to the barracks and take stock of the situation.

'Christ,' said Duffy, replacing the receiver, 'that's torn it.' He rarely gave way to profanity. He looked at his watch. It was half past nine.

'What is it, Sergeant?' asked the constable, looking up from his paper. He had never seen Duffy look so agitated.

'The fools,' said Duffy vehemently. 'The bloody fools.'

The constable waited. 'The sergeant in Balbriggan has been injured in a shooting and his brother, the DI, murdered. And they with a gang of Black and Tans.'

'Jesus,' replied the constable, sucking the breath through his teeth. He could feel the warmth draining from his face.

'We'd better get over there smartly. There'll be hell to pay now.'

The constable was not so sure. 'Isn't there enough of them there to look after things?' After a lifetime in the force without serious incident, he saw no reason to go looking for trouble in the twilight of his service, as it were.

Duffy was on his feet and strapping on his holster. 'We'll take the taxi,' he said without debate. 'Get your gun and let's be off.'

The taximan, a genial and portly gentleman, recently graduated from horse transport, was slightly taken aback when told that his services were being requisitioned by the forces of the Crown, at short notice, but Duffy's urgency imparted an air of importance to the occasion which appealed to his sense of the dramatic. As a devotee of the writings of Zane Grey, he subscribed to the notion that the mail must get through, whether by pony express, by diligence or by iron horse. Transposing this to his own situation, although he carried no saddlebags of precious despatches, it was his duty to see to it that his passengers arrived, or rather got through, in safety. 'A pint in meself and a pint in the oul' motor and we'll go anywhere,' was his observation, as he wound up the hood and swung the starting handle, with thumb well back to avoid a rebound.

The trees at Strifeland reached up, black against the clear

237

starry September sky as the taxi rattled along. Through the isinglass panel in the hood a distorted pinpoint of light, from Bennett's cottage on the point, seemed to flicker and beckon. Duffy watched it as it approached and drew abreast of them.

'Stop for a minute,' he ordered the driver.

He ran quickly down through the stubble field and tapped on the door. He heard voices within.

'Who's there?'

It was Bennett's voice, he noted with relief. 'It's me, Tom, Sergeant Duffy. Open the door for a minute.' Silently he drew his pistol.

'Hold on a minute, Sergeant,' came Bennett's voice again, accompanied by the rattling of a bolt. 'Ye can't be too careful, this weather.' There was a soft laugh and the door opened. Bennett's eyes widened in surprise and his jaw dropped at the sight of the gun barrel glinting in the light.

'All right Tom,' said the sergeant, stepping into the room, 'you're under arrest.' He looked at Clara, who had risen from her chair by the fire. The boy was still sitting at the table, staring in alarm. It was all a bit dramatic.

'What the hell is this all about?' Bennett bristled in anger. 'You can't just come in here.' He searched for the word: 'Grounds. Ye have to have grounds, a warrant. I've done nothin' that concerns you.'

'You'll know all about grounds, soon enough, boy.' He gestured with the pistol. 'And this is my authority, right now, so let you not give me any trouble. You know me well enough, to be sure that I'll blow your brains out, if I have to.' There was a look in his eye that said he would take no argument. 'I'm sorry Mrs Bennett, but I have no choice.' Deftly he slipped the handcuffs over Bennett's wrists and prodded him towards the door.

Bennett glared furiously at him and felt a twinge of fear. He had heard stories of the knock on the door in the middle of the night and bullet-riddled bodies on the side of the road, but Duffy — it was difficult to believe.

Clara was almost speechless with fright at the suddenness of it all. 'But he's done nothin',' she stammered, thinking of the dynamite, but that was all forgotten.

'You'll be furnished with all the necessary information in

due course,' replied the sergeant, retreating into the ponderous language of the law. He closed the door quickly and almost ran with his prisoner back to the car. 'Turn around,' he ordered the driver. To the constable's puzzled look he replied: 'Take this fellow back with you and keep him under lock and key till I return. I'll go on myself on foot.' He took his greatcoat from the seat and threw it over his shoulder.

The constable, not loth to comply with these instructions, bundled the angry Bennett into the back seat and sat in beside him with his pistol at the ready. 'No buck from you now,' he warned the prisoner as the driver reversed into the gateway.

Duffy smiled in the darkness at Bennett's 'Kiss me arse', and set off rapidly towards the distant town.

The Auxiliary officer raised both hands, calling for attention. The crowd of men gradually quietened down into a sullen silence. They were in no mood for speeches. A brother officer had been shot down by the enemy. There could be only one response.

'I won't detain you gentlemen for very long. We all know what has to be done. We want the culprits, and by God, we'll get them.' A growl of assent rose from the crowd. They resembled a mob, more than a disciplined force, but there was no doubting their determination, fuelled as it was, for many of them, by spirits. 'We're fighting fire with fire here, gentlemen, if you take my meaning.' A roar ascended from the crowd. 'Right then,' the speaker concluded, 'let's get on with it.'

His words were lost in the cheer as men scrambled for the lorries. The great Crossley engines thundered into life and the headlamps sliced through the darkness. The officer regretted that he had not had time to expand on the image of fire, smoke out the vermin, cauterise the sore, something along those lines. He checked his pockets for ammunition, and the spare naggin that sat so snugly beside his wallet.

Duffy could hear the shots long before he reached the outskirts of the town. There were sustained fusilades and then sporadic outbursts, as if a fullscale battle were in progress. As he drew nearer he could hear the sound of engines, outbursts of cheering and the crash of breaking glass.

It seemed as if the world had gone completely mad. From the square down to the bridge and up Drogheda Street, gangs of uniformed men were rampaging, smashing windows with their rifle butts. Lorries dashed up and down the narrow street, their wheels crunching on the shattered glass. The men clinging to the bars on the backs of the lorries were firing their rifles indiscriminately into the air and into the windows on either side of the street.

'What the hell is going on here?' Duffy seized a man by the shoulder. 'Who's in charge?'

The man rounded on him violently and then recognised the uniform. 'Here, have a snifter, mate.' He grinned and held out a bottle.

Duffy heaved him to one side and the man lurched against the wall. 'Get away, to be fucked,' snarled Duffy, almost incoherent with fury. He strode on towards the barracks.

Men serving the same cause as himself were tearing the shutters off a public house on the corner of Clonard Street. Further up the street the work of destruction continued unabated, but now civilians were emerging onto the streets, pathetic groups, many still in their night attire and bare feet. The crying of children and the sobbing of women added to the din. He saw a man being brought to the ground by a blow from a rifle and two men kicking him several times as he lay in the gutter.

There were four of the regular constables inside the barracks. The injured sergeant, who had been seen by a doctor, was unconscious upstairs. The constables were standing around aimlessly and looked at Duffy in surprise. In a way they had hoped not to see anyone who knew them, like conspirators caught in some mean and degrading act.

'There was nothing we could do, Sergeant Duffy,' said one of the men miserably. 'There's a whole army of them out there. They're as drunk as lords.'

It was true for him too, but Duffy could not accept it. As yet he could not believe even the evidence of his eyes. 'Phone Gormanston. Get the CO,' he shouted.

The man leapt to the instrument. It was dead. 'The lines must be down,' he mumbled.

Duffy felt his resolution slipping away from him. He could

think of nothing to do.

'Jaysus,' said one of the constables, they've set the town on fire.'

'Come on,' roared Duffy, starting for the door, but no one followed him. He had no idea what he intended to do.

Clonard Street was ablaze. The low thatch roofs of the cottages had been doused with petrol and were now burning fiercely. Showers of sparks and blazing straw swarmed skywards on the whirling, heated air and drifted down to ignite the roofs of neighbouring buildings. The dry straw of generations burst quickly into flame and the aged rafters crackled and collapsed inward, engulfing the few bits of furniture in torrents of fire.

The pub on the corner was an inferno. Bottles of spirits popped like fire crackers, and now and again a cask exploded with a muffled detonation, and gouts of flame leapt through the gaping windows. Gradually the ridge began to sag and tiles showered down into the street to shatter amid the glass. With a deafening crash, the roof collapsed and the building imploded on itself, folding inwards into a heap of blazing rubble, with only a few obelisks of wall left standing and the mottled outline of a charred rafter glowing like red snakeskin against the darkness.

'Why are ye doin' this to us?' There was a woman clutching at his sleeve. She was only half-dressed. There was an infant wrapped in the shawl that covered her shoulders. 'This child isn't well. He shouldn't be out.' Her face was streaked with smoke and tears. Her expression was one of incomprehension. 'He shouldn't be out,' she repeated.

It was as simple as that, thought Duffy. A sick child should not be out in the cold. He tried to disengage himself from her hand. People were staring at him. They knew him. No, he thought, they couldn't believe that I would agree to this.

'Get these people to the Fair Green,' shouted a foreign voice behind him. An officer waving a pistol, was giving orders to about a dozen men with fixed bayonets.

They began to herd the people along the street. They were laughing, and some of them swore when people stumbled or fell behind. The heat from the burning houses was intense. The adults appeared stunned by the destruction and the children clutched at them in terror.

'What are you doing?' shouted Duffy, grabbing the Auxiliary by the arm.

The wretched procession and their captors had moved further down the street.

'Scum,' said the man. 'Traitors, every last one of 'em. Amritsar, that's the only way.' He laughed, showing a gold crown on one of his teeth.

Duffy felt tears of rage blinding him. He grabbed the man by the shoulders and smashed his forehead into the laughing face. He brought his knee up savagely into the groin and the man crumpled to the ground. Duffy drove his boot into the belly of his groaning victim. A murderous rage flooded his veins, but there was no time. He felt his hobnailed boot connecting with the blood-spattered face and had time to think, with satisfaction, that the Tans might get around more quietly on their rubber soles, but a good layer of leather with tips on toe and heel left a better mark on a man. 'Be ready Wednesday', old Grady always said, through a mouthful of brads. This bastard wouldn't be ready Wednesday, or for a good while after.

Amritsar. The word came back to him. He had to get to the Fair Green. He felt the panic rising in him again. In Dublin Street a line of men, kneeling with rifles to their shoulders, watched the column of civilians passing by. Another officer waved them along impatiently. Burning cottages lit the scene like a vivid nightmare.

'What are you going to do with them?' gasped Duffy. He was almost exhausted by the sudden release of adrenalin and the violent exertion.

'Nothing at all, Sergeant, just give them a bit of a scare. We have the ones we want, down in the barracks.' He laughed good-naturedly, all boys together having a bit if devilment, but Duffy was too sickened to react.

He turned back again to the barracks and the ruined part of the town. Beyond the houses a factory was in flames, throwing the buildings beneath it into startling silhouette. Flames burst from all its storeys and greedily devoured the roof timbers. The very economic heart of the town was being destroyed. Even at a distance he could read the legend painted in bold letters on the brickwork of the second floor: 'Deedes Templar & Co.' Hardly the names of typical Irish terrorists, he reflected.

The barracks was thronged with Black and Tans. Some were in a state of high excitement, while others had lapsed into morose silence. The attention seemed to be centred on the inner rooms. Duffy pushed his way through the crowd, until he could see what was happening. In one room a man sat on a chair. His face was bruised and bleeding. Several Auxiliaries were shouting questions at him but he seemed unable to speak. When his lips moved, Duffy could see that his teeth were jagged and broken. Blood trickled from the corner of his mouth.

In a second room there was a man on the floor. His head and neck were pouring blood from several deep lacerations. Duffy recognised him as Lawless, a local barber, a quiet-spoken fellow, with a large family. He had some involvement with republican politics in a kind of a clerical capacity. As Duffy pushed his way into the room, one of Lawless's interrogators was in the act of withdrawing a bayonet from the unfortunate man's thigh. The blood followed the steel, in a bubbling red fountain. The man made to drive the bayonet in again. Duffy sprang forward.

'Shtop,' he roared and made to grab the weapon. In his excitement the accent of his home place re-asserted itself after years of attrition. 'Shtop, or I'll fire.'

He felt a heavy blow on the back of his head and a blinding silver light dazzled him. Darkness closed around him as he sank to the floor. The bayonet descended again and the man on the floor twisted in dumb agony.

243

CHAPTER 21

Clara and the boy were standing at the door of the cottage as Frank approached. He could see their white faces turned towards the distant fires. They withdrew quickly when they heard his footsteps, but opened the door again when he spoke softly, reassuring them.

'Oh Mr Surtees,' she sobbed. 'What's happening at all? Everything is gone wrong.'

He could see that she was trembling. He asked for Tom and she told him what had happened.

'I don't know what to do.' She wrung her hands in her apron. 'Maybe he's been murdered.' She broke down and sobbed again.

Frank patted her shoulder awkwardly.

The boy was watching him intently. 'Do you think my da is all right, Mr Surtees?'

Frank considered for a moment. 'If Sergeant Duffy has him he will be safe enough. Duffy is an honest man. If he's done nothing wrong he'll be safe,' he repeated. They seemed reassured to some extent. 'I don't think it's safe for you to stay here tonight. It's too isolated.' An idea struck him. 'Why don't you come up to the house. It's well off the beaten track. You'll be safer there.'

'Supposin' Tom comes back. I'd want to be here if he comes back.'

'He won't be back tonight. Not if he's been arrested. He's safe enough where he is. You're the ones I'm worried about. Please come up to the house. Lock up here and come at once.'

Clara hesitated again. What might happen to their home if it was left empty? It was all they had in the world. 'All right,' she agreed reluctantly. 'I'll just put a few things in a bag.'

There were people crouching behind a wall at the footbridge, a man and a woman and three small children. The smallest was almost buried under a bundle of belongings in the pram. They seemed shocked into silence, although the children whimpered from time to time and complained of the cold. They started in alarm when the three figures emerged from the shadow of the trees. Frank told them not to be afraid and asked who they were and where they were going.

'We don't know,' said the man miserably. 'They thrun us out and burned the house down. That's all we have left.' He gestured to the bundle in the pram.

'There was people murdered, I heard,' said his wife. 'I don't know what we're goin' to do.' Her voice trailed off in despair.

'You'd better come along with us for the moment. There's plenty of room up above.' Frank told them to bring their belongings but to leave the pram for the moment. He took up one of the children and led the way across the bridge and up through the plantation.

The front door gave at his push and he brought them into the great dining-room. Acutely aware of danger, he closed the shutters before striking a light. His mind was racing ahead. 'We don't want to attract attention to ourselves,' he said by way of explanation.

There were folding beds in the cellars since the time of the Red Cross, and mattresses too, though unfortunately no blankets. By the light of the candle he could see the faces of the children were mottled with measles. Their noses streamed from the cold and from crying. 'Mrs Bennett, get a fire going there. There's kindling in the grate and logs in that box. Come with me,' he ordered the man. 'There are beds and mattresses in the cellars.

He directed the woman to the kitchen where she could get some hot water to make a pot of tea. She could heat some milk on the range for the children. They were glad to fall in with his directions and by the time they had rigged up the bunks the chill had begun to leave the room and the children had, for the moment, stopped their snivelling.

The pale grey light of morning was beginning to creep through the window when Duffy finally awoke. He felt a searing pain in the back of his neck and wondered at first if the vertebrae had been crushed. Gingerly he moved his head. The pain was excruciating. His exploring finger found a lump on the back of his head and he felt the hair matted with congealed blood. The room was empty but there was some activity in the day-room. He looked around for his cap, through force of ingrained habit. It lay crushed in the corner under the bench. Slowly he bent and retrieved it, tapping it into shape and dusting the nap with his sleeve. Pensively he replaced it on his head and adjusted it to a suitable angle. 'When you're on parade you're *on* parade,' they always said. His pistol was still in its holster.

'You all right Sergeant?' It was one of the local constables, anxious to make amends. 'Can I get you a cup o'tea maybe?'

Duffy declined.

'There was nothin' we could do Sergeant. There was nearly a hundred of them.' The man's voice was strained with guilt.

'Aye lad. There was nothing anyone could do. Not then. What's the situation now?'

'There's still a good few of them around but they've quietened down a bit.'

'What about those two men, Lawless and the other man?'

'Gibbons.' The man paused. He could not meet Duffy's eye. 'They're dead,' he mumbled, almost inaudibly. 'Down by the bridge.' He coughed harshly.

'Gibbons? The dairyman! Jesus Christ.' Duffy passed a hand over his forehead. He pressed thumb and forefinger into his eyes. He felt old and tired.

There were very few people on the streets, a few clusters here and there, looking disconsolately at the smouldering ruins. There were some lorries, patrolling with groups of Tans, who looked less fearsome now, in fact rather down at heel, but still defiant. Duffy found a knot of people standing by one of the legs of the railway viaduct that straddled the harbour.

They fell silent and shuffled as he approached, but seemed to relax slightly when they recognised him. A man stepped forward and addressed him.

'Look what they done to the poor men, Sergeant.' There were tears of impotent anger in his eyes.

The bodies had been removed but the marks of the atrocity remained. There were splashes of blood and grey matter on the limestone pillar. They seemed to fit in with the orange and grey lichens that grew in round regular patches on the rough-cut stone. Duffy wondered how there could have been any blood left in the men he had seen tortured the night before. Everyone said about beating someone's brains out but it was not meant literally.

'They didn't even shoot them. They bet them to death.' The speaker claimed to have seen it from his own bedroom. 'One of them picked poor Gibbons up on a bayonet, be the neck, to see if he was dead. I seen it, I tell ye. Like ye'd pick an oul' nowd up be the gills.' He shook his head. 'I went to school with him. I'd know him anywhere.' He seemed to need to reassure himself that it had not all been a dream. 'Picked him up like an oul' nowd and thrun him down again. They're not policemen, Sergeant, nor soldiers. They're gutties, nothin' else.'

In less than an hour Sergeant Duffy had covered the distance to Skerries, passing groups of straggling refugees who watched him sullenly as he passed.

Tom Bennett sat glowering in the one and only cell. The handcuffs had been removed. He had obviously had breakfast, to judge from the greasy plate and the cup.

'Right now. What's been goin' on?' he demanded as Duffy entered. 'There's been comin's and goin's here all night.'

'Will you be quiet a minute and let me explain.' Duffy opened the door and entered the cell. 'I know you too well Tom. If you hadn't been locked up, this last night, 'tis stretched out cold you'd be in Balbriggan today, with two harmless poor divils that you know well.'

He explained as coherently as he could the events of the previous nine hours or so. Bennett was speechless. Had it not been for the sergeant's haggard appearance and red-rimmed eyes he would have found it impossible to believe. Clara and the lad, were they all right? Duffy assured him that the cottage was untouched, that the trouble had been confined to the town. The fields, he said were full of people sheltering in the hedges and under trees. They had not been pursued. Bennett clenched and unclenched his fists in rage.

'Let you cool down now Tom or I'll have to lock you up indefinitely. There's precious little you can do now except stay out of trouble. All I can do myself is make my own report to the authorities. There will have to be an investigation.' He didn't place much hope in that prospect, but they would have to go through the motions.

'You can't hold me here. I haven't done anything.' Bennett was still defiant.

'Tom,' said Duffy wearily, 'I can hold you here as long as I want. Don't you realise? I'm about all the law there is around here — and that's not sayin' much,' he added bitterly. 'I have all the law I need right here.' He patted his holster. 'Now what use will you be to your family with your brains all over the road? Not that I think you have many.' He grunted at his wit.

'Aye,' said Bennett. 'I suppose I'm sort of obliged to ye then. I see what ye mean.' He stood up and stretched himself with a loud clicking of bones. 'The oul' sea air', he said by way of explanation, 'gets into the joints.'

'Arthuritis,' agreed Duffy. 'I'm gettin' a touch of it meself.'

Bennett extended his hand diffidently. 'I'll be off then if it's all right with you.' They shook hands.

'Aye. Right so. A bad time Tom,' said the sergeant sadly.

After Bennett was gone, he sat at his desk and drew a sheet of paper towards him. He opened the ink bottle and stared at it for a long time. At last he picked up a pen, a J nib, he noticed absently, his least favourite, and began to write.

The military stopped the car on the main road and enquired where they were going.

'There's been a bit of bother,' the soldier said. 'It might be better if you went back to Dublin for the moment.' He seemed unwilling to offer any further information.

Eventually they deduced that there had been some kind of battle around Balbriggan the previous night, but that they could proceed at their own risk.

'Well,' said the old man, 'since we've come this far, we might as well go ahead. What do you say?' He did not consult the nurse.

Anna replied that she wanted to go on to Strifeland, suggesting that they go up over the back roads. 'Frank will be expecting us.'

There seemed to be an air of gloom about the countryside. The few country people they saw stared at them with silent curiosity, devouring the sight of the grand motorcar and its strange occupants. High on the shoulder of a hill they stopped, at a place called the Cross of the Cage. Legend reported that criminals had hung there in times gone by, their skeletons a rickety warning to evildoers; that Cromwell had hung men there in cages, until famine had clung to them, eating the flesh from their bones, until the breeze sifted them through the bars and played with the tattered rags of their garments. It was a bleak and lonely place. Far off they could see columns of smoke rising into the still September sky. Anna shivered. She thought of McSwiney enduring his agony in Wormwood Scrubs at that very moment, starving against his enemy, like the ancient Gaels.

There was noise and activity in the house as the car drew up on the gravelled drive. People were standing around watching them and some men came forward, touching their caps when they recognised the old man. They were embarrassed, as if they had been caught trespassing. There was hardly a man there who had not climbed over the high boundary wall at some time in quest of chestnuts or the occasional rabbit.

'What are all you people doing here in my house?' There was a flash of the old anger in the colonel's eyes. 'What's the meaning of all this?'

'Ah, well ye see, Colonel,' one of the man began. He had removed his cap and was looking awkwardly around for support. 'We were sort of burned out last night, like.' He said it apologetically, sorry to be the cause of annoyance.

'Anderson, isn't it?' retorted the colonel. 'I know you. What have you been up to?'

'Nothin' sir, honest. The Tans burned half the town down.'

'Nonsense, man. Don't exaggerate.' He struggled sideways to slide himself into the wheelchair.

Frank emerged from the door, with his sleeves rolled up. Anna noticed that his braces were twisted. He was glad to see her.

'He's come on a bad day though,' he said, nodding towards the old man. 'We've been collecting people from the hedgerows all morning, Tom Bennett and myself. The place is full. It's a very bad business indeed.'

The colonel was shaking his head in disbelief, looking at the groups of people standing aimlessly around. Children clung to their parents, staring at the new arrivals, or chased each other through the long, echoing corridors. Quite a few of them were mottled with measles. 'Extraordinary,' was all he could say. He had not expected his prophecy to come true quite so soon. 'We had better go and see for ourselves, Surtees. This is difficult to credit.'

'A very poor showing I'm afraid, Colonel,' said Frank grimly. 'No way for any force to behave.'

They moved towards the car.

'I'm afraid you won't like what you're going to see.'

Two men stood on the pavement, looking at a shattered window.

Frank accosted them, 'Do you men know what happened here?'

'As much as anyone, I suppose,' replied one. He glanced at the motorcar, bending slightly at the knees to see who was inside. 'Mr Surtees, isn't it? Aye. I was just sayin' if the huers thought they could drink it they'd of took it.' He indicated the broken window and the wrecked interior of the shop.

In solitary state on the shelf in the window stood a bottle of hair oil, miraculously untouched by the havoc.

'How did it all start? There must have been some reason.'

The man leaned forward, lowering his voice confidentially. 'Somebody shot the DI above in Smiths', last night. I don't know, maybe he deserved it, but it turned out a bit expensive in the long run. My family hasn't a buckin' roof over them, on the head of it.'

'They'll be singin' ballads about whoever done it, in ten years' time,' chipped in the other man, 'but me and the missus have to spend the night in a hayloft.' He looked around at the

250

devastation, aggrieved and mystified. 'Me buckin' job went up in smoke too. I don't know the rights of it at all.'

'I wouldn't hang around here too long if I was you,' advised the first speaker. 'They keep comin' back in their lurries, firin' guns all over the place. We was tryin' to find a few bits an' pieces. We're goin' out the fields again before it gets dark. People won't stay here after dark.'

'Do you know anything about inquests or funerals? I mean, surely there will be some investigations.'

'There's been talk of a big funeral with flags and all, y'know, but now they're sayin' that Canon Byrne has been told the Tans will come back and level the town if there's any demonstrations.

'There's not goin' to be any inquests neither,' added the second man. 'This whole thing'll be swept under the carpet. Wait till ye see.'

It would take a deal of sweeping, reflected Frank. In fact there was a man engaged already on the task, sweeping the splinters of glass from the pavement in front of his boarded-up shop. He had chalked 'business as usual' on the makeshift shutters.

'I haven't any stock,' he said catching their eye, 'but I won't let a crowd of bowsies close me down.'

*　*　*

They buried the local men on the Wednesday. It was to have been a small private funeral, at the request of the families, but almost the whole town turned out to line the streets and follow the cortège to the little country graveyard. Ostensibly it was not a political occasion but it said more about the feelings of the people than all the flags that were ever waved, or all the graveside orations ever spoken. As the cortège approached the barracks the constables, under Duffy's watchful eye, emerged in their best uniforms and stood to attention. As the procession passed they saluted smartly, staring rigidly ahead, not meeting the eyes of the mourners.

There seemed to be reporters everywhere. Camera flares popped alarmingly, immortalising urchins in caps many sizes too large and women in long brown dresses and white aprons. Readers throughout the world became familiar with the *bric à brac* of domestic life in Balbriggan, laden on donkey carts or stacked on the side of the pavement, a broken cot, a hand-basin, an armchair with its springs exposed to the elements. Even the London papers compared the scene to wartime views of Belgium and spoke of 'undisguised Prussianism'. *The Manchester Guardian* compared it to the action of the Turks in Armenia and spoke of government by terrorism. *The Times* spoke of a sense of shame, while the *Daily News* pronounced that the Irish Question had been 'poisoned to the roots'.

Controversy raged throughout the realm, inflamed, whenever it looked like dying down, by some insensitive or bellicose remark from persons in positions of authority.

General Macready, the Commander in Chief in Ireland, made the gloomy comment on the human species that it was in fact 'human nature that the men should relieve their feelings at the expense of the civilian population', admitting at the same time that any attempt at disciplinary action would be a risky business.

Not everyone agreed with him, even to the extent that seven Black and Tans from Gormanston resigned in protest.

The attention of the press began to turn to other matters. The blood of St Januarius liquefied punctually at Naples, heralding a protracted era of peace in the world. As reprisals, counter-murder and destruction hit Trim and Mallow in succeeding days, it seemed as if the decent man might have saved himself the bother.

Archbishop Mannix voiced his opinions on the conduct of affairs in Ireland and the papers announced his exclusion from the country. They also mentioned racing at Gowran Park, two o'clock (new time) and a sale of ewes, hoggets and wethers in Lusk.

CHAPTER 22

With hindsight we speak of inevitability. With Mohammedan fatalism, we say 'it was written'. We turn to the next chapter in the history book and regard it as the logical outcome of what went before. Headings and marginal notes nudge us towards the conclusion that what happened had to happen, as part of a great pre-ordained pattern. The writer of fiction will merit our anger if he departs from these rules. The heroine must not turn her foot on a stone and tumble down a precipice as she hurries to a tryst with her lover. However entertaining the villain may be, and villains are rarely dull, they must not be permitted to triumph over virtue. A struggle for freedom must succeed because it is the destiny of a risen people, not because of the myopic incompetence and gratuitous arrogance of the oppressor. Hindsight leaves nothing to chance.

Sergeant Duffy encapsulated these thoughts in the one terse 'I knew it', as he put down the receiver. A remarkable invention, the telephone and a terrible curse too. Wearily he rose and put on his cap. There was never anything but bad news nowadays. He took up his old overcoat. The good one had disappeared on that dreadful September night. 'I'm going round to Drew's,' he said to the constable. 'There's been more trouble.'

'What's that old scoundrel been up to now?' enquired the constable. He showed no eagerness to come along and busied himself with whatever he had been writing.

'Oh, nothin'. Nothin' at all. I just want a lend of his lurry. There's been an accident.'

Mr Drew was not too pleased to be called upon and demanded to know the reason. The sergeant assured him that he would know soon enough. He was in no mood for either argument or conversation. In a sullen silence they jounced along the coast road until they reached the level-crossing. There was a small crowd standing at the low platform. Some of the figures were in khaki. Mr Drew swore under his breath.

The corporal came towards them. He was a young fellow, grey in the face with fatigue or shock. It was difficult to say. He spoke excitedly, anxious to explain the exact circumstances.

'Honest to God, we didn't start it. He just came at us with this thing.' He held up a bill-hook. The blade flashed silver but it was still streaked with red, although someone had tried to wipe the blood off in the grass. 'Honest to God, Sergeant, we didn't start an'thin'.'

'All right, all right. Calm down son, and just tell me what happened.' Duffy drew him to one side.

Gradually he learned that the patrol had been coming along the track and that there had been a man cutting the hedge with the bill-hook. Apparently he had made some remark as they passed and one of the soldiers had replied in kind. A big fellow he was, the corporal emphasised. Dangerous looking, he added strengthening his case. Someone had laughed and that had done it. Suddenly he was on top of them, jumped down off the bank like a lunatic, shouting about turning children out of their houses in the middle of the night. There was only one shot, that was all, but there were two soldiers nearly killed with the slash-hook. He nodded towards the platform.

'And the man?' Duffy asked, although he knew the answer.

'He's dead, Sergeant. Back there in the trees. Honest to God we didn't look for any trouble. There's a woman with him and some other people.'

Duffy was silent. He looked at the two injured soldiers. One had a severe wound on his arm and was unconscious from loss of blood. A companion had made a tourniquet with a strap and was holding it tightly with finger and thumb. Every now and again he relaxed his grip. The other soldier had a field-dressing covering a gaping wound on his neck. The air

254

whistled strangely through the gash and the wad of lint was stained scarlet with bright arterial blood.

'Who shot the man?' asked Duffy, not that it would make a lot of difference.

The soldiers looked at each other. One of them replied: 'This bloke 'ere. It was self-defence. More of an accident really.' Either way it was obvious that he would soon be out of reach of any retribution.

'These soldiers need a doctor, Drew. You'll take them back to the camp.'

Mr Drew looked alarmed at first but quietened when he saw the look in Duffy's eye.

'Put those men in the lurry,' Duffy said to the corporal, 'and our friend here will take ye to Gormanston. I suppose that's where ye were headed anyway.'

The corporal nodded, relieved that someone had taken the situation in hand.

'These people here will help me with Tom,' said Duffy to Mr Drew, who was fumbling with the catches on the tailboard. 'And see you come back here on your way home.' He wondered sourly what theory Drew would advance to explain the whole affair to his unexpected passengers.

Tom Bennett's body lay in the long, dry grass on the railway bank, as if he had lain down for a snooze in the weak autumn sun. His waistcoat was open and his shirtsleeves were rolled. His knees were drawn up and death was already stiffening into them. The posture emphasised the awkward strength of the man. There were no other marks of violence besides the dark stain on his shirt-front. He looked strangely at peace.

Clara was there with several other people, who stood about wanting to offer comfort but unsure of what to do. 'It was bound to happen, Sergeant Duffy,' she said abruptly, 'being the kind of person he was.'

'I'm sorry for your trouble Mrs Bennett,' he said gently. 'I had hoped it wouldn't come to this.' He marvelled at her control.

'It preyed on his mind, you see. He talked about the childer with the measles. He kept sayin' it was wrong to turn them out. He was always very fond of childer, said they should all get their chance.' She spoke as if she were looking back at something that happened a long time ago.

Duffy had heard how Bennett had gone around gathering in people from the fields and the sheds. He had taken his duties very seriously but there had been a terrible anger inside him all the time, as if he had been personally humiliated.

'I prayed that he'd keep out of trouble. I begged him not to get involved but he always believed in fair play.' She spoke it like an epitaph. 'It wasn't like him though, to hurt anyone. I saw what he done to the soldiers.' She wanted to talk it out for herself. 'It's the times that are in it. People aren't allowed to be themselves.'

'We'll get him away from here Mrs Bennett.' Duffy sent two men to find something to carry the body.

Clara waited silently until they returned with a hurdle. She stared at the familiar blackened sleepers. 'He never let me go for the coke, these last couple of years. I used to walk along here every week.' Her voice trailed off. 'What will I say to Davy?' she said faintly, and her reserve crumbled.

'Let ye take her home,' said Duffy to the country people, 'and some of ye women stay with her. I'll be along later.' God dammit, Tom, he thought, you're a hero now to some people and a murderer to others, but I have to clean up after you either way and your family has to pay for it. He spat on his hands and took hold of the hurdle.

* * *

'I was very proud of you this morning,' said Dolores. 'You looked very well with your firing party.'

'Ah the poor divil,' said Kit, 'I suppose it was the least we could do.'

The store smelt its usual ripe smell of fruit and grain.

'You know, he once threatened to give me a right kick in the arse.' He had always been a bit wary of Tom Bennett. A hardy man they said. A fierce man, all right. He laughed drily.

She got a whiff of drink.

'Makes you think all the same.' He left the thought unconnected, hanging in the air.

'You can stay here if you like,' said Dolores. There was a slight tremor in her voice. 'You can let yourself out in the morning. I'll be up early.' She was talking too much and she checked herself.

'Aye,' said Kit. 'That's not a bad idea. It was strange though, to see all the people there, even the old colonel fellow from Strifeland.' He could not forget the scene, the sea of faces, the sharp command and the rattle of rifle shots, the crows rising in protest and wheeling around the old dark pine trees.

'There aren't any rats,' she added trying to lift his dark mood. 'You needn't be afraid.'

'Rats.' Kit shivered. He threw back his shoulders. 'You're talking to a hero of the Movement,' he said not without irony. 'There's very little that frightens me.' Rats scuttled in his mind, pinpoint eyes shining.

'I might,' she said, coming towards him, turning her face up to him.

'You might, at that,' he said, feeling the tension go out of him. 'I've been thinking a lot about you lately.'

'Oh yes?' A pulse beat at the base of her throat, accentuated by the flickering candle flame. 'And how might I frighten you?'

'Well now,' he teased, putting his arms around her, 'if I don't make an honest woman of you before I lose the run of myself, you'll end up in a convent and I'll have to take the boat to England. Think of the scandal.'

She laughed softly pushing her body against him. 'Do you call that a proposal or what? I always imagined that I would be proposed to in a garden.'

'We could go out in the back yard.'

'Too cold,' she said dismissively. 'This will have to do.'

His hand found her breast under the thin dressing-gown. She had nothing on under it except some kind of a chemise or whatever, slippery like silk. 'It's no wonder you're cold,' he said and kissed her with sudden urgency.

'Anyway I accept,' she said, slipping her hands under his shirt. 'I've been waiting for years for you to ask.'

'What about the convent?' he asked, his voice catching in his throat.

'I'll risk it,' she said drawing him gently towards the pile of sacks.

The candle flame flickered wildly in the last dregs of grease, whirled around and slowly succumbed. The room was suddenly dark.

* * *

'Bloody Sunday, they're calling it already,' said the guard on the early morning train.

Frank looked at the paper in stunned disbelief. Twenty-six people had died violently, some shot as spies and others in terrible reprisal, when a crowd at a football match was fired upon.

'I don't know, so I don't,' said the guard in his Northern twang. 'Where is it going to end at all? We're that sick of it too, stoppin' and startin'. We don't usually stop here anymore. Just, you can't be too careful, can you?'

'Quite right,' answered Frank, scanning the page. He was only half-listening. His eye caught a familiar name: 'Bennett, killed in an ambush . . . prominent member . . . " he frowned. 'No, no,' he shook his head at the distortion. 'That's not how it was.'

The guard looked at him in puzzlement.

Tom Bennett, the personification of autumn, standing high on the cornstack, pitching the sheaves; riding in the milk cart with the little fair-haired boy beside him; Tom that went out with a lantern at lambing time in the dead of a February night; Tom who thumped the bejaysus out of the big drum, as he said himself, and never had the slightest notion of his own merits. 'No,' he said again, handing the newspaper back to the guard. 'That's not the way it was.' He looked around him at the fields and the big old house. It was a bleak and alien scene. 'It's time to go,' he said to no one in particular.

'Aye, that it is,' said the guard, nodding agreement. The line was clear. He gave a shrill blast on his whistle, to be answered by the ritual 'toot' from up front.

A cloud of grey-green lapwings rose in alarm from the field beside the track and wheeled overhead, piping forlornly at being disturbed from their feeding grounds. Strifeland's birds, Frank thought, watching them, wondering where they would settle.

* * *

Kit blinked in the light. It was morning. Dolores was shaking him by the shoulder.

'We fell asleep,' she whispered. 'You'd better go quickly.'

He sat up and began to button his shirt. 'Christ,' he said looking at her in alarm.

'Will you be back?' she asked awkwardly. 'I mean after all this.'

'Back? Of course I'll be back.' He grinned, his old, open, cheerful grin. 'I'll have to come back anyway to look for the top of my head. I think it flew behind the sultanà boxes at some stage.'

She stifled a giggle and then became serious. 'Be careful though. I couldn't bear it if anything happened to you.'

'I'll be careful, don't you worry.' He stroked her cheek with the back of his forefinger. 'I love you,' he said simply and lifted the latch on the door into the yard.

EPILOGUE

'Mrs Bennett,' said Frank, 'do you remember us?' Clara turned in surprise. Her thoughts had been elsewhere.

'Oh, Mr Surtees,' she exclaimed, 'and Mrs Surtees. I'm very pleased to meet you again. And are these your little children?'

The children held grimly to their parents' hands and stared back at her, a small dark eyed boy and a girl two or three years older, fair-haired like her father.

'We felt we had to come,' said Anna. 'It must be a very important day for you and Davy.' She nearly said a happy day, but that was hardly the case.

Clara looked confused for a moment. 'It was very good of you,' she said, raising her voice slightly to overcome the buzz of conversation.

The crowd was gradually dispersing. The bandsmen trooped past to a soft chamade of side drums.

'It was justly deserved,' said Frank. 'Your husband was a fine man.'

'It's just that I'm a bit confused by the turn-out,' she admitted. 'I'm just going home now, if I can find Davy.' She looked anxiously. 'Oh there he is, shaking hands with Master Sweeney.' To her, old Sweeney would always be the master, despite his elevation to greater things.

Davy came towards the group, recognising them suddenly. He had grown into a tall, serious-looking young man. He looked vaguely annoyed.

'You remember my son Davy,' said Clara proudly.

'How are you?' said Davy shaking hands formally. 'It was good of you to come today.'

'It was the right thing to do,' said Frank quietly.

Nevertheless it had saddened him to see the old mansion fallen on evil days. The doors had come off the hinges and the building stood open to the elements. Slates had become dislodged after the lead had been stripped from the roof, and rainwater stained the plaster of the ceilings that hung in folds from the mildewed rafters. Fungi proliferated on the exposed woodwork, great pendulous growths that told of irreparable decay. Piles of straw stirred in the draughty corridors, evidence of jackdaws' nests in the elaborate mouldings. Grit and broken glass crunched under their feet in the hallway. Anna had drawn him away. 'Too many ghosts,' she had said. Below the house were the neatly fenced fields of the smallholders and down by the railway the mutilated barn had taken on a stagger, as rust attacked its main supports.

Clara interrupted his thoughts. She was enquiring about themselves.

'Well,' said Anna, 'it's been up and down you might say. Frank was going to try for the Civil Service but they say that the Free State is going to insist on Gaelic. Anyway an office would never suit him.'

'I suppose not,' agreed the older woman.

'We've been in England for a few years.'

'No, said Frank. 'In fact we've decided to go out to Africa, I've been offered a job in Kenya, something similar to what I was doing at Strifeland, in a way.'

'A bit warmer though,' suggested Clara.

'And yourselves?' asked Frank.

'Well, you know how it was, of course. When the old man died they found there was nothing left in the kitty. The estate was caught for two sets of death duties. You see he had signed everything over to his son years ago,' she explained, in answer to their puzzled looks. 'The Free State took the land anyway, instead of the money. We had the field of course. That stayed with us. I have it out on conacre now.'

'He would be pleased about that,' said Anna.

And Frank added that he would probably have been pleased

that there was no money left for the government, irrespective of what government it might be. 'A comical huer,' he added, 'as Tom would have said.'

'Aye Tom,' said Clara and sighed. She looked old and tired, but there was pride in her eye. 'Everyone tells me he was a war hero, but I'd much prefer if he was the one bangin' the big drum today. He would be proud enough about Davy and the way he's won a scholarship.'

'A scholarship,' said Anna. 'But that's wonderful. And what are you going to do with it?' She turned to Davy.

'I'm going to be a teacher,' replied Davy levelly.

'Ah, following in your old master's footsteps I take it.'

'Not exactly,' replied the boy, 'I'll be a teacher all the same.'

'And the painting? Do you still paint?'

'That I do,' said Davy, and he smiled for the first time.

'And thanks to yourself again,' cut in his mother, proudly. 'He's going to make a great name for himself someday.'

Davy shuffled in pleased embarrassment. 'I'll send you some pictures, if you give me your address.' He had always wanted to do so, remembering those early days.

'I should like that very much,' Anna said, touched by the offer. 'It would be good to see the place through the eyes of a real artist.'

Davy beamed with pride. He was not such a serious young man after all.

'You must excuse us, Mrs Bennett,' said Frank, taking his small son in his arms, 'but we have a train to catch. I expect it will be crowded too.'

They shook hands again for the last time and Davy took his mother's arm. The group of dignitaries had forgotten about them and had moved away in search of refreshment.

Anna saw him, pushing his way through the crowd on the platform, before he caught her eye. Kit had filled out. He looked very much the prosperous businessman, but when he removed his hat the hair fell down over his forehead. He gave the old grin and took her hand.

'I was hoping I'd catch you before you left.'

'Frank, you remember Kit Donovan,' she said, turning to

her husband who was observing them with interest. She was still holding Kit's hand.

'Yes, of course,' he said coming forward, 'an old comrade in arms.'

Anna stood back, looking him up and down. 'You look quite the man of affairs. Things must have worked out well.'

'I can't seem to help it,' he said. 'If you have time I'd like you to come back to the house for a drink. I'd like you to meet my family,' he added with a note of pride. Momentarily he wondered if Dolores would be quite so pleased as he said she would be. She could be a bit caustic at times.

'You own a public house too, I understand. I'm impressed.'

He fingered his nose. It looked like a boxer's nose. He laughed. 'It was the only way I could get a drink there. I was barred you see.'

She told him of their plans and asked about his family. 'And your little brother? Does he still follow you around?' She laughed gently, then stopped, seeing the look of pain. 'I'm sorry,' she said. 'I shouldn't have asked.'

'Ah no,' said Kit, 'poor Joey. He was the unlucky one. We had to pack him off to sea for a while, for his own good. A very useful man but could never accept the Treaty. He took the other side, you know, in the Civil War. His health has never been good since — life on the run and that. Got to be a very bitter man.'

'What will he do?'

'I want to pay for him through university. He should have gone years ago, but he hardly talks to us at all.'

'I am sorry. Maybe in time.'

'Aye, maybe,' he sighed. 'I'll keep trying.'

They could see the smoke of the locomotive rising from Strifeland woods. Heat rising from the cinder heaps made the air shimmer. The approaching train floated on the haze. The brakes screeched, making speech impossible. She stood on tiptoe and kissed him on the cheek.

The last glimpse she had of him as the steam swirled around him, he was holding his fingers to the spot and gazing wistfully, like a small boy, after the dwindling train.

* * *

263

All agreed it was a fine piece of stone, a fitting tribute to the man himself, solid as a rock. It was a pity though the harp got a bit of a knock when Mr Drew was bringing it from the stonemason's yard. It was just a chip off one of the strings but it sort of spoiled the effect.

'All the same, if that's all we have to complain about,' said one man, thoughtfully regarding the collar on his pint, 'it wasn't too bad a day.' Understated as usual: it had been a great day altogether. The band had been in powerful form.

'That's a grand tune, "St Patrick's Day", and right for the day that was in it, our own national saint,' said another, 'and our own parish saint too.' Homegrown saints, like most other things, are always better than the foreign variety, Italians, bleeding all over the place, with their eyes rolling in their heads, young ones that never got a hoult of a man in their lives being martyred as virgins. There was something blasphemous, maybe, in his point of view, but worth thinking about. A decent saint that would let the odd roar out of him, or maybe a few curses, was worth ten of the other kind.

'But he wasn't an Irishman at all,' interpolated another, more for the hell of it than in the interests of historical accuracy, 'he was an Englishman.'

A pause. The theologian took a long and disparaging pull at his drink. He replaced it on the counter, wiped his sleeve across his upper lip and regarded his interlocutor. 'He was no such thing,' he explained, with long-suffering patience. 'He was an ancient Briton, a Celt like ourselves. Do ye never read books? More important, he was a fuckin' Catholic.'

'Well then,' conceded the other, 'I suppose he was all right, but wouldn't ye think he'd allow us a jar on his own feast day?' It was a serious flaw in any saint's reputation, particularly an adopted Skerryman, a flaw that might yet come to the attention of the Devil's Advocate in any serious re-examination of Patrick's cause. 'I mean, slidin' in the back door. It's a bit undignified.'

'Jaysus,' snorted the theologian, 'you lose none of your nimbility over the years when it comes to slidin' into pubs. By the way, Skinner,' he continued, noticing Ned for the first time, 'I remember you was barred from this place.'

'Barred, how are ye?' expostulated Skinner in outrage.

'Barred! Kit Donovan isn't the man to bar his old comrades. You can take that back for a start.' He made as if to rise from his stool and the theologian backed away. Skinner subsided again.

'I often meant to ask,' said another, 'what brought yourself into the Movement anyway, Skinner?'

Skinner drank slowly from his glass, then wiped his mouth. He furrowed his brow and spoke deliberately. 'Well,' he began, 'when the Donovan lads went into it, I figured I'd better go along, just to keep well in. I mean, if the boss ever married into the Donovan family like, it would do no harm.' He laughed, gargling his porter and the others laughed too. Skinner had mellowed with age. His eyes misted over with a kind of wonder. 'She still gets the sweetbreads. True love is a marvellous thing.'

There was a reverent silence. They could not divine whether he was serious or not.

'Did I ever tell yiz about the time we burned the soldiers out of the Wireless Field?'

'Aye. Wasn't there an enquiry or somethin' about that?'

'Sweeney wanted to know how the soldiers got away, seein' as how we burned the huts and took the rifles off them. It was level peggin', three against three, but we got the rifles.'

'Aye, but how did they get away?'

'Well there y'are,' said Skinner. 'That's just it. Out comes a white flag and Kit just walks up to the door and tells them to throw out their weapons. "Hold your fire," he says to us.' He sighted along an imaginary gun-barrel. 'I had one of them in me sights. Had him dead to rights.'

'And what did Sweeney say to all this?'

' "Well," says Kit, lookin' him in the eye, "I was the officer on the spot. We achieved our objectives, didn't we?" and he throws the rifles on the table. Sweeney never said another word about it. Aw, we was a team, I'm tellin' yiz.'

'But why did you join, really?' asked the original questioner.

Skinner scratched his head. 'I dunno,' he said half-apologetically, 'I suppose — the lads, like, y'know.' He shrugged and addressed himself to his drink.

The door opened a fraction and Mr Drew entered, with a practised glissade, closing it behind him so quickly that one could not have been entirely sure that it had ever opened. It was a movement of which any matador might have been proud, less flamboyant than the *veronica* perhaps, but with the economy of effort that is the mark of the true artist.

'A black an' tan,' he said to the man behind the bar, and turned to survey the company, old comrades together, enjoying the day of reminiscence.

'A great day Mr Drew, considerin',' the theologian greeted him.

'Considerin'?' inquired Mr Drew and waited.

They thought they had him at last. 'Well considerin' the fact that the memorial to Tom Bennett was damaged before it was even unveiled.' Let him wriggle out of that one.

Mr Drew gazed into vacancy. His voice was heavy with solemnity, hushed with awe. 'God moves in mysterious ways,' he said.

There was obviously more to come. Silence settled on the room.

'A Greater Hand than mine was at work today.' He spoke in capital letters, holding his gnarled and calloused hand aloft for their inspection. 'The harp of Erin, and one of her strings broken. What more fitting symbol for a dead patriot? It's symbolic don't ye see?' There was a tremor in his voice.

The men looked at each other uncertain as to whether he was pulling their legs or not, but reluctant to be the first to laugh. He had done it again.

'That was a damn fine speech Mr Sweeney made though,' said the theologian, acknowledging defeat. Not Master Sweeney anymore, now that he was an elected representative of the people and a man of some weight in the community.

'A fine speech,' they agreed. Mr Sweeney could put the words together.

'A nice touch, the few words in Irish at the start,' said another man, savouring a phrase: ' ". . . proud to number Tomás Bennett among my friends and proud to have worked with him in our common cause." Them's the words that'll stick in the mind for many a long year.' He nodded appreciatively.

They were silent for a time, remembering. Captain McNaughten drew out his knife and pared pensively at a finger nail. Idly he regarded the heathen symbols on the ivory handle. A Lascar or a Chinaman; it was all the one now.

'Funny when ye look back,' mused Mr Drew, 'but weren't we the unlikeliest crew to take on the greatest empire in the world. Look at yiz.' He encompassed them all with a gesture. 'Fishermen, tradesmen like meself, men that looked at the back end of a horse all their life. Do yiz ever think about the significance of it all?'

'I don't know about significance, but we bet them. That's all I care about.'

'Aye,' volunteered another, 'I carried that banner up the street this afternoon with *Fingal Brigade* on it, and I'll tell yiz one thing, I held the oul' head up high. I was a proud man today.'

They murmured assent.

'That's what it was all about, holdin' your head up in your own town,' Mr Drew stabbed his stubby finger dogmatically on the counter.

The talk drifted to other matters until one of them mentioned Duffy.

'I needn't tell ye I was surprised to see him standin' there in the crowd today.'

'Who? Duffy?'

'Where did he go after he left here?'

'Aw, down the country somewhere, where he belonged. He had a terrible down on poor Tom Bennett. Tried everything to catch him out. He never managed it though. Tom was always a jump ahead. Nearly drove the sergeant mad.'

'You know,' said one of the men, 'they wouldn't take him into the Civic Guards.'

'Is that a fact?'

'That's true,' nodded Mr Drew. 'I remember now. He wrote a long report after Balbriggan was burned and there was a big enquiry into what he was doin' there at all. It seems his coat was found with blood on it. The enquiry wasn't finished when they handed over, so the matter was dropped, but the Civic Guards wouldn't have him.'

'Proper order,' said a voice. 'Damn lucky he wasn't shot.'

'That reminds me.' Mr Drew resumed his function as chairman. 'Did I ever tell yiz about meself and Tom and the dynamite? Well,' he was determined to tell it again, anyway, 'there was an argument about whether dynamite blows up or blows down.'

They drew closer around the speaker, those who had heard him tell it before and those who had heard only a version, distorted and refracted by usage. In the smoky atmosphere, he recalled to them the time and its uncertainty and grief. An explanation here, an embellishment there, allowed him to build the legend in their minds, a truth greater than mere facts.

The story warmed them and they gradually expanded with pride, knowing that here, in the drab grey streets and the narrow country roads, amid the hardships and vicissitudes of their workaday world, they had indeed known heroes and had walked with titans.